MW01047104

The Seventh Messenger

The Seventh Messenger

Roland McElroy

Published
by
McElroy & Associates, Inc.
Falls Church, Virginia

The Seventh Messenger
Published by McElroy & Associates, Inc.
www.mcelroyassoc.com

Printed in the U.S.A. by
United Book Press, Inc.
Baltimore, Maryland

Cover Design and Layout
by Jason Alexander

ISBN: 978-0-9673917-3-1

First Edition

For Bettie

Contents

Lake Michigan's Beaver Island Archipelago

Chapter One
Night Dreams

What's the difference between snow peas and green peas?" Abby Finlay put the question to her Aunt Jo O'Neil, as they sat shelling peas on the porch of the Finlay's Saint Louis mansion. A large kitchen bowl, lodged precariously between her legs, was already half full of peas.

"What'd you say?" Abby's startled aunt leaned forward in her rocker.

Abby leaned forward, too, and picked at the paint, peeling from the base of the nearest porch column. "What's the difference between green peas and black-eyed peas?" Abby's dry, monotonous tone never varied. She pulled tight the silk scarf that kept her ponytail in place.

"Child, where is this coming from?"

"What's the difference between black-eyed peas and chick peas?" Abby purposely withheld all energy from her words and leaned over the bowl of peas to roll up the bottom of her denim jeans. "Do you think rolled up jeans are cool?"

"Abigail Finlay, what's wrong with you?"

"I'm bored. Bored to death." Her hands slowly sifted through the peas piled in her bowl, and her eyes wandered to the front walk. "Wait—who's that?"

"That? Where?"

"There!"

The two of them had been sitting on the porch for hours, shucking corn and shelling peas. Neither had noticed the uniformed, young man who stepped out of a black sedan just outside the gate and was fast approaching along the serpentine brick walk.

"Special Delivery! Anyone here named …uh, Abigail Finlay?"

"Yes! Right here!" The peas that had been in Abby's lap spilled all over the porch as she jumped up and leap frogged down the steps, two at a time, hands outstretched to accept the Special Delivery missive.

"Sign here. I have to have a signature," he said, straightening his tie.

Abby grabbed his pen and dashed off her name.

Who could have sent this? Who . . . ? She felt the blood drain from her face as her eyes caught the postmark for the first time. "Aunt Jo, it's from Robert!" Her voice was suddenly very much alive.

"Now Abby, don't do this." Jo shook a long, thin finger at Abby.

"No, no, look, it *is* from Robert."

Jo stood with hands on both hips. "Abby, it's been ten years since Robert was killed at Normandy; don't be foolish."

"It's a letter, not a body, Aunt Jo. I always knew he'd return to me. I suspect Robert is not far behind his letter."

"And all I see is a woman who won't move on with her life." Jo's tone was deadly serious as she glared at Abby.

Abby sighed. She'd seen it before. "Not again, Aunt Jo, not again." Abby couldn't tell the many nay-sayers why she remained faithful to her Lt. Robert O'Donnell. She vowed to hold that announcement until he came home.

For the first few months after the war ended, she sat on the front porch of the family home, waiting for some word from Robert. When none came, she watched for the man himself to appear. She convinced herself it was just a matter of time. She would be patient. But when the months became a year, she reluctantly accepted her father's persistent invitation to assist in his medical practice. "Just for a short time," he had said. "You can be my apprentice."

Abby had agreed, certain that her wait would end soon. But the years rolled by and neither letter nor man appeared—until this day.

"Look—in the upper corner of the envelope—I can still make out the three dots he put there," Abby said. "Those three dots always mean 'I love you' and—don't you see?"

"I see them," Jo said, "and . . . and what's that brown stain?"

"I don't know." Abby rubbed the stain with her finger.

"Looks like dried blood to me," the courier said.

"You've done your duty, young man." Jo jumped in and waved the man off. "Haven't you any more letters to deliver today?"

The courier tipped his hat and made a quick about face. The two women ignored him as he pulled the gate shut, with a loud screech of its rusty hinges.

Abby tore into the letter like a five-year-old opening gifts at a birthday party. Water stains made the words barely legible to Abby's eyes. Her tears didn't help. She wiped them away frequently and whispered over and over, "Robert, Robert, my dear Robert."
Suddenly, she stopped. "Aunt Jo, listen to this." Slowly, to absorb every word, Abby began to read.

> *"Dearest One,*
> *I love you so much it hurts. Your love is all I feel this day. It*
> *is the reason I draw my next breath. Your love gives me*
> *strength for each day and soon will carry me back to your*
> *arms again. Please keep the enclosed piece of paper for me.*
> *I'll see you soon…and explain. It's a clue that's supposed to*
> *lead us to a cache of gold hidden by Beaver Island's King*
> *Strang before he died in 1856. You remember those old*
> *stories, don't you? I always thought they were crazy, but*
> *another soldier – he said he is a descendant of ole Strang –*
> *gave it to me. It may be a hoax, but then again, maybe it'll*
> *help start our new life together, that is, if the gold is hidden*
> *as I've been told. I must go, but believe me when I say, I*
> *love you now more than when I started this letter a few*
> *minutes ago. Remember, "I'll be seeing you in all the old*
> *familiar places," especially those familiar places around the*
> *Pine Lake Club. Look for me there soon.*

*One more thing: on the other side is a speech General
Eisenhower delivered. You might want to share it with your
folks.
Robert ...*"

As Abby folded the letter, a yellowed piece of paper fell to the ground.

"What's this?" Jo bent over to retrieve the scrap of paper. "The clue?"

"It must be," Abby said. "The clue to King Strang's hiding place."

Jo opened the yellowed paper and began reading.

*"Day follows night, Old Pine, thy gate to open wide,
The Kingdom awaits all when the rocks begin to slide.
Whoso shall publish peace, to him it shall be seen,
Our lives pass away quickly, as unto us a dream."*

She scanned the note again before giving it a dismissive wave with the back of her hand. "Gibberish," Jo said, and gave the note to Abby. "Just who was this direct Strang descendant, I'd like to know. That gold was never more than a rumor. No one ever proved that old goat buried any gold before he was murdered. Anyway, all that took place a century ago. A tall tale, if you ask me, like the ones your brother used to tell about the fish he caught." She spread her hands as far apart as she could stretch.

"Robert is nobody's fool," Abby said. "If he is convinced the gold exists, it does! Imagine what we could do with that treasure."

"Abby, James Strang was nothing more than a delusional egomaniac." She flicked her fingers into the air as if removing an imaginary pest.

Abby sniffed. "I don't care; I'm taking the Resort Special to Michigan—to Charlevoix."

"What? Now?" Jo stared at Abby in disbelief. "Abby, what do you *really* expect to find there?" Her voice was heavy with desperation. "If Robert was alive, if he was coming home to you, wouldn't he come here, to your home in Saint Louis? Why do you think you'll find him in Charlevoix, at the Pine Lake Club?"

Abby became very quiet as she recalled the glorious days she enjoyed with Robert on the grounds of the Pine Lake Club. And there was that one afternoon under the pines, an afternoon of "precious, unadulterated joy," Robert had said.

"If Robert is struggling to find me this many years since the war ended, there must be a reason, and I know he'll find his way to Charlevoix and the Pine Lake Club." There was a note of sadness in her voice.

"But Abby–" Jo grabbed her niece by the shoulders, and turned her around until they were face to face.

Abby knew that look and wanted none of it. "Aunt Jo, I can't sit here on this porch shelling peas the rest of my life. You said yourself, I should move on." Abby lowered her voice as she turned toward the gate. "I should have made the trip long before now. Robert and I were never happier than when we were together on our…our…Park Island."

"Abby, your brother is not there, remember? He had to sell the cottage to pay debts your father left behind, and he told you he would never return to Pine Lake. If you go, you'll be alone."

"Not if Robert meets me there."

"But what if he isn't there? What will you do?"

"Robert is always with me. He's never left me alone." She turned to Jo in time to see her eyes close and her mouth open. "Don't try to stop me, dear auntie. And, if he's not there, maybe someone will have heard from him. I don't know why I didn't think of that. Besides, Pine Lake is the only place I *haven't* looked for him."

Jo pursed her lips and shook her head.

"Don't look at me that way. I'm not a child anymore." With that, Abby raced into the house in search of her purse. She wanted to make sure she had enough money for a train ticket to Charlevoix. A moment later, the door opened, and Abby bolted for the gate, her ponytail swinging wildly.

"To Union Station," a jubilant Abby shouted over her shoulder, "for a ticket to Charlevoix." She held her fist high in the air as if it already held her ticket.

"Wait! Abby, I think you should slow down and—"

But Abby had made up her mind.

**

At Union Station, the agent told her the resort train had been reduced to a single weekly run and wouldn't depart for another three days. "I've waited ten years; I can wait three more days," she told the agent, as she grabbed her ticket and put it in her purse. She thought the inconvenience only minor, considering whom she expected to find at Pine Lake Depot.

But the wait turned out to be the longest three days of her life.

"Christmas comes faster," she told her aunt, as she began packing her steamer trunk with an end-of-season wardrobe. "Late August, early September, I might need everything from a light wind breaker, for sailing days, to a heavy wool coat for chilly nights." She twirled around the room and stopped in front of her armoire, with eyelashes bouncing up and down. "Of course, Robert will expect me to have a bikini for the beach, and an evening gown for a night at the Club's casino." She threw a bikini toward Jo, who caught it in mid-air.

"Scandalous thing," Jo said. "Where is your mother—your father, too? That damn ice storm—took 'em both that night. You wouldn't be doing this if they were—"

"Now, don't try that guilt thing, auntie. It won't work. Not this time."

Jo threw the bikini back to Abby, who grabbed it in mid-air and winked.

Three days later, Abby sat at her upstairs bedroom window, overnight valise in her lap, hoping to be the first to spot the taxi coming down the street. "There he is!" Abby shouted to Aunt Jo. "Why is he driving so slowly?" Valise in hand, Abby ran from the room and bounded down the stairs just in time to hear the door's first chime.

Jo grabbed the handrail and followed. While the driver struggled with Abby's trunk, Jo put her arms around her niece and whispered, "Be careful. I don't have a good feeling about this. Be very careful."

"Don't be silly." Abby pulled the door tight behind her. A second later, the door opened again, just a crack, and Abby's face peeked around it. "I *will* be careful, auntie, I promise."

And she was off.

**

A tall gentleman, in a black fedora and light brown trench coat, got out of a Victory cab and made his way toward the ear crushing noise emanating from Union Station's Great Hall.

"What *is* that?" He cupped a hand around his ear. "God save the Queen! It's an assault on the sensibilities of all good men." A facial tic caused his left eye to twitch at the sound.

A band of street musicians were gathered directly ahead of him, and as he approached, they launched into their version of one of 1954's biggest summer hits.

> *"I believe to my soul you're the devil, and now I know*
> *Well, the more I work, the faster my money goes…"*

The gentleman hurried by, ignoring the baseball caps the musicians had spread before them to collect change from passers-by. He stopped just long enough to hail a porter.

> *"I said shake, rattle and roll, shake, rattle, and roll*
> *Well, you won't do right to save your doggone soul…"*

"Quit listening to that doolally music, my dear man. Grab my grip, and follow me." One of the porters picked up his "grip" and followed as closely as his short legs would permit. The British accent caused the other porters to roll their eyes and nod to each other. When the porter reached for his leather briefcase, the gentleman pulled it close, shoved it under his arm, and gave it a firm pat. "I'll keep this one with me."

"All Abo-o-o-a-r-d!" The conductor's voice cut through the cacophony of sound in the hall.

Three giant strides more, and the gentleman leapt aboard the *Spirit of St. Louis* bound for Chicago, followed by the porter who quickly handed him his "grip." In exchange, the passenger placed a fifty cent piece in the porter's palm.

"A Walkin' Miss Liberty!" The porter didn't get a fifty cent piece every day. "Thank you, Mister, uh . . . ?"

"You don't need to know, dear chap." With that, the gentleman turned on his heels.

Two blasts from the engine's whistle rattled every window in the Pullman. The gentleman stopped, set his "grip" on the floor of the Pullman's vestibule, and leaned out to watch others boarding. He searched every face, looking for just one. "She'll make it," he said. "The reward on the other end is too compelling." Both eyes twitched as he waited. A few moments later, he caught a glimpse of a young lady with long, golden tresses. "Ah, yes, and lovely she is," he said, as she came more clearly into view. "Just like her photograph. Miss Abigail Finlay."

Abby glanced down the line of rail cars just in time to see a black fedora disappear onto the train. *Don't see many of those around here.*

"'Board!" The conductor's booming voice echoed to the end of the platform. The clock at the end of the platform showed three o'clock exactly.

"Sounds like he means business," Abby said to the approaching porter. "It won't leave for another two minutes but the way that locomotive is hissing and clanking, you'd think it was already moving."

A crack in the wooden platform caught Abby's left heel and held it. One step more and she left the satin pump behind and tottered forward, trying not to fall. She grabbed the porter's shoulder, steadied herself, and squeezed her toes back into the shoe.

"Is this yours, Miss?" The porter picked up the ticket Abby dropped when the platform caught her shoe. "I found it right here."

Abby looked at her hand as though it had betrayed her. "*Yes*, that's mine! What would I have done? Thank you."

The porter flipped it over and checked her reservation. "Miss Finlay, you'll be in roomette sixteen." He placed the step stool next to the Pullman entrance and offered Abby his hand. She missed the stool entirely on her first attempt to step up to the Pullman. "Slow down, miss, this old train won't leave without you," the porter said. "I don't know who's waiting for you on the other end, but he'll wait—if he has any sense at all."

Abby smiled and wondered if her excitement was that obvious. *But why shouldn't I be excited?* She was on her way to her family's summer retreat—the place where she met the love of her life, Lt. Robert O'Donnell. Along came the war, and Robert left with the others, promising to return soon and pick up their lives. His letters came regularly until the Allied assault at Normandy. After that day, there were no more letters.

"God's ways are not our ways," her father told her.

"If that was supposed to make me feel better, it didn't work," she remembered telling him. Abby switched her overnight valise to her left hand and began searching for roomette sixteen. From the corner of her eye, she spied the approaching conductor who had just pulled out his watch.

"Last call! *Spirit of St. Louis* to Chicago. Last call! 'Bo-aard!"

He squeezed by her, and she continued searching. Thin strips of light leaked from around the doors of occupied roomettes. "These grand old cars now look quite a bit the worse for wear," she said. "Time has taken its toll." She smiled as she thought of the many times she made this journey with her mother—and why. *I got motion sickness when we came by car. The train was more civilized, anyway.*

A second porter in a starched, white jacket appeared and reached for her valise. "Excuse me, Miss Finlay, but your berth is ready." He motioned for her to follow.

"Thank you, but I've decided to go to the parlor car to read awhile. Take my valise, if you will, to my roomette, and come for me in about half an hour."

"Yes ma'am," the porter said, nodding.

"And, oh yes, please ask someone to bring me a cup of hot tea with lemon. I do need to unwind a bit."

The porter nodded again and disappeared down the aisle.

As soon as she settled in the first vacant chair, out came Robert's letter for the umpteenth time in the last three days. Every word reminded her of a time when they were making plans for their future. *But that was before that June night in '44.* She remembered Ed Murrow's radio report from London as if it were yesterday. She squeezed her eyes shut, the better to recall Murrow's exact words.

> *"I'm standing on a rooftop looking out over London. At the moment, everything is quiet. For reasons of national, as well as personal security, I am unable to tell you the exact location from which I am speaking . . ."*

Abby leaned toward the loudspeaker to hear more clearly the voice of the famous war correspondent, but Murrow's voice faded into the ether, replaced by loud, popping static.

Her father jumped up and pinched the aerial, with a thumb and index finger, to improve reception.

". . . [b]ut the guns are so far away that it is impossible to hear them from this location. About five minutes ago, the guns in the immediate vicinity were not working."

Again, the signal faded away. Abby sat frozen, staring at the loudspeaker, but she heard nothing but static. "What guns? Where? Father, can't you do something?"

When her father shook his head, Abby ran from the room.

She pulled out Robert's letters and read them all—again. This was her habit when she could not sleep because holding his letters kept her close to him. Finally, she crawled into bed, pulled up the covers, and prayed sleep would come quickly. But it never did.

Abby was never told the exact whereabouts of her fiancé. She knew only that his Missouri National Guard unit was in England, training for the day when the allies would make their assault on the European continent.

Finally, after tossing in bed a few hours, Abby tiptoed into the living room and once again turned on the radio.

"Leo Diamond and His Harmonaires" were entertaining, when suddenly, the music stopped.

"We interrupt our program to bring you a special broadcast. The German News Agency, Transocean, said today on a broadcast, that the allied invasion had begun. I repeat.

The German News Agency, Transocean, said today in a broadcast the allied invasion had begun. There was no immediate allied confirmation."

In the blackness of the early morning hours, Allied forces had already made the brief sail from Weymouth, England to Normandy, France.

My heart aches. I feel physically sick.

Trembling fingers reached for the knob on the radio and turned it counterclockwise until it clicked off. She climbed back into her bed where exhaustion finally saved her, at least for the remainder of that night.

The house was dark.

**

A sudden bump on the rails and the jostle of a teacup brought Abby back to the parlor car. She folded Robert's letter as a waiter arrived with the tea she had ordered. "Just place it on the table, please." She squeezed a few drops of fresh lemon juice into the tea, and. as she sipped, she pondered again the hand written verse Robert had included with his letter.

"Day follows night, Old Pine, thy gate to open wide,
The Kingdom awaits all when the rocks begin to slide.
Whoso shall publish peace, to him it shall be seen,
Our lives pass away quickly, as unto us a dream."

Abby shut her eyes and had another one of her imaginary conversations with Robert. Such conversations, she found, always brought her a measure of comfort. At times, she thought she even heard his voice. *Oh, Robert, I want to help, but I don't even know what it means. I spent a whole day in the Saint Louis Public Library reading everything its archives held on James Jesse Strang. The buried gold is mentioned as a rumor in virtually every book or newspaper account of his years on Beaver.* She was quiet for a few minutes, then whispered aloud, "I'll be there soon, dear Robert, very soon."

The porter tapped her on the shoulder. "Excuse me, Miss Abby, it's been more than half an hour, far more."

"I'll be right there." As she held Robert's clue, she examined both sides again. *Where has it been all these years?* Slowly, she folded the clue and returned it to the worn, brown envelope. She examined both sides, then waved it at the porter. "Where has it been all these years?" He didn't answer, but she didn't expect one. She followed the porter to roomette sixteen, closed the door, and began unbuttoning her blouse. Undressing in such cramped quarters, however, proved to be a challenge. *There used to be more room in here.* She smiled, twisted her torso, and with some effort, unzipped her corselette. *You almost have to be a contortionist to make this work.*

A few minutes later, she was snuggled under the Pullman's salmon-colored, wool blanket. The back and forth, constant swaying of the old Pullman, soon lulled her to sleep—a fitful sleep.

In the restlessness that followed, she relived a dream she had dreamt nearly every night for the past decade. *I'll never forget that Sunday, that summer.*

**

"Come on Abby, we're going to Park Island."

"Be right there!" Abby picked up her swimsuit and grabbed a towel. "Mother, don't hold dinner!"

"Dinner will be at seven." The edge in Frances Finlay's voice said, "Seven p.m. sharp."

"Sure, sure." Abby was out the door.

With Abby sitting in the bow of his little canoe, Robert was soon paddling the shallow waters of Old River, up the little channel behind Park Island, and away from any prying eyes on the Pine Lake shore.

"C'mon," Abby said. "Hurry!"

"I'm paddling as fast as I can."

Under the pines of Park Island, their first kiss had set off a chemical reaction that produced all the ingredients for cementing their relationship. "It was magical," Abby had told her mother, "and wonderful."

But I didn't tell her that Robert has the best hands. With only a touch, he brings every nerve ending in my body to attention, and I don't want him to stop—ever.

Abby knew she couldn't go "all the way," as the other kids referred to the act of having sex. She always called a halt before things got completely out of hand.

"I'm a virgin, Robert."

"So am I."

"We're Presbyterians for heaven's sakes, what would John Calvin say?"

"Quite a bit, I suspect." Robert smiled. "In my family, sex before marriage is strictly taboo."

"My mother wants us to wait until you come home." Abby gently traced her finger along his chin, a bit rough with whiskers, and smiled. "I don't want to wait, but she does, and I guess that's that."

"But that's too long." Robert looked straight up. "God can be witness to our love, to our promises to each other." Pulling Abby close to him, he whispered, "Can you think of a better witness?"

Abby shook her head. "I . . . guess not."

"No, of course not." Robert spun around 360 degrees. With arms outstretched, he asked, "Have you ever seen a more natural cathedral?"

Abby blushed. Robert grabbed her hands and pulled her to him once more. "We're surrounded by gorgeous white birches, a wedding gift from Mother Nature herself for the commitment we're about to make, and she took the time to arrange the birches against a backdrop of the tallest pines you've ever seen. And here—look at the bridal bier—a bed of pink and white wild flowers. They probably have a name."

"Lady's Slipper, silly."

"Oh, of course. And the music, we need some music. There's no orchestra, so I'll try to sing something, uh, accompanied by the breeze in these pines. There's only one song appropriate for this occasion. Are you ready?"

Abby shook her head. "No, but I don't dare stop you. This should be good."

Robert cleared his throat and began to sing his version of a tune they'd heard many times on the radio.

"I'll be seeing you,
In all the old familiar places—"

Then, he forgot the words.   After a moment of hesitation, he picked up the tune, inserting lyrics he made up as he went along, forcing a squeeze into each line.

"In Schroeder's café,
Park Isle across the way,
In maple trees,
A summer's breeze,
The rustic bridge,
The terrace ridge."

Abby laughed. "I don't think it goes that way."
"Wait, I'm not through."

> *"At Pine Lake Beach,*
> *My lovely peach,*
> *Come what may,*
> *I'll always think of you that way,*
> *And I'll be seeing you—every day."*

And with that, they melted into each other's arms for the rest of the afternoon.

"Oh, how I wish I could make the earth stand still for one more day," Abby finally managed to say, as the sun fell behind the trees.

"As do I, my love, as do I," Robert whispered in her ear.

Long shadows covered the little island before their bodies finally separated. Robert pulled Abby to her feet. "But we have to go. Didn't you tell me your mother expected you at seven for dinner?"

"Oh, my gosh!" Abby grabbed her blouse and slipped into her penny loafers. "Our parents are already suspicious. We've gotta' go!"

Another surprise awaited them, as they reached the beach and began removing branches that hid Robert's canoe.

"Who's that?" Robert pointed to a large group of children walking along the beach. One adult chaperone was trying, unsuccessfully, to keep them together.

"Pine Lake brats! Probably looking for wild things— deer, muskrat . You know, plenty here." Abby looked about her nervously, hoping no one else was there.

"Do you think they spied two love birds?" Robert winked. "The pines aren't thick enough to hide everything. God may not have been our only witness." He gave his canoe a push into the water.

"I hope not, but if they did, they likely just giggled and ran away to tell their chaperone." Abby jumped aboard, trying to keep her feet dry, but in her hurry, failing.

A beaver slapped his tail against the water as their little canoe pulled out onto Old River.

**

Without warning, the Pullman lurched to one side, took two sudden jerks forward, and another backward.

"Screeech! Schliipisssssh! Plang! Plang!"

Sounds of steel scraping steel, coupling and uncoupling—Abby knew the sounds well. The Pullman was being pushed along a siding by a switcher locomotive. *Unwillingly, I'd say.* She covered her ears. *They're moving the Pullman cars to the C&O Resort Special for the final leg.* Abby dropped her hands and cocked her head to one side. *Did I hear someone?* The next moment, the Pullman stopped with a sudden burst of steam.

"Robert, is that you?" She was surprised to hear a noise that sounded like a voice. "Are you there?" She heard only the sound of her own breathing. "Robert, I have something to say, something I haven't shared with you but should've long ago." Abby took a deep breath. "Ten years ago . . ." She swallowed hard, but couldn't hold back the tears. "No, no I can't; it's just too awful. I'm sorry, but I can't speak the words. I want to tell you. I do, but I'm ashamed to speak the words— and afraid you won't understand—and worse, afraid you won't speak to me again." In the stillness, with the Pullman now parked on the siding, she pulled the blanket over her head and held it tight, as she retreated from the pain of her private thoughts.

Finally, the Pullman began moving again, jerking and swinging back and forth as it picked up speed.

After a long while, she peeked through the window curtains and tried to identify images on the passing landscape. The blackness of the night hid the monotonous sameness of the row houses, lit here and there by naked bulbs on front stoops, little flecks of light not much brighter than fireflies. Soon, the row houses gave way to endless miles of barbed wire fencing, guarding field after field of late summer corn.

"Please come home," she whispered to the night. "I am so alone . . . . so alone."

The regular rhythm of the Pullman registered the passing of each rail, and soon brought her back to the present. She loved railroad tracks; they always kept their promise. Railroad tracks didn't go tearing off through the woods for no reason at all. And they certainly didn't run off to war, never to return. "We were so happy," she whispered.

Abby turned out the light and pulled the blanket up tight. Around the edges of her window curtains, she caught the occasional snap of lightning in the distance and could hear the rumble of thunder that accompanied each strike. *Sleep will be difficult tonight.*

In the roomette next to hers, the gentleman with the brown trench coat prepared for what he hoped would be a good night's sleep. He had watched Abby's every move since boarding, from parlor car to Pullman berth. He made certain she did not change her mind and disembark before the train pulled out of Saint Louis. As he closed the doors to his own roomette, he noticed Abby's light already out. "The bait has been taken," he said aloud. "Now, James Strang, King of Beaver Island, you, sir, will help me reel it in slowly."

Chapter Two
A Priest, a Legislator, a Conqueror

1826 – Chappaqua County, New York

I will suffocate and die if I become a farmer, bureaucrat, or even a lawyer. I am unable to think on such lowly endeavors." James Strang sighed and threw his schoolbooks on the kitchen table.

His mother, her back to him when he came through the door, put her soup ladle down and turned to face the young James. "You're just thirteen years of age, James." She leaned toward him and looked him squarely in the eyes. "Thirteen! Don't you think it a bit pre-mature to be excluding such honorable professions from your career?" This was a conversation they'd had many times.

"No, Mother, I do not." He slumped into the nearest chair. "I do not."

His mother picked up the ladle and stirred the soup again while James stared at her back. Finally, she turned to him and, in a near whisper, asked, "Do you have something . . . you want to do . . . above all else?"

James nodded slowly.

"Well, write it down," she said. "Think about it every day, and dare I say this: pray about it."

James pulled himself out of the chair and dragged himself to his room. "No answers have ever come to me while praying," he said, as he walked away. "I might as well be an atheist."

"*James Strang*! I never want to hear you say such a thing again—*ever*," his mother said. "Shame on you for having such a thought."

In his room, young James picked up his diary and began to write. "My overriding ambition is . . ." He scratched his chin, then dashed off, ". . . to accomplish something grand with my life." He was barely a teenager but already impatient to achieve success. "Some days," he wrote, "I am overwhelmed by the unlimited possibilities the future holds for me."

His mother opened his door a crack and peeked in. "One more thing, James. 'Add to your knowledge, self-control.' That's from the Book of Proverbs."

"I know where it's from, Mother. It's Second Peter 1:5 – *not* Proverbs – and there is more to it. 'And to self-control, add patience, and to patience, godliness.'"

His mother was quiet for a moment. "James, you know so much about the Bible already; perhaps you should become a great preacher."

"I don't think so, Mother. There is no such ambition in my soul." *Why did I feel a sharp twinge at her suggestion?* James became very quiet. He put his pen down, then, picked it up again. "No such ambition at all." His feet shuffled back and forth under the desk.

His mother, at last, broke the silence. "Well, whatever you settle on, you'll do well to be diligent in your studies. All that you seek will be out of your reach if you fail to exercise self-control over your ambitions."

"Did Napoleon limit his ambitions? I think not."

"But Napoleon's ambition was his undoing, my sweet James." She reached over and gently caressed his chin.

"I'm smarter than Napoleon, my dear Mother." He put his hand into his shirt jacket and stood at military attention, as he had once seen in a portrait of Napoleon.

His mother could only shake her head. James sat down and picked up his pen again. As his mother started for the door, she paused just long enough to close the conversation. "I suspect Napoleon knew nothing of Proverbs *or* Second Peter." And then, she was gone.

James laughed and closed the door after her. "I know only one thing," he wrote in his diary. "I am surely destined to be a general in the army, a great political leader, or perhaps a religious leader with a large flock of believers. Yes, even a preacher. There is across the country, in this very time, a revivalist fervor racing through the land like a fever."

**

Three years later, young James was still undecided about his future. He had no confidence in his father's advice and filled his diary with thoughts of his father's weaknesses. His father was short in stature, little more than five feet tall, but known in the community as a "kind and charitable" man. *Of what use are such people?* James asked himself. His father was a devout Baptist, of that he was sure, and on occasion, a strict disciplinarian.   But worst of all, James found his father's incessant questioning about a career path a bit tiresome.

"You spend too much time in your room, James. What do you do in there?" Clement Strang asked him the same question nearly every day.

James always gave him the same response: "Studying, thinking and planning my future."

"Have you asked your teachers for their counsel regarding the vocation you should pursue?" Always, that was his second question.

"My teachers are inexperienced and ill qualified to offer advice on any subject. If I am to have any insight on such things, it will come from within or perhaps from a Divine source. I do believe, most devoutly, that God anointed me at birth with Divine insight."

"Preachers are poor men," his father would say. "You are an able debater, and more than glib. Your voice reflects a maturity beyond your years. Perhaps the study of law is for you?"

Father always points me away from religion. James would shake his head. "I enjoy reading, Father, but not the law." James tried to change the subject. "Give me the works of Thomas Paine and Walter Scott, and I am quite happy."

"Walter Scott? What has he written that inspires you?"

"'He that climbs the tall tree has won the right to the tall fruit.'" James enjoyed quoting Walter Scott. "And I shall climb the tallest tree, my Father. I shall become a better writer than Scott most certainly—and *I will* pick the tallest fruit."

That's when his father would shake his head and quietly retreat from the room.

**

By the time James' family gathered round the kitchen table to celebrate his nineteenth birthday, he could not contain the many ambitions that burned within. "I ought to have been a member of the Assembly or a Brigadier General before this time if I am ever going to rival Caesar or Napoleon as I have sworn to."

The family laughed, and his cousin slapped him on the back.

"Now James," his mother said, as she placed the birthday pound cake before him, "it's fine to be mediocre or ordinary in some things, isn't it?"

"Curse me eternally if mediocrity be my fate," James replied, slamming his palm on the table so hard, the salt shaker turned over. "Mediocre? Never! Here, look at this!" He held up a sheath of paper for all to see. "I have spent this entire day contriving a plan to persuade the heir of the English Crown to join me in marriage. It is a difficult business for me, but I shall try if there is the least chance."

Suddenly, all were quiet. His father put a hand on James' shoulder. "I do not wish to discourage you, my son, but do you think it rational that the Queen would entertain the idea of making a young man, from the back woods frontier of New York, her prince?"

James stared at his father, squinted, and in a calm voice, said, "Do you think me a fool?" James ducked from under his father's arm. "My mind has always been filled with dreams of royalty and power— and why not? Why not?"

There was a ripple of nervous laughter from those around the table. His mother shushed the group as James flew away from the table, leaving nineteen candles burning. In his room, James snatched the pen off his desk and poured his dreams of marriage to Queen Victoria onto no less than ten additional pages.

His many letters to Queen Victoria did not elicit so much as a polite acknowledgement. *Since my entreaties were never returned, I shall continue to believe she must have all my epistles under consideration.*

Chapter Three
A Diamond between Two Sapphires

Abby tossed back and forth in her berth, frequently fluffing her pillow, struggling to find a position that would permit sleep— even for fifteen uninterrupted minutes. Well before dawn, she gave up, got out of her berth, and packed her bags. She was fully dressed and ready to disembark, long before the train reached Traverse City. The old track, uneven and bumpy, had the rail car swaying from side to side, as it had done, Abby thought, most of the night. A brass rail along the Pullman's narrow corridor gave her welcome stability. She stumbled her way to the dining car where cooks, still bleary eyed from a short night's sleep, welcomed her as the first diner of the morning.

"Well, at least the eggs ought to be fresh," Abby joked to the porter holding her chair. "Make mine scrambled, with an English muffin and cherry preserves on the side. And, oh yes, tea with lemon, please."

The early hour afforded her the opportunity for a second and third cup of tea before the conductor strolled through calling out her destination. "PINE Lake! PINE Lake! And SHAR-lee-VOY!"

Two stops, recalled Abby, and both nearly within sight of each another. Through the window, Abby caught a glimpse of the old, wooden semaphore, its arm pivoted downward in the traditional position for a stop. Pangs of nostalgia pricked her brain as she realized she was about to step again on the manicured grounds of the Pine Lake Club— and her memory swirled with images from the past. Smiling, she picked up her coat, handbag, and scarf, and moved closer to the door, impatient for the end of her journey.   Finally, the brakes of the old Pullman squealed to a stop.

Abby blew a kiss to the Club's red and white burgee, flying high above the depot. The burgee meant she was home—home on the Pine Lake Club. The Club took its name from the body of water on its eastern boundary that was known as Pine Lake in the Club's founding year, 1878. When town fathers renamed the lake in the 1920s, Club members stuck with Pine Lake Club. Abby was told about the decision some years later, but wasn't surprised. *Change doesn't come easily at the Club.*

The Club sat on Round Lake, with Lake Michigan less than half a mile to the west and Lake Charlevoix on the eastern shore. Round Lake connected both of the larger lakes by way of Pine River, a narrow channel that runs through downtown Charlevoix.   Abby couldn't remember who first described Round Lake as "A diamond between two sapphires," but that bit of hyperbole always brought a smile to her face.

"And there's our cottage, *Sunrise*," she told the porter, who had appeared next to her holding her overnight valise. "Just a little Queen Anne dollhouse." Abby pointed to the white cottage, with teal trim, next to the Hotel. "What a gorgeous view of Lake Charlevoix." The Club's sprawling, two-story Hotel was just coming into view on the left side of the train. "I love its gingerbread trim, but—" She accepted her valise from the porter. "But, I shall truly miss my beloved *Sunrise*."

She didn't share that her brother had been forced to sell the cottage to pay the outstanding debts her father left behind when he died. She smiled to think of her father's lifelong penchant for generous and charitable giving. *He didn't charge his patients when they were down and out, and he kept even fewer records of such.* She sighed deeply. *But I wish he had. God bless him.*

Abby had always been first off the train since she was a little girl, but today, as she stared into a sea of faces on the platform, she only had questions. *Do any of them know my worst secret? Will they see me and think, 'there she is; she's the one we've heard about.'*

She shook herself. *Get yourself together, Abby girl. Take that first step.*

The conductor placed his stool near the Pullman's entrance, and Abby stepped down into the cool, invigorating embrace of the early morning Charlevoix air.

Not far behind her, a passenger pulled on his trench coat and cinched the belt tight as he stepped off the train. He stopped only long enough to light up a cigarette, and a cloud of smoke soon hid almost all of his face, but he never took his eyes off Abby.

The livery driver offered her a ride, but she waved him off. She preferred the walk. It was, after all, only a short distance from the depot to the Hotel. People rushed by her in their hurry to greet arriving guests and family members. She recognized many—the doctor from Ohio and his artist wife, and that musician from Benny Goodman's band. She was sure their names would come to her later. Abby glanced up and down the platform.

Ah, well, no sign of Robert. Two steps more, and she couldn't resist stopping to take a look at the old railroad swing bridge a few yards beyond the depot. She remembered sharing a final goodbye kiss with Robert at the exact spot where the bridge crosses the channel. Her eyes drifted left, past the Casino, and down the embankment to Old River, where it emerges from behind Park Island and empties into the channel. Tears blurred Abby's vision. *Old River, have you kept all the secrets we share?*

28 || Roland McElroy

Chapter Four
Courtship of Mary Perce

1836 – Cherry Creek, New York

Is that a letter from the Queen?" James' mother teased, as she placed the laundry on the kitchen table where James was slowly unfolding a letter.

"No, Mother, definitely not the Queen." It had been a long journey from thirteen to twenty-three years of age, and James had long ago given up realistic expectations that the Queen would answer his many expressions of interest. "No, Mother, not the Queen, but it is from William Perce, father of Mary."

"Oh, yes–Mary, your intended."

James looked up on those words, and smiled broadly.

"Good news?" she asked.

James held the letter high in the air. "I was confident I could win her affections if she would reserve enough time for prudent reflection. Apparently, she did."

"And?" His mother leaned across the table to replenish his glass of cider.

"And now I have *this*, a letter from her father giving his approval." He waved the letter as if it were a trophy.

His mother stood beside him, gave him a hug, and a kiss on the cheek. "You have passed the bar, established a practice, and now you are blessed by this young lady who has agreed to marriage. I am so proud of you."

Without smiling, James folded the letter and returned it to his pocket with a secure tap of his hand. "I remember the day I first met Mary. It was the wedding day of her aunt, Freelove Perce. You were there, Mother. Mary was already a full flower." He smiled ever so slightly and turned toward his mother. "That day, no one was more radiant, not even the bride."

His mother stopped folding the laundry. "I thought you seemed perfect for each other." She threw down the sock she was holding. "I can't find its match."

"Here, Mother." James picked up the missing sock from the floor. "Now you have a perfect match . . ." He smiled again. ". . . and so do I."

His mother picked up another sock and again began searching for a match. "But James, your father was not amused when the two of you became engaged. He thought your pursuit of Mary was reckless."

"Perhaps, I was. But if Mary mistook my aggressive pursuit for an undisciplined nature, she was mistaken in her judgment, and I, disappointed that she would adopt such a shallow reason to break off our first attempt at engagement."

"I am convinced some socks are not meant to be matched." His exasperated mother threw the second sock down. "I give up." She put another stick of wood in the kitchen's old potbelly stove. "Your father thinks Mary has a rather mercurial personality, an unpredictable nature."

James shook his head. "I do not see her that way." He checked to be sure the letter was still in his pocket and gave it another couple of firm taps. "I am determined that she not be my Waterloo." James gulped down all remaining cider in his glass and placed it next to the pitcher. "I never gave up. Even as she resisted, it was in her best interest that she agree to be my wife."

"And what does Mary say? His mother filled his glass a second time. "Have you talked with her?"

"In our last conversation, she said she was willing. And now her father, who is away in Virginia building a canal, has given his consent." James pulled out the letter again. "Hear his exact words: *'I fervently hope neither of you may have cause for sorrow and that you may not be disappointed.'"* He held up a second page. "And, my dear Mother, there's this–a copy of the words he wrote to Mary: *'I am now about to surrender my authority, but you must not forget that your part is still obedience. You have been a dutiful daughter. Do not let me hear that you are a stubborn wife, but remember to make your home pleasant for your husband.'"* James could not resist another broad smile. He folded the letter again and placed it in his pocket. "I like her father very much. God *is* good to me."

His mother nodded, but said nothing.

**

The marriage took place at the Presbyterian Church in Cherry Creek, New York, on a cold day in November, 1836. Skies were heavy and completely overcast as guests arrived. Mary's aunt whispered in her ear as she was about to walk down the aisle. "I hope your marriage will be brighter than this dreary day." She squeezed Mary's hand as if to guarantee better days ahead.

But it was not to be. After the marriage, James worried constantly about Mary's health, which was never good, particularly in the early years of their marriage. Her letters to James, when he was away, included frequent references to her health problems. "The doctors say it is a respiratory problem that affects my 'vital capacity,'" she wrote. "They are at a loss to give their diagnosis a name. As for me, I know only that this terrible malady visits me altogether too frequently. I am some melancholy this evening." She added a postscript: "Your brother, David, has encouraged me to give up my studies of science. He says I deplete your resources and that my studying may be the cause of my ill health. I must tell you that my studies bring me more happiness than anything, except your appearance at the door."

James sensed that something else troubled his wife. *Her letters reflect the sad spirit of one who is lonely and depressed.* He read aloud the words he had just received: "*'I am some melancholy this evening.'*"

In response to her letter, James struggled for several days to find words that Mary might find uplifting. "*Continue your studies, if they bring you happiness,*" he finally wrote. "*New quills are enclosed for your use. But do be careful with your health, my dearest, and follow the physician's directions in everything. I fear you will not be careful enough.*"

James thought childbirth might give her more happiness. "It imposes a regimen to life, and a new joy that cannot be explained to the childless," he said to Mary, when she told him she was expecting.

Any chance for Mary to experience a "new joy" vanished when their first child died in infancy. James could only watch, as Mary fell into a deep depression. He continued to believe that a healthy baby would be the best antidote for her spells of depression. In the spring of 1840, they welcomed a baby girl into their lives. But the birth of Myraette Mabel did not diminish Mary's periodic bouts with depression. At times, James found Mary inconsolable. When the news of Mary's chronic condition reached her sister-in-law in Wisconsin, Myrtle wrote to invite them all to move to the Wisconsin Territory.

"Come and enjoy the peaceful prairie," Myrtle wrote in 1843. "Your brother, Benjamin, will welcome James' assistance in selling real estate."

Her invitation came at a propitious moment for the Strang family. James had lost his position as postmaster in Ellington, New York. None of the work he was doing as a lawyer brought him any satisfaction. Even the newspaper he founded did not fulfill his ambitions. In James' view, 1843 had become yet another low point on a career path he had hoped would bring him great honor and glory.

Still, he was reluctant to drop everything and dash off to the Wisconsin Territory. "I am waiting for Divine Providence to reveal his plan for my life," James told Mary, as they sat around the hearth one night, weighing their decision.

"Why, James, are you so hesitant to accept Myrtle's invitation?" Mary asked. "You have always possessed the most confident and ambitious spirit."

He took a long sip from the cup of soup he was holding, and then, began cradling the cup, first in one palm, and then, the other, blowing steam away with each exchange of the cup. "I'll go," he said, at last, staring into an empty palm. "I do not know what awaits us in Wisconsin, but surely it will be a higher calling than selling real estate. It must be."

"You are ever the dreamer, James, ever the dreamer," Mary said, smiling. "I believe God will provide an answer to your prayers in Wisconsin. Just remember to 'Trust in the Lord with all thine heart, and lean not upon thine own understanding.'"

That night, they began packing their belongings for the long trek to Wisconsin.

Chapter Five
The Darkening Mist

More than a few heads took notice as the Saint Louis beauty, wearing the latest silk chemise, stepped toward the Hotel's main entrance. She looked stunning, as if she had just stepped off a Christian Dior runway, not the C&O Resort Special.

To her left, next door to the Hotel, Abby spied *Sunrise,* the summer home of her youth. *Hmmmm . . . gingerbread trim needs painting, but there's the rocking horse swing my brother made. Not much more than a scrap of carpet nailed over a two-by-four . . . . but might as well have been a Kentucky thoroughbred for all the fun we had.* She always hoped her own children would enjoy it. *But now, maybe not . . . maybe not ever.*

Just as Abby placed a foot on the stairs that climbed the Hotel's terrace, a familiar face peered over the railing that guarded the second floor veranda. *Julius Mooney! I'd recognize that white suit and Panama hat anywhere.* A second later, the face disappeared.

Abby couldn't remember how long Julius Mooney had been the Hotel's manager, but she knew he had been the Club's sailing instructor for at least two dozen years before that. The outside staircase took her straight up to the second level where she found Julius settled in his favorite Carolina rocker. *I believe that's where he was sitting the last time I saw him, ten years ago, and he's still wearing those snakeskin boots.*

Julius Mooney started to get up as Abby approached, then hesitated.

"Hello, Julius, I don't think you remember me."

Mooney jumped to his feet. A knowing smile spread across his face. "As I live and breathe, I think it's that little girl I used to call 'Miss Gingerbread.' Where're your pigtails? What'd you do with those freckles? I reckon you can still run faster than any of the boys; am I right?"

"No, but you're still a tease, Julius." *And he still has that permanent sneer up the left side of his face. Mother said it was like a lopsided smile that made half of his face look happy, while the other half looked as if it just paid the tax bill. Father, the doctor, was not so kind. He said it was a problem with facial muscles—some stronger than others. Whatever the reason, it always made him look unhappy with the world.*

Mooney extended his arms for a bear hug, but Abby only gave him a demure smile while extending her hand, which he shook vigorously. "I wasn't sure we would see you again. I heard about Robert."

"Have you seen him? Has he been here?" Of all the people she might encounter on Club grounds, Abby knew Julius Mooney would know if Robert had been around, if only for one day. Hardly anything escaped his curious eye.

Mooney gave his suspenders a quick pull and released them with a loud snap. "No, Abby, I haven't seen him. I was about to extend my condolences."

He hasn't seen Robert. That's not what I expected to hear. Abby slumped in the nearest rocker.

"The Club feels different to me, Julius, as if something major has changed. Everything looks the same, but it certainly doesn't feel the same."

"As the lake changes with the weather of the day and seasons of the year, Miss Gingerbread, so does the Club change with the chapters of one's life."

Abby shook her head. "Look who's talking. You sit in the same rocker, at the same hour of the day, every day of every summer."

"You're not the first to make that observation." Julius pursed his lips several times in quick succession. "I work plenty hard all day, but I'll have you know, I sit in this Carolina rocker on doctor's orders. Best thing for my back." He leaned forward, was quiet a moment, and the tone of his voice became quite serious. "I've changed, Abby. Believe me, I've changed." He stared out toward the lake. "We all change, even you."

Abby thought the wrinkles on Julius' face seemed longer and deeper than she remembered.

"Abby . . . " Julius lowered his voice to a near whisper. "We *must* change, or change will be thrust upon us."

Abby decided to change the subject. "And how *is* your wife, uh, Henrietta?"

"Oh, Abby, you haven't heard," he said, his voice barely audible and shaking with emotion. "My Henrietta, my wife and helpmeet for more than forty years, one bright mornin' four years ago, stepped off this planet into 'the undiscovered country from whose bourn no traveler ere returns.'"

Neither said anything more for several minutes.

Then, as if someone had turned a switch, Julius turned abruptly to Abby. "Your father is not here, Abby, so I'm gonna' tell you like your poppa would: don't get caught up in this search for King Strang's gold. Fool's gold if you ask me. Doesn't exist. More trouble than it's worth even to think about."

Abby was surprised to hear Julius mention King Strang's gold without any prompting from her. *Where'd that come from? Surely no one could have told him the purpose of my visit. No one knew.*

"And one more thing," Julius said. "Stay out of the Darkening Mist."

"The what?"

"The Darkening Mist. You wouldn't like it. You wouldn't like it at all." His eyes tightened into tiny slits on his last words.

"Thank you, I'll . . . I'll keep that in mind," she said, and took a few steps backward. *That was more than a warning—more like a threat.* "Excuse me, Julius, I must go to the front desk and check in."

Julius nodded, and then, with a heavy sigh, he settled back in his rocker.

As Abby left the veranda, she walked past an open dining room window and was bombarded with the aromas of lunch being prepared. She sniffed the air and tried to identify dishes familiar to her since childhood. "That's gotta' be a Smoked Ham Steak, or maybe . . . " A moment later, her entire face lit up. "Beef Liver with Onions, my father's favorite." She peeked through the window and inhaled the aroma of all those dishes baking, stewing, and being stirred.

The Ham Steak makes me homesick since that's what the whole family enjoyed every Sunday after church. For some reason, Abby thought of *Brigadoon*, the Broadway musical she enjoyed two summers ago, a fantasy about a Scottish town that disappeared into the Highland mist and returned for one day every hundred years.

In a sense, Pine Lake is not unlike Brigadoon in that it awakens each summer for three glorious months, before closing its eyes again for nine months. And each time it awakes, it's paradise once more.

Abby walked into the lobby of the Hotel, and her *Brigadoon* moment was almost complete. When she left Saint Louis, amateurs in Union Station were singing one of the new rock and roll hits by Bill Haley's band, but now, down the hall, someone was playing the music of Fred Waring and his Pennsylvanians.

The music warbled, slowed down, and a moment later, she heard the ratcheting sound of someone winding up an old Victrola. Abby smiled when the music resumed its normal tempo. *The timeless classics of days gone by always make me happy . . . and sad...very sad.*

In the lobby, she spied the candy counter she visited so often as a child, and walked right up to see if the same treats were on display. For a moment, she was almost that little girl again, allowing her tongue to trace her bottom lip, the better to resurrect the memory of lemon flavored

Necco wafers—always her favorite candy. Their tangy tartness stayed with you all afternoon.

"What'll it be, young lady?" A voice from behind the counter brought her back to the present.

"Oh, Xeno Miller, it's you. I'm so glad to see you're still here." Abby was relieved that she recalled the name of the blind attendant behind the counter. Xeno always amazed the children in the Club with his ability to tell the difference between a one dollar bill and a five dollar bill, just by its feel.

"Why, of course, I'm always here. And you're gazing at my selection of sweets with that same look you gave them in your childhood."

"Now, Xeno, how can–?" Abby's eyes had taken in everything under the glass counter, but she was amazed that somehow Xeno knew.

"I can't see, but I can *hear* what you're looking for in your voice." Xeno reached under the glass and pulled out two packages. "For example, one of these is your favorite, right?" He opened his fist to reveal a roll of Sugar Daddies and another roll of Necco Wafers.

Abby giggled like the schoolgirl she used to be when she stood before the candy counter. "Necco Wafers! I used to buy a whole roll just for the one lemon flavored wafer inside."

"Now you can buy a whole roll of the lemon flavored wafers. Say, where's that Robert? He always came with you. He always asked for the same thing, a pack of Black Jack licorice gum."

"I thought you knew," Abby sighed. "Robert was at Normandy on D-Day. He hasn't come home . . . yet." She was tired of revisiting the story, but never tired of reminding others that she still expected Robert to return.

"Abby, forgive me. Mr. Mooney told me the news a long time ago, and I forgot. We lost so many members of the Club that day. You know, Robert came by to see me before he left and bought a pack of gum. He said it was to remember the Club and especially the girl he planned to marry one day in the gazebo on the Old Rustic Bridge."

Abby managed a faint smile even as she held a hand to her mouth to suppress the urge to cry.

"I can tell I've made you sad." He pulled a Kleenex from a box near the cash register and held it out. When she reached for it, Xeno placed the roll of Necco Wafers in her palm and closed her fingers around it. "Here, take this. It's on me. They're *all* lemon flavored."

"Wh-what happened to your hands, Xeno?" Abby had not seen his hands until that moment, but she could see that both hands were wrapped in bandages from his knuckles to his wrist. Xeno jerked his hands out of sight and placed them behind his back, but Abby had seen enough. "Are you hurt badly?"

"Uh, no, no. Abby, I didn't mean for you to see; the drawer of this old register was stuck the other day. I gave it a hard bump with my knee, and it slammed shut with my knuckles caught underneath. It's not too bad. My fault, I guess. I should have asked someone for help. Anyway, don't worry about me. You're here . . . at Pine Lake . . . and for a reason, I'm sure. Come to see me if you need anything, anything at all."

"I will," Abby said. "I will." She turned and waved the Necco Wafers in the air. "Thank you, Xeno. And please, be more careful!" *I feel foolish waving something in the air as if he can see, but I swear, sometimes he acts just like he can see everything around him.*

Xeno gave her a faint smile and a half-hearted salute.

As she approached the registration desk, she recognized the grey haired clerk, Harry McPheeters, a family friend for nearly half a century. Harry had what the ladies called "that Vitalis look." Just enough hair product to slick his hair back and keep every strand in its place. Abby thought he could have just stepped out of a haberdashery. He had the right amount of cuff showing at the end of his jacket sleeve, a perfect Windsor knot in his tie, and a sharp crease in his trousers—perfectly groomed in every way.

"Abby Finlay! Mr. Mooney told us you were coming. I've saved the best room for you—east side, facing the lake."

"Thank you, Harry."

Harry gave a smart tap to the desk bell. "Louis, show Miss Abby to room 202." The sharp click of heels behind her told Abby the bellman was at the ready. "Your trunk has already been delivered to your room."

Abby did her best to keep up as the bellman walked briskly through the Grand Foyer, on a straight line to the antique elevator tucked back in the corner. Once aboard, the brass door clanged shut. The "lift" began an excruciatingly slow ascent to the second floor, crawling upward, jerking, stopping abruptly, starting again.

"I *still* don't know how Julius knew I was coming to Pine Lake." Abby wondered aloud.

"What's that, ma'am?" the bellman asked.

"Oh, nothing, Louis. Nothing. Can't you make this thing go any faster?" She was ready to unpack and get out of her traveling clothes. But to herself, she said, *I'll find out who told him – and why.*

In the lobby, the passenger from the train, still in his trench coat, was settled in one of the overstuffed wingbacks. As Abby walked past, he pretended to be reading his newspaper. Just as the elevator door clanged shut, he picked up a house phone. "Outside line, operator; connect me to 3671." When his party answered, he spoke briefly. "You were right. Julius is more than interested in Miss Finlay's visit." He paused, listening. "But it's not in his interest to become a problem for us." He listened, then suddenly restless, stood up, shifted his weight back and forth several times, took a deep breath, and sniffed. "Don't worry about Julius Mooney. He's not as clever as James Strang." With that, he unceremoniously pressed the button on the receiver to end the connection.

Chapter Six
From Postmaster to Prophet

1843 – From Ellington, New York to Burlington, Wisconsin

Early on the morning of May 5, 1843, James Strang packed his wife and all their worldly possessions into a one-horse carriage and prepared for the journey from New York to the Wisconsin Territory. Strang handed their second child, Myraette Mable, up to Mary, and the three-year-old, nicknamed, Nettie, quickly snuggled up beside her mother on the carriage seat.

The last item to be loaded was a plain, but sturdy oak chest, about eighteen inches square and six inches deep. James had kept it under the floorboards of their kitchen, well-hidden from unauthorized inspection. He had made sure the kitchen's woodbox was placed over the hiding place and always overflowing with kindling and short sticks of firewood. No one, not even Mary, was allowed a peek inside.

When she asked about it, he snapped, *"Never* attempt to open it." Strang gave her a penetrating stare from his deep-set, unblinking, brown eyes. The longer he stared, the tighter the slits through which he examined her face. *Could she have attempted to discover what lay beneath the floor boards?* "You have not disobeyed me, have you?"

"No! Never. I thought only to—"

"We shall not discuss the keys to the kingdom, which Almighty God has entrusted to my keeping. In due time, I shall reveal the contents to you."

James gave the horse a command to move forward. The heavily loaded carriage refused to move at first, but with some effort, the horse finally stepped off. Mary and James rode in silence. James was content to be left to his own thoughts, but from time to time, he glanced in her direction. *She may be wondering if the marriage has been a mistake for her. I sometimes wonder, too. But all shall be revealed in God's own time.*

In the silence, James thought not of their personal relationship; rather, his mind was again occupied with thoughts of how little he had accomplished with his life. *But surely that will change in Wisconsin. Some will hear of my great works and marvel. Others will doubt my greatness and ask, "Can anything good come out of Wisconsin?"* He smiled and flicked his whip near the ears of his horse. *"'Twas the same question Phillip asked Nathaniel, yes?"*

"What's that, James?" Mary had been dozing and suddenly sat up when she heard his voice.

"Nazareth was not special; Nazareth was a small rural village unknown to most citizens of Judea. No one expected anything good from Nazareth. The Wisconsin Territory is the Nazareth of our time." James urged his horse to pick up the pace.

"And do you expect–?"

"Yes! The heavens shall open, angels will descend, and God will grant us a blessing in Wisconsin." His eyes glistened with excitement.

"Amen," Mary said.

Little Nettie smiled at her mother and echoed, "Amen."

**

Aaron Smith, a devout Mormon and brother of Joseph Smith, happened to be in the Wisconsin Territory, actively recruiting converts, when he met James Strang. "Mormonism is not new to me," James told Aaron. "I heard plenty about it back in New York, but I have questions." James invited Aaron to his home that night for a discussion of religion, and specifically, the Mormon faith.

James was just seventeen years of age when he first heard the story about Joseph Smith being led by an angel to a buried chest filled with golden plates, each inscribed with an alien language, a language that Joseph Smith translated. "I was told the translated text became the Book of Mormon," Strang said, "but it seemed an extraordinary tale."

"Extraordinary and wonderful," Aaron said, as they sat around the hearth after dinner. "All that you have heard is true. The golden plates the Prophet found explained it all."

"But a whole church founded on such brief writings?" James made no effort to hide his doubts.

"The plates contained the history of a lost Hebrew tribe that came by boat to the Americas six hundred years before the birth of Jesus Christ," Aaron said to a suddenly wide-eyed James Strang. "Many have a hard time believing that fundamental tenet of the faith, but it was written on the plates."

James leaned back in his rocker as Mary approached to fill their glasses for the last time, before retiring for the evening. "It seems a bit far-fetched."

"You are not the first Doubting Thomas, but hear me out," Aaron continued. "The tribe split into two clans. One clan became known as Nephites and the other, Lamanites. After his resurrection, Jesus Christ paid the tribe a visit, urging them to live the life of the chosen people they were. Alas, it was not to be." Aaron kicked a hot coal that popped out on the hearth back into the fire. "Their disagreements were many, and over the years, many lives were lost. Unfortunately, their Judaic heritage was lost as well."

"What happened to the two clans?" James asked.

"The Nephites did not survive. The last of them to die was Moroni, the son of the tribe's final and most revered leader, Mormon."

"And the Lamanites?"

"The Lamanites became the forerunners of the Indians you see in the wilderness today. All of them are descendants of the Lamanites, the lazy side of the tribe."

"So, when Moroni appeared to Joseph Smith and showed him where the golden plates were buried–let me understand this–that was God's way of saying 'the time has come to restore the true faith?'"

"Indeed! And with the Book of Mormon as his guide, the Prophet Smith laid a foundation for the Church of Jesus Christ of Latter-day Saints."

"And all this was written on the plates?" Strang's voice indicated some doubt remained.

"Yes, all of it," Aaron said.

"And, where are the plates today?" James took a sip of cider. He would really like to examine them personally.

"When Prophet Smith finished his translation, he gave them back to the Angel Moroni," Aaron said. "No one has seen them since."

All the cider Mary left for the men had been consumed by the time their discussion of Mormonism ended. "How I yearn for a similar experience," James told Aaron. "I was a doubter when I first heard the Prophet's message, but his doctrine fills my heart, fills my spirit. I cannot deny it."

"Then, you shall meet with the Prophet immediately," an excited Aaron Smith said.

James Strang and Aaron Smith left the next day for Nauvoo, Illinois, headquarters for Joseph Smith's Mormon Church. The Prophet greeted Strang warmly.

I feel an immediate brotherhood with this man. Perhaps it is because we share humble origins in New York, or perhaps God has had a hand in our mutual destiny this day—a meeting of the two men God has chosen to lead.

Prophet Smith related his lengthy journey from New York to Ohio, then Missouri, and finally, to Nauvoo where his followers settled on the banks of the Mississippi River.

"I firmly believe none of us take a step without the guidance of Divine Providence," Strang said. "God Almighty has brought us together at this moment, in this place, for His purpose."

As they talked, the Prophet was impressed by Strang's understanding of Christian doctrine. In the days that followed, the two of them enjoyed many hours of theological discussion. *My upbringing in a strict Baptist family has paid dividends.*

James Strang was baptized by Prophet Joseph Smith on February 25, 1844.

"The most blessed day of my life," James said to Mary, as he described the experience.

Mary put down the needlework in her lap. "Are you sure, James? Are you sure?"

James detected more than a hint of doubt in Mary's voice.

"Are you convinced this is your destiny?" She was Protestant through and through. This would be a different path for their lives. "You have been disappointed so many times before. I should not like to witness your disillusionment again."

"Mary, the Prophet has made me an elder and asked me to establish a stake in Voree. This is an opportunity to join something important. Mormonism is a religious movement of unknown potential."

"Are you sure?" she asked again.

James had heard her questioning tone before. "Yes, Mary, I believe this calling is the Divine sign I have patiently awaited."

"Are you going to tell the Prophet you once considered yourself an atheist?" Mary asked. "You were, after all, expelled from the Baptist Church in New York for expressing atheistic views."

James cleared his throat a couple of times. "I don't believe it prudent to express doubts once held by me," he said. "Those doubts are no more. I am convinced the Mormon pulpit holds the key to the power that has eluded me."

**

In the weeks that followed, Strang devoted much of his time absorbing the doctrine of the new church, directly from the Prophet Smith. "Voree is our 'Garden of Peace,'" Joseph Smith said to Strang, on the morning he sent him off to establish a mission church in Voree, Wisconsin.

Less than six months later, Strang was stunned when the news reached Voree that Joseph Smith had been murdered, while incarcerated in a Carthage, Illinois jail. James immediately sought out his brother-in-law, Benjamin Perce, to share the news and solicit his views on how such a fate could befall the Prophet.

"God knows that anything is possible when evil consumes the hearts of men," Benjamin said. They sat down before Strang's fireplace the next night to discuss the sudden turn of events and Strang's options.

"There is more than evil at play, my friend," Strang said. "Fear of the true power of Mormonism *and* prejudice against anyone who harbors such beliefs are likely the root of the trouble."

"What will you do?" his brother-in-law asked. "Do you have a course of action in mind?"

"Perhaps it is my destiny to assume the mantle of leadership and continue the Prophet's struggle to bring more converts to our faith."

"You?" Benjamin was incredulous. "Mary has told me of your ambitious nature but—"

"Why is that surprising?" Strang asked. "Do you not remember what they said when told that Jesus came from Nazareth?"

Benjamin nodded. He had heard Strang tell the story many times, and he knew it was time to leave.

"I need say no more, my friend," Strang said, with a strong tap to Benjamin's shoulder, as if placing a period there.

The men soon parted, but James sat before the hearth until the last ember turned cold. By morning, ambition had overtaken James Strang. He was full of questions, which he launched rhetorically into the air at breakfast. Only Mary heard him.

"Who shall succeed the Prophet? Who shall the Quorum select? By the Will of God, did Joseph Smith choose any of the elders to succeed him? Who, indeed? Perhaps there is a record somewhere of the Prophet's choice?" James Strang had decided overnight to seize the opportunity before him. "Yes, perhaps there . . . is . . . a record." As he stirred the eggs on his plate, his intellect and energy were already focused on devising the surest method of sealing his selection as Smith's successor.

Chapter Seven
Blue Hair Vandivare

Try as he might, the bellman could not turn the brass key far enough to unlock the heavy oak door to Abby's room.

"Here, Louis, let me try," Abby said. The bellman shrugged his shoulders and backed away, leaving the key in the lock. A bump from Abby's hip, as she turned the key to its most extreme position, was all she needed to swing the door open.

"See, that wasn't so bad." She dug into her handbag for a tip. "Thank you, Louis, for your help." Abby turned around, expecting to find the bellman with his palm open, but he had already disappeared. "Hmm…that's unusual."

Once inside, her eyes fell upon a note someone had slipped under her door. *What's this, a welcome note?* The message she read was printed in block letters on Hotel stationery, the Hotel's watermark so faded, it had almost disappeared.

> *"Fear the Seventh Messenger,*
> *For him alone the gold is saved."*

She plopped on the bed and dropped her handbag to the floor. The only sound in the room came from ancient springs under the mattress, springs so worn they squeaked in agony with even the slightest shift of her weight. No one knew she was here except Julius Mooney, and now, a couple of employees of the Hotel. "Seventh Messenger?" She read the note again, desperately trying to make some sense of it. She wanted to believe it was a joke, and hoped she could find someone who would tell her she had nothing to fear, someone who knew the Club and all its history. She folded the note and slipped it into the zippered, side pocket of her handbag. *Most importantly, I need someone I can trust.*

Only one name came to mind: Blue Hair Vandivare. Her real name was Josephine Vandivare, but almost everyone knew her as Blue Hair. Abby picked up the house phone and asked to be connected to the cottage of Josephine Vandivare. As she waited for an answer, Abby wondered if Mrs. Vandivare would remember her. *And will she be willing to hear me out?*

When a familiar magnolia-laced voice answered, Abby immediately felt reassured.

"Mrs. Vandivare, this is Abby—"

"Abby Finlay! How *are* you? Where have you been?"

Abby thought she seemed genuinely glad to receive the call. "I finished college since I saw you last. And how are *you*?"

"Fit as a fiddle." Mrs. Vandivare cleared her throat. "And I'm sure you graduated with honors, yes?

"As a matter of fact, I made Phi Beta Kappa."

"Your parents would be so proud of you—and so would Robert, wouldn't he?"

"Well, Robert is the very reason I have called you."

"Do tell."

Southerners never talk business until they've covered all the social bases, and Mrs. Vandivare traces her family all the way back to Mississippi. Abby smiled. *We had plenty of bases to cover.* But she was impatient for a face to face meeting. "I'd prefer not to talk about Robert on the phone, Mrs. Vandivare. Would you have time for a confidential chat?"

"But, of course! Let's have tea in the Solarium Lounge of the Pine Lake Hotel at three o'clock."

"Three o'clock, it is." *That was surprisingly easy.* Abby hung up and busied herself unpacking her trunk.

At precisely three o'clock, Abby entered the Solarium, only to find Mrs. Vandivare already there, settled into one of the blue, upholstered, wingback chairs she liked so much. It was Mrs. Vandivare's habit to dress after lunch for visitors, those with appointments and those without. By two o'clock, she would be appropriately dressed to see and be seen. Hats, furs, and shoes all played important roles in the fashion stamp of 1954, and she chose hers with great care. She was going to the Hotel for afternoon tea, so her long, white gloves would complete her ensemble.

Her perfectly coiffed hair, muted blue, crowned a statuesque figure more than six feet in height. Her blue hair was the result of some beautician applying too much Goldey Hair Blue Rinse. Abby smiled as she recalled the story of how two pre-adolescent boys saw Mrs. Vandivare as she was leaving the beauty salon, and pointedly shouted, "Look at that Blue Hair!" Mrs. Vandivare told her friends she liked the color and decided to make it a permanent fashion statement. *She was never easily embarrassed.*

From across the room, Abby admired the stylish, sophisticated air that seemed to surround her. *No wonder father called her the Pine Lake Countess.* There is that face the men so enjoy, a face with the perfect symmetry of a Hollywood starlet. And look at that nose—a classic Italian shape like Sophia Loren's—long, thin, gently flared, suggesting strength of character. *Ah, to be more like her.*

"Abby!" Mrs. Vandivare waved her over with both hands in motion.

Damn! I forgot my white gloves. But of course, she didn't.

"Did you notice the Manchester medallion? Isn't it a masterpiece?"

Abby turned toward the center of the room and searched for a piece of fine art. Fresh cut flowers, cultivated in the Hotel garden, adorned every available table. Floor lamps, more than one could count, stood by sofas, chairs, and gaming tables. Oversized picture windows brought in more than adequate light from the garden. "I don't see a medallion of any kind."

"Oh, I thought I saw you admiring the ceiling medallion. Well, never you mind. No one ever notices that gorgeous piece of work in the middle of the room. Such a pity; it is simply elegant."

Abby finally spied the medallion. *It does seem rather unorthodox.* For a moment, she couldn't turn her eyes away. Two concentric circles surrounded an angelic figure, its head crowned with a rainbow. The angel held an open book in one hand, her right foot firmly planted on the land, and her left foot on the sea. Both feet seemed to be on fire. The angel's face, exaggerated in size, was painted a bright gold. *Bizarre,* Abby thought. She really did not know how to comment on such an unusual feature.

Blue Hair interrupted her thoughts. "You know, my dear, for a moment, I thought I saw your mother. You have the same unblemished complexion, the same smile, the same hair as—"

"But, Mrs. Vandivare, my hair is blonde; Mother's hair was auburn."

"My dear, I know a thing or two about the color of hair, and I say you look just like her. What a great friend she was to me." Blue Hair smiled. Her eyelids closed slowly, and Abby thought her fingers seemed to nervously touch the diamond brooch around her neck.

Is she trying to clear a few cobwebs from her memory, perhaps the better to recall someone else from her past, someone with blonde hair? I wonder.

"Anyone can be your friend in good times, but your mother was always there for me in the rough times. When my Bob died, your mother was first to come over. Of course, her political philosophy was exactly the opposite of mine."

"She never cared about such things," Abby said.

"I know, and I loved her for that. We were just two people sharing our lives and simply enjoying each other's company."

"And she loved you like a sister; that's what she told me."

At that, Mrs. Vandivare reached over and squeezed Abby's hand. "You *are* just like her." A waiter appeared at that moment and offered them a cup of tea from a silver tray. "Tea is the best beverage to facilitate an informal afternoon tete-a-tete between friends, don't you think?"

Abby smiled. "Of course, that's what I was taught."

Mrs. Vandivare poured cream into her tea, and Abby stirred sugar with lemon into hers. As Mrs. Vandivare sipped a polite, single sip, she nodded approvingly. "Mmmm, just right." She took a deep breath. "Well, I can see you have something quite serious on your mind."

"Indeed." Abby got straight to the point. "What do you know about a man named James Jesse Strang?"

Mrs. Vandivare laughed and put her cup down quickly to avoid spilling her tea.

At that moment, the patio doors burst open, and a boisterous party of three swaggered into the Solarium. Howard Hancock stumbled through the doors, accompanied by two female companions, no older than Abby, one on each arm, and both giggling uncontrollably at something he had just said. All were dressed in tennis whites, undoubtedly, Abby assumed, having spent most of the day on the adjoining clay courts.

"Hellooooooo," Howard yelled across the room. "Blue Hair, you lovely creature, who is that gorgeous waif with you?" As they approached, Howard stared directly into Abby's eyes. "Don't hold back; *who* is this fantastic ingénue?"

"Howard, I can't believe you don't recognize Frances Finlay's daughter, Abby, all grown up."

"Oh my, more than grown up, she's absolutely stunning," Howard said. He felt a tug on each arm. "Oh yes, let me present the Gambrelli twins. First, Gina." He gave the twin on his left a squeeze around her tiny waist. "And this is Lola." To the second twin, a peck on her cheek. "They beat me at tennis today, but I'll earn my reward by giving them a sailing lesson this afternoon." His eyebrows flew up and down in Groucho Marx fashion before he turned to Abby and winked. "Give me a call, Abby."

"Ta-ta, Howard." The disdain in Mrs. Vandivare's voice was palpable. Abby giggled as they walked away, and Mrs. Vandivare said "good-bye" with a back-of-the-hand wave that continued until Howard and the twins had walked through the Solarium doors. When they were out of earshot, she added, "Yes, ta-ta, you incorrigible ass." She pulled Abby closer and lowered her voice. "Howard would be ashamed if he had any shame in him, but he doesn't. Those two young ladies married the Gambrelli brothers five years ago in a joint ceremony right here in this very room. Earlier this year, they divorced the same brothers. On the same day! Have you ever heard such? Scandalous! Howard, as you have seen for yourself, wasted no time."

"But they must be at least thirty years his junior."

"Disgraceful, isn't it?" Blue Hair put her tea down. "Now, where were we?"

"Mrs. Vandivare, I'm grateful for your time, and I really have only two questions. First, James Strang and second –"

"Well, I suspect you will have more than two questions before we're done." Mrs. Vandivare took another sip of tea. "James Strang was an enigma to all who knew him or ever heard of him. Born in New York, I was told, and—" She paused. "But why you are so interested in him?"

"Surely, you will keep our conversation confidential?" Abby asked.

Mrs. Vandivare tilted her head and gave Abby a nod. "My dear, most assuredly."

Abby pulled Robert's letter from her purse and described its contents, including the clue Robert had entrusted to her. "Robert's letter was written on D-Day, perhaps just hours before the assault on Normandy." She placed the folded letter and clue in Mrs. Vandivare's palm.

"Ah, the Old pine clue," Mrs. Vandivare said, as she glanced at the clue and put it aside. "I've seen it before." She carefully unfolded the letter and began reading.

Abby was surprised to discover Mrs. Vandivare was familiar with the clue. *I think she's more interested in Robert's letter.*

She finished reading the letter, folded it, and then touched the back of Abby's hand. "What a wonderful man to write you such a sweet epistle." She picked up Abby's clue, and turned it over several times, as if, Abby thought, looking for additional information. Suddenly she looked away, and stared toward the lake. "I wonder if–no, it couldn't be. Couldn't be."

"What couldn't be?"

"Not long after the war, a man came through town looking for your Robert. He said he was an old war buddy; I believe he called himself 'Sergeant Strang.' I tried to find out if he met Robert at Normandy, but he couldn't seem to talk about anything except the Battle of the Bulge. We know Robert wasn't there for that one. Maybe he met Robert in boot camp, or maybe not at all. Hard to say, because he just didn't seem right, if you know what I mean. He never seemed to complete a thought without wandering into another subject."

"But his name was Strang, and he knew Robert from the war!" Abby jumped up. "Isn't that proof that Robert survived?"

"Abby, don't get excited." Blue Hair motioned for Abby to sit again. "I talked with him two or three times, and then, he just stopped coming by. They say he worked at Griner's Garage for a while. But then, he just disappeared. No friends, I understand."

"But he knew Robert, and he was a direct descendant of James Strang." Abby waved her hands in frustration. "Surely, that's enough to prove he knew Robert . . ."

"Even if he was the soldier who gave the clue to Robert, he's long gone now, and you have the clue. Just forget him." With a deep sigh, she handed Robert's letter back to Abby. "I've been hearing about that gold all my life. Rumors circulated around the Club for years that Strang left a clue—probably two clues—pointing to the location of his, ahem, 'Royal Treasury.' You have one, the Old Pine clue, and Howard Hancock *says* he has another. But, I've never seen it. You'll have to ask him about it. Maybe you can get him to share it."

"I *will* ask him." Abby moved to the edge of her seat. "But please tell me all that you know about the mystery surrounding Strang's gold."

"Abby, most of what I know was told to me by a certain John Johnson, one of the early caretakers of the Club. He was the first, I suppose, starting way back in 1878. Born in '36, he came to the Club when he was around forty or maybe forty-two years of age, and he died right here at the Pine Lake Hotel in 1937."

"1836 to 1937? That would make him 101 years old when he died."

"Yes."

"Remarkable. Do continue." Abby leaned forward. *Anyone with that many years with the Club must have heard all about Strang's gold.*

"Mr. Johnson was a young man, about twenty, when Strang was killed." Slowly, Mrs. Vandivare picked up the large linen napkin in her lap, and with exaggerated care, she folded and unfolded it, before placing it again in her lap. "The trouble all started when Strang came west, from New York to Wisconsin, in 1843. That's when he met Joseph Smith, founder of the Mormon Church. Smith made him an elder and—oh, well—it wasn't long before Smith got himself murdered, *in jail*, of all places, by a mob of folks who didn't think he ought to be President."

Abby's mouth dropped open. "President of what? The United States?" She chuckled in disbelief.

"That's right— in 1844. Smith's presence in the race made a lot of people unhappy, as you might imagine. They didn't like the idea of a Mormon in the White House." She took a deep breath. "Where was I? Oh yes, Strang immediately returned to Nauvoo to claim the mantle of church leadership. What an ego! He told church elders Joseph Smith planned to make *him* the leader." She laughed. "Did you ever hear such?

Well, they asked for proof, and to their shock and amazement, he produced the proof."

Chapter Eight
Joseph Smith's Letter of Appointment

1844 – From Voree, Wisconsin to Nauvoo, Illinois – and Back

As James and Mary sat before the hearth, late on the night the news came that Joseph Smith had been killed, James spoke excitedly of his ambition to succeed Smith. He admitted it would be difficult to convince the elders that he should be chosen to lead the Mormon faithful.

"They will be looking for a Prophet," Mary said. "Aren't all prophets chosen by God?"

"Or one of God's angels." James smiled, as an idea began to form.

"I don't know what you have in mind," Mary said, "but be aware some will doubt you, no matter what you do or say."

"Yes, some will question my motives, and others will say I am too new to the faith." He grabbed a log and placed it on the coals. "Those who question my motives are jealous, already, of the high esteem with which I was held by our Prophet during his days on earth. I can handle their jealousy, but how do I prove, without a shadow of doubt, that I am the chosen one?"

"I do not have an answer to such a question," Mary said, and touched his arm. "But I have no doubt God will provide an answer. He always does." She kissed his forehead. "Good night; don't stay up too long."

James didn't hear her final words. His mind was already devising a plan to convince the Quorum of Twelve that he, James Strang, should be chosen to succeed Joseph Smith.

By dawn of the next morning, Strang had moved to the kitchen table, and his plan was almost complete. Mary was surprised to find him still there when she entered to make their breakfast. "Have you been here all night?"

James muttered something unintelligible.

Nettie, their four-year-old daughter, trailed along behind Mary, rubbing her eyes with one hand, and dragging a small blanket with the other. James brightened when he saw her and pulled her into his lap. "Look, my dear Nettie." And he tapped the document he held in front of her. "This is where the Quorum shall read and hear the Prophet make his wishes abundantly clear."

Strang's words meant nothing to young Nettie, but Mary, startled, turned to James immediately. "What is that document, James?" She stopped tying her apron and sat down in front of him.

"A letter, my dearest, but not just any letter. I have the Prophet's own words in *this* letter, in his own hand, and they shall not be misunderstood by any member of the Quorum. His letter of appointment shall be proof enough to carry the day." Strang laid the document on the table, and with a final flourish, he affixed the signature of Joseph Smith. "I shall date it June 18, seven days *before* the Prophet's death. That should seal my appointment for all eternity."

"Will it not be easy enough to determine the letter a fraud?" Mary stood and tied her apron in place and turned her attention to preparing breakfast.

Strang held his anger. "Mary, a postmark will provide the most important evidence when the letter is examined," he said, in as calm a voice as he could muster, given the excitement welling up within. "As postmaster in New York, I canceled postage with a mark I cut from cork. That cork had a star carved on the bottom, but for this document, I have carved a flag, a waving flag, just as I have seen on letters from the Post Office in Nauvoo."

He began shuffling through several stacks of correspondence on the table. "Where is that red ink pad? Ah, here." With the cork suitably inked, he pressed it across the front of the envelope. A moment later, he held it to the light to assess his work. "My time as a postmaster was well spent," he said, and blew on the artwork to hasten its drying. His final act was to affix the date under the canceled mark, June 19, 1844. "Yes, a day later than that of the letter." Strang stroked his beard slowly, several times as he admired his work.

"James, why is this matter so important to you?"

"Mary, all of the vocations I have pursued were chosen for me by others." His lip curled in disgust. "I detested them all. My newspaper in New York struggled; I lost the postmaster's job in Ellington; and my law practice here in Wisconsin is undistinguished. Now, at last, God has opened the door to my true calling, and I must reply as Samuel did, "Here am I, Lord. Here am I."

"And here is your breakfast, James, here is your breakfast." She smiled, but James didn't think her words amusing at all. He scowled at her attempt to ridicule him.

"You underestimate me, Mary!" James knew what she thought of his ambitions.

Once, he had overheard her telling a neighbor, "James' ambitions far exceed his station in this life." James Strang felt his wife underestimated his considerable talents of persuasion. *I will prove her very wrong, and soon.*

He used the rest of the day to prepare for the journey to Nauvoo and the biggest day of his career. With a fist in the air, his eyes locked on Mary's, he seemed to be taking an oath. "I shall speak before the Quorum of the Twelve Apostles. I shall speak convincingly, and by their wise choice, I shall realize my true destiny."

"What about Sidney Rigdon and Brigham Young? They are not likely to let you have the leadership without a fight." Mary turned to

Nettie and gave her a smack on the rear. "Get dressed. We have to go to town."

"I care little about the aspirations of Rigdon and Young," James said. "Their feeble attempts to sway the Quorum will be for naught, after the Quorum reads the letter I will present, the Prophet's own letter of appointment."

Though he left at the crack of dawn, the sun had nearly set by the time Strang caught his first glimpse of the still unfinished Mormon temple at Nauvoo. As he crossed the Mississippi River, the imposing temple, the center of his new faith, left him in awe. "Solomon, in all his glory, did not enjoy a temple such as this." High on a bluff, overlooking the river, the Mormon temple was radiant in the late afternoon sun. Strang couldn't take his eyes off the structure. *It might as well be a gateway to the afterworld, and perhaps it is.* He followed the temple as long as the light of day permitted.

**

When the appointed hour for deliberations arrived, James Strang entered the temple to find a packed meeting room. The Quorum of Twelve Apostles sat in a semi-circle at the front of the room. Each had a small table positioned at his right hand. A glass of water and Book of Mormon were the only items on each table. Behind the Apostles, an oil lamp burned bravely, one moment brightening, the next, dimming its light. Strang felt the single light was an intentional effort to give the twelve a certain mystique, for there was no other light in the room.

All three contenders for Smith's title were dressed in black. Each wore starched white shirts with black ties. None presented a physically towering figure like Prophet Joseph Smith. Rigdon and Strang stood between five feet, five inches and five feet, seven inches. Young was slightly taller and portly, but all three were shorter than Joseph Smith, who was fully six feet tall and lanky.

Sidney Rigdon was first to address the Quorum. The former Baptist preacher had followed Joseph Smith from New York to Illinois and was the only remaining leader from Smith's presidency. He spoke for almost ninety minutes, quoting the Book of Mormon often, and though he made many references to his close relationship with Joseph Smith, he failed to convince any of the Apostles that he should be handed the mantle of leadership.

James Strang was second. When his name was called, he walked to the center of the room, and began in low, somber tones.

"Dear Saints: Thy most humble servant, James Jesse Strang, stands before thee extending felicitations from a sincere and devout heart. My words will be few." He pulled his jacket tight, though it fit snugly already. "The Prophet Smith will speak for me. Prophet Joseph Smith took me aside prior to my departure for Voree and in most explicit terms asked that I take the mantle of leadership should…great…evil…befall him."

He paused to let the last words settle on the ears of his listeners. There was a murmuring among the Quorum.

"My initial reaction was to recoil from accepting such responsibility, but I felt it my duty to God to respond in the affirmative, for I trusted that my God – and thy God – would walk beside me each step of the way, guiding my footsteps, answering my prayers."

Strang's voice was slowly building in intensity.

"To seal his promise, our blessed Prophet Smith, on June 18 last, wrote this letter to me in Voree. I received it one week past. If thee will indulge me, I shall, a portion of his message, share with thee."

Without taking his eyes off the Quorum, he reached into his waistcoat, pulled out the three-page letter, and with a snap to the first page, he began reading:

> "'I have long felt that my present work was almost done, and that I should soon be called to rule a mighty host, but something whispers to me, it will be in the land of the spirits, where the

wicked cease from troubling, and the bands of the prisoner fall off.
I bowed my head to the earth and asked only wisdom and strength for the Church.
The voice of God answered. 'My servant Joseph, thou hast been faithful over many things, and thy reward is glorious; the crown and scepter are thine, and they await thee. And now, behold my servant James J. Strang hath come to thee from far, for truth when he knew it not, and hath not rejected it, but had faith in thee, the Shepherd and Stone of Israel, and to him shall the gathering of the people be, for he shall plant a stake of Zion in Wisconsin, and I will establish it; and there shall my people have peace and rest and shall not be moved.
So spake the Almighty God of heaven. Thy duty is made plain, and if thou lackest wisdom, ask of God, in whose hands I trust thee, and he shall give thee unsparingly, for if evil befall me, thou shalt lead the flock to pleasant pastures. God sustain thee. Joseph Smith'"

When he finished reading, Strang held the letter up for all to see. "And here is the signature of our dear Prophet Joseph Smith." Strang turned slowly in all directions. He made sure all could see the signature of Joseph Smith. And to make certain all had heard him, he cleared his throat, and in tones most stentorian, read from the third page of the letter once again: "'. . . If evil befall me, thou shalt lead the flock to pleasant pastures.'"

The murmuring continued among those gathered. Strang knew there would be doubters. He listened quietly as the murmurs grew louder in the room as each Apostle read the document. Some of them read aloud portions of the letter before handing it to the next Apostle. In the dim light of the room, Strang saw many spectators shaking their heads, but he had prepared for this moment. He waited until the room was quiet, and concluded his remarks with what he was sure would be his best and most convincing argument.

"Most reverent Apostles, it is my duty to report to thee all the circumstances surrounding this matter. Therefore, for thy further elucidation, an angel of the Lord appeared to me at the hour of half past five o'clock, in the afternoon on June 27, prior to the Prophet's death that very night, and anointed my head, proclaiming me the Prophet's successor."

Some in the room gasped. Two or three elderly men wiped their brows with handkerchiefs pulled from breast pockets. Strang distinctly heard someone say, "No, no!"

Undeterred, Strang cleared his throat. "The angel of the Lord, most reverent Apostles, spoke these words:

"Grace is poured upon thy lips, and God blesseth thee with the greatness of the Everlasting Priesthood. He putteth might and glory and majesty upon thee, and in meekness and truth and righteousness will he prosper thee."

Strang paused, and turning about the room, he looked each man in the eye and repeated the angel's words ". . . *'in meekness and truth and righteousness will he prosper thee.'"*

Someone in the back of the room shouted, "Blasphemer!"

Strang had been called worse in a courtroom, and thus was not rattled. "If you need further proof, I have brought witnesses who will speak in turn, and with glad hearts, attest to this event which occurred prior to receiving news of the murder of Prophet Smith." He raised his arm as high as he could reach, and with a final thrust of his finger toward heaven, uttered in a loud voice, "It is verily so!"

And with that, Strang slowly walked to his chair and sat down, satisfied he had demonstrated his charismatic best for the Quorum of the Twelve Apostles. He made no further eye contact with anyone, bowing his head, to demonstrate devout contemplation of the responsibilities the Quorum was surely about to place on his shoulders. The murmurs

Strang heard now had the ring of approval. The mood in the room had changed.

An ever so slight smirk appeared on the face of Brigham Young as he rose to his feet. Strang had caught a glimpse of Young's contempt for him during his speech, but the mood in the room had changed. Strang knew Young's response would have to be convincing, as the letter would be hard to refute.

When Young walked to the center of the room, he pulled himself up to his full height and buttoned his jacket.

He's trying to make himself look like Joseph Smith.

"Grace, mercy, and peace to all." Young began with a slight bow of respect to the Apostles. Unlike Strang, Brigham Young brought no documents to the deliberations. His hands were empty as he continued. "All of you know full well of my devotion to the Prophet Smith. My affection for him has always been . . . deep and unswerving. His theological tenets are mine . . . his steps are mine. We are more than brothers . . . . our souls beat in unison and harmony . . . with love for our God."

Young took a deep breath after each phrase, lending further authority to his speech. His voice settled on the faithful, with the weight of Joseph Smith himself. Many of those present sat transfixed, as if listening once more to their departed leader.

Look at him. He is trying to sound like Smith; even his mannerisms are Smith's. What's that? Something new? Why, he's even had a tooth removed on the same side of his face as the Prophet.

Young saved his best for last and summarily dismissed Strang's claim of appointment by letter as a forgery. "In all the crowd of evil and wicked men that the world is pestered withal, there is none so stigmatized for unworthy villainy than the imposter, James J. Strang. Those who knew Joseph Smith well—and Elder Strang did not—will never believe Prophet Smith chose such a weak means of making his succession known. Indeed, he would not choose a man so weak in the faith."

Turning directly to Strang, Young focused a burning stare on his red headed rival. "James Strang is a forger who has saved his best forgery for this day. And if not by his hand, perhaps the letter is the work of Voree counterfeiters, of whom there are many. For this sham alone, he should be deemed unworthy of the leadership."

The Quorum of the Twelve Apostles voted 10-2 in favor of the selection of Brigham Young as their second President, Prophet, and Seer.

"This is not over," Strang said, loud enough for Young to hear when the vote was made final.

The rejection would have destroyed an ordinary man, but I am far from ordinary. As he returned to Voree to consider the decision of the Quorum, Strang pushed his horse aggressively. He was driven by one thought: *God chose me to succeed the Prophet Smith and lead the Mormon Church. The foundation of the true church will be laid in Voree.*

Two months later, Brigham Young announced that James Strang had been excommunicated from the Mormon Church. Strang let it be known he was not upset; he was elated. He was now free to develop his Mormon following without anyone looking over his shoulder.

Chapter Nine
Master Manipulator

W hat a despicable man." Blue Hair frowned, and began wringing her hands as if, Abby thought, the whole subject was repugnant to her, something she wished to avoid but knew she couldn't. "Vile and despicable." Blue hair spit the words out.

"Really?" Abby raised her eyebrows. *I've never seen Mrs. Vandivare so grim.* "In what way was he vile and despicable?"

"Listen, child, James Strang was a calculating individual who sought only to control his people with his pernicious teachings. He was a skilled orator, no doubt about it, with the talent and wit to captivate any audience. The larger the audience, the better. But, in my view, he was a short little man with an insatiable need for adulation and attention." Now she began to wring her hands even more vigorously. "He abused his followers, especially the women, with his polygamous ways. No wonder his own followers conspired to get rid of him." And then, she was calm again.

Her long nose was high in the air and more than gently flared at the end. "He set up the 'Kingdom of God on Earth,' as he saw it." She inhaled deeply, which elevated her nose even higher. "I'm not sure God would have recognized the 'kingdom' created by the self-anointed King Strang, if God bothered to look Strang's way at all." She stopped, looked down that nose again, and glared into her teacup. "Strang claimed to be on the receiving end of Divine revelations from God." Her lips tightened in disgust as she shook her head.

Abby held up her hand, as a student might to ask a teacher, to clarify a point. "I'm sorry, but this sounds simply unbelievable."

"I didn't think you would believe it; I should stop." She reached for her tea.

"No, no, please continue."

"Well, if you found that hard to believe, Abby, I suggest you suspend all rational thought to the end of this story."

"I'm suspending, right now," Abby said, and pulled her chair closer. "I want to hear all that you know about this strange man. Don't hold anything back."

"To start with, James Strang was a man of great talent. Unfortunately, he was also a man *possessed* by his talent."

Chapter Ten
Brass Plates of Voree

1845 – Voree, Wisconsin

A year after Strang returned to Voree, the number of congregants in his stake had diminished substantially, and new recruits to his version of the Mormon faith were few. Some of his flock, he suspected, were growing restless. A disappointed James Strang watched as his followers talked among themselves after worship in whispered tones. Their lack of enthusiasm for his preaching was a grave concern to him.

"I must do something to cement their belief in me," he shared with Mary one Sunday at dinner. "I am their leader and *true* Prophet of the Lord. A true prophet can see beyond the horizon. If the spirit of God abides in your heart, you can see what others cannot." With that, he fell silent and sat, shoulders slumped, staring at his plate.

"Perhaps you should pray for an experience like that of Prophet Smith," Mary said, "who was led by an angel to discover the golden plates . . . on a hillside . . . very near Palmyra . . . back in 1830."

James sat up straight in his chair. "Yes, that's it!" Suddenly, his face was beaming, his heart racing.

"But, if you had such a vision and found such plates," Mary said, "you might need a seer stone or two, like the Prophet used back in Palmyra to translate the original scriptures."

"Forget the seer stones," James said, as he dug into his supper, "*this* Prophet will not require such a secular crutch."

**

At the next meeting of his followers, Strang told them about a recent vision, in which an angel of the Lord appeared before him and spoke of the ancient record of a people who had ruled the continent before them. "The angel took me away to the hill in the east of Walworth, against White River in Voree, and there he showed me the record, written on metal plates, and buried under an oak tree as large as the body of a large man." Several people gasped, but Strang continued. "It was enclosed in an earthen casement, and buried in the ground as deep as to a man's waist, and I beheld it, as any of you might see, a light stone in clear water."

Immediately, the people gathered around him with many questions. "Where is this place?" one of the elders asked. "Take us to it," another insisted, "if there is such a place." Strang was momentarily taken aback by the hostility in their questioning. Someone pulled on his jacket and asked, "Are you sure this was a vision?" Before Strang could answer, someone in the rear shouted, "We demand to be taken to this spot to see for ourselves if there is any truth behind your vision."

Strang began to stumble, "Well, uh . . ."

"Take us! Take us!" came from every corner of the crowd, about half of whom Strang could see, and all were shaking their heads in disbelief.

He raised his arms to silence them, and that gave him a chance to regain some semblance of control. "Four of you shall be selected in due course and shall accompany me to claim the truth, as revealed by the angel of the Lord." He lowered his arms about half way, and dismissed them. "Go and be blessed by your Lord."

Two weeks later, Strang was still conspiring with his real estate partner, Benjamin Perce, brother of Mary, to devise an infallible means of convincing the people he had truly experienced a Divine revelation. "This will not be an easy task," Strang told his partner. "There are many doubters."

"We must bury the plates in a manner that will not disturb the ground where they lay, for that would betray our mission," said Benjamin.

"Yes, but how shall it be done?" Strang was already knee deep in the fraud but had not given much thought to their next steps.

"Leave that to me, Brother Strang. Leave that to me."

"You are devilishly clever," Strang said, "and thus, I give you my blessing to proceed." Strang knew Perce would be an eager accomplice. Both of them, especially Perce, would realize a substantial financial gain if the number of Strang's followers grew. "If we are successful," Strang said, as he stopped Perce, preparing to depart for his home, "demand for the acres we hold jointly will surely follow, but I see by the smile on your face that you have already thought of that prospect."

Over the next few days, Perce cut apart an old kettle and flattened the pieces in the shape of rectangles. Strang personally engraved each of the rectangular plates. For the message, he copied hieroglyphics from a book his father-in-law had given him before he and Mary left New York. When the engraving was finished, Perce poured acid over the several plates, "to give them a look of antiquity," he explained to Strang.

At the next full moon, Strang gathered his handpicked group of four and bade them follow closely as he led them to a hill south of White River Bridge. Suddenly, he stopped and held his arms out, as he thought Moses must have done when he approached the Red Sea. And there before them, was a giant oak, its gnarled limbs stretching nearly forty feet to the edge of the oak's crown. So great was their length that some limbs touched the ground in several places, attempting to take root on their own. A gentle breeze blew, but not strong enough to remove the mist that hid the highest branches. Tiny flickering lights in the distance peeked from around the oak's great girth. "The will-o-the-wisps are out tonight," Strang said. "We shall go no farther, for to do so would risk our falling into the clutches of the bog."

Strang's followers did not seem worried about the bog. Several were already stumbling through the oak's exposed and twisted roots, trying to avoid breaking a leg—a fate that awaited any man who made a misstep in the darkness.

"Yes, this is the tree I beheld clearly in my vision," Strang said. He spread his arms as if embracing the tree. "The Spirit lives in this one." The group silently moved closer to the base of the tree, their boots sinking into the soft ground cover. "You are stepping on the detritus of thousands of seasons past," Strang said, as if he had always possessed total knowledge of this place.

"There is no *evidence* . . . of any *saint* . . . standing *here* . . . for two thousand *years*." He spoke in staccato fashion, emphasizing the last word of each phrase. He wanted the others to hear a voice of absolute authority. The others nodded as Strang said, "Verily, I say to you, this is the spot where God's message is buried."

Strang offered shovels to two of the men, and they began to dig. While struggling to cut through the matted forest floor, Strang heard one say, "The grass is deeply rooted here. It resists our shovels." The second said, "Reminds me of the virgin fields we tilled last summer." When they tired, the second pair took their place. "Just roots here. We're digging through roots, that's all."

"Thunk." One of the men had hit something hard. He tried again, and once more his shovel stopped with a dull "thunk." Excitedly, all began to dig with their hands, and there, with roots of the tree wrapped all around and holding it tight, was an earthenware box. With great difficulty, the men cut away enough of the roots to free the box and pulled it to the surface. Inside the box were three brass plates – dirty, old and corroded.

"But, I can't read it." One man looked at Prophet Strang, quizzically. "What does it say?"

Strang had told them to expect a message from God, but he did not tell them it would be written in a language none had ever seen. As he wiped the dirt from each plate, he tried to reassure them. "God shall reveal his message to me—in time. I shall take the plates home, translate them, and deliver their meaning to all of you—in time."

When members of Strang's church saw the plates for the first time, several let it be known they were not convinced of their authenticity. One skeptic turned a plate over and over, with his eyes less than an inch away from the plate's surface. "It doesn't look very old," he said.

"Brothers," said one of the men Strang had taken into the forest, "we took the utmost care in digging." He looked one skeptic in the eye, and said, "We will take an oath that no part of the earth through which we dug exhibited any sign or indication that it had been moved or disturbed at any time previous."

That seemed to silence the doubters, and Strang breathed a sigh of relief.

Three months later, Strang called the faithful of his church together to hear a "true revelation from God." Every bench in their simple, white frame church was filled, as Strang announced he had completed his translation of the plates. "I have determined the plates contain the testimony of one who lived here centuries ago, one who wanted those who followed to know of his devout allegiance to the one and only true God."

Strang titled the translation, The Voree Record. "It is as strong a statement of faith as I have ever read," he said. As he came to the end of the text, Strang paused, and took a breath before reading the last line.

> *"The forerunner, men shall kill, but a mighty prophet there shall dwell. I will be his strength, and he shall bring forth thy record. Record my words, and bury it in the Hill of Promise."*

Strang's translation of the ancient text left little doubt that "the forerunner" was Joseph Smith and the "mighty prophet" to follow him was James Strang.

When he finished, one of the Apostles slowly stepped upon the platform next to Strang, put his hand on Strang's shoulder, and said, "You are truly a Prophet and Seer of the true God." He shook Strang's hand. "May God Almighty continue to guide you and give you wisdom in his service." From every corner of the little church came a chorus of "Amens."

When the crowd dispersed, Strang walked out with Benjamin Perce. "You must be our guest for supper this evening," Strang said to Perce, who wore a satisfied smile. "We have much to discuss."

At the appointed hour, the two men settled around the table, and Mary heaped their plates with Wisconsin potatoes and brisket stew. Before Perce could take a single bite, an impatient Strang asked, "I must know, my friend, how you managed to conceal the plates so well?"

Perce picked up his fork, and slowly twisted it in the air. "I took a large auger, put a fork handle on the end, and bored a long slanting hole under the oak, laying the earth in a trail on a cloth as I took the earth out." Perce picked up an empty saucer, stacked another on top and pretended to put them in an invisible hiding place under the table. "Next, I put the plates in, tamping all the earth around in a manner that would not leave a trace of my work." He tamped the table above the saucers and let out a hearty laugh.

"But how did you arrange for the appearance of the will-o-the-wisp?" Strang asked.

"I did not; God did."

"God's name be praised!" Strang clapped his hands. "May He bless you always."

Strang was so confident of his creative work with the plates that he offered them for examination by many scholars in the days that followed. He took every opportunity to tell anyone who asked that experts had deemed the plates authentic.

But there was always someone near, casting doubt on the authenticity of the plates or their translation. "The seeds of dissension are sown constantly, and I am kept busy stamping out the weeds that sprout from them," he said to Mary, one night as they prepared for bed.

"If only it were possible for you to escape with your followers to a place far from the devil's emissaries, so that all could experience a rebirth of their faith." She sighed, and tied her nightgown around her waist. "But, I know of no such place on this earth."

"A Garden of Eden," Strang said, his eyes dancing with excitement. "Pure, pristine, isolated, and far from the temptations of the devil." Strang got down on his knees. "Father, I have seen the Garden of Eden you have set aside for your new kingdom on earth," he prayed, "and I ask only that you guide us there safely—and quickly, Holy Father. Amen."

A month later, Strang stopped in the middle of a Sunday sermon to reveal yet another vision from an angel of the Lord. This one surprised his followers even more than the first. "I was praying last night, as is my daily practice, and I beheld a land amidst wide waters, covered with large timbers, with a deep broad bay on one side. And I wandered over the land, upon little hills and among rich valleys, where the air was pure and serene, and the unfading foliage, with fragrant shades, attracted me till I wandered to bright clear waters, scarcely ruffled by the breeze."

His people were perplexed. An elder in the back of the church stood. "We know not of such a place in these parts, Prophet. Where is this land 'amidst wide waters?'"

Prophet Strang pointed over their shoulders in an easterly direction. "There, dear saints, across the great lake." He held his hand to his forehead as if shading his eyes and stared at the far wall. "Paradise awaits all of you on the shores of your new Beaver Island home." A broad smile spread across his face, and he squinted as if he could actually see their new home. "There. Paradise awaits!" And he took a deep breath as if breathing the purest air of heaven.

Chapter Eleven
Sanctum Sanctorum

Blue Hair gazed deeply into her tea and tapped the lip of her cup. "He played his followers for fools, I tell you." She took a quick sip.

Abby had another question, but Blue Hair held up her hand, palm turned outward for silence. "This is the best part: Strang told some of the doubters that his brass plates were part of the original set given to Joseph Smith by his Palmyra angel. That took real gumption, don't you agree?"

Abby, at first, had no reaction; she was thinking how strange to hear Blue Hair use gumption in a sentence. *Doesn't sound like her.* Finally, Abby nodded her agreement.

"He preyed on those poor people like a flesh stripping vulture," Blue Hair said, "taking his time."

Now that sounds like her. Abby smiled, then pressed on. "Did his people follow him to Beaver Island?"

"Not all, but enough. About two hundred made the commitment to follow him." Blue Hair took another deep breath. "He called Beaver Island his *Sanctum Sanctorum*— his 'Holy of Holies.' He fully expected to establish a new kingdom of God on Earth." Another sip of tea, and then, "May I see that clue again?"

Abby placed the clue in her palm. Without opening it, Blue Hair closed her eyes and recited the clue in dull, sing-song fashion.

"Day follows night, Old Pine, thy gate to open wide,
The Kingdom awaits all when the rocks begin to slide.
Whoso shall publish peace, to him it shall be seen,
Our lives pass away quickly, as unto us a dream."

Opening her eyes, she returned to the magnolia voice Abby knew so well, and asked, "Did I get that right?"

"Yes, but how did you remember?" Abby was astonished. "You've only seen it once."

"My child, as I said, this clue has been around a very long time. My father gave it to *me* when I was a teenager."

Abby dropped her head and stared at the floor.

"Don't be disappointed; Robert couldn't have known all the kids had it." Blue Hair took another sip. "Getting cold," she said, and put the cup down. "Well, as Marc Anthony once said about another man, 'the good is oft interred with their bones.' And there are good things to say about the bones of James Strang. He was not altogether a bad sort, just misled by his own mental state in pursuit of what he considered a true calling from God." With that, she touched her lips politely with her napkin as if to put a proper punctuation on her description of James Strang.

"But, you said he was a 'despicable man.'"

"Indeed, but he also built schools, established a newspaper, and started a saw mill. If you go out there, you'll see the remnants of all of them, mostly stone foundations now." Blue Hair grimaced as if in pain. "I *am* trying to say something good about the man." She picked up her tea and gave the dark brew a timid sip. "Utterly vapid, and now, *completely* cold."

Blue Hair tugged at her gloves, which Abby thought might be a signal that Blue Hair was ready to terminate the discussion. "Permit me one last question." Abby handed Blue Hair the note someone had slipped under her hotel room door. "What do you make of this? I found it on the floor of my room when I walked in today. Who is the Seventh Messenger?"

Blue Hair read the note silently. As she finished, she reached for her teacup again, but stopped before she picked it up. Abby noticed a tremor in Blue Hair's hand. "Seventh Messenger? Sounds like a ghost that comes in the night, you know, like the ones that visited Ebenezer Scrooge. I've heard it said there is a ghost in the Hotel who doesn't pay rent for his room."

Abby did not smile. *Why is she trying to dismiss the note with a joke? Her trembling hand tells me there is more to this than she wishes to share.*

"I'm sorry, Abby, I didn't mean to be flippant. I haven't a clue to its meaning, but I urge you to be careful. Sounds like someone doesn't want you snooping around." With one hand, she brushed her hair back, and with the other, she pushed a couple of wandering strands back in place. "Enough of this, my dear young lady. I've told you all I know, but Howard Hancock—shameless fellow that he is—might be able to shed light on the gold *and* this Seventh Messenger business. Howard was one of those who got caught up in the search for Strang's gold, but he never found it. He once told me Strang's treasury was hidden on High Island, just west of Beaver. When you see him, ask him about that. Ask him to show you the clue he says he has but has never shown anyone."

"I will. I will." Abby sat forward, and was about to stand.

"And ask him if he knows anything about a Seventh Messenger. Let me know what he says. It's bound to be more than a little amusing."

"I will definitely ask him," Abby said, rising to her feet. "Thank you for your time, Mrs. Vandivare." Abby took a step toward the door.

"Abby?"

Abby turned her head. "Yes?"

"Call me Blue Hair. All my friends do."

Abby felt her cheeks redden. "They may, but I can't."

"I understand, and thank you. You *are* your mother's daughter." With careful emphasis on each word, she added, "Yes, you are." Smiling, she touched Abby's arm, and her voice grew softer. "I always knew Robert was in love with you from that day the two of you went cruising with my family on the *Frolic*." Blue Hair stopped and cast her eyes to the floor for a long moment.

Abby wondered if she was thinking of her own personal loss. Her husband died of pneumonia early in their marriage, and she never remarried.

"I know something of your pain," Blue Hair said, looking up. "But you must find a way to put this chapter behind you."

Abby quickly wiped away the tear that slipped down her cheek. Any reference to Robert seemed to bring a tear, and she wished it didn't. "If only it was that simple."

"Well, let me start over." Blue Hair cleared her throat. "It's all about love, my dear Abby, love. The kind you give away—unconditionally, unremittingly, unselfishly. Robert knew that, and in your heart, you know it, too. And now, the love you knew with Robert has turned to a quiet pain, a pain that prevents you from knowing the love Robert would have you know, again." She touched Abby's cheek and brushed away a tear with her thumb. "I say, let yourself breathe again." She took a deep breath and released it. "Keep putting one foot in front of the other; soon you will find yourself in a different place, a better place."

"I know you're right, but I can't. I just can't. Someday I'll tell you why, and you'll understand." Abby cast her eyes downward and smoothed out the wrinkles in her sundress. Without looking up, she said, "But this—this is not the time."

"I would be pleased to have tea with you again, anytime." Blue Hair rose from her chair.

Abby thought it appeared as if Blue Hair was being lifted on air, ascending, not standing on two feet. *But maybe her height created that illusion.*

"I'm here for you. Remember that," Blue Hair said, and she touched Abby's forearm. "Such a beautiful child. That's what I always told your mother."

When she stands up, she's almost at attention.

"Your mother once said 'bad times never pick a good time to call.' To which I might add, bad times are like a wave you don't expect to hit you, when you're walking down the beach. You know you could dive right through that wave and come out safely on the other side, but you don't trust yourself, so you don't do it. The wave—in your case, your unexpected loss—controls your life."

"An unexpected loss is one type of wave, and is difficult enough, but what if the wave is a problem you created yourself?"

"It makes no difference." Blue Hair cleared her throat. "Dive right through them all." She cleared her throat again.

Abby thought her question must have surprised Blue Hair. She decided to give her mother's friend a reassuring embrace, and as she did so, she whispered, "No wonder you and Mother were so close."

Blue Hair nodded and kissed Abby on the cheek. "Abby, some day you will discover that the advice I just gave you is worth more than any king's gold. Don't be afraid to dive through the waves." She put her hands together as if about to dive through an imaginary wave. "Hold your nose if you must, and just dive."

"I'll try it," Abby said, smiling. "And you're sure this fellow, Sergeant Strang, doesn't live around here?" Abby didn't want to let go of the idea that meeting Sergeant Strang face-to-face might provide news of Robert's whereabouts.

"Positive. Forget him."

Chapter Twelve
Holy Island Gallows

1850 – Spring

The fog was beginning to lift around Saint James Harbor. "Hotels and restaurants on the mainland are waiting for today's catch," James Strang said, as his hands pushed upward, pretending to lift the denseness surrounding him. A dozen of his men stood along the Beaver Island shore, waiting for enough light to launch their fishing boats. The morning silence was suddenly broken by the sound of an approaching boat. "What's this?" The thin outline of a fishing boat gradually emerged from the fog. "Damnation, here they come! And that's John Dixon from Pine River in the bow of the boat! They're early this year. Ready the weapons, men." The men sprinted to the central meeting hall where all their weapons were kept. Only Samuel Chichester, Strang's young assistant, remained by the side of his Prophet.

"Every spring, the gentiles come out, Samuel, and try to drive us off the land which the Lord, our God, has given us. And every spring, we have to teach them a new lesson." When the men returned, Strang pointed to the rocks along the shore. "Quick, all of you, get behind those rocks. Dixon, and the scoundrels who accompany him, are almost upon us." Strang called to the tallest defender. "McClennan, do you see any Indians?"

"No, Prophet, none so far," McClennan said.

"Good. Last year, they came with Indians from Little Traverse Bay." Strang never took his eyes off the approaching boat. "I suppose

Dixon did not offer the Lamanites enough to drink." He whispered, "I see no more than two of them."

"Two?" Samuel asked. "Are you sure? And who are the Lamanites?"

"I will explain later, but for now, there is Dixon and beside him, his neighbor, Andrew Porter. Neither has the courage to present any hazard to us."

Dixon's fishing boat made a loud, crunching noise as it slid up the rocks and onto the shore. Strang silently motioned his men forward on the beach. Dixon and Porter jumped from the boat, grabbed lines on either side, and pulled the heavy wooden craft as far as they could out of the water. When they turned around, they found themselves staring down the barrels of loaded rifles, held by a dozen men, fingers already tight around a dozen triggers. The men stared silently at Dixon and Porter and waited for instructions. From out of the fog, Strang emerged on the beach, shotgun in hand, and stood in their midst.

"Ready arms," Strang said. "Six of you will shoot them." He pointed, one by one, to the six closest men. Rifles and pistols made loud clicks as they were cocked, a sharp noise that seemed to echo in the fog. "And the rest of you will bury them." With a wide sweep of his hand, Strang included the remaining men.

"Ready!" Strang raised his arm.

"No, no!" Dixon's voice trembled. "Don't shoot! You misunderstand our intentions."

Strang walked over to Dixon and placed the tip of his double-barreled shotgun under Dixon's chin. "Just what *are* your intentions, John Dixon? State them, and be quick about it."

"We came here to discuss how best to live peaceably with you."

Strang scoffed and gave them a derisive laugh. "You want no such thing. You want our fishing grounds, our timber, our boats, our women, and our property. Now, get off our island." He poked Dixon in the stomach with his shotgun. "I will spare your lives this final time. You have five minutes to leave."

While Strang was talking, several of his men removed the sails and oars from Dixon's boat.

"What are you doing?" Dixon protested.

"I'm putting you adrift," Strang said. "Others have not fared as well."

Dixon stumbled toward Strang. "No, please! We'll end up on the rocks."

Strang grabbed Dixon's arm and gave him a push toward his boat. "Be glad you're not dead already. Leave now, or you will be in hell before daylight."

Suddenly, several of Strang's men picked up Dixon and Porter, threw the two men into the boat, and gave it a hard shove into the lake. From the shore, Strang saw Dixon pull a couple of oars from the bottom of the boat. "Thomas, did you leave those oars behind?" Strang asked. Thomas Bedford was one of the newer recruits to the faith, and Strang was not yet convinced of his allegiance. "Your silence proves your guilt, sir. That will be twelve strokes with the leather strap tonight after dinner." Bedford retreated to the rear of the group, shaking his head.

"They will be back, Prophet. They will be back," Samuel said.

"There was never a chance for peace," Strang said. "Of course, they will be back. They will never tolerate our religious differences. Yes, they will be back, but their attempts to drive us out will be futile. If they persist, these times will not end well for them."

**

The next Sunday, Prophet Strang surprised many of his flock at worship with an announcement. "If we expect to grow beyond this small island and extend the kingdom to all the Earth, we must search for a new home on the mainland. We will have need of such a home very soon." As they murmured among themselves, he continued. "Tomorrow, those of you who have been chosen, shall go with me to Pine River. This time, you shall not destroy the homes of those who wish us ill. Your mission will be to find a suitable place to establish a new and permanent home for our faith."

The following day, as the Mormons sailed their boats past the community of Pine River, Strang watched local residents gather on the dock. "They worry about my every move," Strang told Samuel, "but their worry does not bother me. God is for us; what care have I if they are against us?"

As the little stream of water emptied into the larger lake, Strang began to laugh. "Mormon Lake is most tranquil today. The gentiles are not aware that we have renamed these waters, but they shall learn soon enough to call it by its proper name. They will regard Mormon Lake as a Divine gift, for indeed, it is." He stared across the placid waters, and watched as several fish jumped in front of the boat. "If we weren't so far from Jerusalem, I would take an oath that this area may have been part of the first Garden of Eden."

Off the starboard side of the boat, Strang heard the mooing of a milk cow on the mainland. "And there, dear saints, is another gift. A gift, perhaps, from John Dixon, for that cow has strayed too far from Dixon's barn." Strang pointed to a black and white cow near the trees, a loose tether hanging from her neck. "Saints, we are blessed. There is no bell on this one. Our receipt of this wonderful gift shall be without incident." The men nodded. Quickly, they tied a stout rope to the cow's neck and led her on board.

When they were about fifty yards from shore, Strang saw Phoebe Dixon running down the hill, wading into the water, and yelling all the while at the top of her lungs. "Thieves! Pirates! Devils! Come back here with Old Daisy!"

"That we cannot do, madam," Strang yelled back. "Old Daisy is to be our guest at dinner tonight."

"Mister Dixon will hear about this, and you will rue the day," Phoebe shouted.

Strang cupped his hands to his mouth and shouted back, "You'll have to come with him, madam, or he won't have the courage to object," Strang shouted.

Phoebe waved her fist in the air. "You, son of the devil!"

The next morning, with Strang in the bow, the Mormons returned. But this time, one of their boats was towing several long timbers. As they passed the Dixon farm, Phoebe stood on the landing and called out, hands on her hips. "You may frighten my husband, James Strang, but you don't frighten me. Where are you going with those timbers? I know you are up to no good, you scoundrel."

"Although it is none of your business, madam, we are on our way to Holy Island," Strang smiled. "You must know that Old Daisy was the perfect guest at our feast last night." He reached below the bow, pulled out a large bone and threw it overboard.

"You bastard," Phoebe yelled. "May the devil take your soul." Phoebe stamped her feet.

"To Holy Island, men." Strang pointed down the lake. "To our new home."

At Holy Island, the Mormon men spent most of the morning pulling the timbers from the water and dragging them to a clearing in the middle of the island. By early afternoon, they were ready for Strang's next instructions. "We shall erect a gallows, thus to send a message to John Dixon and any man foolish enough to follow in his footsteps."

One of his men, standing atop the gallows, called to Strang. "Prophet, I think we are being watched from the mainland." He pointed to two figures darting from rock to rock along the shore.

"That is as I planned." Strang turned back to the construction site just in time to see his men executing their first test of the working gallows. There was a "snap," followed by a horrible "thud," each time the men pretended to execute someone, by permitting a potato sack filled with rocks to drop through a trap door—a substitute for human weight. And each time, Strang looked toward the shore to see if anyone dared peek, to witness their morbid business. "I do not see anyone now, but they are there." He chuckled to himself. "When we depart, dear saints, they will come out to see your handiwork."

Strang busied himself writing on a piece of parchment. When the Mormons finished the gallows, Strang handed young Samuel the message he had written. "Nail this parchment to the gallows that all might understand our purpose."

Samuel held the message high and read it aloud as he nailed it to one of the large support beams. *Thus is the fate that awaits all who violate the laws of Mormon.*

In late afternoon, while his men boarded their boats and prepared to cast off, Strang walked back to the gallows and personally posted a second message: *Dixon, in his dying hours, abandoned by his friends.*

The Mormon boats were a few hundred yards away from Holy Island when Strang asked young Samuel if he had heard a noise from the island.

Samuel was quiet as he listened. "No, Prophet, not a thing."

Strang cupped a hand around one ear and waited. From a distance, he heard a woman screaming, "God does not know you, James Strang."

Strang heard the cry clearly. A satisfied smirk crawled up the left side of his face, and he blew a kiss in the direction of Holy Island. "I do love these gentiles," he said, sarcasm dripping from every word. "They are so predictable."

Chapter Thirteen
Raconteur, Bon Vivant, Man About Town

You are very kind to agree to see me on such short notice." Abby cradled the phone between chin and shoulder as she wrote down the hour of her appointment. "Seven o'clock. Are you sure this is a good time?"

"Yes, yes, this is a very good time," Howard Hancock said to his caller. "The daughter of Elisha and Frances Finlay is always welcome here. *You* never have to call."

What a flirt. "Well, I promise not to stay longer than it takes to enjoy one cup of tea."

Howard laughed. "I'll put a kettle on right now. Maybe you'll decide to have two cups. Toodle-loo, sweetie."

Howard Hancock lived by himself in *Seven Seas*, one of the smaller cottages on the Club's "back row." Abby has heard that Howard was once considered for the role of Tarzan in the movies. *I'm not sure if that's true, but I know many women at the Club still talk about his "perpetual good looks," even though I'm sure he must be pushing seventy.* She decided to "dress down" for this visit. No need to encourage him. The coral pants will be fine with flats, she thought, and a light sweater over that high collar blouse. *Howard won't like the pants.*

Abby and her girlfriends had passed Howard's cottage many times in their youth. It was directly in the path of their shortcut to the lake, across the Old Rustic Bridge.

Abby smiled ever more broadly with each step across the bridge. *I still feel a tingle down my spine when I think about that ugly troll my brother used to describe, the one who lives under this bridge. That was my brother's story and all the kids were silly to believe him. None of the kids took the bridge after twilight. I guess it wouldn't hurt to step lively now.*

With her hour-glass figure, Abby's weight was hardly enough to put a strain on the bridge. Nevertheless, she thought it seemed to creak and groan a lot under her weight. She quickened her pace and was nearly running by the time she reached the other side. *There it is—Seven Seas— and, what's this? A new Dodge parked in the driveway? Howard only drives Cadillacs.* At that moment, the car sped away with only the driver aboard. She couldn't see well enough in the twilight to identify the driver.

A ten-foot totem pole stood guard at the door and greeted Abby as she approached *Seven Seas.* A solitary bird totem sat on top, displaying multi-colored wings and a bright yellow beak.

"What in the world . . ."

Howard was known by Club members as an eclectic collector. *But look at this . . . stuff all over the porch. Souvenirs from his many global excursions, I suppose.* Abby gave a sharp rap to the door.

"Billy, rise please. Our guest is knocking."

Was that Howard? Is someone with him? Abby was about to give the door another rap, when the screen door opened so quickly, it nearly knocked her down.

"Abby! You are the prettiest Miss America I have ever seen." Howard ignored the fact that he nearly hit her with the door as he grabbed both of her hands, kissed them several times, and finally kissed both cheeks. "I've been watching since you rounded the corner at the Stanton cottage."

"Is that so?"

Howard moved into the light, and Abby got her first good look at the seersucker blizzard of many colors he was wearing. She couldn't remember ever seeing a jacket quite like it in the Club. *Not one color complements the next.* Abby tried to look past it and tried harder still, not to laugh.

"I have not seen you since your father's funeral in '47," Howard said. "Please, come in."

"Forty-seven, it was. You have a memory like an . . . " Abby blushed as she realized she was about to say the word everyone tried to avoid speaking in Howard's presence. She knew that to say "elephant" would risk having to sit for hours, as Howard told yet another tale about his many elephant encounters across the globe.

"Elephant?" Howard laughed. "You can say it." He took a seat on the flat surface of a wooden elephant bench about two feet high. "I know what people say about me. I have ears, though not as large as . . ."

Now, they both laughed.

"Howard, I thought I heard you speaking with someone a moment ago. I can come back." She started to turn toward the door.

"Oh no, that's just Billy Merrill. He's out in the kitchen. Too shy to come say 'hello,' even though I told him you wouldn't mind."

"But father told me . . . Billy drowned . . . a long time ago . . . and . . ." Her voice slowed on each phrase as she tried to think of a proper way to continue.

"Yes, the reports are true," Howard said. "Billy has left this dimension, but that doesn't mean he isn't with us in this very room. Isn't that right, Billy?" He looked toward the kitchen and seemed to be listening to someone. He stared into the blackness a long time before finally blinking and turning back to Abby. "Billy wants you to take a seat. He says I should be embarrassed for not offering you a seat as soon as you came in." Howard pointed to another elephant bench, and Abby took her seat.

I'll just humor him, at least until I get what I came for. She was aware of his elephant fetish, but as she glanced around the room, she was not prepared for the display of ivory elephants everywhere—marching, standing, sleeping, and in a hundred more action poses. *Most are small, hardly more than two or three inches. There's even an elephant sugar bowl on the table, and . . . what? Two seem to be procreating by the hearth*. Her eyes grew wide.

"I'll give those to you as a wedding present, and a matching set when you and Robert have your first child."

. She was not prepared for his comment and was taken aback. "But Howard, Robert hasn't come home. I haven't heard from him in ten years. I'm convinced he'll return, but what makes *you* so certain?"

"He said he would, and he will," Howard said. "Billy Merrill came back; Robert will, too."

Oh my, what have I gotten myself into? Abby stared first at Howard, then at the empty hallway. Finally, she fixed her gaze on the elephants on the hearth and sighed.

"I do like 'em," Howard said. He jumped up, stood in front of the nearest mirror, and began combing his thick, black hair. "I wish I could find a good Republican to leave 'em to." He pushed a dark cowlick from his forehead back into place. "My good friend, Adlai Stevenson, says I oughta' give 'em all to George Romney—you know, the head of American Motors. He's a good Republican and a Mormon. Nothing wrong with that, of course, but I can't give 'em to a guy who drives a Nash Rambler. No sir! No, I'll probably give 'em to Barry Goldwater. You know, the Senator from Arizona. He's gonna' be President one day, sure as you're born." He wagged a finger in Abby's direction. "Besides, he had the good sense to marry one of our Pine Lake girls, that pert little Peggy Johnson from Muncie. Cute legs."

"Why don't you give the elephants to Adlai?" Abby knew Howard and Adlai had become close during the many summers Adlai Stevenson visited his grandparents at Pine Lake.

Howard ignored her question as he turned sideways to the mirror and flexed the muscle of one set of biceps. "Charles Atlas has nothing to compare, isn't that right, mirror?" A turn in the opposite direction was next. "Look at that, Abby. Still eighteen years of age."

His preening before the mirror, taking an inventory of all he perceived in the reflection, was disgusting to Abby. *How do I get him back into this world? How do I—?*

"Give 'em to Adlai? A Democrat? He'd probably use them as kindling next winter." Chuckling, he turned towards the lake, where long shadows from shoreline pines stretched their full length across the water. "I wonder if James Strang was a Democrat." His chuckling evolved into uproarious laughter, which ended only when he heard the high-pitched sound of a tea kettle's whistle. "As promised, ye ole kettle is ready," he said, and walked briskly into the kitchen. "I'll be right back with our tea, and then we'll talk about James Strang. That is today's subject, isn't it?"

She had not mentioned the purpose of her visit, but it didn't surprise her that Howard already knew. People asking questions on Pine Lake always came to Howard's attention.

"Yes, Howard, as a matter of fact, it is."

Howard quickly retrieved the waiting pot from the kitchen, and two cups. He put a tea bag in her cup and another on his saucer next to his cup. Abby wondered why he didn't put his tea bag in the cup and pour hot water over it. She watched as he poured his cup full of hot water, then, with a deft flick of his wrist, dipped the tea bag in the water for three seconds, and removed it just as quickly, declaring, "Ah, this will be good."

"Howard, it's not tea until it changes color," Abby teased.

"So *you* say." Howard filled Abby's cup and sat down. "People are allowed to have different tastes, aren't they?"

"Yes, of course." *There's no point in getting into a discussion with him about tea, his fashion tastes, or really, anything at all.* "And I'm sure your tea is just fine." Abby poured hot water into her cup and stirred it gently. "Okay, let's talk about James Strang. What can you tell me about the rumor that he buried a treasure, a chest of gold, or something like it on Beaver Island before he died?"

"Not a rumor; 'tis true. But no one knows the location, and it's certainly not Beaver Island." Howard got up, opened his desk drawer, and shuffled through a loose stack of paper. "I've got *the* clue to its whereabouts here someplace."

"Not the Old Pine clue?" Abby asked. The thought had occurred to her there might be two . . . or more.

"Everybody has the Old Pine clue. It's worthless. I have *the* clue."

"In that case, do you mind if I see yours?" Abby reached across the desk with her palm open.

"I'm looking for it. I'm looking for it." Howard lifted a stack of papers. "Several folks 'round here got their hands on the Old Pine clue and tried to find the gold long ago." He lifted another stack of papers. "It's 'round here someplace." He searched for another few seconds in vain, and then shoved the drawer shut. "I went myself with Billy Merrill back in the '20s. We checked out every rumor, including one that had the gold buried way out on High Island."

"Really?" She was amazed at the number of threads people had followed over the years in searching for Strang's gold. "Why did you think the treasure might be on High Island?"

"The rumor was that Strang, or one of his lieutenants, buried the gold exactly 'thirty paces from a large tree,' supposedly visible from a point high above the island's western shore. Billy and I went out there looking for it, but we forgot that the island had been clear-cut several times in the years after the king's assassination. There was no chance anyone was going to find the gold if they expected to use the 'large tree' as a landmark. No sir, no chance."

"Where else did you search?" She was starting to think this was going to be more difficult than she imagined.

"Well, I've never told this to anyone. You probably don't remember the stories about the *Keuka?*

Abby shook her head. *Why do I feel like I'm in the middle of a game of Twenty-One Questions?*

"No? Well, the *Keuka* was a big old lumber barge someone converted into a floating dance hall, complete with a . . . whatchamacallit, cabaret. During Prohibition, the *Keuka* was extremely popular 'round here. Locals called her a "blind pig." I don't know why. She came to a rather undignified end one Sunday morning when she sank right there in the middle of Lake Charlevoix. I watched her go under. She's there to this day, about forty-five feet down."

"Go on. Go on." Abby shifted back and forth in her seat.

Howard got up to look at himself in the mirror again. "I'm just happy I'm not struggling with thinning hair like most men my age. Doesn't run in my family. We all have Ronald Reagan's hair—you know, full and thick."

He didn't seem the least bit concerned with Abby's impatience. "The *Keuka*, Howard." She slapped her forehead. "What happened out there?"

"Immediately, the rumors started." Howard spoke excitedly, as if there had been no interruption. He waved both hands above his head. "One rumor had the local temperance league doing her in. Another said federal revenue agents did the deed. But the one that got my attention said Strang's followers, who did *not* drink alcohol, by the way—well, not openly—found the treasure and hid the gold on board, intending it for safe passage down the lake to a bank in Boyne City."

"Did you believe it?"

Howard gave Abby a sideways, questioning glance. "Indubitably," he said, with absolute certainty in his voice. "Billy made several dives to look for the gold, but the only discovery he made was finding the dance hall structure gone! Disappeared!" He paused. "Say, did you know Billy invented the first scuba diving gear?

"Howard!" *This is exasperating.* "The cabaret was gone?"

"That's what I said. Some believe the Mormon's Angel Moroni came back and spirited the gold away. For Pete's sake, what use would an angel have for gold, or for that matter, an entire dance hall?" He chuckled. "I never attended a single dance there."

"So, neither you nor Billy ever found the gold?" Abby refused to engage Howard in idle conversation about a lost dance hall.

"Everybody knows that, Abby, but we actually found something even more valuable."

"Okay, I'll bite," Abby said, against her better instincts. "What's more valuable than gold?"

"How 'bout safe passage through Devil's Reef? We threaded the needle and came home without a scratch."

"Not possible. No one was ever crazy enough to try such a stunt. There's a reason it's called Devil's Reef, you know.   Too many rocks, and most of them out of sight just beneath the surface."

"Yes, but Billy said the Indians taught him how to run the reef safely. There's a large rock at the western entrance to the reef. If you take a 150 degree heading from that rock, it'll lead you in a straight line to another large rock, where the reef widens into the lake again. I'll have to admit, when Billy told me we had to follow marks left by Indians on the rocks, I thought he might have been confused."

Abby twirled a finger in circles and pointed to her head. "Crazy is more like it."

"Crazy? Oh, no, not at all." Howard laughed. "I just kept telling myself if the Indians followed the marks, we could, too. Anyway, we decided to try it." He looked down, back and forth from his seat to the wall, as if reliving the experience of watching for hidden rocks on either side of the boat. "We scraped a few rocks along the way, but we survived."

"Both of you were insane!" Abby could see Howard's eyes dancing with excitement as he retold the story.

"We always survived, Abby." He grinned from ear to ear. "Of course, the Coast Guard never believed us, and never put our discovery on any charts. In fact, they warned us not to try it again. Billy went out to the reef later and painted large white circles on the two rocks. I guess that was better than tomahawk marks."

Abby threw up her hands. "What does this have to do with the gold?"

"Nothing; I just thought you might be interested." He gave her a puzzled look. "Say, are you aware there is not a single blemish on your skin?" He leaned forward and seemed to be examining both sides of her face.

Abby shook her head. "The gold, Howard, the gold." *I can't take much more of this.*

"Well, we never found the gold, and I stopped searching, but Billy didn't—unfortunately." Howard got up and looked out the front window. "Getting dark . . . can't even see the Old Rustic Bridge anymore. Did you know the elders 'round here want to take that old bridge down? Yes, they do. Can't leave well enough alone. Besides, where's that troll going to live?"

"Howard! I don't have all night!" Abby put her tea down with a loud clank in her saucer. "What did you mean by 'unfortunately?' Is this when Billy . . ."

"Drowned? Sadly, 'tis true. I was on a cruise when Billy went out to Skillagalee Island and searched the belly of that old shipwreck, *The Patchin.*' She sank off the island's western tip—oh, about 1850. Anyway, Billy went too deep. Never came up. They say he got caught in the ship's rigging and, who knows, he may be there still. Very sad. We called him Billy Too because everything he did was *too* much, *too* extreme, but mostly *too* fast."

Howard glanced toward the hall. "Ah, Billy Too, we had a lot of fun, didn't we?"

Abby looked toward the hall, too, but seeing nothing, returned her attention to Howard, who was smiling broadly. *I think he's amused that I looked for Billy in the hall.* "Howard, if I could talk with Billy, I'd ask why he thought the gold was in a shipwreck. Has Billy ever answered that question for you?"

"Abby, Billy's, uh, *dead.* He's not here." Howard gave her a most perplexed look. "He's *really* dead." His arched eyebrows seemed to question her sanity.

Or is he simply trying to determine if I think him unstable? Well, I do.

"Natalie Nash also had the skin of a fine porcelain doll. What a doll she was. There was that night down by the old railroad trestle." He paused, eyes closed. "My Pierce Arrow got stuck, and when I got out to push, she—"

"Howard!" He was about to launch into another unrelated tale, and Abby wanted nothing of it. "Back up! Why was *The Patchin'* part of Billy's search?"

"The clue clearly points to *The Patchin'*," Howard said, his eyes wide in amazement at her question. "Clearly." He shrugged his shoulders. "It's a miracle *more* people didn't die swimming 'round that old scow." Back into the drawer he went for another search. "Ah, here 'tis." From the back of the desk drawer, Howard pulled out and read aloud the clue Billy Merrill had given him decades earlier.

> *"Deep within The Patchin' lies a Spirit House of old*
> *Drink of it, lost prodigal, and risk thy very soul.*
> *From heaven's gate, Divine One descends to aviary white*
> *Trust but one – thy Father – he will keep thee in the right."*

Abby's jaw dropped. It *is* a different clue, she wanted to shout.

"So, you see, the wreck of *The Patchin'* seemed logical," Howard said. "It sank not too far from the Beaver. Strang would have no trouble hiding his gold there, and he could have done it quickly." He pointed to the first line. "Right there, you see where it says, *'lies a Spirit House of old'?* Spirit House was the name the Indians gave to their cemeteries, and *The Patchin'* was a cemetery all right."

"Okay, but what about the last two lines; what do you make of them?" Abby was bubbling over with questions. *Two clues! Now I have both! Robert would be so proud of me.*

"The last two lines? I've never been able to divine their meaning. I think those two lines represent the Baptist in him. Wasn't it a dove that descended to earth when John baptized Jesus?" He drew the sign of the cross in the air in front of him. "Or maybe the lines mean nothing at all."

"Do you think it possible that King Strang wrote even more clues, perhaps one for each of his children?" Abby asked.

"I hope not. They say he had ten children." Howard, wide-eyed, held up ten fingers. "Or maybe more. He was, they say, an energetic little fellow." Howard chuckled as he looked at the two ivory elephants having sex on the hearth.

"Ten children? Do any of them live in the area?" It hadn't occurred to Abby that descendants of Strang might be around.

Howard shook his head. "Most of them scattered to the four winds after his assassination." He took a sip of his tea. "Who could blame them? The gentiles were none too happy with the Mormons."

"That's too bad because—"

"Wait!" Howard put down his cup and held up an index finger. "There might be one!" He scratched his chin. "Billy once told me the publisher of the Charlevoix newspaper is himself a descendant of the old king. I don't know it for a fact. But, even if he is, he didn't find the gold."

"How can you be so sure?" Abby put her tea down.

"Well, if he'd found it, he wouldn't likely be a small town newspaper publisher, now would he?" Howard laughed. "No sireee!"

Abby stood up. "I have another call to make." She folded her napkin and placed it on the table beside her. "Thank you for the tea, Howard."

"Well, there is something else that might be of interest," Howard said. "Maybe nothing to it, of course . . . probably nothing. But my old buddy, Ransom Olds—you never knew him—I called him Ranny. He was older than me by a good twenty years, and he knew a lot about Strang. Ranny, of course, was the creator of the first Oldsmobile."

Howard truly is the world's biggest name dropper. She managed a polite nod.

Howard rummaged around his desk again and smiled with delight when he pulled out an old photo. "There's Ranny and me sitting in his 1912 Autocrat Speedster, right there in front of the Pine Lake Hotel. Most of the elders around here were adamantly opposed to automobiles on Club property. You won't believe this, but when they finally got around to approving cars, the board reserved the right to regulate them. Regulate them? Can you believe that? 1912. Ranny died a few years ago; I was sorry to see him go." He tapped the corner of the photo. "I miss him. I do. Anyway, where was I?"

"Not sure," Abby said. "How about this: Did Ranny know King Strang?"

"Oh yes, *that's* it. Ranny's father spent some time on Beaver Island teaching Strang about mechanics. Kind of odd, don't you think? Pliny Fisk Olds—that was his name—went to his grave to be forever known as blacksmith, machinist, *and* teacher of old King Strang." Howard laughed heartily again. "They probably met in Lansing when Strang was in the Legislature. That's another story, too. Anyway, Ranny said King Strang was a quick learner, but his father also made clear he thought Strang was pluperfect crazy. Very smart, but crazy."

"You don't hear much about James Strang's physical appearance. Did Pliny ever describe King Strang to your friend, Ranny?"

"Funny you should ask. Pliny said Strang was kind of compact, you know, short and stocky, with deep-set eyes, thick red hair, and a red beard. And he scratched that beard a lot, or stroked it, whatever people do with beards. Pliny said he would never forget Strang's eyes, too small for his head, but piercing. You know what I mean?"

"Sounds scary," Abby said, nodding. "I wouldn't want to look him in the eye." As she opened the door, she remembered the question Blue Hair suggested she ask. "Howard, what do you know about a Seventh Messenger?" She held the door just short of its latch and waited.

All of the blood drained from Howard's face. "W-why do you ask?"

"I received a brief note of welcome from him—or it—upon arrival at the Hotel."

Howard stepped closer. "Some people say the Hotel is haunted. If any unexplainable activity goes on there, the staff, I hear, usually blames the Seventh Messenger."

"Now, Howard." Abby tilted her head to one side and gave him a raised eyebrow. "Be serious. Is there anything else I should know?"

Abby noted an ever so brief pause before Howard spoke, but it was the kind of pause that speaks volumes. *He definitely knows something he's not willing to share.*

"Look, even if you were to find Strang's gold, be aware that the Government might have an interest in it, too."

He seems a little too anxious to change the subject.

"My old friend, Sam Martino—you know him, I'm sure—is the head of the Federal Reserve. Sam told me a large cache of gold sovereigns, minted in London, was stolen from a bank in New York while Strang worked there. I believe it. Anything Sam says you can take to the bank." Howard chuckled. "Get it? Bank?"

"Yeah, I get it." She pulled the door open again. "What about these gold sovereigns?"

"Did you know Sam and I were doubles partners in the 1926 US Open? We were. He had a great backhand!" He scratched his head. "Uh, where was I?"

"Why don't you start with 'Gold sovereigns disappeared from a New York bank where Strang worked,'" Abby said. *Could the sovereigns be the actual source of Strang's gold? The pieces are starting to make sense, or my imagination is working overtime.*

"Correct. And not long after they disappeared, Strang packed up and headed west, rather abruptly, in the summer of 1843. Sam said Strang worked at the bank only three months. If he was the culprit, his sudden departure was understandable. The Feds never proved anything."

I can't believe this. Abby had never taken her hand from the doorknob and now gently closed the door. "How much would the gold sovereigns be worth today?"

"Well, I heard there might've been as many as 200 coins. Gold, of course, is currently going for $35 an ounce. How much does each gold coin weigh? That's one thing you need to know, but not the only thing. The total value would surely be a king's ransom—pardon the pun." He slapped his thigh and gave a satisfied guffaw. "But it'd be a nice nest egg for someone. How would you like a nest egg worth maybe half a million dollars?"

"Whoa. What do you mean? How did you get to half a million dollars?"

"These were not just any gold sovereigns. *The New York Times* reported the coins were minted in 1839 and 1841. Today, they would be worth a lot more than face value, which was about $20 each, and far more than the value of the gold in them. Far more. Coin collectors have long ago run the price up because the gold sovereigns were part of a limited run from the London mint; probably less than half a million coins were minted, total."

"You learned a lot about the missing coins, didn't you?" Abby knew the best way to get information out of Howard was to flatter him.

"Well, years ago, between seasons, when I wasn't on a cruise or here at Pine Lake, I spent some time in New York researching the stolen coins. I really don't know how much they are worth today, but it is safe to say quite a lot. Most of them had an image of Queen Victoria on one side and the Shield of the Crown on the other. The bank never said exactly how many were stolen, but if it was two hundred or more, I would estimate the value of whatever King Strang hid to be about $500,000."

"Incredible! But why would there be British sovereigns in a New York bank? How would gold sovereigns from London find their way to an American bank?"

"I have no idea. None, whatsoever. The *Times* never said or maybe, never knew."

"Owww!" Abby's foot struck a cast iron elephant doorstop, and she almost lost her balance. "You should move that thing, Howard. People are going to hurt themselves."

"Not if they step around it." He made no attempt to move the iron elephant. "That's what I do all the time."

"Gotta' go, Howard," Abby said, as she pulled her scarf around her shoulders. "I have a publisher to see."

As she walked toward the Old Rustic Bridge, Howard called after her. "But who knows, a museum in London or New York might be willing to pay even more than half a million dollars."

She waved an acknowledgement as she reached the footpath, then paused. *What's that?* She thought she heard Howard's voice again.

"Yes, Billy, she is lovely. My eyes are still eighteen years old; why not the rest of me?" Then, silence, followed by a burst of laughter.

He's becoming nuttier by the day. Abby squinted into the darkness to find the outline of the bridge. "That bridge always looks more ominous at night," Abby said aloud, as her favorite shortcut came into view. "If not for that lantern in the middle of the bridge, I'm not sure I'd be willing to walk this way after dark."

All of her brother's tales about the troll under the bridge came flooding back. *No matter how many times I told myself that none of his stories were true, he always succeeded in scaring the living daylights out of me.* The memory of those times made her smile, as she passed the lantern that burned in the gazebo in the middle of the bridge.

"What's that?" There was a loud creaking behind her. The bridge appeared to sway from side to side, as it might if someone heavy was walking across, his weight shifting from one foot to the other.

"Who's there? What—?" The lantern that had been burning brightly was suddenly snuffed out.

The air, mild a moment ago, feels ice cold, Abby thought. She grabbed the handrail and used it as a guide to quickly reach the end of the wooden walkway. As she stepped onto solid ground again, she turned in time to see a shadowy, white image around the middle of the bridge. *Someone in a white robe? Someone trying to scare me?* In the next instant, the white robe flew into the trees, disappearing into a canopy of leaves about fifty feet up.

"Well, *that* worked!" Abby said aloud. Adrenaline flowing, she raced toward the Hotel. "Where . . . where is that Hotel?"

Chapter Fourteen
Elvira, My Queen

1850 Summer – Kingdom of Beaver Island

It is time for my coronation and for you to become my queen." James Strang was bursting with excitement. "I have long anticipated a royal coronation for us." He kissed Elvira, his secretary, on her face, neck, hands—wherever he could find bare skin to kiss.

"But, James—"

"It will do you no good to object, my queen." Strang was nearly finished with his dictation for the day when he reached over his secretary's shoulder and took the quill from her hand. "Let's put your quill away."

Elvira Field, twenty-year-old secretary and confidant to the king, turned to face her lover. "But that will mean announcing to the world that you have taken another wife," she said, as she covered her ink well and put the unfinished parchment in her desk.

"Yes, and a more proper occasion for the announcement could not be imagined," Strang said. "We have been married for most of a year already, and it is time to tell the world."

"What about Mary? What will she say?" Elvira asked. "After all, for a year, I have been careful to maintain my disguise as your secretary and nephew, Charles Douglas." She closed the ledger book in front of her. "It has not been easy to live my life as a man, but the disguise has worked; no one suspects, not even Mary."

Strang smiled. "If they suspected, they dared not speak of it."

"Only Thomas Bedford had the temerity to ask why I did not grow a beard," Elvira said. "I told him, 'facial hair is not my preference,' and that seemed to satisfy him. But James, what will you tell Mary?"

"Mary has been a good wife, but I believe the condition of multiple wives is a Divine requirement."

"I am not confident she will agree." Elvira turned to put the ledger on the shelf behind her.

"Look at me, Elvira." Strang puffed his chest out, raised his arms as high as he could, and spoke as if issuing an official proclamation to all his followers. "The taking of additional wives is simply a continuation of a tradition practiced by Father Abraham. As I, and the rest of the men, take more wives, the women shall be elevated and liberated to choose the best possible mate based on their requirements for compatibility, even if that mate is married to another." Slowly, he brought his hands together and shook them to signify the finality of his statement.

Elvira fidgeted with her vest buttons, pulling on each one as she spoke. "I do not question your decision," she said, "but I worry that Mary will react adversely to your news."

"Your buttons are secure, my dear." James put his arms around Elvira and gave a playful tug to her vest. "Do not be concerned about Mary; she will understand. If she does not, I shall send her to the mainland. A separation enforced thusly will most surely engender a change of heart."

"I hope you are right," Elvira said. "I hope you are right."

"Of course, I am right. It is time to tell everyone our plans," Strang said. "There will be a coronation on the eighth day of July, in the year of our Lord, 1850. I chose your birth date intentionally. It shall always be known, henceforth, as a day of celebration and honor. And I shall be known as the 'King of the Kingdom of God on Earth.' *You* shall be my queen." With that pronouncement, he gave Elvira a deep and passionate kiss.

In the days that followed, Strang prepared for the royal event by enlisting the aid of a traveling actor, George Adams, whom Strang first met in Nauvoo. "My good friend, you must use all your skills to create a ceremony befitting the occasion, a ceremony filled with royal pomp."

"I'll do my best," Adams promised. He rummaged through his traveling trunk, full of costumes and props, and from near the bottom, he pulled out a red, flannel robe trimmed in white.

Strang smiled his approval when Adams held it up. "And for a scepter?"

"This two foot wooden pole will be your scepter, sire." Adams said. "I'll decorate it to make it more, uh, royal."

"Very good," Strang said, "but the ceremony cannot be complete without a crown. I will require something most appropriate." He ran his fingers through his hair as if preparing to receive the crown.

"That's going to take some time, your majesty, but do not worry. I shall have something appropriately royal for you by the date of your coronation." A deep bow from Adams followed as he backed out of the room.

Two weeks later, two hundred of Strang's most loyal followers gathered in an unfinished meeting hall. He waited until all were inside before signaling Adams to begin the coronation ceremony. A single bagpiper played "Scotland the Brave" as Strang ascended the makeshift stage. With a great flourish of his robe, Strang took his place on a moss-stuffed seat in the middle of the stage. Across the platform, he spotted Elvira and motioned for her to join him. Dressed in a plain, white, poplin skirt, Elvira Field stepped upon the stage and took her assigned seat slightly behind, and to the right of the soon to be anointed king.

At that moment, Mary Perce leaned forward, then, clasped her hands to her breast. "Oh, James, my love," she whispered. "I cannot abide this."

Strang knew he should have told Mary before the ceremony began but could not find the courage. In the end, he said nothing. A moment later, he caught a glimpse of Mary as she left the room. For a few moments, he felt the pangs of a coward's guilt. However, his ego took control again as soon as Adams approached with the royal crown.

"Kneel, your Royal Highness." Adams spoke the words as though he were in the middle of *Macbeth*. He raised high the crown he had made from a discarded coffee kettle. Around the edges, he had glued a row of stage jewelry, mostly cut glass of red and green, with an occasional clear stone.

As Strang knelt on one knee, Adams said, "I crown you 'King, Cawdor, Glamis.'" And he placed the crown on Strang's head.

Strang wasn't sure what the title meant, but he knew it sounded magnificent to his ears. He straightened his spine to attain the fullest height possible from his short frame, and slowly turned to allow all to appreciate his royal visage. Bathed in a chorus of approving cheers, he realized that the ambitions of his youth were being fulfilled, and he exulted in the moment. Holding his scepter high above his head, Strang slowly lowered it until he tapped Adams on the shoulder. "And you, the right honorable George Adams, are hereby named my prime minister and chief counselor." More cheering ensued.

Every family brought a dish to share in the celebration. A heifer was slaughtered and offered as a burnt offering. "The burnt offering is made in the tradition of our biblical ancestors," Strang explained to the gathered faithful. "With this offering, we do honor all the saints who preceded us."

As everyone cheered, the feasting and rejoicing began for all but one. Mary retreated to their home, fed supper to their three children, and tucked them in bed. And then, she sat down before the fire to wait for her husband's return.

But the newly crowned King of Beaver Island did not come home that night. Around mid-morning the next day, James Strang walked the long path to his house, but from a distance, he sensed something was amiss. *There is no smoke from the chimney and no sign of any living soul. By this time of the morning, those three children should be outside doing their chores.*

When Strang opened the door, there was no sign of life of any kind. On the kitchen table, he spied a note Mary had written during the night, folded and placed against a candleholder at the spot reserved for the head of the household. With so little light in the room, Strang unfolded the note and walked near a window to read it.

"My dearest husband, I cannot accept your rationalization of the act of taking more than one wife. I do not wish to disobey, but your action does nothing to elevate a woman. Only through respect and the mutual sharing of affection between two people—and only the two—shall a woman's life be lifted up. Your Divine imperative is demeaning to any woman who must suffer such, and I believe it is an abomination in the eyes of God. Your decision leaves me bereft of all happiness."

She hadn't taken the time to sign it. As Strang folded the note, he heard a knock at the door and looked to see the familiar face of his neighbor, Julia Campbell, peering in. "If you were expecting Mary, I'm afraid she is well on her way to the mainland by now."

"What! Did you have a hand in this mischief?" Strang reached for the cane strapping he kept near the table.

"No, although I can't say as I blame her." Julia took a small step back to the entrance. "Mary stopped by my house this morning with the children, all wearing their traveling clothes, and she asked me to give you a message."

"Well, what is it?" Strang whacked the table top with the strapping. "Speak up!"

Julia opened the door and stepped across the threshold, pausing just long enough to say, "Mary's message was: 'Good bye.'" With that, she stepped onto the porch and slammed the door behind her.

Strang whacked the table again, grabbed the candleholder and threw it at the door. But a few minutes later, a much calmer James

Strang began to smile. He flung the door open and bounded down the steps in the direction of the celebration still underway. James, the king, and Elvira, his queen, enjoyed the celebration on the green three additional days.

Chapter Fifteen
A Spicy Little Paper

G old lettering on the door was fading, but still legible:

The Charlevoix Sentinel - "A Spicy Little Paper"
Founded 1869

The rusty knob on the badly warped door resisted Abby's firm twist, so she gave it a swift kick near the bottom. The old door swung open wildly.

"DING! DING! DING!"

"Good grief. What's that?" she said aloud. *That thing clangs like a fire alarm.*

"DING! DING! DING!"

Abby glared at the bell on the back of the door, as if that would make it stop.

"You like my bell?" a voice from the back of the room asked. "She's a beauty, isn't she? The Smithsonian wanted it but I said, 'no thanks,' and—"

The disconnected voice was suddenly connected to a young man emerging from the shadows, his arms and face streaked with black grease.

Younger than I expected, but why all that grease?

"Good morning—I mean—good afternoon. Come in. Come in."

Abby thought he sounded a bit nervous. "I'm in, sir. I'm in," Abby said, in her sweetest most reassuring tone. "And pray tell, why would the Smithsonian be interested in *your* bell?

"Used to be on Number 161, the first engine to pull Pere Marquette's Resort Special into town back in 1892." His voice was full of pride. "I'm Mark Day, editor, publisher, and chief bottle washer, at your service." Mark rolled down his sleeves and straightened his tie.

Abby glanced about the room, trying to avoid looking straight into his intensely blue eyes. "What is that smell?" she asked, as she fumbled for words to open the conversation. "Is something burning?"

"No," Mark laughed. "That's just my linotype machine. Every small town newspaper in America has one and they all smell the same. I wish I could afford a new one."

"I thought the building might be on fire."

"Hardly; that's a combination of hot oil and molten lead. Without that smell, the type doesn't get set, and the paper doesn't go out."

She wrinkled up her nose. It was a smell she would not soon forget.

"You don't look like a linotype salesman," Mark said, putting his hands behind his back to be sure his shirttail was tucked in. "In fact, you look like one of those Breck models, you know, the ones on the back of the Saturday Evening Post, with every hair in place and a flawless complexion. You've seen them."

"Oh, my no. I'd rather be a linotype salesman than one of those artificial models." She flipped her hair to one side as if she wanted to brush the compliment aside. "No one is that perfect."

"Of course not." He gave her a slightly exaggerated bow.

Time to move on. Abby straightened her back and extended a hand.

"I'm Abby Finlay and—may I sit down?" *He doesn't look like the green eye shade editors I've seen in movies.*

Mark motioned to his desk in the corner and simultaneously pulled up a chair, dusted it off with his bare hand, and slipped it under her, as she, with perfect timing, sat down, but only on the edge of the seat, her back, ramrod straight. She straightened the pleats in her day dress and tried to look as business-like as possible. Directly in front of her was an angel—a statue, really, about five feet tall—which someone had placed in the corner behind the editor's desk. The figure appeared to be flying, holding an open book in one hand and a trumpet in the other.

"Just an old weathervane," Mark said, following her eyes, "carved by some unknown craftsman more than 100 years ago. Been in my family a long time. I haven't figured out what to do with it. I just know the family would never forgive me if I threw it away. But I'll cover it if it frightens you?"

"No, uh, it's very, umm . . . interesting," Abby said, "but it looks like much more than a weathervane. I suspect there is another story behind it."

"To be perfectly honest, there *is* another story, but probably not very interesting to the average person—not that you're average, of course not," he said, a little pink in his cheeks.

"Of course not." Abby smiled at his embarrassment. "Perhaps we'll have time later for you, Mr. Day, to tell me its full history."

Mark gulped hard. "But right now, you have a question about another matter, yes?"

"Yes, Mr. Day, several questions actually." She pulled out a pad and pencil. "You are the editor, right?"

"Editor, typesetter, press operator, and circulation manager, at your service."

"Well, the lettering on the door says *Sentinel,* but I remember a paper here by the name of *Clarion;* when did it change?"

"Abby, you must call me Mark, or I won't answer any of your questions," he said with a grin. "As for your first question . . . hmmmmmmmm . . . where to start? The *Sentinel* was the first newspaper established here in 1869." Mark got up and walked to a wall display featuring full-length portraits of elderly gentlemen. "My grandfather," he tapped the first portrait, "Charles J. Strang, set up another, *The Charlevoix Journal*, in 1883. The name was changed to *Charlevoix Clarion* in 1884, but the *Sentinel* was first." He tapped the next portrait.

"My father, Seth Day. He was the one who told me the *Sentinel* was known as 'a spicy little paper.' So, when I found that old door, the original door, in a consignment shop on Van Pelt Alley, I had to have it. For me, it's a reminder of the personality of early newspapers around here." He straightened his father's portrait and turned to Abby. "But I can't believe that's what you came to ask me?"

"Well, no, I came—"

Suddenly, the conversation was drowned out by the clackety-clack of the linotype machine in the next room. Abby looked toward the sound, and Mark started to get up. The machine seemed to hesitate a moment before stopping altogether. Mark took his seat again. "Please, pay no attention to that infernal device; go on."

"I came for another reason, actually. You've already said Charles J. Strang was your grandfather. Was *his* father, by any chance, James Jesse Strang of Beaver Island fame?" Abby gave a quick glance toward the next room, as if that would keep the linotype machine quiet a while longer.

"Well, yes, he was. In fact, that little angel behind me was the weathervane on top of his temple on Beaver Island. My grandfather had only girls, my mother one of them. She married Seth Day, whose family ran the sugar beet factory until it went bust." He squinted into her eyes. "Why do you want to know about me?"

"Oh, it's not *you* who piques my interest." *Did I just flirt with him? What's wrong with you, Abby Finlay? You better get to the point.* "I want to find out if King Strang really did bury any gold. At the least, I'd like to get to the bottom of the mystery. There may not be any gold at all, but then again, if . . ." She paused a moment. "A direct descendant of James Strang might have a claim to at least some of it, don't you agree?" She didn't want to appear as if pleading for his help, but she sensed the young editor might be her best hope of solving the riddle of the two clues now in her possession. "That gold might buy a very fine linotype machine, and besides, I have a clue that's *guaranteed* to lead someone to the gold."

"Guaranteed?" Mark raised his right eyebrow. "Well, that's certainly worth my attention." He sat back in his swivel chair. "I'm not sure if going over this ancient story again will pay dividends for either of us, but I'm willing if you are."

"I'd be delighted," Abby said. "Where do we start?"

"Look, a newspaper office always has ears to hear things it shouldn't." Mark sat up in his chair and stretched his neck in all directions as if searching for an eavesdropper. "Let's go down to Schroeder's. I'll buy you one of his patented milkshakes and tell you everything I know." He opened the bottom drawer of his desk and pulled out a cotton cloth and small mirror. "But I have to get back by four o'clock. The linotype machine is working sporadically, as you can hear, and I'm expecting a repairman from Traverse City this afternoon." He quickly wiped away as much grease as he could see on the face reflected in the small mirror, then dropped the cloth and mirror back into the drawer. "I've still got a paper to get out this week."

"Surely our conversation won't last 'til the end of the week," Abby said, as they started for the door. She blushed when she realized she may have sounded a bit flirtatious again.

Mark jumped ahead to grab the door and hold it open for her.

"DING!" DING!" "DING!"

"I'm gonna' get rid of that bell tomorrow," Mark said, as Abby looked askance at the misfit bell. She didn't mind the bell but was amused that Mark thought the bell annoyed her.

Speckled sunlight danced across Abby's face as they walked under the shade of Mason Street's white birch trees. They walked in silence for a minute or two as Abby tried to think of something they might have in common. Mark saved her.

"Schroeder's was my hang out as a kid," he said, pointing to the drug store sign ahead. "At lunch time, my friends and I raced from school to try to find an empty stool at the counter. We always looked forward to 'drug store lunches,' malts and potato chips. Of course, in the middle of winter, we were stuck at the school with cafeteria food."

Abby laughed as she realized she seldom thought of life in Charlevoix at any season other than summer. "How cold does it get in the winter?" she asked.

"How does five degrees Fahrenheit and four feet of snow sound to you?"

"Sounds too cold for Abigail Finlay."

"And too cold for locals if they're honest," Mark said, as they approached Schroeder's. Mark gave a heaving push to the drug store door, which squeaked open with a sound only an antique door can make. "Not very welcoming, is it?"

"It reminds me of the door that opens each week at the beginning of radio's Inner Sanctum," Abby said.

"I agree, and isn't it an awesome sound," Mark said. He had to give the door another equally hard push to close it.

"Not sure I would say it's 'awesome,' but it does need a little oil."

Inside, four twisted wire chairs with plain, oak, panel seats, much worse for wear, surrounded a matching circular table with glass top.

"Those chairs don't look strong enough to hold anyone," Mark said.

"They never did," Abby said. Black and white square tile covered the floor; embossed tin covered the ceiling. "Not one thing has changed since the first time I came through that door." They slipped onto two well-worn, red-vinyl top stools at the counter. It had been a long time since Abby sat at the counter, and she took it all in: the soda jerk washing glasses, the pharmacist at his mortar and pestle in the rear of the store, and the lady buying film for her Brownie Hawkeye.

And that smell, Mercurochrome, everywhere. It's strong—gives the whole place a perpetual medicinal smell.

Mark's nose wrinkled up in disgust. "I can almost taste it. Smells like a cross between a hospital ward and, uh, that gargle—what's it called—oh yeah, Klenzo mouthwash. Blech!"

"It's not that bad," Abby said, giggling. "Mercurochrome healed every scrape I got when I was growing up."

"I'll keep that in mind if you fall off that stool." Mark gave her arm a teasing push. She laughed, and he raised his index finger to single the soda jerk. "Around here," Mark said, "a raised finger is the accepted signal to begin creating Schroeder's Marshmallow Cream Milkshake."

I wish he would stop staring at me like a teenager. Still, it is flattering.

They swiveled awkwardly for a time on their stools before Mark finally glanced at the clock. "I have to keep an eye on the clock so that I don't miss . . ." He stopped and took a deep breath.

"So that you don't miss . . . what?" Abby asked.

"So that I don't miss that smile—no, I'm sorry, my appointment at four." The room was suddenly warmer, he was sure. "Say, you know what's in the 'Jeff'?"

Abby knew but thought she would play along. "No, I can't imagine," she said, smiling.

"Schroeder adds three scoops of bittersweet chocolate to a regular milkshake before he puts it in the mixer, but the secret is in the final ingredient—I think it's the extra marshmallow cream—about three scoops. That cream really makes it pop."

He talks a lot when he's nervous. Abby smiled at his schoolboy charm. *I recall another boy who called to ask me for a date; he talked a mile a minute and hung up before he got to his question. Thank goodness Robert called back.*

"Oh yes, I remember the 'Jeff'," Abby said, still smiling. "A smoother shake was never made."

With an exaggerated flourish of both hands, the soda jerk launched a completed 'Jeff' down the counter with just enough momentum to bring it to a stop in front of Mark.

"Get ready for yours!" Mark pointed to the end of the counter. "Get ready!" Another 'Jeff' followed the first with equal accuracy. Lost in the blur of motion was a hand that inserted two straws. They applauded the soda jerk's practiced precision and giggled like two teenagers as they put their lips around the straws and began to extract the Jeff's legendary sweetness from deep within those extra-large soda glasses.

A moment later, Mark pushed his straw aside, the better to access the foamy goodness at the top of the glass. "Nothing like it," he declared as he looked up.

Abby laughed at the white chocolate moustache on his upper lip. "You did that on purpose."

"Did not." He grinned broadly. "Okay, maybe I did. But I just wanted to see that marvelous smile again. You're far too serious, Abby Finlay."

"I haven't had much to smile about in a long while." She stared at the counter top. "But you can help by telling me what you know about King Strang's buried treasure."

"What do you want to know?" Mark turned from his shake and looked straight into her eyes. "You don't seem the type to chase a wild goose, or to be more specific, to follow some never heard of clue to some never heard of place in search of treasure that might not even exist."

"Robert O'Donnell, of the Pine Lake O'Donnell's, is my fiancé." Abby emphasized the present tense when referring to Robert. "You may have heard of him or his family."

Mark put his glass down. "Well, yes, I, uh . . . I think I've heard the name once or twice."

He bit his lip as if he was about to say something else, but decided against it. Why?

"Robert was in London, or at least, England, in the weeks leading up to D-Day. We were to be married when the war was over—

the minute it was over." She closed her eyes. "I heard from him nearly every day, but nothing after June 6, 1944, nothing until this letter came." She pulled the letter from her purse. "And inside, he put this clue." She handed the yellow scrap of paper to Mark. "Tell me what you make of this."

Mark read the clue quietly. Finally, he looked up. "Well, you have what's been called the 'Old Pine' clue," Mark said, staring back at the words. "I've seen it many times." He nodded. "No doubt about it." He scanned the lines several times.

"But in his letter, Robert says he was given the clue by a descendant of James Strang. He gave it to Robert just hours before the D-Day invasion. Doesn't that give it a little extra cache?" Abby hoped Mark would reconsider any conclusions he may have reached about the value of the Old Pine clue. "His buddy wanted Robert to have the clue in case he didn't make it. I don't know what happened to his friend, but Robert was declared missing in action not long after D-day."

"Abby, I think you should know . . ." Mark hesitated, and Abby, with a glance in Mark's direction, saw a face that was devoid of expression. She decided she didn't want to hear whatever he was about to say.

"I never believed it." Abby was adamant, her voice strong and unwavering. "And now," her voice suddenly weaker, "all that I have is this—this obscure and mysterious clue."

"As I was about to say, I think you should know, no one has found the 'Old Pine' clue of much use in locating Strang's gold, if there is any. I'm sorry to disappoint—"

"It *must* mean something." She suddenly got up and walked toward the magazine rack. "Perhaps there's more to know."

"Well, what more can I tell you?" Mark swiveled on his stool to face her.

"I understand your grandfather, Charles J. Strang, moved to Charlevoix not long after his father's death. You have said he came from

Beaver Island and set up the local newspaper." Abby walked halfway back to the counter.

"That's right."

"I'm curious; did your father or grandfather ever speak of King Strang?"

Mark pulled on his straw, his milkshake half empty, as Abby slipped back onto her stool. *Mark knows something he doesn't usually reveal.* "They tell me he was a charismatic man but absolutely devoid of any sense of humor."

Mark shook his head. He turned toward Abby, but said nothing.

Again, the staring. Abby blinked and waved her hand across Mark's face, trying to wake him from his daze. "Yes?"

Mark blinked and raised his eyebrows. "I'm not going to bother you with anything but the truth. That's all any of us have a right to anyway." He tilted his head from side to side. "There are at least two perceptions of James Jesse Strang. Both, it may surprise you, are accurate. I can say with confidence that Strang was gifted and articulate, perhaps even a compelling intellect. But in many ways, he was an utter fraud. One thing is certain: when he crowned himself king of Beaver Island, he became the only king ever in the history of the United States."

"But no one can crown himself king," Abby said. "That's worse than attempting to secede from the Union, and that's been tried."

"Not in 1850," Mark said. "Imagine what President Fillmore must have thought when he heard someone claimed sovereignty on an island in the middle of Lake Michigan. There weren't many national stories in newspapers in those days, but this one made all the papers. Even Stephen Douglas wrote the President to express concern. I think Douglas didn't want to give the South a secession movement to point to in the North. That's all that was needed, I suspect, to prompt President Fillmore to instruct his Attorney General and the Secretary of the Navy to arrest the king."

"And did they?" Abby asked.

"Indeed, they did, and it wasn't long before the Feds had the king in custody and brought him to Detroit to stand trial for a series of crimes ranging from counterfeiting to stealing timber from federal lands."

Chapter Sixteen
Persecution in Detroit

June 20, 1851 – US District Court, Detroit, Michigan

A s James Strang waited for Judge Wilkins to enter the courtroom, he told his attorney that he would offer his own defense when the proceedings called for it.

His attorney shook his head. "I strongly advise against it," he said. "Surely, you've heard the old saw that any lawyer who represents himself in court has a fool for a client."

"I have been in jail more times than I can remember," Strang said, gritting his teeth. "I have no fear of another incarceration, but it shall *not* happen on this occasion."

"This is likely to end badly for you," his attorney said. "I repeat: I *am* against it. I predict the entire affair will be over in short order, and a guilty verdict returned." He slammed a raft of paper on the table.

"I *will* rise to defend myself." Strang put his hand over his heart and puffed his chest out.

When the prosecution rested, Strang was quick to his feet. "Members of the jury," Strang began, in his most convivial tone, "I have no doubt about your verdict. I know that I face an honest jury, and your verdict shall be justified by the evidence in the case, and in keeping with every principle of right and justice." He leaned forward toward the jury box. "As I look into your eyes, I know that it cannot be otherwise."

Strang paused, then slowly began to pace back and forth the full length of the jury box, pausing from time to time to stare purposely into the eyes of each man sitting there.

"You have heard a one-sided and bitterly prejudiced version of the affair, from a prosecutor who would take great satisfaction in learning you have pre-judged the case and condemned the parties charged." Strang turned to the prosecutor. "Sir, I must report to you that the jury has not judged anyone. Every man has spoken to me through his eyes, and each seeks to hear only the truth. That truth, I will now gladly reveal." With that, Strang turned again to the jury, and spoke in a sinister tone. "Emissaries of President Millard Fillmore came to Beaver Island as thieves in the night."

Many jurors sat on the edge of their seats. Strang, with his tiny, deep set eyes, stared into every set of eyes and never blinked at any.

"With warrants in hand, and accompanied by a company of Marines and U.S. Marshals, they slipped into the harbor of Saint James and crawled . . ." Strang stared at the prosecutor. ". . . like the Devil serpent himself, toward the only light still glowing in the night, a single lantern on the table of my modest log cabin, where I sat reading the Scriptures." He waved his finger at an oil lamp burning on the courtroom wall, walked over to it, and pretended to open a Bible in its light and read, "*Judge not that ye be not judged.*" He pretended to close the Bible and walked back to the jury box. "No one discharged a firearm. Of that there was no need. I was arrested, as I have been on many occasions when the gentiles have mustered the courage to harass me by perverting the laws upon which this country was founded." With a flourish, Strang pulled a copy of the U.S. Constitution from his vest pocket, and held it high. "And this book sits next to the Bible in my house, just as it must in the houses of each of you." Strang pointed the long index finger of his right hand to the face of each juror.

"My persecutors should be as ardent in support of this document as they are in persecuting innocent people whose only purpose in life is to become closer to their God."

Strang cleared his throat.

"The evidence presented, dim and shadowy as it is, falsely portrays my followers as being so sunk in infamy and crime as to be beyond the pale of human sympathy. My accusers have seen fit to provide fourteen indictments, but they have no evidence of any offense. None! Indeed, before this trial began, as you have heard, of the fourteen charges, only three have been saved for your consideration: counterfeiting, treason, and trespassing on Government lands. All of these charges—these persecutions, to be more precise—I have heard before, many times. Always, they have been dismissed."

Strang paused, then dramatically heaved a deep sigh. "The government has expended more money in this attempt to crush the infant settlement than the whole of Beaver Island would sell for." A little boy sat with his father in the first row of spectators. Strang walked over and patted the boy on the head. "In some countries, governments are instituted for the protection of the weak. I have even heard old people say that such was the purpose once entertained by the founders of the United States, but I do not have personal knowledge of it. I pray, however, that all of you will subscribe to that underlying principle when your verdict is rendered." He gave the little boy another pat on the head.

Nearly every member of the jury nodded, as Strang stared into their faces once more. Over his shoulder, he raised an eyebrow and glared at the prosecutor who was squirming in his chair. Next, Strang slowly walked to an empty seat on the other side of the courtroom and picked up a newspaper someone had left behind. "The only entity to find the Mormons of Beaver Island guilty of any charge is the Detroit newspaper, *The Advertiser*," his voice rising on each word, until he was nearly shouting at the end. He slapped the newspaper into the palm of his hand. He turned to the editorial page and, holding it up for all to see, pointed to the lead editorial. He slammed the paper on the table with a loud "shmaaack," and spit out his next words. "The editorial of yesterday described me as the Prince of Darkness. I am only surprised the editor did not call me Lucifer by name." He sneered at the paper as he picked it up again. "Satan may be familiar with the lives of a few editors, but he has never been welcome on Beaver Island." He walked to the nearest trashcan and released the paper as if it held a dead rat. Pretending to wash his hands, he smiled and turned back to the jury. "If perchance Beelzebub should visit us one day, he would find a simple folk and James Strang, a devout man, worshiping together and following the precepts of their God in the sanctity of Beaver Island."

Strang heard a few jurors murmuring softly, and sensed the jury had moved to his side. "You may have knowledge that *The Advertiser* has called me a king. If that is so, I am the first foreign leader to be escorted into a country on a national vessel, the *USS Michigan*." The courtroom erupted in laughter. Everyone was aware that the *Michigan* had been sent to Beaver Island to bring Strang to Detroit to stand trial.

"Order! Order in the court!" Judge Ross Wilkins banged his gavel. "Members of the jury, the prosecution was notified this morning that the charge of treason is invalid. Neither Mr. Strang, nor his followers, have engaged in war against the United States or aided enemies of the nation in doing so. Therefore, Mr. Strang cannot be convicted of treason."

Applause erupted from Strang's followers in the back of the courtroom.

"Order!" shouted the judge. When the applause faded, the judge continued. "Further, the charge of counterfeiting is dismissed as well. Yesterday, the government's witness, Mr. John Smedley, admitted that he, in fact, had not been a witness to the work of counterfeiters on Beaver Island. Indeed, he testified that he made up the entire account."

As Strang's followers began stamping their feet, Strang decided not to say another word. He moved quietly to his seat, and gave a broad smile to his attorney.

The judge banged his gavel again. "Now, Mr. District Attorney, do you have further evidence to bring to the attention of the court in the matter of trespassing on federal land, specifically, the cutting of timber on Government lands?"

"Yes, your honor." The prosecutor soldiered on. "Mr. Strang, do you deny *that* charge as well?" he asked, putting his finger in the face of James Strang.

Very slowly, Strang pushed the finger away from his face. "No, I do not deny it, Mr. Bates."

"Aha!" The prosecutor whipped around a full 360 degrees, his finger high in the air.

The room fell silent. Strang showed no signs of worry or concern. "Your honor, may I address the court?"

"Please proceed," the judge said, "if you have anything to say in your defense."

"In the rugged hills of Michigan, such an offense hardly merits more than a frown. Far from theft of government timber, when my followers cut timber on federal land, they were merely improving the property of which they hope to take ownership in the future. Is the court not aware of such a practice among frontier settlers?"

The judge cleared his throat. "Ha-rumph." He smacked his gavel on the rostrum. "Do you, Mr. Strang, have anything further?"

"Just this, your honor: I have given my followers strict orders." Strang placed his hand over his heart. "'You shall preserve the trees by the wayside, and if there be none, you shall plant them.'" He lowered his hand. "That is all."

Hearing Strang's final comment, two Democrats on the jury allowed a smile, and a couple of the Whigs nodded.

The next morning, the jury delivered a verdict of "not guilty" on all counts. The *Detroit Free Press* carried a story about the trial a couple of days later, concluding, *"That the Mormon defendants were Mormons was the only crime fully substantiated."*

As Strang folded the newspaper under his arm, he smirked. "My enemies, President Millard Fillmore, U.S. Marshal Charles Knox, and U.S. District Attorney George Bates, have only succeeded in securing for themselves a place in the Temple of Infamy."

The morning fog was beginning to lift as Strang walked toward the docks to await transport back to Beaver Island. *If I am to rule this country, it will be a hard struggle if I do not make myself one of the judges of the Supreme Court within one year.* He smiled. *Yes, that shall be my plan.*

A day later, Strang reached Beaver Island, and while still far from shore, he could see a large crowd gathered at the docks of Saint James Harbor. *The news has preceded me. I pray the malcontents will be silenced at last.* At first he heard nothing, but as the vessel neared the docks, the unmistakable chant of "Not guilty! Not guilty!" welcomed him home. He stepped ashore to the chant, "Victory! Victory!"

At the top of the gangway, Strang surveyed the crowd, threw open his arms as if attempting to embrace them all, and in a loud voice said, "Blessed saints of Beaver Island, I am honored to be your king. When history is recorded, all of you will be listed as first citizens of the new Kingdom of God on Earth. Let our work begin!"

Confident his power base had been secured, Strang laid plans to run for a seat in the state legislature. A year later, in Lansing, he was sworn in, the first Mormon to win a seat in the Michigan Legislature. "It is not the Supreme Court," he told Elvira, "but it is another step in that direction."

Chapter Seventeen
"Whoso Shall Publish Peace . . ."

The two milkshakes were nearly drained. Mark pushed his away when the soda jerk approached, and it was quickly whisked away. Abby wasn't quite finished with hers.

"Supposedly, my grandfather, Charles J. Strang, was the king's favorite, not only because he was the first born son of his relationship with Elvira, but because he expressed an interest in becoming a journalist. King Strang published the only newspaper on Beaver Island, and he believed Charles was destined to succeed him—*if* he used his writing skills to proselytize a bit."

"The Old Pine clue mentions something about a destiny for the one who 'shall publish peace.'" Abby held out her clue. "Right here, see." And she pointed to the line.

"It helps to get in his head, and I think you've made a good start. I should also tell you that his newspaper, the *Northern Islander*, was the theological arm of the church while Strang was alive. He was a prolific publisher of his personal doctrine."

"His theological ideas don't interest me unless they have some bearing on understanding the clues," Abby said.

"And they may," Mark said. "They may."

"Very well, we'll get back to his doctrine later, but for now, what can you tell me about his children?"

"Well, his greatest hope was that Charles, Clement, and Eva— his children by Elvira—would forge a partnership, and continue his work on Beaver Island. He had other children, I was told, but was partial to

Elvira's three. Unfortunately, those three children seldom agreed on anything, a sore spot with their father. Strang knew he had to be creative, or there would be no family succession in the leadership of his church."

As Mark explained Strang's plan, Abby felt drawn to him by something more than his smile and affable nature. *Both are more than enough to hold my interest, but there's a devilish charm about him that is, well, hard to resist.* She found it easy to believe Mark Day was a direct descendant of the charismatic King Strang, but was surprised to find herself staring, hanging on every word, as he spoke. *What is it about this man that attracts me?* She felt a stirring somewhere inside and took a deep breath. *And those eyes, piercing blue, the color of a Charlevoix sky in summer.* An instant later, she felt a gentle ache within her chest. *I've felt it before. Why?*

"What's wrong, Abby? That wistful smile is gone, again. Try one like this." Mark flashed a wide grin that wrinkled the corner of his eyes.

When he smiles, those eyes seem to increase their blueness, their intensity.

"You're still not smiling," Mark said. He reached over and pretended to pull up at the corners of her mouth.

"Oh, I'm sorry. It's just that . . . waiting for Robert . . ." Abby gave a deep sigh.

"I'm sorry, too." Mark touched the back of her hand. "Believe me, I understand."

How could he? How could anyone feel this pain that cuts so deep?

Abby looked around the drug store and watched as the last customer bought a pack of cigarettes from the pharmacist and left the store. Mark sneaked a peek at the Coca Cola clock over the soda fountain and checked his watch. It was already after four o'clock.

This is not going to get any better unless I stay focused. "So, how did King Strang ensure his three children would work together when he died?" She pulled on her straw a final time, and was embarrassed to hear that final slurp she always tries to avoid.

Mark smiled. "I knew you would enjoy the 'Jeff.'" He signaled the soda jerk to bring him the tab by pretending to write on his hand, and then he turned to Abby. "The answer to your good question is part of the murder story."

Abby winced as she pushed away her empty glass. "Horrid. Simply horrid." She pushed her glass even farther away.

"You might not feel that way if you lived on Beaver during Strang's time. Everybody knew, if you disobeyed Strang's orders, you might be excommunicated from his church, or worse, you might be on the receiving end of a public flogging."

"That must have upset quite a few of the islanders," Abby said, "not just members of his church."

"Yes, and Thomas Bedford was one of them. Eventually, 'ole Tom had enough of Strang's edicts. With three similarly chastened members of the king's church, they devised a plan to get rid of Strang once and for all."

"But, a cold blooded murder?"

The Coca-Cola clock chimed once at four-thirty p.m., and Mark jumped off his stool.

"I know you have to go," Abby said, "but stay long enough to finish the Bedford story."

"I'll try to make it quick." With a twist, he was back on the stool. "Tom concluded there was no other way to resolve their 'Strang problem,' as he often described it. There had to be a murder; there was no way around it."

Chapter Eighteen
Assassination of the King

June 16 to July 9, 1856 – Beaver Island to Burlington, Wisconsin

B y the spring of 1856, James Strang was aware that forces were beginning to conspire against him. It had been a bitter winter. Ice in Saint James Harbor had been almost three feet thick. The brutal weather had confined most of the island's residents indoors for nearly six months.

"Hibernation may be good for bears, but not for people," Strang said to his assistant, Samuel Chichester. "When people are confined too long, the malcontents among them are emboldened in their ways and will insist on being heard."

"But it has been desperately cold, Prophet. Surely they can be excused if—"

"Silence! I'll hear none of it. We did not choose this place of dwelling. God chose it for us. Those who disagree had best choose a place for themselves somewhere else."

Through the winter, Strang heard the rumors that some of his church members had used alcohol, and it was quite obvious to Strang that some of the women had refused to wear bloomers, in willful defiance of his most recent decree. "Now, Samuel, sit down and tell me what you have learned with those two fine ears of yours."

"As you have commanded, Prophet, I have observed Thomas Bedford and his friends from afar." He hesitated a moment, then stood up and walked to the fireplace. "But it is as you have feared. They are planning an assassination attempt." And he took a step toward the fire.

Strang's anger was well known among his following, but in this case, he answered Samuel in a most reserved voice. "And how, my son, have you come by their diabolical plans?"

Samuel took a step closer. "At Johnson's store, they met just yesterday—four of them—sitting around the pot belly stove, drinking cider. The storeroom was as close as I dared approach, and I could not catch all that was said."

"Sit down, Samuel. I'm not upset with you." Strang wanted Samuel to tell him all that he knew. "When will they attempt this deed?"

Samuel chose to stand with his back to the fire a while longer. "That is not clear. They make no mention of a date. The only thing certain is that they have been practicing with a pistol in the woods north of the harbor for several weeks."

"Where did they get this pistol?" Strang demanded to know.

"Bedford said one of the Irish fishermen left it here. I cannot be certain of that, but he did tell his friends, 'With the help of the Irish and our just God, we shall soon be rid of the plague among us.'"

"What! He called me a plague?" Strang slammed the table with his fist. "Samuel, please sit down."

"Yes, a plague," Samuel said. "If it's all the same to you, I prefer to warm myself by the fire."

"Very well. Who else is involved in this devil's enterprise?" Strang was becoming more agitated with each passing minute.

"Sitting around the stove with Bedford were Dr. Hezekiah McCulloch, Franklin Johnson, and his son-in-law, Alexander Wentworth."

"A cauldron of evil," Strang said, with disgust in his voice. "McCulloch drinks too much, Johnson is a deadbeat, Wentworth chooses his company badly, and Bedford – well, he's one of the malcontents I mentioned. I have already excommunicated most of them from the church. I shall have to do more if they attempt to carry out their plot." Strang tapped his fingers on the table and contemplated his next move. "I gave Bedford thirty-nine strokes with the blue beeches a fortnight past. That should have been a lesson to him, but it appears it was not harsh enough."

"Prophet, many thought he had been killed," Samuel said. "I was there; he was tied between two trees like a suckling pig."

"The evil in that one is not so easily extinguished," Strang said. "He deserved thirty-nine more."

"Prophet," Samuel said, with a timid voice, "I am reluctant—"

"More? Speak, Samuel. Tell me all."

"I've heard several of the women say they will never wear pantaloons or anything that pinches or compresses the body." His face turned red as he told Strang this news.

"What?" Strang popped out of his chair and grabbed Samuel by his shoulder. "The women are wrong, Samuel. Mrs. Bloomer has said that wearing pantaloons is more practical for women, and healthier, too."

The fire's crackling echoed about the room. Samuel added nothing more, but leaned over to place another log on the fire.

"They have a pistol, do they?" Strang asked, at last.

Samuel nodded.

"And ammunition?"

Samuel nodded again.

"Do you think any of them could hit the broadside of a barn?"

"They are fishermen, Prophet," Samuel said, with a smile. "The answer is no. Only by the best of Irish luck could they be successful."

Strang walked to his straight back chair and sat down hard. The cane bottom seat sagged under his weight. "When Johnson came by last week to lodge a complaint about taxes due the kingdom from his dry goods store, he left with a direct threat to my wellbeing."

"What did he say?" Samuel asked.

"'Now it is you and me; you will destroy me, or I shall destroy you.' I laughed in his face and told him, 'Do your worst, Franklin.'" The fire had become a bed of glowing coals and ashes. In a low voice, Strang added, "I don't believe there is one of them man enough to pull a trigger."

Samuel gave a little nervous laugh as he headed for the door. "I will keep you informed if I should hear anything further about the assassins' plans."

"You do that, Samuel," Strang said, patting him on the back. "But, be on your guard. Bedford will not take kindly to the decree I will issue tomorrow."

The next day, Strang posted a single sentence edict on the tabernacle entrance: "All Gentiles must move out, or go to the temple to be baptized into the Church of Zion." As Strang stood back to admire his work, he smirked. "Now, we'll see what those four devils are made of. I shall make an example of all four very soon."

As soon as the co-conspirators learned of Strang's decree, Bedford called them together at Johnson's store. Again, Samuel overheard the conversation and reported as much as he could remember to Strang. "They said you were tightening the noose around them, but seemed uncertain in their plans. Dr. McCullough took great pains to withdraw from whatever action Bedford planned, but he was willing to go to the mainland to seek help from the Governor. That's what he said."

Strang stroked his beard several times when he heard Samuel's report. "Just as I thought, only Bedford is willing to go forward. Wentworth and Johnson were quiet, yes?"

"Yes, they said nothing."

"McCullough has already gone to the mainland," Strang said. "I gave him permission. He will come home, no doubt, with bandages to bind up wounds, that's all." He reached for Samuel's hand and shook it vigorously, and laughed. "He will need all of his bandages when I get through with the four of them."

Samuel left for the night and Strang gave no further thought to the conspiracy.

Several weeks later, the *USS Michigan* steamed into the island's harbor with a company of Marines waving from the rail. Strang was sitting on his front porch, reading his Book of Mormon, and looked up only briefly as the ship tied up. "Just a routine stop, I'm sure, to pick up wood for the boiler." But there on the rail, Strang spied Dr. McCullough waving to someone on the dock. "I hope the doctor brought plenty of balm with him. What a fool he has been to question my authority." Strang turned back to his reading. "All of my authority comes from God."

In mid-afternoon, a messenger from the ship's captain appeared at Strang's door with an invitation to come aboard for a visit with Captain Charles McBlair. Though he had accepted such invitations in the past, Strang was suspicious of this one. He sent the messenger back, declining the invitation.

Before the messenger was out of sight, Elvira brought Strang's coat and chimney pot hat to him. "This is no time to be inhospitable, James. We need good relations with the US Government. I think you should go, but you shouldn't tarry long. You can take your leave by explaining you have duties at the tabernacle."

"You are right, my dear. There are times when my proclivity for caution prevents seizing opportunities to make friends where friends are needed." With that, Strang was off for the short walk to the wharf.

It was a warm summer afternoon with not a cloud in the sky. High above, the screeching of a cormorant echoed across the harbor as it swept low and settled in the water a few feet beyond the *Michigan.* Strang smiled as the cormorant landed with hardly a ripple. *God has blessed us with a sliver of his own paradise, and a promise that we shall one day see his paradise in its entirety. I pray that day will come soon for all the faithful.*

Strang stepped briskly onto the dock and missed entirely the moment when Wentworth and Bedford stepped behind a stack of nearby cordwood. Bedford cocked the one pistol in their possession, and as Strang passed, he stepped out to fire. Wentworth reached for Bedford at that exact moment, but Bedford twisted away and fired a shot.

Strang, stunned, stood frozen for a moment. He touched his temple, and his fingers came away covered in blood from the path of a bullet that just grazed him. "The devils have done their worst." Before he could turn, he felt another bullet, and another. Strang's hat plopped into the water. He thought it odd that he didn't hear the sound it made when it hit the water. In the next instant, someone grabbed him from behind and pushed him forward hard. He fell face down, motionless, but still conscious. As the two assassins stepped over him, he reached out and grabbed the leg of Wentworth who let out a yowl. Bedford, halfway up the gangway, heard Wentworth's scream, and ran back to help his friend.

But Strang had a tight grip. *This damn devil will pay. I'll not release him until he is ready for hell.* A blow from the butt of Bedford's pistol forced Strang to relinquish his grasp. *Why can't I move?* Strang struggled to make a sound, to scream, anything, but couldn't. *Eternal God, my refuge, help me.*

Several of the Marines picked up Strang and carried him aboard the *Michigan*.

"Take him to my cabin," Dr. McCullough said. "I'll tend to him."

As the Marines delivered him to McCullough's cabin, Strang opened his eyes and locked onto McCullough. His voice suddenly returned. "God will avenge me," he said, and closed his eyes.

Strang was not dead, but McCullough soon determined he was mortally wounded. As McCullough attempted to remove Strang's coat, a hand written note fell from Strang's vest pocket. McCullough picked it up and read aloud, *"I have made my mark upon the times in which I live, which the wear and tear of the unborn ages shall not obliterate."* McCullough handed the note to Captain McBlair, who had entered the berth just as the doctor was reading the note. "I doubt, Captain, the world has seen an ego larger than that of the one lying here."

Through the night, Strang was in and out of consciousness. By morning, the head wound had closed of its own accord. When Strang felt Dr. McCullough touch his head, he whispered, his eyes still closed, "Take me to Mary."

"What's that, James?" McCullough put a hand on Strang's shoulder.

"Take me to Mary," he whispered again.

"Who's Mary?" asked Captain McBlair, who had just stepped in to ask about the patient.

"There is only one Mary with whom I am familiar," McCullough said, "Strang's first wife, Mary Perce. She returned to the mainland several years past, went back to Burlington when James took a second wife." McCullough wiped Strang's forehead. "James, are you sure you want to travel to Burlington?"

"Take me to Mary," Strang said. His eyes barely open, he grabbed the doctor's arm. "I *will* survive."

"James, I have always been honest with you." McCullough wiped Strang's brow with a cool cloth. "You will surely die if we move you to the mainland."

"He's going to die anyway," the Captain said.

"Shhhhhh!" McCullough gave the Captain a look of total disdain. "Sir, don't you have a course to map out?"

The Captain nodded and left the room.

"James, you have a bullet in your spine. That's the honest truth. It cannot be removed and—"

"Take me to—"

"Very well." The doctor whispered in Strang's ear, "James, I promise we will take you to Mary."

An hour later, the *USS Michigan* was steaming out of Saint James Harbor with Strang, the two assassins, and Dr. McCullough aboard. Mackinac was their first stop, and they were only there long enough to hand Bedford and Wentworth over to the local sheriff. Another day of steaming brought them to Milwaukee Bay on the west side of Lake Michigan.

At the dock, Strang was loaded into the only available transportation McCullough could find, a railway baggage buggy. "This will have to do," McCullough said, as he motioned for a few of the men to lift Strang into the buggy.

The jostling woke Strang who muttered, "Touch not mine Anointed, and do my Prophets no harm."

"Will you ever stop quoting Holy Scripture, James?" McCullough asked.

"Not until mine enemies breathe their last," Strang whispered, "or . . . I do."

"It's a full half day from here to Burlington, James, but I'll stay with you," the doctor said, "until I can turn you over to the healing hands of Mary."

Strang smiled. That was all he asked for. "And where are the assassins?"

"We turned them over to the authorities at Mackinac," McCullough said. "Justice will be served."

"Hailed as heroes, most likely," Strang said, coughing hard. "Cigars and whiskey all around."

**

Mary Perce was standing on her front porch when the wagon carrying James Strang appeared on the rise just down the road. "Oh, my Lord. Save us!" she screamed, and ran down the road to meet the wagon. "Have they finally done it, good doctor?" she asked when the doctor was within earshot.

"No questions now, Mary," McCullough said. "Come quickly; he has been asking for you every day."

Mary jumped into the wagon, gasping in horror when she got a good look at his wounds. He was still wearing the same blood soaked clothing from the afternoon of the assassination attempt. For a long time, Mary cradled his head in her arms, and repeated, over and over, "James, my dear James." She touched his hand and began to stroke it gently.

"Mary, we weren't sure you would be glad to see him, considering the circumstances of your last parting." McCullough pulled the wagon to a stop at Mary's front gate.

"My good doctor, I have loved James dearly and always will," Mary said. "I could not divorce him because no action on his part, no matter how undisciplined, could diminish my love." Tears cascaded down her face. "Please, if you will, take him upstairs to my room. Place him gently on my bed."

"Mary, thank you, but you should know he will not recover from his wounds. He has been struck with a bullet that lies next to his spine, and it cannot be removed."

"Good doctor, tell me not of these problems; they are yours, not mine." And for the next two days, Mary Perce never left the side of her husband, James Jesse Strang.

On the evening of the third day, Strang opened his eyes, and the face he saw was that of his devoted Mary. He managed a wan smile. "I knew you would take me in, dearest Mary." He struggled to expand his lungs for air. "But, I do not have much time. My Heavenly Father is calling . . . and I must go soon."

"Don't try to speak." She wiped perspiration from his brow and cheeks.

"I must. I must. Do you still have the diary I gave you?" He grabbed her forearm and tried to sit up.

"Yes, but most of what you have written cannot be read. You have employed a strange language. I cannot read one word of it."

"Shhhh. Be silent, my dear, and listen." His head fell back on the bed.

Mary leaned forward to catch every word.

"They think I made no plan for someone worthy to follow me . . . . and as they often are . . . they are wrong. I beg you, open the diary to the last page."

Mary quickly retrieved Strang's diary from a shelf across the room. She kept it next to the *Complete Works of Shakespeare,* which he had given her as a wedding present. When she returned with his diary, she found Strang, still on his back, had somehow raised himself on his elbows.

"Someday there will be an heir . . . who will decipher the words . . . I have written . . . and the words . . . my words . . . will be a blessing to a new generation. Open it. Open it."

As Mary opened the diary to the last page, as instructed, three small envelopes fell out. On each, Strang had written the name of one of Elvira's three children: Eva, Clement, and Charles.

"What's this?"

"Keys to the kingdom, my dear, keys to the kingdom."

"But, I do not understand. I . . . " The lump in her throat held her voice for a moment. "Dear husband, you are making a bequest. Have you forgotten the children you had with me? Are they not worthy?"

"It is not yours to understand," he whispered, "or to ask questions. It is yours only to obey. Give each to the child . . . whose name appears thereon . . . on the occasion . . . of that child's . . . twelfth birthday. Say this . . . and this alone . . . to each." Strang took several large gasping breaths.

> *"Thou shalt wear a cloak of gold, my kingdom to restore.*
> *Trust but one, thy Father, and live forever more."*

The next day, the remaining four wives arrived with most of their children in tow, and all gathered at the foot of Strang's bed. He wanted to say something to each of them, but didn't have the strength. When one of the women mentioned that all of them were expecting a child "by his seed," he gave them a weak smile and a gentle nod of approval.

On July 9, his mother arrived and stationed herself at the foot of the bed. Phoebe, his fifth wife, sat closest to his face and held his hand. "Are you going to leave us, James?" she asked.

"Yes," he said, in an extremely weak voice. Strang suddenly coughed and grasped Phoebe's hand.

Several hours passed, and Sarah, his third wife, asked, "Is there anything you wish to communicate?"

There was silence, but after a long while, and with great effort, he nodded, "Yes." It was his final word.

One of the elders reached over the bed and closed his eyes. The time was nine forty-five p.m., July 9, 1856.

Chapter Nineteen
Truth or Hoax?

Clouds gathered in the southeast, dimming what little ambient light remained in the drug store. Abby swiveled back and forth on the vinyl-topped stool. "The sun, I fear, has gone home for the day," Mark said, and pushed his empty milkshake glass toward the soda jerk. "I must return to my office." Mark plunked a dollar fifty in change on the counter. "That should take care of it."

"Wait. You must tell me; what was the bequest Strang made?"

"I was told that Mary opened each of the three envelopes and discovered he had left a clue to the whereabouts of the gold to each of Elvira's three children." Mark stood and buttoned his jacket. "And he included in each envelope a single gold coin as proof, if they needed any, that the rumors they had heard about the gold were true.

"If he liked Elvira so much, why did he entrust the clues to Mary?" Abby was fascinated by the machinations of such a dysfunctional family.

"Mary had helped him bury the gold shortly after they arrived on Beaver in late 1848. She was the only one who knew precisely where it was hidden, and the only one who could have found the gold without a clue."

"Did you ever consider that Mary came back and moved the gold to another location long before Strang was shot?"

Mark unbuttoned his jacket and sat down again. "But there is no evidence she ever returned to Beaver or any of the other islands before or after Strang's death. That's what my mother told me before she died."

"Okay. So, let me get this straight: there were three clues altogether?" Abby was so excited she kept reaching for her milkshake and pulling on a straw that failed to deliver anything from her empty glass. "A gold coin for each of the three children, and a clue?" Another attempted slurp on her straw followed.

"Well, there were at least two clues," Mark said. "I have one and you have another, the Old Pine clue. If there is a third, no one has seen it."

"And yours is different from the Old Pine clue?" *He probably has the same clue as Howard.*

"Yes, and . . . " Mark looked deep into her eyes. "I've never shared this with another soul."

"Everything we do in this search, as far as I am concerned, is confidential between us." She drew a finger across her lips.

The soda jerk came over with a half filled pitcher. "Look, I've been watching you try to extract more 'Jeff' from that glass. I don't have much left, but you're welcome to it. It's on the house." As he talked, he poured the rest of the "Jeff" in her glass.

Abby blushed and tried to explain why she kept pulling on an empty straw. "When I get excited, I tend to snack on what's handy or drink from what's available."

"No need to apologize to me," Mark said. "My stories bore most people. It's great to meet one person who thinks they're exciting."

"I should say!" Abby took a long draw on the straw. "Now, if we could find one of those coins, that would prove . . ."

"Well, I know the fate of one of them. Mother told me that her father, Charles Strang was twelve years of age when he received a single gold coin in the mail and a clue to the whereabouts of Strang's gold. Mary Perce sent it, and by that time, she was living somewhere in Illinois. Mary apparently *never* told Elvira about the clues or the gold."

"Where is the coin today?" Abby asked.

"The story told by mother was that he gave his gold piece to the Mormon Church sometime in the late 1880s. The elders, fearing it might be evidence of a theft, melted it down in the late 1800s to gild the figure of the Angel Moroni when it was installed on the Salt Lake Temple."

"Really?"

"Really."

"Are you telling me the evidence of Strang's buried treasure now stands atop the Temple in Salt Lake City?"

"Yes," Mark said. "And it may be the only evidence. The coins given to the other children have never been accounted for."

At first, Abby was speechless. She wanted to shout, but was afraid they would cause a scene in the drug store. Instead, she leaned over and whispered loudly into Mark's ear, "The . . . gold . . . exists!"

"Yes, I know that, but we don't know where it is. If I knew where Strang buried the gold, I would already have a new linotype machine humming in my office."

"Or getting a suntan on Waikiki Beach while your assistant runs the presses." She smiled, beaming toward the sky as if basking in the sun herself.

"Not a bad idea," Mark said, "but that suntan will have to wait until we have all three clues. I have one clue handed down through my family, the Charles Strang branch, and it is quite different from the 'Old Pine' clue, which came down through the Clement Strang side. There has never been even a rumor about the whereabouts of the third clue, the one given to Eva, and that could be the most illuminating of all."

"Is it possible that you have the same clue in Howard's possession?" Abby is growing more giddy by the minute.

"No, not possible. I know Howard. He talks a big game but never produces anything. If he has one at all, it's bound to be the 'Old Pine' clue, that's for sure."

"Or the Eva clue," Abby said, with a tone of conviction. She couldn't hide the excitement in her voice any longer as she began to absorb the very real possibility that they possess all three clues.

"I'd have to see it to believe it," Mark said.

"I don't have it," Abby said, with a smile.

"I thought so."

"No, I have it memorized. Would you like to hear it?"

Mark had been skeptical until this moment. But what if he was wrong? He simply nodded and gave Abby rapt attention as she recited Howard's clue.

> *"Deep within The Patchin' lies a Spirit House of old*
> *Drink of it, lost prodigal, and risk thy very soul.*
> *From heaven's gate, Divine One descends to aviary white*
> *Trust but one – thy Father – he will keep thee in the right."*

"The Eva clue!" Mark whispered, his eyes wide open. He leaned over and whispered so loudly in Abby's ear that he almost burst her eardrum "We have all three clues!" From his wallet, Mark pulled a scrap of yellowed paper, worn and frayed, like the one Abby possessed. Held together by many pieces of Scotch tape, Mark began to read:

> *"Granite turns to emerald when Divine Orb glows green*
> *Brighter eyes than thine have the drumlin never seen.*
> *Welcome all ye faithful, the right hand of Jesus beckons*
> *A rising sun bears witness, thy sins are now forgiven."*

"Different, yes?" Mark asked with a quizzical look.

"*Yes*! Quite different!" Abby nearly fell from her stool. "*Yes*!"

The pharmacist looked up from his mortar and pestle.

"Shhhhh! You're attracting attention," Mark said. He touched her arm, very gently.

Abby felt a warmth in her heart she had not felt in a very long time. His touch conveyed a sense that it was okay to be here at this moment.

"Abby, I have something else to tell you, and I ask you to forgive me for what I am about to say because the news I have may be connected to your clue, and your Robert."

Abby winced. She wasn't sure she wanted to hear this, but she let him continue. *I've got to be willing to hear everything, but this—this has an ominous feel.*

"Several years ago, a Sergeant Strang came by my office to talk about Strang's gold. He claimed to be a great-grandson of King Strang. The sergeant wanted to know if a Lieutenant Robert O'Donnell had been around looking for him. He said he had given the Old Pine clue to the lieutenant in England, but they were separated the night before the Normandy invasion and never saw each other again."

"Are you serious? Did he think Robert *wasn't* at Normandy?"

"Not sure, but apparently Robert wasn't in the first assault wave. The sergeant said Robert was proficient in Morse Code and was pulled out of their unit at the last minute for duty in the Signal Corps. He didn't say much more, except he was mad as hell that Robert was probably going to survive the next day, and he wouldn't. From that day forward, the sergeant said he was determined to get back to Charlevoix, find Robert, and make him split the gold with him."

"Oh my God," Abby exclaimed. She had begun to accept the fact that her Robert might really be dead. He didn't meet her at the train station; he wasn't at the Hotel; no one, not even Mrs. Vandivare had seen him. "But, now . . . . now this!"

Mark tried to slow her down. "Abby, you should know . . ." Mark lowered his voice to soften his next words. "The sergeant concluded that since Robert never returned to Charlevoix—not even to look for Strang's gold—that he must have died at Normandy or soon thereafter."

"Mark! How could you say such a thing?"

"Abby, I'm not making this up." He gently put his hand on her shoulder. "That's what the sergeant said. He claimed he gave the clue to Robert directly."

Abby closed her eyes and slowly shook her head.

Mark put his arms around Abby's shoulders, pulling her slightly toward him in a comforting way. He didn't say another word.

After a long while, Abby opened her eyes. Through clinched teeth, she asked, "Are you trying to tell me you believe Robert really was killed that day?" Without waiting for a response, she pulled away and declared, "No! Robert *will* come back." Defiance was embedded in her every word. She slapped the counter with the palm of her hand. "He *will* come back." And she burst into tears.

Mark dabbed away her tears with his handkerchief.

Abby tried to collect her thoughts. *I tell everyone Robert is alive, and yet, deep inside, a part of me knows that he is gone—gone forever. Publicly, I say one thing, but my mind, when it yields to rational thought, says another. And now, Mark confirms my worst fears. It is hard for any part of me to deny the truth anymore.*

"You deserve to know all that I know," Mark said, "and I'll gladly share the rest of the story, but it won't answer any of your questions."

"I want to know everything," Abby said. "Whatever you know, please share it."

"Sergeant Strang made several trips to my office. Often, he seemed confused, unable to put his thoughts together. I'm certain the war left him shell-shocked. At one point, he brought in a journal—I use that term loosely—and he asked if I would write an article about his experiences at the Battle of the Bulge. I accepted his material just to get him out of my office. Before I could write anything for the newspaper, he disappeared."

"Maybe he found the gold and left the area?" Abby shrugged her shoulders and looked up at Mark. "Is it possible?

"I don't know," Mark said. "One day, he didn't show up for work at Griner's Garage, and nobody saw him again. I heard one of the regulars at Whitney's Pub say he saw a man walking the beaches of Garden Island, but later, when he told the story again, he said it was High Island, not Garden. He probably made it all up."

The soda jerk interrupted, "Mr. Day, your office called. The linotype repairman can't find that special oil you use and wants you to come right now. He said to remind you he is being paid time and a half."

Mark looked at Abby and slipped off the stool. "Gotta' go."

"But I have more questions." Abby said.

"Tell you what, let's have dinner tonight and share our combined knowledge. I have something incredible to tell you about my clue."

"Even more incredible than what you have already revealed?"

"Oh, yes. You may not believe it."

"Then, I'll agree to it," Abby said. "Would you like to join me at the Pine Lake Hotel?"

"Why, yes," Mark said, smiling. "It'll be my first time in the Hotel dining room."

Abby, brushing her hair back as she had seen Mrs. Vandivare do earlier, slipped off the stool, took Mark's outstretched arm, and together they stepped through that ancient door again.

Mark turned left; Abby turned right. As he released her hand, he gave her palm a slight squeeze.

Now who's flirting? God, why do I feel this way? I can't explain it; I only feel it.

"See you at seven," Mark said. His voice betrayed his excitement.

She waved. "Seven, it is," and she began the short walk back to the Club. At the traffic light, she turned to watch the young editor stepping briskly back to his office. *He's late, I guess, but he sure walks fast. He's almost skipping.*

As she reached the old birch tree near the entrance to the Club, what had been a gentle breeze suddenly increased in intensity, gusting from the southeast, and the highest birch limbs twisted and turned. *A sure sign of rain.* Behind the birch, a pile of leaves rustled unexpectedly, as if someone had just walked through them.

"Is anyone there?"

She heard only the wind.

"Damn!" As the wind crept up her arm, Abby wondered if she should have told Mark about the note she received from the Seventh Messenger.

Chapter Twenty
Dinner for Two at the Pine Lake Hotel

When Abby peeked into the dining room, she hoped to find Mark already there, but he was nowhere to be seen. *Has he changed his mind? I wouldn't blame him, but I wonder . . . oh . . .*

A little girl pulled on Abby's arm, then danced in a full circle around Abby, her pigtails swinging around her head as she searched for a place to hide from her brother. He was busy running from table to table, lifting up each tablecloth in a vain search for his sister. From behind Abby's long skirt, the wide-eyed little girl dared a peek, only to find her brother standing there, hands on hips, staring into her eyes and laughing. The little girl let out a squeal of delight and dashed away again.

Abby didn't mind the noise. It reminded her of the many evenings her family dined in that room when she was young. *Father patted the toddlers on the head as they walked by. "That's the next generation," he always said. I do miss the Johnny DiCicco Trio. They were always playing hit tunes just outside the dining room.* The smell of dark, roasted coffee put her sense of smell on high alert. She smiled as she remembered better times at the Hotel.

Abby motioned for the Maitre'd to come closer and was about to ask if a Mr. Mark Day had arrived, when the Maitre'd nodded and smiled to someone behind her. "Good evening, sir, are you looking for this lady?"

Abby turned to look into those intensely blue eyes of her new friend. "Among other virtues, I see you are punctual, too," she said, returning his smile.

"A good reporter is always on time," Mark said. "In the news business, too early is a waste of time, too late will cost your job, but on time earns a scoop."

"If we succeed in this adventure, you will definitely earn a scoop, and more," Abby said. *What am I doing? Why did I say that?*

Mark smiled and buttoned his dinner jacket. The Maitre'd signaled them to follow. Faces turned toward Abby, as she and Mark strolled through the room, faces well known to her. She was glad she had taken the time to select the proper evening wear for such an occasion. The long skirt, with fitted waist, was simple but elegant and would work for more than one evening event. As she scanned the room, she wondered if anyone remembered her name. After all, ten years had passed since her last visit. A few waved politely, but Abby sensed all were bursting with curiosity about her handsome escort for the evening. Eyebrows were raised by some, while others seemed to be whispering behind their menus.

"I hope you don't mind," Abby said. "I reserved a corner table in the back for us. We can have an uninterrupted conversation, but most important, we'll be safely away from unwanted ears."

One member of the wait staff, his gray hair a reflection of his senior status, stepped quickly ahead of the others.

"Hello, Miss Abby. So good to see you."

"Why, hello Sam. It has been such a long time."

It was the same greeting they had exchanged every summer since she first dined at the Hotel almost twenty-five years ago, a time when she and her family were regular guests for dinner.

"Sam, I haven't been here in a decade. How did you remember?"

"Miss Abby, you're talkin' to Old Sam; he doesn't forget anyone. Do you also wish to have the broiled white fish with parsley and lemon?"

"That's my favorite dish." Abby handed the menu to Sam. "I don't think it necessary to say another word." She unfolded her napkin and smiled. "Sam, you are simply amazing."

Sam nodded, and turned his attention to Mark. "And you, sir?"

"Make it two."

As soon as Sam turned toward the kitchen, Mark placed their two clues on the tablecloth while Abby retrieved a menu from an adjoining table and began writing Howard's clue on its back. Mark also pulled out a pocket version of the Book of Mormon and fanned its pages. "Just in case we need a spiritual reference to help interpret, uh . . . " He tossed the book on the chair next to him. " . . . anything."

Another waiter placed a serving of stuffed green olives on the table for an appetizer.

Abby stared at the Book of Mormon. "A spiritual reference?" She shook her head and finished writing Howard's clue. When she finally looked up, she reached over and put a finger on Mark's clue. "What about this clue, Mark? This afternoon, you said you had something incredible to tell me. Does that something lead to another of your dead ends or perhaps buried treasure?"

"Abby, my clue holds the key to the entire puzzle, and your friend, Howard Hancock, gets at least part of the credit." Mark popped a stuffed olive in his mouth.

"I find that hard to believe, but go ahead."

"Howard takes an annual winter cruise, usually on the *SS Rotterdam,*" Mark said.

"Yes, I know. He's convinced that living on a cruise ship is cheaper than buying and maintaining a house." Abby rolled her eyes. "I never believed it."

"Don't be such a quick skeptic," Mark said. "I decided to take a cruise myself, test his theory, and do a story for the newspaper."

"You didn't." Abby shook her head in disbelief.

"Hear me out. Last winter, I booked passage on the *SS Rotterdam* while Howard was on safari in South Africa. For many years, Howard returned from his winter cruises regaling everyone with tales of a green flash he'd seen on the horizon at sunset. From Howard's perspective, if you have not seen the green flash at the exact moment the sun sets, your ability to perceive 'regularly occurring natural phenomena,' as he called it, was sorely lacking. He swears he's seen the green flash at sunset many times, implying that he possesses some sort of astrological insight the rest of us do not."

"What does the green flash have to do with finding Strang's gold?"

"Well, take another look at the first line of my clue." Mark's finger traced the words across the paper.

"*Granite turns to emerald when Divine Orb glows green,*" Abby read. "What does that—"

"When atmospheric conditions are right, a green flash will appear on the horizon at the exact moment the sun drops out of sight. It's been called a 'flash' because it's only visible for about a second, and then it's gone." Mark looked up from his clue. "Some people see a green dot and think that's the flash. It's not. A green dot will appear in anyone's vision if he stares at the setting sun too long. That green dot is the after image of the sun burned on the retina. There's a difference, and you'll understand the difference the first time you witness a true green flash."

"And you have actually seen it?" Abby asked.

"Yes, absolutely. Anyone can see a green flash at sunset *if* conditions are right, but that's not the most amazing part." Mark sat back in his chair and rearranged his napkin.

"No?"

"I was leaning against the granite bar on the upper deck of the *Rotterdam*. The sun was setting, and purely by chance, I turned my head toward the sun at the exact moment it disappeared. For one very brief instant, I saw a bright green flash." Mark's eyes brightened as he relived the experience. "I turned around and the granite bar was green for a full second."

"Mark, this sounds like the beginning of a snipe hunting expedition. I don't think I want to be part of— "

Mark laughed. "I would never do that to you. I don't blame you for doubting. I didn't believe it at first, but Abby, the granite bar turned *green*! In that blinding flash, for some inexplicable reason, a line from my mother's clue came to me *'Granite turns to emerald when Divine Orb glows green.'*"

"I get it, but I don't believe it." Abby tapped her fingers on the table.

"It was as if James Jesse Strang spoke to me," Mark said, his eyes closed tight.

"Do I have this right?" Abby asked. "*If* I were standing at sunset near the spot where Strang buried his gold, and *if* I saw a green flash at the moment the sun disappeared on the horizon, a granite rock or boulder nearby would turn green, or emerald in color and . . ." She paused because her own words sounded incredulous to her.

Mark said nothing at first, but then, "Yes?"

"And, would I be near the gold?"

"Yes, my little leprechaun, you would be very near King Strang's gold."

Abby doodled on her menu as she contemplated Mark's explanation. "That's a stretch, a real stretch," she said. "Did it get you any closer to the location of the gold?"

"Well, not yet. I've seen the green flash several times while searching on and near Beaver Island, but I've always come up empty."

"Maybe, the gold is not on Beaver," Abby said. "Maybe the location can be found in one of the other clues. Maybe—"

Mark raised an index finger to his lips. "Hold that thought." He nodded in the direction over Abby's shoulder. "Sam's coming this way."

A moment later, a small silver plate appeared in front of her as Sam announced, "A note left for you at the front desk."

"Who–?" Abby hesitated to open it. "I'm not expecting a note–or anything–from anyone. Mark, please, open it."

"Well, whoever it is didn't bother to put your name on the envelope, just your room number and, well, let's see." He opened the note, read it quickly to himself, then handed it to Abby. "Somebody has a very weird sense of humor, or doesn't want you searching for old Strang's gold."

Abby read the words in a whisper.

"Seal up those things which you have seen. Write them not.
The mystery of God will soon be finished.
-- The Seventh Messenger"

"Mark, this is the second note I've received from this Seventh Messenger character. Another one was slipped under the door of my room just after I checked in."

"What? You should have told me. What did the first one say?"

"Wait, I have it right here." Abby pulled the note from her purse and read it aloud.

"Fear the Seventh Messenger.
For him alone the treasure is saved."

"I asked Mrs. Vandivare about it," Abby said. "She told me many people believe there is a resident ghost in the Hotel who does not pay for his room and—"

"Abby, you must consider these notes a serious threat. I don't know who's behind them, but I think you're in real danger." There was none of that infectious smile from Mark that Abby had already grown accustomed to.

"Well . . . " Abby slowly tossed her head from side to side. She wasn't quite sure what to make of this new, expressionless demeanor.

"I don't want you to go anywhere from this point on without me to protect you, okay?" Mark grabbed her hands. "I'm serious," and he stared into her eyes.

She wasn't quite sure how to react. After a moment, she attempted a deflection of sorts. "Don't be so melodramatic."

Mark squeezed her hands again, even tighter than before.

"Oh, all right, if you say so." She pulled her hands free, and gave him a gentle wave. "You talked me into it." *Maybe I should be afraid, but I'm not going to show it.*

"Good." Mark took a closer look at both notes from the Seventh Messenger. "If I didn't know better, I'd say this is the work of Ian Mooney, half-brother to Julius Mooney. Sounds just like him, but Ian died on Iwo Jima. Around town, he was known as a genuine rapscallion. The rumor was, he sowed his oats up and down Lake Michigan's shore for quite a while after he returned from the First World War. He came back a decorated hero, so I guess he thought everyone owed him something. He was a colonel by the time he left again for WWII. His only redeeming quality was that he was very close to his brother, Julius."

"I never met him, fortunately," Abby said, "but if not Ian Mooney, who is this Seventh Messenger?"

"There is some mention of a Seventh Messenger in the Bible— Revelation, I think—and wait, speaking of Julius, he's coming over." Mark quickly put away all of the clues.

"I suspect he's been watching us since we sat down," Abby said, "and probably couldn't contain his curiosity any longer."

"Shuusssh–here he is."

When Mooney arrived, he pulled a chair from the next table, reversed it, and sat down with his arms folded over the back of it. "Good evening, Abby. I wanna' tell you again how great it is to have you back. And good evening to you, Mr. Day. I commend you for your good taste in dinner partners."

"Thank you."

"You know, young man, you could improve your newspaper a great deal if you'd divide it into four sections: truths, probabilities, possibilities, and lies, the same divisions Thomas Jefferson recommended to editors in his day."

"Julius!" Abby said. *I don't like the direction this conversation has taken. If I have to talk to this man, I may as well learn something useful.* "When I first arrived, you mentioned that people have been looking a long time for King Strang's gold, 'fool's gold,' I believe you said. What else do you know about James Strang?"

At first, Julius said nothing. Finally, a kind of crooked smile crept up the side of his face. "Everyone who knew him said he could talk the hind leg off a mule. You've seen Oral Roberts on television, haven't you? Well, everything I've read about Strang tells me he was a hundred times more powerful as a preacher, a hundred times more influential on the lives of his followers."

He's ruminating freely, Abby thought. *Good.*

"There was a religious fervor about him, in my view, that bordered on the blasphemous."

"In what way?" She was desperate for any small tidbit of information that would shed light on their clues.

"In his newspaper, the *Northern Islander,* he described himself as 'the enlightened one,' and 'a vehicle of God.' They've got copies at the Historical Society if you wanna' read about it for yourself. He was constantly testing the beliefs of his followers and imposing penalties on those who questioned his authority. If you ask me, his entire life was a blasphemy." Julius smiled and looked at Abby. "You don't have to be a chicken to know a rotten egg."

"What about his children? Didn't he have a daughter?"

"Uh, well, yes – Eva, I believe."

He doesn't want to talk about her; I wonder why? Look at him, fidgeting in his seat.

Julius cleared his throat and got out of his chair. "Well, enjoy your dinner." And then he was gone.

As Julius walked away, Abby leaned closer to Mark. "Never mind him. What do you know about the Seventh Messenger?"

Before Mark could answer, a waiter appeared and placed a cup of hot tea before Abby. Mark waved him off before he could place a second cup down.

"In the early 1920s," Mark said, in a near whisper, "a religious group established itself on High Island. It was called the House of David."

"Wait a minute," Abby said, "Another religious group, another sect? Not Mormon?"

Mark tilted his head to one side and smiled. "That's right."

Abby sat back in her chair. "What is it with these islands that makes them so attractive to religious zealots?"

"To be honest, the islands offered a perfect sanctuary for them—isolated and far from curious eyes."

Abby sat up again. "And safe from the law, I suppose."

"Of that you can be sure," Mark said, as he shuffled through the clues once more.

"Tell me about this High Island group; what'd you call it, House of David?"

"Yes. Well, back in the '20s, about 150 members of the House of David called High Island their home."

"Let me guess," Abby said, "and the Seventh Messenger was their leader?"

"Yes! An ordinary man—uh, damn, I forget his name—called himself the Seventh Messenger." Mark slapped his forehead. "According to the Book of Revelation, there will be Seven Messengers sent by God over a period of time to save the world. Supposedly, when the Seventh Messenger arrives, all who are faithful believers at that time will be granted eternal life."

"Where are the island faithful today?" Abby asked. "Are there any left out there?" She put down the tea the waiter had delivered only a few minutes earlier.

"Oh gosh no, they left in the late 1920s over some sex scandal," Mark said. "The story was told that the Messenger kept a harem of young girls in an underground chamber."

"Why does there always have to be a sex scandal around these religious pretenders?"

"Maybe it's in their blood. All I know for sure is that every time the authorities showed up on the island to question him about his, uh, religious practices, he seemed to disappear." Mark shrugged. "Seems like these stories almost always involve a preacher, a politician, or traveling salesman."

"Well, they're all selling something, aren't they?" Abby chuckled and threw her head back. "Tell me, Mark, where'd they finally catch him?"

"I think they finally caught him in bed with one of the girls."

"I am *so* surprised," Abby said, her voice dripping with sarcasm.

"Well then, I think you will also be surprised to learn that the sexual misconduct charges were never proven in court."

"But they found him—*in bed*—with one of the girls!" She held her palms in the air. "What more proof did they need?"

"That should've been enough," Mark said, shaking his head. "But it wasn't. They did find him guilty of fraudulent business practices."

"What happened to those poor girls?"

"When he was arrested, the girls, many of them pregnant, scattered to the winds."

"But he's back," Abby said, holding up the note just delivered to their table, "and he lives around here." She glanced over her shoulder, as if expecting to spot someone who might be a possible suspect.

"The Messenger is long gone, Abby, but someone could have decided to pick up the mission where the Messenger left off, and he could be the one writing you these notes."

"I don't believe I'm in any immediate danger." Abby put the notes back in her purse. "Just the same, maybe we should expedite our search. What do you think?"

"Absolutely! Not worth the risk." With that, Mark picked up the clues and spread them across the table again.

As he put the first clue down, he said, "We know Strang was an organized individual, a planner who tried to anticipate the action of others." Mark placed the second clue next to the first. "Strang also was aware that enemies of Joseph Smith were still around and fully capable of carrying out another murder if necessary." The third clue he carefully lined up next to the others and leaned over to examine them closely.

"Are you saying he expected someone to shoot him?"

Mark looked up from the clues. "I am."

Abby rubbed her forehead. "I can't get into his mind."

Mark laughed. "I've tried many times with very little success. But I know the planner in him would have left nothing to chance, certainly nothing as important as his financial legacy."

"And so . . . ?" Abby picked up a stuffed olive and popped it into her mouth. "And so he would have selected a hiding place secure enough to prevent anyone, except the owner of the clues, from finding it, right?"

Mark nodded. "Sure."

Abby was silent and finally swallowed the olive whole. "Mark, have you ever had a burst of inspiration when you thought, 'ah, *that's* the place?'"

"Yes, but so have many others." Mark reached for another menu, turned it over, and began drawing an outline of Lake Michigan with several islands bunched together in the middle near the straits. "Some have searched Beaver Island, here, and Holy Island, here." He put one finger on Beaver Island in his crude drawing and another several inches from the menu. "This spot, Holy Island, would be on the mainland, down near the middle of the South Arm of Lake Charlevoix." He tapped the drawing in several places. "But the 'X' spot could be anywhere in between."

Abby gave him a perplexed look. "That's quite a range of geography."

"I've personally looked all over Beaver, Fisherman's Island, Michigan Beach, and even Pine River, with no luck. I've thought about the surrounding islands, but there're at least a dozen in the archipelago," Mark said. "We could spend the rest of our lives looking."

"Billy Merrill even went searching near that little spit of land they called Skillagalee Island." Abby smiled. She enjoyed saying the word. "Skillagalee."

"Well, that's a new one."

Abby recounted the ill-fated attempt by Billy Merrill to search the wreck of *The Patchin'*, the old side-wheeler mentioned in the second clue.

"I knew Billy drowned out there, but I never knew what he was up to," Mark said. "Anything so obvious was clearly designed to throw undeserving treasure seekers off the trail. Strang was not that obvious, ever."

"Let's take another look at all three clues," Abby rearranged them as she spread them across the table again. I don't think there's any particularly order to them." She began to read aloud.

"Day follows night, Old Pine, thy gate to open wide,
The Kingdom awaits all when the rocks begin to slide.
Whoso shall publish peace, to him it shall be seen,
Our lives pass away quickly, as unto us a dream."

"And *if* the rumor is correct," Mark said, "that's the clue handed down from the Clement Strang branch of the family."

"Now, the *second* clue," Abby said. "Howard never told me or anyone, as far as I can tell, where he got it. Let's call it the Eva clue for now." She began to read slowly.

"Deep within The Patchin' lies a Spirit House of old,
Drink of it, lost prodigal, and risk thy very soul.
From heaven's gate, Divine One descends to aviary white,
Trust but one – thy Father – he will keep thee in the right."

"Finally, the third clue," Mark said. "My mother's clue. She received it directly from her father, Charles J. Strang, eldest son of the king." And Mark began to read.

"Granite turns to emerald when Divine Orb glows green,
Brighter eyes than thine have the drumlin never seen.
Welcome all ye faithful, the right hand of Jesus beckons,
A rising sun bears witness, thy sins are now forgiven."

"Very little, if any, of that makes sense to me," Abby said, "no matter how much you explain the green flash to me." As she spoke, she underlined the most perplexing words in the first line of the verse. "Just makes no sense at all."

"I'm confident," Mark said, "that each clue holds at least one key to the location of the gold. Some lines seem thrown in to mislead us, sort of like detour signs along a road. But unlike a true detour, it's up to us to determine which path to take. So far, most have led to a dead end."

"I think we ought to focus on eliminating what you've described as the detour verses, lines written to mislead anyone not considered worthy," Abby said. Sam placed their entrees in front of them. "Thank you, Sam."

"He hoped his children would be worthy, but if not, he was satisfied to let the gold sit in its hiding place forever." Mark shoveled a fork full of potatoes into his mouth.

"That's a mouthful," Abby said. A red-faced Mark glanced her way. "No, I meant that was a great analysis." She laughed as Mark swallowed hard and put down his fork.

"I guess I'm not very hungry." Mark picked up the Old Pine clue. "This one has little value, in my opinion, because it's too obvious. Old Pine could be Pine River itself or even Charlevoix, the town, since both shared the name in the mid-nineteenth century."

"As I look at the 'Old Pine' clue," Abby said, leaning over and touching Mark's arm, "it seems the only real help is offered by the second line: *'For the Kingdom awaits all when the rocks begin to slide.'* To take it literally, we would assume there are rocks near the gold, and when they 'slide,' or fall, or maybe just move in some way, that's where the gold will be found." She let her hand rest on his shoulder. "What do you think about that?"

"I like that," Mark said. "One thing for sure, the last two lines just don't work, even though I'm drawn to the line which seems to suggest special insight will be given to the one who, quote, *'shall publish peace.'* That's a reference to scripture from 1 Nephi in the Book of Mormon. I've got the original verse here."

As Mark flipped open his Book of Mormon, a faded bookmark fell out. "Mother must have put this little item in the book before she gave it to me. Look, the all-seeing 'eye of God' on one side and—what's this on the back—a verse, barely legible, but I think it's written in mother's hand." Mark read the verse softly. *"The Divine One will return as a white bird from Heaven to gather the faithful to him, and they will find their reward at the right hand of Jesus."*

"Sounds like a verse from Scripture all right," Abby said. "Probably familiar to James Strang, too. Say, wait a minute. Take another look at Howard's clue. *'From heaven's gate, Divine One descends to aviary white.'* Could Jesus be the *'Divine One'* who returns? Or, to put it another way, *'descends to aviary white?'*"

"Oh, my God!" Mark slapped the table. "I think we've just been told that an 'aviary white' is where we'll find the gold. Talk about a burst of inspiration! How'd you come up with that?"

"Howard reminded me that a dove descended on Jesus' head when he was baptized," Abby said. "Maybe there's a symbol of Jesus at the site. After all, '*the right hand of Jesus beckons.*'   That's what the clue says."

"You . . . are . . . unbelievable!" Mark put his arm around her shoulders and pulled her to him in what, Abby thought, was an impulsive but, nonetheless, celebratory embrace. Abby didn't pull away until Mark sat straight up. "An aviary is a place for birds!"

"Of course. And?" Abby thought his excitement was going to erupt.

"In these parts, there is only one common white bird, the sea gull, and where are there more sea gulls than people? Gull Island! Forget dinner, we're heading for Gull Island."

Abby put down her fork. "But, if you are correct, where on Gull Island is the gold?"

"You must think I know everything, Miss Abby. Well, my guess goes like this: we'll find the gold near a symbol of Jesus that beckons us when granite turns emerald after we witness a green flash. How's that?"

Mark squeezed her hand.   She squeezed right back.   *I'm beginning to think we might actually find this gold.*

Mark then gave her a quick kiss on the cheek.   In the next instant, he was out of his seat, pulling her toward the door, as he swiped a cherry from the top of the parfait Sam had just delivered to their table.

"Where're we going?" Abby asked.

"Neff's Grocery store stays open late. Tomorrow, we're heading to Gull Island. I'll pick up enough provisions tonight to hold us for several days."

"Several days?" Abby was suddenly not thinking of food but what she would wear if she had to stay on a remote island with no running water for more than a day.

"Fishing is good on Gull Island, but fish is all we would eat if we don't take provisions. My boat's at O'Malley's Marina. Come as early as—well, I guess I should ask if you would like to accompany me tomorrow to Gull Island. We could—"

"Try and stop me," Abby said.   Wardrobe aside, she was not going to miss this adventure. "What time shall I be there?

"We'll push off in *Holly-Hoo* as soon as you arrive."

"I'll be there at six!"   On a typical morning, she was never up before eight. *I'll have to set two clocks to be sure I'm on time.*

"By the way, Howard was right," Mark said, as they passed the Maitre'd. "Living on a cruise ship all winter *is* cheaper than owning a house."

Chapter Twenty-One
The Beavers

The northwest wind bit the back of Abby's neck and sent a chill to her toes. Her cardigan sweater and windbreaker were no match for the wind. She pulled the ties of her upturned collar tight but couldn't shield herself from the spine numbing blast. She even cinched the waist tighter, but it wasn't enough to stop the wind from creeping under, around, and through the windbreaker. *Is there no way to escape this chill?* Her skirt didn't help, even though it was mid-calf in length. *I hope I chose the right ensembles for this trip. Shorts if it's warm, jeans if it's cool. I suspect I'll be in jeans the whole time . . . if I survive today.*

The marina was finally visible to her teary eyes, and she picked up the pace. A moment later, as if on cue, the sun appeared, a yellow crack on the horizon.

"I guess that's all we get this time of year," she said. The sun was mostly hidden by a tangibly thick mist that clung like cotton candy to the surface of Lake Charlevoix. "Sea smoke," she said, smiling.

"Mark?" she called out, as she stepped aboard and dropped her overnight bag.

Mark's head popped up in the companionway. "Down here, Abby. I'm giving the bilge pump and engine a once over before we get started. She's reliable, but burns a little oil." He pulled out a rag and started to wipe oil off his hands. "I just want to make sure we have enough for our return. Don't want to get stranded . . . wow!" He stopped in mid-sentence, took a deep breath, then finished. ". . . in the middle of Lake Michigan."

Abby gave him her most demure smile.

"Gosh, *are* you beautiful at *every* hour of the day?" Mark's face suddenly turned pink. Abby watched, smiling, as he attempted to recover. "Of course, you are. You must be. I mean, I know you are." His face was now quite red.

Abby purposely cast her eyes downward to hide her amusement at his impulsive comment.

Mark finished wiping the grease from his hands, stuffed the rag in his back pocket, and quickly offered Abby a hand to steady her down the ladder. "Welcome aboard *Holly-Hoo,*" he said, cheerily. "You look great!"

"Thank you, captain." She tried to match his cheerful tone and give him a chance to start the conversation again without any further embarrassment for either.

"The mist is evaporating fast this morning; it's going to be a spectacular day." Mark gestured to the captain's chair beside him. "Have a seat." He patted the cushion, and Abby plopped into it.

"Full speed ahead, captain."

"I'm anxious to get underway, too," Mark said, "but we've gotta' take our time motoring through the channel; we don't want to make a wake in Round Lake." Up ahead, the town's only bridge, a drawbridge, came into view. It spanned the channel, connecting the north to south highway above them. As they passed under, they waved to a couple of early risers walking across. Soon they were clear of the channel, greeting the first waves of Lake Michigan, and following a course for Gull Island, seven miles west of Beaver.

"You must be very proud of *Holly-Hoo*," Abby said. "From the looks of her, I'm sure she's had a fascinating history.*"* Abby glanced at her reflection in the highly polished brass work.

Mark loved his boat and never missed an opportunity to show her off. "Several years ago, I was faced with choosing between buying a two story house in town and *Holly-Hoo.* I chose *Holly-Hoo,* as you can see, and decided to rent a one-bedroom apartment near the marina to keep an eye on her. I figured I'd rather spend my leisure time on the water than pushing a broom around a dusty old house."

"You made an excellent choice." Abby loved sailing, but she also had an appreciation for the classic wooden powerboats that were almost extinct on the lake.

"And just look at her, handcrafted from mahogany, personally selected by her creator, John Hacker." He reached over the wheel to give the *Holly-Hoo* an admiring stroke. "Thirty-two feet of muscle and art."

Abby knew something of *Holly-Hoo's* history and a little of its reputation. "When I last saw her, the Wynn Brothers, from the family that built the Old Rustic Bridge, were the owners."

"That's right," Mark said, "and when she finally came on the market, I snatched her up. In my view, she is nothing less than a nautical Mona Lisa." He gave *Holly-Hoo* another loving stroke, as if she possessed heart and soul.

"Is she also hiding a secret," Abby asked, with a playful tone, "as some have speculated about the lady in the painting?"

Mark raised an eyebrow and shrugged his shoulders. "Maybe. Why do you ask?"

"My father said the *Holly-Hoo* was used during Prohibition by rum-runners hauling illegal booze from Canada to Harsen's Island." She decided to lay the most common rumor out there, all of it, to see how Mark would react.

"Yes, I've heard that tale," Mark said, calmly and almost matter-of-factly.

"C'mon, Mark." She gave him a "you can do better than that" sideways glance.

"Okay, I won't deny it, but I don't care about her history. Look at her now. Five years of elbow grease, and a few new parts have given her a new life."

"I heard she was fast." Abby enjoyed watching Mark open up a bit. "What do *you* say?"

Mark laughed. "People do talk, don't they? If brought to court, I guess I would plead 'very fast' to the judge."

"I see." Abby turned her head to one side, away from the wind. "And just how fast is 'very fast?'"

"Well, *your* Honor," Mark said, in a somber tone. "I replaced the original Scripps engine with a '53 Ford Flathead V-8, and let's just say she'll do considerably more than twenty-five knots."

"Great! I love anything that's fast." *Whoa, Abby. Too much.* She shook her head in criticism of her own thoughts. *Try something else.* "Maybe you can demonstrate her speed, Mark, before we're done."

"Nothing like the present." He pushed the accelerator lever to full throttle. "Hang on!"

The waves that had been pounding the bow since they left the channel, at little more than idle speed, were soon tamed as *Holly-Hoo* reached its planning speed and skimmed across the top of the lake, *Holly-Hoo's* bow completely out of the water.

"Okay, I believe you." Abby held onto the brass rail with one hand and made a futile effort to keep her blonde hair out of her face with the other. "She's very fast," Abby shouted, above the engine's roar.

Mark backed off *Holly-Hoo's* speed a bit. "She's fast but also old. We best save a little something for later."

Abby rubbed her arms up and down and tried to keep them warm.

"Didn't you bring anything warmer?"

"I thought this would be enough. I'll change into jeans when we get to Gull."

"It's not the middle of summer anymore," Mark said, "it's early September, and you'll need your jeans. You'll also need this." He threw a man-sized, bright yellow, foul weather jacket to her. "It's too big for you, but it'll keep you dry and warm."

Abby put the jacket on quickly. "It's so big, it even reaches half way down the length of my skirt." She laughed to think of how silly she must look.

"You look . . . warm." Mark smiled at her, checked his compass, and motioned for Abby to take the helm. "Hold this course."

"Are you sure?" She'd been a sailing instructor for the Club years ago, so being in command of a boat was a familiar experience. This, however, would be her first time at the helm of a powerboat.

"Yes, of course, but you'll need to stand while holding the wheel in order to see, and avoid any boats in our path."

"Are you sure?" she asked again. She was nervous about being responsible for a valuable antique boat.

"You'll do fine." Mark gave her two thumbs up.

Abby's hands were shaking as she stood at the helm. When she closed her fists around the wheel, she felt a good bit of vibration. *Excessive, not like Father's Cadillac where the wheel never vibrates.*

Once she felt comfortable at the wheel, she looked around to become more familiar with other equipment she might be asked to master. "And what's the purpose of this chrome stick thing?" She had already decided not to touch it.

"Don't worry about that. It's the gearshift–only two gears, forward and reverse. All you really need to know is this: the accelerator is mounted here." Mark reached around her waist to put her hand on the steering column lever that controlled *Holly-Hoo's* speed. They were suddenly very close.

Abby thought he seemed to linger longer than necessary but didn't mind.

"What's that you're wearing?" Mark asked, as he finally stepped back.

"Oh . . . uh, I don't remember." Abby blushed as she realized how close they really were.

"Smells like a southern gardenia to me, or maybe . . ." Abby was sure he was just pretending to be thinking of another name.

"It's by Chanel, if you must know," Abby said, "but you need to keep your eye on my driving." She pointed at the wheel. "Am I doing this right?" Abby increased their speed, sliding the lever up ever so gently, and scanned the horizon ahead.

"Perfect," Mark said. "You're a natural." And he pretended to hit a home run with an invisible baseball bat. "But remember, you're not *driving*. You're at the helm, and you're *steering*. There is no driving on the water."

"I'll remember that," Abby said. "My father would frown on my . . . uh, *steering* a power boat. He called them stink pots."

"I've heard worse."

Abby loved being on the water. "On a clear day, we used to stand on the bluff above the channel and try to spot 'the Beaver,' as we called the island. Did you ever do that?" she asked.

"No, but we 'townies,' if we could find someone willing to loan us his boat, would motor out and count the islands."

"Why'd you do that? They're always twelve, aren't there? Or is it fourteen?"

"That's right."

"What's right?"

"It could be twelve or fourteen; it depends."

"On what?"

"The actual number of islands changes, depending on the cyclical rise and fall of water levels on Lake Michigan. About ten years ago, we counted only ten islands in the archipelago. Beaver, of course, has always been the largest." Mark glanced at his watch. "Oh, heck, Abby, it's not even noon. Let me have the wheel, and we'll take a spin around Beaver. I'll show you all the old familiar places I visited as a boy."

Abby was delighted to relinquish the wheel. Besides, Mark's reference to "old familiar places" struck a melancholy chord in Abby's chest. Suddenly, she remembered all the times she and Robert danced to "I'll Be Seeing You," but most of all she remembered Robert's singing his own version of the song on that special day when they were together on Park Island. A tear materialized in the corner of her eye and was quickly wiped away.

"I'm glad I took the wheel," Mark said. "You look like you needed relief."

Abby nodded, stared at the distant horizon, and stood motionless. *Oh, Robert, I miss you so much. But this man, this Mark, if you are not coming home . . .* She was suddenly overwhelmed with guilt—again—for letting herself think such thoughts. *Robert, what am I to do . . . ?*

Slowly, Abby closed her eyes and tried to imagine him, the two of them, in one of the thousand images stored in her memory. She cherished all of them because they kept her close to Robert and made it easier for her to remember his voice and her love for him. But today, the image she saw was from a place she'd never seen, and it startled her. There was Robert, holding her hand, the two of them walking barefoot through ocean surf, searching the shallow water for shells.

"Look, a perfect specimen," Abby called out as she leapt ahead of Robert to rescue a shell before the tide swept it back into the ocean. As she stooped to pick it up, a rogue wave broke behind her and knocked her face down in the surf. She came up sputtering and spitting out seawater, but turned just in time to see Robert dive, head first into the next wave approaching, and disappear. "Robert!" She called his name over and over. "Robert!" There was no sign of him. She searched desperately across the full expanse of water, and then, there in the distance, Robert appeared, waving for a brief moment before swimming away, as if nothing had happened. Abby squeezed her eyes tight, but the scene was gone. She opened her eyes and looked to see if Mark was still beside her.

"It's a good thing I took the wheel," Mark said. "Your eyes were closed a long time. You must have been a million miles away. What were you thinking?"

"I don't know what I was thinking," Abby replied softly. "I really don't know." Her mind swirled. *So many images . . . stealing a kiss under the trestle, together on Park Island . . . yes, but never in the surf. Why that image? Knocked down by a wave . . . Robert swimming away . . . farther . . . and farther away.*

"It's okay, Abby. It's okay." Mark gave her a gentle touch on the shoulder. Abby interpreted his touch to mean, "I understand." *Whatever he meant, I'm glad to be with such a man right now.*

"Look, over there: Saint James Harbor," Mark said, as he caught a glimpse of the largest community on the island. "We'll go around the northern tip of Beaver in a minute and head west toward High Island. Since we talked about the Seventh Messenger last night, I wanted you to have a glimpse of where he lived and—what's the matter?"

Abby frowned and stared straight ahead.

"Whoa, what happened to that smile? I liked it much better."

Abby felt a shiver. "I don't know. I'm just not sure I want to see High Island."

"Don't worry. Nothing's going on there today. I've heard there's an old Indian living there who—"

"Mark, over there." Abby interrupted and pointed to a dark cloud over the island's northeastern tip. "Why is there a bluish mist hanging over that side of the island?"

"Oh, that's the Darkening Mist," Mark said. "It was said that House of David sinners were banished to the Darkening Mist to repent of their sins. The only person allowed there was the Seventh Messenger himself, and he always accompanied transgressors—always women, by the way—on their 'journey of repentance.' I don't know anyone who has been in the mist, but it's said some sort of atmospheric anomaly causes the area to be perpetually covered in a dark blue mist."

Abby's face turned ashen, and a chill shook her spine. "Oh, no," she mouthed as Mark looked at her.

"Don't tell me you've heard about it?" he said.

"No, I, uh . . . well, I *have* heard about it . . . and recently," Abby said. "Julius mentioned it to me." She became very quiet as she remembered the warning Julius gave her the day she arrived. "Tell me, Mark, what do you know of Julius Mooney's past? It seems to me that members of the Club know a lot about each other but very little about our current Hotel Manager."

"I've probably heard the same stories you have, that his family came north from Alabama in the 1920s and settled in the region. That's all I know; you'll have to check with Club members for any other details."

Abby nodded. "I will certainly do that."

"One other thing…probably untrue…but not long ago, there was a rumor going around town that Mooney was spotted wandering East Park in the middle of the night and—get this—dressed head to toe in a white robe." Mark chuckled. "Whoever reported it said they called out to Mooney but he didn't answer. His eyes, they said, were fixed as if he was in a trance."

Abby shook her head in disbelief. "That doesn't sound credible enough to be believed for even a minute."

"I'm sure you're right." An unusually strong wave pushed *Holly-Hoo* closer to the High Island shore. Mark grabbed his binoculars and began scanning the sand. "Keep your eyes out for a piping plover."

"A piping, what?"

"It's a bird. Some beaches here are covered in them, running around in short starts and stops. It's like a sparrow. Hard to see, really, because it's the same color as the sand."

Abby squinted into the sun. She didn't see any birds at all on High Island beaches, as they passed its western tip. She turned her gaze toward the open water. "There, Mark, in the distance—it looks like a tiny speck of land."

"Gull Island," Mark said. "We don't have far to go; hold tight." As he increased *Holly-Hoo's* speed, he placed Abby's right hand on the wheel. "Hold 'er right there." The bow was now just slightly out of the water. "You're doing great!"

And then, she noticed no vibration at all, and their speed seemed to increase. *Holly-Hoo* was almost gliding across Lake Michigan.

Sailing has its virtues, but speed is not one of them. With this boat, we'll be there in no time.

That green speck had now become a large glob of land. To Abby's eye, it was a jumble of tall pines, sedge grass, and sand. *Not very attractive.*

"Isolated, virtually abandoned," Mark said. "Gull Island is a perfect hideaway for a pot of gold."

Abby had picked up the binoculars and was focusing on the beach ahead. "Why, it's covered in snow. Totally white." She handed the binoculars to Mark.

"That's not snow. Keep watching." He reached around Abby and gave the engine full throttle for a moment. The additional noise reverberated across the water. Suddenly, the snow Abby thought she saw began to move. It wasn't snow, but seagulls.

"They're everywhere!" For a moment, Abby covered her ears. "What a racket!" The overrun rookery made it hard for her to hear anything but the cackling and calling of the gulls. "Sounds like an orchestra where half of the players are out of tune." Abby pointed to a double crested cormorant about a quarter mile down the beach. "Ugliest bird I've ever seen. Its beak is much too long." One of the cormorants took off, flew inland, and soared over a tall balsam fir. Her eyes followed the cormorant until it landed on the only evidence of previous human habitation she'd seen thus far. Abby pointed to a gray, stone chimney, peeking a few feet above the pines and leaning dangerously. "What do you make of that?"

"You're looking at the remains of a cottage, probably built by fishermen decades ago. When Strang was around, this was the best fishing ground in the world. But it's the same old story: the islanders got greedy and overfished the waters."

"Did some of those fishermen leave a campfire burning?" Abby pointed to a plume of smoke rising into the sky near the chimney.

"Hmmmm . . . I don't think so," Mark said. "Nobody is supposed to be here. Let's check it out."

Mark slipped behind Abby to take the helm from his much relieved first mate. They slowly circumnavigated the island before discovering a dilapidated old dock. Most of its planking had disappeared into the water, when nails holding it rusted away and fell into the lake. What remained was held in place mostly by gravity.

"It's where we want to be," Mark told Abby, who gave him a raised eyebrow.

"Are you sure?" She gave the rickety planking a dubious look. "How will I get ashore?"

"Carefully. Very carefully." Mark steered *Holly-Hoo* until she was snug against the dock on one side and within reach of a large balsam fir, half submerged, on the other side. Next, he secured bow and stern lines to the dock. "Unless we get a really stiff wind, we're set for the short time we'll be here." He motioned for her to crawl out on the bow. "Go ahead."

For a moment, she considered the best approach. "I wish I was in jeans. Nothing about this looks safe." She tested her saddle shoes for traction. "Thank goodness for rubber soles." She held *Holly-Hoo's* rail and stepped toward a narrow span of timbers that had been the weight-bearing portion of the old dock. "I do *not* want to fall in."

"One misstep and you'll spoil our entire adventure."

"Oh, great," Abby said, her left hand held a vice grip on *Holly-Hoo's* rail and her right arm wrapped around the remains of a piling. "You're not very reassuring, captain." But a quick step later, and she was on dry land. She smacked her hands together in triumph. "I knew it would be easy."

Mark laughed. "That isn't what you said."

"Stop talking and jump. We need to check out the source of that smoke and get back before the sun sets." Once on dry land, her enthusiasm for the expedition had returned. "I can't wait to see this crazy green flash you've been talking about."

A moment later, they were headed toward a thicket of hardwood trees near the middle of the island. "See those skinny pines? I think the smoke was coming from over there." Mark led the way, pushing aside small elderberry bushes and speckled alder. Finally, they stepped into a clearing with several well-worn paths through it. Off to one side, the remains of a few crumbling shanties appeared. "There's your chimney," he said. "I think the vines wrapped around it must be all that's holding it up."

"Is it the chimney we saw from the water?" Abby asked.

"We'll soon find out." Mark began down a narrow path in the direction of the chimney.

"The island may be abandoned, but someone comes here often enough to keep this path open," Abby said.

"Probably a fisherman. Say, watch your step there. It looks like an old well." Mark pointed to a depression in the soil. "Completely filled with dirt and trash and . . . look at that, an old plow."

"But, what's this?" Abby kicked a pile of charred wood behind the chimney and stirred ashes someone had left behind.

Mark hurried over and placed his hand over the ashes. "Mmmmm . . . ashes are still warm." He kicked sand onto the ashes to be sure they wouldn't spring to new life. "Last thing we need is a forest fire to deal with. We ought to keep a sharp eye out for a visitor or two."

"Or two?" Abby asked, with an anxious tone. "Two?"

"It's not uncommon for a fisherman or two to visit and wet a hook here, from time to time. I wouldn't be too concerned."

Concern is written all over his face, but for now I'll go along with him. "You're probably right. Just the same, I don't like people who threaten me or hide in shadows."

"C' mon," Mark said. "Let's get back to *Holly-Hoo*."

At the boat, they grabbed a blanket and headed for the shoreline. For a long while, they sat on the beach, staring at the slowly disappearing disk in front of them. Abby finally broke the silence. "James Strang really was an egomaniac, wasn't he? When he wrote, *'Trust but one – your Father – he will keep you in the right,'* it was an intentional double entendre. He wasn't advising his children to trust the Father in Heaven; he wanted them to trust *him*, only him, and '*he will keep you in the right.*'"

"You are finally getting into his head, Abby."

"That's scary. Not sure I really want to do that." Abby chuckled.

"Have your eyes ever enjoyed such a feast?" Mark asked.

"Never. The sunset looks as if a giant hand spilled a full palette of colors across the sky." Abby stood and pretended to erase the sky.

"What are you doing?"

"Smearing the colors to change the hue." She continued to wipe the sky with both hands working feverishly.

Mark smiled. "I don't think old Sol needs so much help."

Abby lifted her arms. "I *love* it, and the air is crisp, clear, and dry."

"Perfect conditions to produce a green flash. C'mon; sit beside me. It's almost time," Mark said, inviting her to sit near him with a pat on the sand.

Their plan was to try to repeat Mark's experience on the *Rotterdam.* They positioned themselves where they would be able to see a large granite boulder on their right at the same moment they saw a green flash.

Abby didn't take her eyes off the sun. A few minutes more, as it vanished over the horizon, she exclaimed, "There, I saw it!"

"No, I'm sorry. I don't think you did," Mark said. "The same thing happened to me the first time."

"But I *did*; I *still* see it." Abby pointed to both eyes.

"That's the green dot I told you about," Mark said. "The small dot burned on the retina when you stare too long at the sun. Unfortunately, it's not the green flash, but I'll tell you this: there will be no doubt in your mind the first time you see it."

Abby sighed. "I guess it would have been nothing short of a miracle if we saw it right away." Her shoulders drooped.

Mark took her hand, and they walked slowly to the edge of the water, spread the blanket again, and sat down to enjoy the twilight. From the plentiful supply of driftwood on the beach, they built a roaring fire to keep them warm. "I know you're in a hurry, but give it time," Mark said. "People have reported seeing the flash even when not looking for it, perhaps especially when not looking for it. I know that doesn't make much sense, but it will when you see it." He touched her chin and pulled it gently upward until her eyes met his. "And you *will* see it."

"I hope so," Abby said. "I really hope so."

In the still of the day's last light, the fire provided a shield against the cool temperatures of the approaching night. The warmth of Mark's touch gave Abby's arm the most goose pimples she'd ever felt. No words were spoken, but Abby felt comforted and safe with Mark beside her. *I'll let Mark make the first move. He knows, I'm sure, that Pine Lake girls are raised to be coy in such matters.*

Mark slowly stirred the fire and watched burning embers flee into the sky like fireflies.

Is he going to kiss me, or not? Abby wondered. *I think he wants to. Should I let him? Oh, Robert, I am so lonely; what should I do? I don't want the fire to go out.*

Mark threw another piece of driftwood on the fire and came back to sit closer still to Abby.

She closed her eyes. *I think I know your answer, Robert; I think I've always known your answer.*

Abby held Mark, and he held her until the last ember died.

"We're going to freeze if we don't get back to the boat," Mark said, at last. He gave her a kiss on the forehead as he pulled her to her feet.

Really? That's it? Abby was disappointed but was careful not to show it. *If he won't make the first move, I'll have to, and will, soon.*

As they walked back to the boat, Mark took her hand and held it tightly. The sand, deep in places, made walking difficult. Abby took off her saddle shoes and emptied the hour-glass fine sand that had collected in them. The sand gave a bit under her weight but never, she thought, in the same direction twice. "Yow! Too much like sandpaper. My feet will never be the same." She was grateful for Mark's steady hand to guide her through the approaching darkness. As they neared *Holly-Hoo*, Abby put her arm around Mark's waist and pulled him closer.

"You take my cabin in the bow," Mark said, as he turned to help her aboard, "and I'll go aft for the single."

I guess . . . not tonight. Disappointed, she smiled, nonetheless, at his adherence to the accepted "dating protocol" at the Club. Her mother always told her "*never* on the first date." *Maybe his mother gave him the same advice.*

Mark was halfway to the aft cabin when he suddenly turned toward Abby. "Say, did anybody ever give you a foot rub?"

"No, but . . ." His question startled her; she really wasn't sure what to say.

"After walking in that sand, I'm sure your feet need one. I'll take care of that tomorrow night. I promise." And then, he disappeared into his cabin.

Abby stared at his door a moment. "Well, uh, okay," she said to Mark's closed cabin. "Good night."

**

The next day, Mark and Abby walked the entire length of the island's western shoreline, their eyes searching for signs of granite.

"Just small rocks and pebbles," Abby said, "and shouldn't there be at least one drumlin?"

"I was hoping you wouldn't notice, but yes, we should see at least one," Mark said. "Those things are strewn all over Ireland and northern Michigan, and yet, not one here."

"Another result of retreating glaciers?" Abby asked. The scene she surveyed was quite unremarkable, just a narrow beach with brambles and sedge grass encroaching upon it.

"Glaciers, undoubtedly," Mark said, shielding his eyes from the sun's morning glare.

"Mark, a campfire site. Is this–?" She kicked a large piece of driftwood.

"Yes, that's ours from last night."

"So, we're back to where we started." Abby, dejected, sat down on the piece of driftwood she had just kicked. "No drumlin, no green flash, and only a few granite rocks, like those over there." She pointed to a row of small granite rocks peeking out of the sand behind Mark.

"But, that'll be enough," Mark said. He lit another fire, shook the sand out of their only beach blanket, and settled next to Abby on the driftwood.

The sun was setting in another perfectly clear, unblemished sky, but Abby had decided to resist looking directly into it. She didn't want to be misled by another green dot burned into her retina. In a few minutes, she was snuggled tight against Mark . . . waiting and waiting.

"Tell me, Mark, what did you do during the war? Were you a clandestine agent for the allies, reporting from the drumlin fields of Ireland?"

With each passing moment, the sun edged closer to the horizon. "Worse. I was a journalist." The sun had become a bright orange disk. "The Associated Press hired several young reporters straight out of college to staff its London bureau. We worked directly across the hall from Ed Murrow."

"No! You didn't!" She sat straight up. "You met Edward R. Murrow of CBS?"

"We called him Ed."

Starstruck, Abby asked, "Did you get his autograph?"

Only one half of the sun was visible now, and the round disk had flattened to an oval. "Only a dozen times," Mark said. "For family back home, you know. Ed was a mentor who had a lot to do with shaping my career in journalism." He paused. "I was interested in moving into broadcast journalism, but Ed said I should spend some time in print first, you know, newspapers. I think he gave everyone the same advice."

"But you took it," Abby said, "and here you are."

"Yes, here I am, still in print journalism." Mark leaned over to stir the fire.

"You seem resigned to it." She pulled him back to her and pulled him close. "I say we *need* more journalists like *you*."

"I love it, but I'm not sure about the future of newspapers." He looked up toward the setting sun. "Radio and television are making serious inroads with our readers."

Only the topmost rim of a very red sun remained visible on the water. Abby pulled the blanket tighter and squinted toward the horizon. "I was one of Murrow's regular listeners during the war, and—"

"*Green Flash!*" They shouted in unison, jumping to their feet.

Mark grabbed Abby and twirled her around in the sand.

"Look at the granite!" she shouted. With the sweep of her arm, she pointed to the rocks nearby. "Did I miss it? Did any of them turn green?"

"No, *not one*," Mark said. His tight lip and wrinkled brow showed his exasperation. "None of it."

"We must be in the wrong spot," Abby said. "Maybe the granite has to be larger than these rocks, perhaps as large as a drumlin."

"We didn't see a drumlin today either," Mark said, squenching his nose to one side. "We've missed something entirely from the clues. Tomorrow, it's back to Charlevoix to reconsider the whole enterprise. We have no other choice."

Abby knew he was as disappointed as she. She hugged him around the waist, her head buried in his chest. He wrapped his arms around her and held her tight for a very long time. Slowly and silently, the two walked back to the boat, occasionally exchanging glances. No words were spoken. None were needed. *We're not teenagers*, Abby reminded herself. *We're mature adults, and if we don't find the gold, maybe we were meant to find something more valuable . . . for two people to enjoy together.*

Once on board *Holly-Hoo*, Mark headed for the stern to make sure the lines were secure for the night, while Abby, in the galley, tried to reconcile all the emotions swirling in her brain. After all, she had made a commitment to Robert, hadn't she? She put her hands to work securing loose objects in the galley. A moment later, she stopped and set the coffee pot down with a firm thud. *It's been ten years, Robert. Ten years.* Abby glanced at Mark, who was retying the spring line amidships. *So damn handsome.*

She turned again to the galley cabinets, and there, in the back of one, she discovered a battery powered AM radio and made several attempts to switch it on. Each time, she made a loud "click."

"It doesn't work," Mark called out. "I tried earlier."

But Abby had already opened the radio and was examining its contents. "Ah, here's your trouble," she said to the radio. "Someone forgot to plug in the speaker before it left the factory."

As soon as the connection was made, the radio immediately jumped to life at full volume, with the announcer identifying the station as "WLS, Chicago."

"How'd you do that?" Mark gave the knot he was tying a final yank, and came forward to the galley.

Abby grinned, turned the volume down, and put the radio on the counter just as Mark arrived. "My father loved the latest electronic gadgets, and studied the physics of radios as a boy. He taught me how they work, and more important, how to repair them. This one didn't need much, just someone to . . . uh, plug in the, uh, speaker." She gave Mark a sheepish grin as she realized how simple her fix must sound to him.

"You absolutely amaze me. You have so many hidden talents." He turned the radio upside down to examine it more closely. "You are simply amazing."

Abby barely heard his last comment. Her attention was focused on the song the disc jockey was playing, the sound, a little scratchy, but the tune, very familiar.

"It seems we stood and talked like this before
We looked at each other in the same way then,
But I can't remember where or when."

She was just fifteen when she first heard it. Her mother called her to the radio and told her how much she liked the song, a new one from the 1937 musical, *Babes in Arms.*

"Some things that happened for the first time,
Seem to be happening again."

Now she felt Mark's arms encircling her from behind, a slight squeeze, and he turned her slowly toward him.

"Sometimes you think you've lived before
All that you live today
Things you do come back to you
As though they knew the way
Oh, the tricks your mind can play!"

They began to dance. He didn't say a word but kissed her cheek, her ear, her neck.

"And so it seems that we have met before
And laughed before
And loved before
But who knows . . . where or when."

By the time the last note faded into the static of the airwaves, they found themselves near her berth in the forward cabin. Without a word, they fell into it as though this was the continuation of a relationship that had started long ago.

Chapter Twenty-Two
Merrill's Mirage

The stillness of the Gull Isle morning was broken when a buck deer, sporting a handsome eight point rack, peeked out of the white cedar forest and spotted something new, bobbing gently in the shallows. The buck sniffed the air a couple of times, then dashed off when Mark and Abby appeared in *Holly-Hoo's* galley.

"It's chilly out here . . . brrr!" Mark was wearing only boxers, and Abby, wearing one of Mark's sweatshirts, threw a second to him, as he reached for a coffee pot.

"Put this over your skivvies, Tarzan, or you'll freeze to death in this chilly air." Abby watched as Mark, laughing, tried to pull it over his head.

"Give me a minute; I'll get the bacon under control."

"I've got the eggs," Abby said, "and I'll be ready for the griddle when you're finished." She turned aside and caught a glimpse of her mussed up hair in the tiny mirror hanging in the galley. Quickly, she ran a brush through it several times. *Presentable, I guess, but barely.*

There was a measure of electricity in the air that wasn't there the day before. The new lovers could not stop smiling. Soon, they could not stop kissing. Abby pulled Mark backward toward her cabin again. "But Abby, the coffee will get cold."

"Let it," Abby said. "I like my coffee cold, so long as everything else is hot." She gave him a playful pull, and together they tumbled into Abby's berth.

An hour later, Mark emerged from Abby's cabin, sipped a bit of cold coffee, and took a deep breath. "Let's go, my little chickadee. The coffee's cold, and we've gotta' get back to Charlevoix to figure out what we're doing wrong."

"*You're* not doing anything wrong, my dear." Abby twirled around in Mark's sweatshirt, stopping short of a complete circle, then with a teasing look over her shoulder, said, "But you did forget that promised foot rub last night."

Mark laughed and waved as he disappeared below to check the bilge pump. "I *will* take care of that tonight."

Alone with her thoughts, Abby suddenly felt a wave of sadness and confusion sweep over her. *Is this real? Do I belong here with this man? Is this the change I prayed would never come, and yet the change I've always known would come?* Her head was spinning. *Robert, I lost you.* She clutched her chest and bowed her head. *And . . . and now, I don't even have—*

A dropped wrench clattered against metal down below followed by an expletive from Mark that Abby couldn't make out in the clatter.

Abby took a deep breath. *Where are those comforting images that always appear in such moments to make me feel better?*

Unnoticed, Mark had slipped up behind her and gave her a lover's squeeze. Startled, Abby stared straight ahead, and screamed.

"I'm sorry, I didn't mean to hurt—"

"No, no, it's not you. Look!" She pointed to a small hand lettered sign someone had planted in the sand during the night, just off the bow. There was no way they could miss it.

> *"Covet not Gull Island, nor anything on it, for the island and all its fullness belong to the Seventh Messenger."*

Abby shivered and hugged herself against a sudden chill. "Since I arrived in Charlevoix, someone has followed my every move, always from the shadows, on the Old Rustic Bridge, from behind the trees near the drug store, and now, whoever it is, has anticipated our search on Gull."

"What do you mean, 'anticipated?'"

"If this person is responsible for the fire by the chimney, he or she, or whatever, knew we were coming here." She turned and crossed her arms with a determined scowl. "I think it's time to get to the bottom of this Seventh Messenger business. I've had enough."

"I agree," Mark said. "First, let's get outta' here." A few minutes later, with the lines free, he pulled the choke out all the way and switched on the ignition. *Holly-Hoo's* engine growled. "She's like that when she's cold, but we're not waiting for her to warm up." He shifted to reverse and backed clear of the dock. Soon, *Holly-Hoo* was at cruising speed for the run back to Charlevoix.

Ten minutes out, the engine began running irregularly—sputtering, running fast, sputtering again—then finally stopping altogether. "Drinks a little oil, but usually runs like a top; she's upset about something. I better get below and talk to her."

In a few minutes, he reappeared on the main deck, his hands dirty with engine grime. Abby could tell by the grimace on his face he didn't have good news. "Someone was busy last night while we slept," Mark said, "and they siphoned away most of our remaining gas. There was just enough to get us out on the lake and leave us dead in the water. Easy enough to do, unfortunately. Access to the tank is right there on the bow."

"What? We're stranded in the middle of Lake Michigan? You seem pretty calm for someone whose boat is bobbing like a cork." Abby was out of her seat and already looking for some form of rescue apparatus or device. "Do you have any paddles?" she asked, with a note of desperation in her voice.

"I guess it's a good time to tell you the rest of *Holly-Hoo's* secrets," Mark said, trying at first not to smile. "You were right about

Holly-Hoo being a rum runner during Prohibition. They said she was one of the best." Now, he smiled broadly and winked.

"What does that have to do with this predicament?" Abby found nothing but life preservers on board, but she kept up her frantic search. "What about your radio; can't you call someone?"

"Whoa, calm down. We're okay; we have something better than paddles or a Coast Guard rescue."

"What are you talking about?" Abby collapsed into her seat.

"Gasoline, my dear. Gasoline." Mark grinned from ear to ear.

Abby was not convinced they should be smiling. "But I thought you said—"

"Yes, wait here. I'll be right back." He bounded down the companionway. "I can't wait to see that fabulous smile again." In less than a minute, he was back. "Just one valve I had to open, and now, the second, if I can find it." Abby watched as he felt under the instrument cluster, found the valve he was searching for, and, with some effort, turned it counterclockwise.

"Sticks a bit, but there you have it—fifty extra gallons, just like that." He snapped his fingers as Abby looked on in amazement. Again, Mark pulled the choke wide open and turned the ignition switch. "If federal agents were hot on your tail between Canada and the United States, *Holly-Hoo* could outrun them, but only if she didn't run out of gas. John Hacker made sure that would never happen, by installing an extra fifty gallon tank between the lower deck and bulkhead."

"So, the rum she carried might have been illegal, but an extra gas tank was not." A relaxed Abby now began to smile.

"That's what I wanted to see," Mark said, as he closed the choke. "Let's go, my little Ford sweetheart, let's go!"

"Cheers to John Hacker," Abby said, as she pretended to lift a glass. "But we may not need the extra gas." She pointed to a boat on the horizon, moving toward them at a rapid pace. "We're about to be rescued."

Mark focused his binoculars on the rapidly approaching boat. "That's no rescue craft. It's an Aqua Cat!" Mark slammed the binoculars on the console and pushed the gas lever forward as far as it would go.

"What's an Aqua Cat?"

"Probably the one boat I can't outrun, that's what. Twin Mercury 80's on the stern. One person in it, and he doesn't look friendly. Keep an eye on him."

Abby picked up the binoculars and steadied herself against the stern, as she gazed at the approaching boat. "He's closing the gap. Can't you give it more gas?"

"No, she's wailing right now with everything she's got," Mark said, shaking his head. "This is not good at all."

"I've an idea," Abby said. "Let me have the wheel." Mark gaped at her, but relinquished control.

"What do you have in mind?"

"I'll explain later. Hold on tight!" she shouted, and jerked the wheel ninety degrees hard to starboard. Now, it was Abby's turn to smile.

"What are you doing?" Mark shouted, over the engine's deafening roar. "You're heading for the Foxes and Devil's Reef!"

"Yes. I know." Abby knew experienced boaters took great pains to avoid the area between North Fox and South Fox islands. The channel between them was wide enough all right, but was strewn with large rocks and boulders lurking out of sight, just beneath the surface, ready to take the life of any careless boater.

"Are you trying to get us killed?" Mark grabbed the rail and held tight.

"No, I'm trying to save us!" Abby was glad for a chance to play the rescuer. "Sit down."

"I'm not about to," Mark said. "This is crazy. Too risky. Too many rocks."

"Howard told me how to pass through unscathed. Billy Merrill discovered it."

"Billy Merrill?" Mark smacked his forehead. "He was crazy!"

"This is the only way to escape that guy," Abby said, pointing over her shoulder. "You got a better idea?"

"Well . . . uh." He couldn't think of anything, so he just shook his head. "Guess we're stuck with Billy's plan. God help us."

She squinted at a large rock with a faded white circle on it, barely visible ahead. "That's it!"

Mark strained to see the rock, but couldn't. "I don't see anything, except rocks!"

"There's a circle of white paint. See, that one?"

"Yes, just barely."

"That's it!" Abby jerked the helm to port. "Gotta' be quick. Now, 150 degrees." She checked their compass. "We should be on a straight line for the next one."

"How do you know the heading?" Mark asked.

"The Indians told Billy a safe course was at 150 degrees from the first rock with a white circle painted on it.

"Do you realize how crazy you sound?" Mark's tone was anything but confident. "Are you sure?"

"No, not sure, but I'm *almost* positive." Abby gave Mark a fleeting smile. "And it's supposed to be a straight shot between two rocks, one at each end of the reef." As soon as Mark began to smile, Abby teased, "But I think you oughta' get out the life vests just in case."

Mark reached under the seats and pulled out two regulation life vests. "Make sure we don't need them, okay?" He glanced over the port gunwale just in time to see the other boat slow down, but now with a sudden burst of speed, the Aqua Cat headed straight for them. "What's that guy doing? Faster, Abby!"

Abby's knuckles turned white. She couldn't hold the wheel any tighter if she tried, and *Holly-Hoo* was at her top speed. Suddenly, several large rocks appeared ahead of them.

"*Which* rock?" Mark shouted. "I don't see another white circle."

"I can't see it either," Abby said. "That's why maintaining a 150 degree heading is critical."

"Holy Mary! I can't believe we're doing this." Mark scanned the horizon. "Nothing. I see nothing!"

"There it is!" Abby shouted. "Dead ahead."

"I wish you wouldn't use the word 'dead,'" Mark said, as his eyes strained to find a rock with a white circle painted on its side. "Yes, there; I see it too!"

Abby felt the blood return to her extremities. "Howard said they told the Coast Guard, but I guess their story wasn't convincing."

Suddenly, from behind them, there was a thunderous explosion.

"I guess nobody told our friend about Billy Merrill's secret rocks," Mark said. "Did you get a good look at him?"

"No. Do you think *that* was the Seventh Messenger?" Abby asked.

"I don't know, but if so, he's also the *last* messenger. No one could survive a crash on the rocks at this speed."

Abby slowed and focused on the approaching second rock. As they passed the painted circle, Abby turned the wheel ninety degrees to starboard and shouted, "Safe water." She motioned for Mark to take the wheel. "Did you know the Coast Guard called it Merrill's Mirage?"

"No, but maybe they'll reconsider, now that it's been officially confirmed, and maybe they'll name it, Abby's Alley," Mark said, smiling. "I'm proud of you for daring to challenge Devil's Reef, but I can't believe you so easily took Howard's word for it."

Abby sat down as the reality of their escapade hit her. "I doubted him, too, but today, I felt we had no choice. It *was* dangerous, wasn't it? What a blast!" She hoped Mark wouldn't notice her shaking hands. She also hoped he wouldn't ask her again if she had any secrets to share. *But let him ask; I'll tell him the truth.*

She closed both eyes as the wind pushed tears into their corners. Her hair streamed wildly behind her. For some reason, her mother's image came to mind, standing at the kitchen sink in the summer cottage, her head tilted to one side, as if listening. Abby looked up as she might have when addressing her mother as a child.

Oh, Mother, what's happening to me? The Charlevoix of my youth is gone, and so are the people important to me. All are gone, with all their wonderful traditions, all their predictability. My new world is utterly unpredictable. Is it wrong to find that...exhilarating? Abby turned toward Mark, and with a toss of her hair, kissed him on the cheek, and he returned the kiss to her lips.

As Mark brought *Holly-Hoo* to planing speed once again, Abby protected herself from the wind by hiding behind him, with both arms around his waist. When the lighthouse finally came into view, Mark turned to Abby. "This Seventh Messenger character has been on my mind all the way back. He, or someone working with him, is trying to do more than discourage us in this little adventure."

"I agree," Abby said, "and I think we're running out of time."

"If we want to expedite our search, we need to bring someone else into our confidence," Mark said. "Who do we know with knowledge of Beaver Island, its king, and his treasure, and most importantly, wouldn't dismiss us as totally crazy?"

They looked at each other a moment and simultaneously exclaimed, "Howard Hancock!"

A few minutes later, they tied up at O'Malley's Marina, picked up a change of clothes for Mark at his apartment, and made a mad dash for Abby's room at the Hotel.

"Baths in the cool waters of Lake Michigan cannot compete with hot, running water when one needs to wash away sticky island sand," Abby said. "C'mon, join me." She gave Mark a playful smack on his rear.

Properly refreshed, they conducted a brief search of the grounds and found Howard Hancock having a late lunch with a young lady twenty years his junior, in the gazebo on the Old Rustic Bridge. As Abby and Mark approached, Howard's luncheon companion seized the moment to excuse herself.

"No, wait," Howard called to his companion. But, in a flash, the lady was off and never turned around.

"Now you've done it," Howard said.

"Done what?" Abby asked, pretending not to notice the young lady's retreat.

"Oh, never mind." His eyes followed his luncheon companion until she was out of sight. With lips tightly pursed, Howard watched her disappear. "Your timing could be better, much better," and he turned again to see if his companion had changed her mind. Sighing, he asked, "So, what?"

In the next few minutes, they shared their combined knowledge of Strang's gold and discussed the three distinctly different clues in their possession. Howard asked only one question: "You didn't find the treasure, did you?"

Mark cast his eyes downward and shook his head.

Abby was quiet a moment. "Not yet. That's why we're here." She looked at Mark, who gave her a nod. "If you know anything at all that might help us unravel the mystery, we'll . . . uh, share the treasure with you, that is, if we find any."

Howard pretended to give it a lot of thought. He reached across the table and picked a couple of French fries from the deserted luncheon plate of his companion. Slowly he placed them in his mouth, and he chewed them even slower. Finally, he turned to them. "Well, why not? I spent a good portion of my youth looking for that damn treasure. You two may be closer to it than anyone has ever been, including Billy Too."

Mark described how they searched Gull Island. He even told of how they had attempted to witness a green flash at sunset.

That brought a broad smile to Howard's face. "You actually believed that old story?" He picked up a luncheon roll, buttered it, and was about to put the whole thing in his mouth.

"It's mentioned in this clue." Mark held up a small piece of yellowed paper.

Howard put his roll down. "It's what?"

"It's mentioned here." Mark pushed the clue across the table and put it directly in front of Howard. "Read it yourself."

Howard read the clue and burst out laughing. "King Strang, you rascal! I thought I was the only one who knew about the green flash." He pushed his plate away. "You damn rascal."

"Never mind that, Howard, we've missed something," Abby said, "and since you're the Club's resident expert on the green flash, we came to you." *A little flattery never hurt relations with Howard.* "We saw the green flash at sunset, but the nearby granite didn't turn emerald or any other shade of green."

Howard scratched his chin, then reached for his buttered roll and took a large bite.

"In addition, we haven't seen anything that can be interpreted even loosely as ' . . . *the right hand of Jesus,* '" Abby said.

Howard closed his eyes and began drumming his fingers on the table.

"And if that's not enough," Mark said, "we think someone is on to us. Someone . . . Howard, are you hearing any of this?" Mark put his hand on Howard's shoulder and shook him vigorously. "Howard, are you there?"

"Green flash?" Howard asked the question aloud several times. "Green flash? Green flash?" Each time his voice rose a bit more. "Green . . . ah, yes!" His right hand shot an index finger high into the air. "I remember." He shook his raised finger, took a deep breath, and looked directly at them. "There was that one summer back in '22."

Abby glared at him. *Another wild story is coming.*

"I took the Pine Lake kids to Michilimackinac, where we planned an overnighter on the beach. The kids went swimming, and I went looking for wild cherries. But, as Robert Burns once wrote, 'The best laid plans of mice and men often go astray,' and uh, well, etcetera, etcetera." Howard took another bite out of the roll. "I have to commend ole' Spec; these rolls are really good."

" . . . '[L]eave us nothing but grief and pain for promised joy.'" Mark finished the quote.

"What? Oh, yes, 'promised joy,'" Howard said. "That's what I hoped to find."

"I hope this 'promised joy' of yours has something to do with a green flash," Abby said.

"Something better, actually. The 'promised joy' I had in mind was a tree full of Michigan cherries, tart and ripe for the picking. The best of the cherries were just out of reach, so I climbed up into the tree. Not far off the ground, a branch under me broke clean away; I lost my balance and fell into some brambles. And then, I felt the stings, stings all over my legs and back. Wild honeybees boiled out of the hive I fell into, and every last one of them was mad as the dickens. I'm not going to tell you the rest. I will say one thing: cussing under such circumstances helps!"

Abby rolled her eyes. She hoped he would get to the point soon.

"I had nothing but a tube of Unguentine with me, so it was a painful night. I really needed bicarbonate of soda, but of course, you know that." He shook his head as he relived the experience. "I hardly slept the entire night."

With hands on her hips, Abby could resist no longer. "Howard! Please!"

"As dawn broke the next day," he continued, unfazed, "I was more than ready to get up, believe me. And I must tell you, I thought it was exhaustion that fooled me into believing I saw a green flash at sunrise."

"You did what?" Abby said. "You didn't!"

"Well, yes, I did." Howard's tone was very matter of fact. "Just before the sun appeared on the horizon, there was an instant when I thought I saw something green. No, I *did* see a green flash! Little Donnie Smith was up by that time; he saw it, too."

Mark's jaw dropped as he started to back away. He grabbed Abby by her arm. "Come, my dear, I think we'll take a look on the *eastern* side of Gull Island."

"Just a minute, my captain," Abby said. "We need to ask Howard about the Seventh Messenger."

"Are we back to that?" Howard asked. "I guess I better order dessert." He snapped his finger to bring a member of the wait staff out to the bridge. "All I know is that whenever something unexplainable happens on Club grounds, someone always suggests the Seventh Messenger is to blame. I'm beginning to think he lives amongst us, or else, he's nothing more than a tall tale—and that, of course, is entirely possible. Entirely. Would you like dessert?"

"No!" Abby got up to signal Mark she was ready to go. *Howard is thinking about food or women or cars all the time.*

"Well, his jurisdiction is now more than the Hotel, and more than the Club," Mark said. "He left us a warning while we were on Gull Island, telling us, in effect, to leave and never come back."

"Yes, and he siphoned fuel out of our boat." Abby began pacing along the wooden railing. "When it ran out of gas, he tried to chase us down, but we outran him." She looked over the rail into the ravine below.

"Don't look," Howard said, laughing. "There might be a troll down there." Laughing heartily, he said to the waiter, "Bring me a hot fudge sundae." With a wide grin, he turned to Abby. "I can see you really do need my help. I'll go with you just in case you actually meet this Seventh Messenger again." He pushed his chair back.

"No, we travel light," Mark said, "but if we're not back in three days, send someone for us. But, uh, don't send Julius."

Chapter Twenty-Three
Where the Rocks Begin to Slide

D awn the next day found Mark and Abby running for the *Holly-Hoo,* snug in its slip at O'Malley's. As Mark prepared the boat for launch, Abby took another look at Mark's clue. "That last line, *'A rising sun bears witness,'* seems to fairly shout, 'Look for a green flash at sunrise.' How could we have missed that?" She threw him the bowline.

"I smell success!" Mark shouted, as *Holly-Hoo's* engine sprang to life. Abby loosened the stern line, threw it to Mark, and leapt aboard. She came better prepared for the wind and wild variations in temperature this time—wool sweater over her blouse and wind breaker over her shoulder to start, and jeans. *At least I'm not wearing pedal pushers like some teenager. Jeans are the only thing that'll work for this enterprise.*

Holly-Hoo easily made more than thirty knots on a calm, almost placid Lake Michigan. Much sooner than Abby expected, she caught sight of the wider beaches on the eastern side of Gull Island. "No docks here, dilapidated or otherwise," Mark said. "I'm going to need your help."

"Aye, aye, captain."

Mark chose a spot on the beach near a couple of cedar stumps stuck in the sand, very near the water's edge, and gently, he nudged *Holly-Hoo* forward. "We want to beach her, but not so much that we can't back off when ready."

"I'm sure you know what you're doing," Abby said. *I hope he knows what he's doing.*

206 || Roland McElroy

With the bow on the beach, Mark jumped into the shallows, and Abby threw him a bowline. He gave the boat a strong tug, easing it onto the beach a few more feet, and tied it off to the nearest stump. Abby followed and waded ashore, feet wet but otherwise, completely dry.

Before dawn the next day, Abby put on every piece of wool clothing she had brought with her. Satisfied with her effort to keep the morning chill at bay, she walked with Mark along the beach, stopping periodically to stare at the horizon, hoping all the while to catch a glimpse of the green flash at the moment the sun broke the darkness.

"I'm not a morning person," Mark said, "so this better be a good idea. Right now, I think this may be the silliest thing I've ever done."

"Wait! There's the sun!" Abby pointed to the horizon. "But, not in the spot I was watching." Her finger traced the horizon a couple of inches to the right.

"I missed it, too," Mark said. "I told you Howard was crazy. It's nearly impossible to determine the exact spot on the horizon where the flash will appear." He shook his head.

"Well . . . maybe. If we should see the green flash, it may be due to luck, pure dumb luck."

"Maybe the bee stings caused Howard to hallucinate," Mark said. "In fact, I'd put money on it."

"Let's give it another day," Abby said, as she tightened her head scarf. "I'm not going back with blisters on my feet and nothing else to show for it." She lifted one foot and then the other. "Yep, two on each foot. We *will* see that green flash . . . tomorrow." Abby's tone was insistent and determined.

The next morning, they walked barefoot in the shallows more than halfway to the far end of the island, with no luck. Abby stopped frequently to scan the horizon for the rising sun, but finally and reluctantly began to think the entire search was, as Julius said, "a fool's errand." *Frustration is written all over Mark's face.* "You look like you'd rather be sipping a gin and tonic on the veranda of the Hotel."

Mark laughed. "At this early hour?"

"Yes, at this very moment." She smiled. "Wouldn't it be great to be there right now relaxing in one of those wonderfully therapeutic Carolina rockers?"

Mark turned to look into Abby's eyes. "Yes, even that would—oh my God!"

His face turned ashen, and for a moment, Abby thought he had stopped breathing. She turned and was surprised to see a dark and oddly shaped rock rising on the distant horizon. The rather large protuberance interrupted what had been a nearly flat and undistinguished landscape until now.

"A drumlin," Mark whispered. "A drumlin!" he shouted. "*'Brighter eyes than yours have the drumlin never seen.'* I thought it might be a decoy, but that, my dear Abby, is a drumlin." He pointed to an oblong piece of land and rock that rose almost sixty feet into the air. "It's flat like, uh, an altar, a granite altar that—whoa! What's that?" His breath came quickly. "Stop right there, don't move!"

Abby stood frozen in place, ankle-deep in water. Not one lovely hair on her head dared to move.

Mark had spotted two large granite boulders: the first, high on the beach, and the second, half buried in the shallows leading into the lake. They were about twenty-five yards apart.

Abby, still not moving, stared at the eastern sky. At first, she saw nothing. Suddenly, there—in a brilliant instant, she saw it. "*Green flash!*" She turned toward Mark who seemed mesmerized by a large boulder in the middle of the beach. "The drumlin is green, *really* green, and so is that large boulder," Abby said, pointing to the boulder that had captured Mark's attention.

"Green at sunrise," Mark said. "Incredible!"

"Is that it?" Abby asked. "Where do we dig? What do we do now?"

"Well, we could dig near that granite boulder, but . . . but it doesn't feel like the complete picture." Mark stared at the large boulder

208 || Roland McElroy

in the middle of the beach, and then another, a smaller one, near the forest. Suddenly, he smacked his forehead. "We need an airplane! If my hunch is correct, we are very close to the gold. I know the guy who brings the mail out to Saint James Harbor every day. He's idle for half a day before he flies back to the mainland. I suspect he'd be glad to earn a little extra cash. Let's find him and rent his plane for half a day.

"Rent his plane? What about *him*? Don't we need a pilot?"

Mark, indignant, pointed to his chest. "Ma'am, you're looking at the best pilot around these parts." He gave her his best John Wayne impersonation and sauntered over to give her a kiss.

Abby was not entirely convinced. "Really?"

"Don't worry; I'm fully licensed. I've been flying since I was a teenager."

He is a most unusual man. Abby pulled him by the arm and whipped off her scarf. "Every pilot in the movies has a scarf. Take mine; tie it around your neck for good luck."

Mark gave the scarf a kiss and tied it loosely, "The better to let the wind have its way." In less than half an hour, *Holly-Hoo* made the crossing to Beaver Island and was soon tight against the wharf in Saint James. "The mail plane!" Mark pointed to a single engine Cessna on pontoons tied to the opposite side of the wharf. They found the pilot sipping coffee at Swan's Coffee Shop, waiting for his scheduled flight back to Charlevoix. A deal was soon struck for a one-hour rental of his plane. "If you're gone for more than an hour, I won't have enough fuel to make it back to the mainland," the pilot warned.

"Don't worry; I'm pretty sure we'll be back in less than an hour. Your Cessna will be plenty fast enough for us."

Mark helped Abby make the giant step into the passenger seat, and then climbed into the pilot's position next to her. "Buckle up." He gave her a pat on the back. "You're supposed to say 'roger' to everything the pilot says."

"OK," Abby said. "I mean, roger." She looked around the cockpit. *Just doesn't look substantial.* "What's this, Mark? Is that coat hanger wire holding the compass in place?"

"It'll be fine, don't worry, and don't touch it."

She gave him a wan smile, and looked around as if planning a quick escape if it became necessary. "Is there a parachute if I need one?"

Mark shook his head. "No need for one in a plane this small; if there's a problem, I'll just land it on the water."

Abby wasn't satisfied. Just the thought of an emergency landing had her looking around the cockpit for a quick escape route.

"The seat is a flotation device, if that makes you feel any better."

"It doesn't."

As they began skimming across the water, Mark patted her hand, and said, "I really do have this under control. Don't worry."

Once in the air, Mark turned immediately toward the Gull Island drumlin. "We'll be there in a minute." At 1,500 feet, he handed Abby his camera. "There's plenty of film inside."

"I see that," Abby said. "What do you want me to shoot?"

"I want you to shoot the drumlin and the beach and the rocks—everything. On the second pass, I want you to concentrate *only* on the rocks." As he dropped to about five hundred feet, Mark dipped the right wing and pointed to a very large rock. "When we pass over, put that big boy in the center of your focus and shoot away. I don't care if you shoot the entire roll."

Abby nodded. The two large boulders were easy to spot, and she snapped away. There was, however, a third, barely visible in the water but in a straight line from the first two. "These two are nearly equidistant from the center boulder, and it's the largest," she said.

Mark nodded and smiled.

A quick scan of the rest of the area revealed nothing distinctive or even slightly interesting, but she didn't stop snapping photos until she captured the entire beach.

When they landed, their first stop was the little photo shop of Beaver Island's only resident photographer, who also owned the island's only dark room. Two hours later, the photographer had developed, dried, and printed their entire roll of film. As he handed the photos to Abby, he smirked, "First time with a camera, eh?"

I don't have time to engage such an idiot, Abby thought, *but I'm glad he looked at our photos and didn't see anything of interest.*

Mark began shuffling through a deck of nearly three dozen images of the drumlin, the beach area, and the two large boulders they had seen earlier. "But what's this? Mmmmm. Let's get back to the boat."

Half an hour later, they were anchored again near the site of the drumlin, at the north end of Gull Island. Abby spread all of the photos under the brightest lamp they could find. "Three boulders in a row, in a straight line?" Abby asked, looking up at Mark. "Could it be some sort of religious symbol? We know this guy was a religious fanatic—"

"Whoa, I know where you're going," Mark said, sitting back in his chair. "Yes, Strang was a fanatic, and he definitely had his own interpretations of biblical truth. But, scratch any thought of the Trinity; he didn't believe in any Father, Son, and Holy Ghost ideas. And, by the way, he also didn't believe in the Virgin Birth of Jesus. He believed Jesus Christ was human, a man chosen by God to save the world, a man who lived a perfect life, and therefore, earned the right to die for all mankind. Jesus was important to him, but there was no Trinity business for James Strang."

"Still, the boulders could be symbolic of something, couldn't they?"

Mark turned back to the photos. He leaned over the table, examining each photo under a magnifying glass, finally stopping on one in particular. "Abby, I think you may be the most perspicacious person I have ever met. Take a look at this one." Mark handed her his magnifying glass.

"What am I looking for?" she asked.

"In reading Mormon history, I recall they used pentagrams and five-pointed stars in the temples they constructed. Even that early temple in Nauvoo, Illinois, featured the pentagram prominently."

"So?" Abby's eyes were just inches from the photo. "I see nothing of interest."

"Keep looking. Consider the drumlin as a headstone, and put it at the top for the time being. This large stone on the beach can be the center, or keystone, and the smaller stone at the bottom, the one partially visible above the water, can be the feet."

Abby dropped the magnifying glass. "The feet? Whose feet? What are you looking for?"

"You've already told me: a symbol." Mark held up his right hand. "Let me show you." He pulled a protractor from the drawer and slowly began to connect the stones. "Watch this." He put the point of the protractor on the center stone, and using the largest of the stones visible in the photo as a radius, he slowly drew a circle around the center stone. Tracing his finger along the circle, two vague but unmistakable dark spots appeared on the arc.

"Two more boulders?" Abby asked. "Completely submerged, just barely visible to the camera." With the magnifying glass, she searched for more boulders in the image but found none. "Two and only two. Mark, no one was going to discover these while walking the beach. No one."

"Yes, and look where they're located," Mark said. "About four o'clock and eight o'clock on our circle if we assume the drumlin is at twelve o'clock. Each is about sixty degrees from the boulder at six o'clock. See that?" Mark pointed to the dark images on the circle. "Now, let's connect the dots."

"Astounding!" Abby put down the magnifying glass. "The peace symbol? I thought it might be a religious symbol."

"It *is* a religious symbol," Mark said. "The peace symbol is only a recent creation. This is something else entirely. Hear me out. Mormons believe in the Resurrected Christ, and in many of their representations of Jesus, he is portrayed as standing with palms outstretched."

"Outwards and downwards." Abby stood and mimicked the position with her own hands placed near her body. "Oh, my God, you don't think—"

"Inviting people to come to Him," Mark said. "Inviting . . . people . . . to come . . . to him," Mark repeated, as he thumbed through the Book of Mormon on the table. "I marked a passage here awhile back, on the hunch we might need it. There are, after all, plenty of hints of some sort of 'invitation' in the clues." He stopped at the only page with a corner turned down, and read aloud:

> *"Behold, he sendeth an invitation unto all men, for the arms of mercy are extended towards them, and he saith, repent, and I will receive you. Alma 5:33"*

"Are you saying the rocks are abstract representations of the risen Jesus?" Abby asked, frozen in place, arms outstretched, palms turned outward, and attempting to understand the image before her. "The image of Jesus returning to Earth to reward the faithful?"

"*. . . [T]he arms of mercy are extended towards them,*" Mark said. "And, what does the clue say?"

"*. . . [T]he right hand of Jesus beckons.*" Abby heaved a sigh, and collapsed in her chair.

"All right then, let's take a walk to the right hand of Jesus," Mark said, giving his best impression of a traveling tent revivalist. Grabbing her hand, they practically ran to the water's edge, where Abby stopped short. She stopped so abruptly, she almost jerked Mark off his feet.

"Now, what's the matter?"

"It's under water!" Abby took a couple of steps backward. "Why would he bury the gold under water?"

"I don't know; but Abby, you saw the photos, you knew it was underwater."

"Yes, but now it looks really deep." She took one timid step forward. "How deep is it?"

"I don't know." He walked over to her, and slowly they walked together to the water's edge.

Abby pulled back at first, then slowly slipped a toe into the water. "I don't swim very well," she said, a bit sheepishly.

Mark clapped his hands in mock relish of discovering something she didn't do well. "You *are* human, after all."

Abby kicked sand toward him. *If only he knew how much my brother teased me growing up. I can't stand to be teased.* "Isn't there another way?" She didn't want *this* problem. "Why would he bury the gold under water?"

"It wasn't always under water here," Mark said. "Right now, the water level is unusually high, but I bet water levels were low in the mid-nineteenth century, about the time old King Strang buried his gold."

"So, we have to look below?" She took another step backward.

"Yes, we gotta' look below."

"Why do you need me to go with you?" Abby made no move toward the water.

"Okay, wait here; I'll be right back." He took a deep breath and dived straight down. The water was clear enough for Abby to watch, as Mark moved a rod of some kind back and forth. It seemed to be holding several rocks in place. At first, Mark couldn't budge it. Just when Abby thought he was about to succeed, Mark burst through the surface, gasping for air. "Someone took great pains to tap a hole through each rock piled there." He was breathing heavily. "The whole pile is only about three feet high, but I needed air."

"Do you think you'll be able to move it?" Abby had walked closer and was standing knee deep in the water.

"Definitely. One more dive ought to be enough." In his 'excitement, he put his hands in Abby's hair, pulled her close, and gave her a deep and affectionate kiss. He released her finally, and said, "Abby, we're about to discover whether Strang was serious about rebuilding his kingdom, or," he took a deep breath, "only serious about pulling off the world's biggest hoax." Another deep breath, and he was gone again.

Mark vigorously rocked the rod back and forth until he was able to pull it straight up, freeing the rocks, all of which tumbled to the lake bottom. Mark was forced to spring to the surface to keep his feet from being struck. At the surface, Mark smacked the water with the palm of his hand, sending spray high into the air. *" . . . The kingdom awaits all when the rocks begin to slide,"* he shouted.

Abby was now about waist deep.

"There's nothing to be afraid of." Mark reached for Abby's hand and began to pull her closer to him. "You have to be with me at the moment of discovery. It's only about six feet down."

"But, I can't." She started for the shore again, but Mark stopped her.

"I can't believe Abby Finlay said, 'I can't.'"

That comment caused Abby to stop and turn around. *He's right; I don't like "can't."* "Well, the water is clear . . . all the way . . . to the bottom, isn't it?" she asked.

"Yes. You can hold onto me the whole time." He pulled her a step closer. "I won't let go."

She took two steps toward the water.

"I'll think you'll like what you see," Mark said.

Afternoon shadows grew long, but Abby, trembling with a combination of fear and anticipation, put her arms tightly around Mark and inhaled deeply. A moment later, they plunged to the bottom, where Mark quickly pushed the last couple of stones away. But there was no chest, no gold, only sand. Frantically, Mark dug with his bare hands until his lungs ached for air. Back at the surface, Mark said, "I was so sure. You saw it: sand, a few rocks, and nothing else under the stones—nothing."

"Do you think it's possible," Abby gasped, "that someone moved it?"

Mark let his body sink into the water up to his neck. "I hate to admit it, but yes, I think somebody beat us to it."

"No, you're not supposed to agree with me." Abby felt her own voice quivering, as she desperately sought a different answer from Mark. "We have the clues, all of them, and they point to this place. *This* place." She pointed a stiff finger to the spot. "The treasure *must* be *right* here."

Twice more Mark dived to the bottom. Abby became concerned on the second dive, when the water became so muddy she couldn't follow him anymore. Each time he came up empty-handed.

"One more time," he said, gasping for air after the third dive. "I'm digging as hard as I can, but something tells me even a shovel wouldn't help." When he surfaced after his final dive, he shrugged his shoulders and waded ashore, holding his empty palms up. "Nothing. Nothing at all."

Abby collapsed on the ground next to the large stone that had been the keystone in the pentagram Mark drew. All the energy she felt on the day Robert's letter arrived was suddenly gone, leaving her an exhausted heap on the sand. *Everything was going so well. Why does everything I start end so . . . poorly?* For the first time in her life, she couldn't think of her next step. *There is no gold . . . and Robert is not here; he's really dead just as the Army said.* The tears began to flow. *I was a fool not to believe it from the beginning.* Her hands dug into the sand, kneading it over and over. Finally, she looked up to the skies. "I can't do this . . . not . . . any . . . more."

"Can't do what?" Mark asked. "Abby are you okay?"

Abby didn't say a word. She stared at her bare toes, wiggled them in the sand, and finally, she looked at Mark. "Never again."

"What do you mean?" Mark asked. She didn't answer. "Where are you, Abby? That look . . . what are you thinking?"

Slowly, she rose to her feet and in a determined voice, said, "Thinking? Not anything anyone has ever told me to think, I can assure you."

"I don't understand. What—?"

"But I'll *show* you what I'm thinking."

She waded into the water until she was waist deep, her back to Mark. As she turned slightly toward him, she said, "Watch this." Inhaling deeply, she dived to the spot where the gold had been buried. Quickly, she moved a few rocks, and dug into the sand with her bare hands. She didn't find the gold, but she didn't expect to. That was not the purpose of her dive. With a push against the bottom, Abby shot to the surface where Mark was standing at water's edge, his mouth wide open. Abby smacked her hands together like cymbals clashing at the conclusion of a Tchaikovsky overture.

"What's going on? I—I thought you were afraid of the water."

"Well, it turns out, I'm not." She laughed, and flipped her soaking hair behind her head. "When I was a young girl, my father warned me not to go near the water, and with each warning, he told me of someone he knew who drowned while swimming. I grew up terrified of water—*all* water more than two inches deep—until today." She stepped back to the water's edge and gave the shallows a defiant kick. "Today, this minute, it has occurred to me that I have spent too much time dwelling on the past and what people from the past have told me to think, too much time attempting to meet the expectations of others."

"And?" Mark sat on the keystone. "What are you going to do about it?"

"Well, I've never taken the time to focus on what *I* might accomplish in the present or, for that matter, the future. One thing I know: living in the past has only brought me regret and pain."

"Is that what you meant by 'never again?'"

"Yes!" Abby radiated a smile. "I think it's time for me to acknowledge that life is not perfect." She grabbed his hand. "Most importantly, I think there are secrets that should *never* be held from those you love, or from those who love you." And she squeezed his hand tightly.

"Do you, uh, have secrets to share with me?" Mark asked.

Abby started to speak but stopped when she heard the sound of a small engine.

"Oh no," Mark said. "Visitors."

A small plane, its engine coughing and sputtering, broke through the clouds. Mark shaded his eyes with one hand as he tried to identify the plane. Overhead, the plane circled lower and lower. "That's *not* the mail plane."

Abby shook a fist at whoever was in the plane. "I'm not afraid of you . . . you…Seventh Messenger."

They gathered their gear and headed for *Holly-Hoo*. Abby stopped when the small plane descended to a few hundred feet above the water. "Is it going to crash?"

"No, no—look!" Mark pointed to the plane as it slowly turned and flew in the direction of the mainland, its engine still running unevenly. "Get on board. *Holly-Hoo* is gonna' make some waves." *Holly-Hoo* roared to life, and Mark steered her quickly toward open water.

"Mrs. Vandivare got us started. Maybe it's time to pay her another visit," Abby said. With both hands, she attempted to wring all the water out of her hair.

"Why not Howard or Julius?"

"I have a feeling she knows more than she has told us. As my father once said, 'She even knows the unknowns no one knows.'" She flipped her hair back and forth several times to aid its drying. "I *do* want to hear about those unknowns."

Mark smiled and stared at the horizon. "Unknowns, indeed."

Abby, left alone with her thoughts, wondered if Mrs. Vandivare "knows the unknown" about the badge of shame Abby wears. *I don't want to keep any secrets from Mark, but I don't see how anything good can come from telling him. And yet, I don't want to withhold anything from him, ever.*

Chapter Twenty-Four
No Exceptions to the Rule

Abby sat in her Hotel room listening to the ringing on the other end of the phone line. "No answer, so far." She hoped Mrs. Vandivare would be willing to break her rule and see them before lunch. "She says her rule is firm," Abby whispered to Mark, who was putting on his jacket. "But, perhaps she'll grant this one exception." Abby held up her crossed fingers. "She must."

The phone rang eight times before the butler answered at Blue Hair's cottage. He listened only a few seconds—Abby never had a chance to finish her request—before he huffed, "Mrs. Vandivare is *unavailable* before noon."

"Please tell her Abby Finlay is calling; I think she will want to hear from me." Abby was not giving up easily.

A moment later, that honeysuckle voice Abby knew so well came on the line. "My dear sweet Abby, you have been very busy, I'm told. What can I do for you now?"

"Mrs. Vandivare, we, that is, Mark Day and I, were very close to discovering the hiding place for James Strang's royal treasury, but it appears someone got there before us. You are the only person I know who can help us. I, uh . . . *we* would like to visit with you right away."

"Oh my, you have been busy," Blue Hair said.

"Perhaps there is some tidbit of information from your memory that will shed additional light on our search." Abby shook her crossed fingers in Mark's direction. "Would it be possible to see you in an hour? We promise to be brief."

"One hour? Oh my dear, I am just out of the feathers. There is nothing so urgent it can't wait until afternoon. Please call at one o'clock, and I'll be glad to entertain you and your friend, a Mr. Day, did you say?" Abby heard the playfulness in her voice. "I look forward to meeting him. I hope he is someone, shall we say, substantial."

"Yes, he is, and we'll see you at one." Abby hung up the phone and with a look of feigned seriousness, asked Mark, "Do you consider yourself 'substantial?'"

"What?"

"Oh, never mind." Abby shook her head. "One o'clock is the earliest—"

"One o'clock is four hours from now." Mark was incredulous. "Dare I ask why?"

"Yes, you may dare, and I shall dare to give you an answer: it's her rule." She wagged her finger at Mark as if he were a student in her class.

"Oh, great." He flopped in a nearby chair. "I can see it would take an Act of Congress to change 'her rule.' I can't wait to meet this person around whom the entire world spins."

At the appointed hour, they arrived at Blue Hair's cottage, and the butler ushered them into the front parlor. And there she was, looking perfectly elegant in her blue afternoon dress, a skirt that fell just past her knees, elbow length gloves, and brimless felt hat adorned with some sort of feather. Abby thought she looked like the Queen, her spine against the back of the chair, straight as a board, in a room decorated almost entirely in shades of royal blue. Blue curtains, blue upholstery, and blue paint. Only the briefest of white lace trim broke the overwhelming essence of blue on all furnishings.

"Please, please have a seat." With a broad sweep of her hand, she indicated they should choose the blue velvet settee near the fireplace.

"Mrs. Vandivare, I would like to introduce my good friend, Mark Day. He's—"

"The Editor of the *Clarion*, I know. I've never had the pleasure, but I have enjoyed reading your editorials, young man. A bit liberal, but entertaining, nonetheless."

"I consider that a glowing endorsement." Mark bowed deeply. "Thank you very much."

Blue Hair leaned toward Abby and smiled. "Good choice, Abby. Good choice." At that moment, the butler entered. "James, bring us three teas," she said. "Abby will have hers with sugar and lemon. And young man, how do you take yours? You do drink tea, don't you?"

"Of course," Mark said. "It's, uh, uh . . . better than coffee." When Blue Hair looked away, Mark rolled his eyes at Abby.

Abby hid her smile behind her hand. She knew Mark seldom drank tea; he definitely preferred coffee.

"Sugar only, please," Mark said.

"Oh my, no. James, put lemon in Mr. Day's tea, too."

Mark started to object, but held his tongue when Abby shook her head. The butler disappeared into the kitchen. He had only been gone a moment before Blue Hair rang the little bell on her side table. When the butler reappeared in the doorway, he was met with an icy reminder. "And James, don't forget the tea cakes, currant tea cakes."

"Of course, madam, of course." With an about face, he was gone again.

"I have to remind him of everything," Blue Hair said. "I don't know why. Now, my dear Abby, what brings you here so urgently?"

"Mrs. Vandivare," Abby said, with a celebratory note in her voice, "we've found the spot where King Strang hid his gold on Gull Island."

A crash from the kitchen stopped their conversation.

"Pay no attention, and please don't say anything about Strang's gold when James returns," Blue Hair said. "Now, Abby, you said you found 'the spot' where the gold was hidden. Wasn't it there?"

"No, and that's why we came here to see you," Abby said, "Do you think it possible that—?"

The butler entered at that moment carrying a sterling silver tray with matching teapot, three cups, and a selection of tea cakes. Blue Hair put two teaspoons of sugar in her teacup and took a sip. "Wonderful, James, wonderful."

Abby chose a currant cake to be polite but had no intention of eating it. She had other business. She waited until the butler left the room before asking in a quiet voice, "Is it possible someone might have found the gold long ago?"

"Maybe." Blue Hair shrugged her shoulders. "But if they did, what makes you think they didn't just run away to live a high life in, perhaps, San Francisco or some such place?" She noticed Mark hesitating as he looked over an assortment of tea cakes. "Mr. Day, I think you will enjoy the huffkin tea cakes; they have a bit of the hops in them."

Mark nodded and selected two of the huffkins. "It would have been in at least one newspaper somewhere," Mark said, as he examined all sides of a huffkin, "and I would have known about it." He slumped in his chair and popped a whole huffkin tea cake in his mouth. His eyes opened wide as a surprising flavor greeted his taste buds. "A bit of the hops, indeed."

"Strang was suspicious of everyone in his final days," Abby said. "Do you think he might have moved the gold to another location?"

"It's possible," Blue Hair said, "but not by James Strang."

"If not Strang, then who?" Abby moved to the edge of her chair.

Blue Hair glanced toward the kitchen to be sure the butler was out of earshot. "Well, there is one old story." She put her cup down and circled the saucer with her index finger. "I told you about John Johnson, didn't I, the first caretaker of the Club?"

Abby nodded.

"And that he heard all the Strang stories in his youth?" She tapped the side of her saucer.

"Is there something more?" Abby was anxious to hear anything Blue Hair knew that might shed light on their search.

Blue Hair, for apparently no reason, moved her cup and saucer nearer the edge of the butler's tray. "Well, there is more to say, as there always is when the subject of James Strang comes up." She smiled and glanced briefly in Mark's direction. "I didn't tell you that Mr. Johnson was on Beaver Island when the king was assassinated, but he was."

Mark sat straight up. "Don't tell us Johnson was involved in the murder."

"No, no, John Johnson was a young man, about twenty years of age in 1856. He was not part of the plot, but I suspect he would have counted himself among plot sympathizers."

"Clearly, not everything to be known about the James Strang story has been written," Abby said, as she took a sip from her cup.

"Oh my, child, no, the worst has *never* been written." Blue Hair leaned over, stared deep into her tea, as if peering into another world. "When Strang's wife, Mary—his only legal wife, mind you—moved back to Voree, Wisconsin, John Johnson visited her from time to time." Blue Hair continued to stare into her tea.

"How do you know?" Abby asked.

"Because he *told* me so, my dear." She adjusted the blue sapphire stone hanging around her neck and folded both hands in her lap. "He told me so."

Abby thought Blue Hair considered the question impertinent. "I'm sorry; please go on."

Blue Hair looked down the full length of her nose at her questioners, and with one fully arched eyebrow said, "They became quite close through their regular correspondence."

"How close?" Abby asked. "Very close?"

"So close that he often visited her in Voree, Wisconsin, then Eglin, Indiana, and the last time, in 1880, when she moved to Terre

Haute, Indiana. That's where, in her final days, when she was very ill, she invited Johnson to visit her once more."

"Her final days?" Abby worried that any story told by a deathly ill woman might have credibility problems. "What was the status of her health when Johnson arrived?"

"She was weak but lucid enough, if that's what you're asking, and ready to talk about James Strang's gold." Blue Hair rang the bell on the table nearest her, and the butler quickly appeared. "More tea, James, for all." Blue Hair stood and walked to the parlor's fireplace, where she gazed at the portrait of her late husband hanging just above the mantle. She never took her eyes off her husband's face while she revealed John Johnson's story for the first time. "Mary moved the gold to High Island with the help of her Indian friend, Ogawee. Upon her return, she wrote a separate clue intended for her daughter, Nettie, a clue written with the sole purpose of guaranteeing her daughter would find the gold, and no one else." Blue Hair turned to Abby. "That's what Johnson reported to me."

"And where is the clue; has any one seen it?" Abby was beginning to think the whole tale had been made up from whole cloth.

"Mary put the clue in Strang's diary, but she also told Johnson the diary was stolen years later when she moved from Voree, to Eglin."

"Without the diary, we won't have the clue, and without the clue we won't be able to locate the gold on High Island," Mark said. "Could she have told anyone else?

Before Blue Hair could answer, Abby asked, "What about Ogawee? Could he have returned and claimed the gold himself?"

Mark jumped in. "Or maybe she simply told her daughter where the gold was buried and Nettie claimed the royal treasure."

"Not likely," Blue Hair said. "Nettie Moved to California after her father's death and never returned to the area." Blue Hair moved back to her chair and took a seat as her butler entered with fresh tea. "As for Ogawee, he disappeared after Mary returned to Voree. His whereabouts have always been a mystery." Blue Hair stirred lemon and sugar into her tea and took a sip. "The British gave us just one decent gift before the

Revolution, tea, but it was worth all the trouble they caused." She put her cup down. "Now, where was I?"

"Why didn't she just tell Johnson where the gold was hidden on High Island?" Mary asked. "No one would need the diary or the clue if she had just told him the hiding place."

"Johnson thought she intended to share that information with him but died before she had a chance. On her final day, she uttered only one word, 'Ogawee,' the name of her Indian friend. Johnson returned to Charlevoix convinced the diary held the key to finding the gold, but he never found it." Blue Hair finally turned from her husband's portrait and looked straight at Abby. "If Mary was telling the truth, the clues written by James Strang were *never* going to yield the treasure," she said, her face a blank expression.

"What about you, Mrs. Vandivare? Do *you* believe Mary wrote a separate clue for her daughter?" Abby wanted to know if Blue Hair thought Mary might have been hallucinating on her death bed.

Blue Hair stared at the parlor's blue ceiling, as if just beneath its glorious blueness were written all the stories ever told about Mary Perce. She shook her head as her eyes dropped to the floor. "I'm far from certain, Abby, especially when you consider the chronic health issues that plagued that poor woman."

"What do you mean?" Abby asked.

"Mary was a woman who dealt with bouts of depression all her life. She was prone to 'fits of darkness,' as someone once described her reclusive behavior."

"So sad," Abby said. Tilting her head to one side, she asked, "And, by the way, you didn't tell anyone about the gold being moved to High Island, did you?"

"No, I never believed it. I think it quite likely that she confused High with another island out there, perhaps Garden or Hog, or perhaps one of the islands completely covered by water today." She flipped her hair to one side.

"Why do you say that?" Abby asked.

"Every corner of High Island was searched, over and over, and nothing but Indian bones was ever found. It is, after all, a Spirit House."

"Thank you, Mrs. Vandivare. You've been most helpful, as always," Abby said. "We may be no closer to solving the mystery than before, but we are gaining a better understanding of the characters involved, and who knows, maybe insight will follow." Abby put her tea down, and Mark stood up. "Please excuse us."

"One more thing." Blue Hair stopped them. "Speaking of characters, I'd like to suggest that Julius might be of some additional assistance. I know you don't like him very much, but he always knows more than he's willing to share. With your eyes, Abby, you should have more success than the rest of us." She cleared her throat. "If you know what I mean." With that, she rang the bell for her butler.

Abby frowned at the suggestion that she must use her feminine wiles to extract truth from Mooney. "That flirtatious habit of his is one reason I've never liked him. He's almost as bad as Howard."

"Yes, but you *need* all that he knows," Blue Hair said. "He's the unofficial keeper of Club records; whatever records exist, he has them in his possession, even the early caretaker files." The butler reappeared from the kitchen. "James, please show my guests out."

"Pretending to be friendly to Julius is more than a little repugnant to me, but I'll do it," Abby said. "I know what I have to do." She took Mark's arm, and together, they followed the butler through the front hall.

"Be patient with him," Blue Hair said, as the two reached the door. "Be patient."

**

In late afternoon, Abby and Mark found Julius relaxing on the Hotel veranda with his usual gin and tonic firmly in hand.

"As I live and breathe, it's Robinson Crusoe and his first mate, Friday," Julius said, as they approached. "Suntanned, windblown, the beachcombers at last come home. But you look a little befuddled, betwixt and between, as they say. What can I do for you?"

"Julius, you know I returned to Pine Lake determined to solve the mystery of James Strang's gold, and, well, we've hit a brick wall," Abby said. "We've looked, but have nothing to show for the effort." She leaned against the railing and gave Julius a strained but coy little smile. "Will you help us?" She added a little sweetness to her voice as she asked the question. "Mrs. Vandivare thinks there might be something in the files of former caretakers, especially the earliest, a Mister John Johnson. Could that be possible?" Again, the coy little smile, her head cocked wistfully to one side.

Mark pulled up one of the rockers and took a seat.

"Johnson, eh? Well, Johnson was right here for a long time, almost sixty years, but he didn't leave many records."

Julius cleared his throat with some unease, it seemed to Abby.

"In his day, folks just didn't write everything down like they do now, but . . . " Julius scratched his chin and gave Abby a sideways glance.

She returned his little peek, let her eyes flutter a bit, and lifted her chin as if to say, "Yes?"

Mooney's eyebrows soared up and down several times. "There is *one* person in the Club who might be able to help you. And, uh, I've never talked about it, but you might as well know . . ." His eyebrows stopped in a way that nearly covered the deep furrows he had created in his forehead. "It's King Strang's granddaughter."

"Here—in the Club?" Abby was suddenly standing straight up. "Now?"

"Maybe I shoulda' told you sooner but, well, it's not something that . . . I don't think Blue Hair knows, but even if she did, she'd not likely discuss it with anyone, even you." He looked directly into Abby's eyes. "It's not something we talk about."

"I don't know what to say." Abby was shocked and not certain she believed her ears.

"I probably shouldn't have told you." Mooney reached into his boots and pulled his sagging socks up as far as he could. The worn out socks disappeared again, almost as quickly as he pulled them up.

Abby stood stiffly behind Mark's rocker, her hands gripping the top rail as a teacher might, when calling an unruly class to order. "Julius! Why is this so hard? If you ask me, Club members need to get over their obsession with hiding Club secrets."

"Oh, all right, I'll tell you this one story," Mooney said, "if you're sure you wanna' hear it?"

She moved to the front of Mooney's rocker. "Yes, we want to hear it!" There were no fluttering eyelashes or coy smiles anymore. "It's always worse, Julius, when secrets have to be pulled out like an infected tooth." She gave Mark an exasperated look. He returned her look by using his hand to signal, "Remember to stay cool."

"This story is worse than an infected tooth," Julius said, "so, I'm just going to tell it once. Elvira Strang came to the mainland after the king's assassination, trying to make a new life for herself. She brought her daughter, Eva, with her. John Johnson was the only person 'round here who would even talk to her. Anyway, Johnson hired Eva to work as a dance instructor at the Hotel, the first such instructor I might add. Just when and where she learned to dance herself is not clear. She was hired for the sole purpose of teaching Pine Lake girls how to dance the Highland Fling. She also taught the boys a sort of Sailor's Hornpipe, probably as much to burn off excess energy as to teach them a dance step or two."

"And, and—?" Abby leaned forward. While the gin and tonic was talking, Abby wanted Julius to reveal every snippet of information he knew about Eva Strang. "And—?" She gave him a circular motion with her hand. "Yes? Keep going."

"I'm going as fast as my old memory will let me. Where was I? Oh, yes, I remember the elders telling the story repeatedly at the Sunday evening hymn singing. Eva married a local bartender by the name of

Zachariah Smith. They had a daughter, Mary Beth, born around 1886, I think. Mary Beth followed her mother as dance instructor for the Club. Now, Mary Beth *was* a dancer!"

"Julius!" Abby held up a stiff index finger. "One story at a time!" She wanted him to finish before he changed his mind.

Julius smiled weakly before a dark frown spread across his face. "Mary Beth never married, but that didn't keep her from being active, no sir." He lowered his voice to a near whisper. "She had a daughter, born out of wedlock, shameful day . . . born, I'd say, around 1908."

Why do the old folks always whisper when they speak of a birth out of wedlock?

"Mary Beth was probably twenty years of age when her daughter was born," Julius said. "But, of course, that daughter would not be her last misstep."

"And *how* is this going to help us find Strang's gold?" Mark asked, as he got up and joined Abby, leaning against the porch railing directly in front of Mooney.

"You two really are impatient." He tipped his Panama hat to the back of his head. "Well, rumor had it Phoebe was fathered by a Pine Lake member. But, it was just a rumor."

"Wait . . . a . . . minute!" Abby moved directly in front of Mooney and put her hands on the arms of Mooney's rocker and stopped his rocking. "You just said 'Phoebe.' The only Phoebe I know in the Club is Miss Phoebe Cooke. Is she Strang's granddaughter?"

"Yep, she's the one. Most folks know her—affectionately, I might add—as the Pine Lake Madam." Mooney sat up, tipped his hat forward, and asked, "Do you know her?"

Of course, Abby knew her. Miss Cooke had been their next door neighbor for years.

Julius scratched his head. "The way it was told to me," he said, "when her grandmother died, Phoebe inherited all her worldly goods, which did not amount to much."

Abby watched Mooney in silence as he moved his mouth side to side. She was sure he had more to share. Finally, he put his drink down beside the rocker and tapped his fingers on the rocker's arm.

"A single box carried most of what she inherited, and as I recall, that box held all that was left of King Strang's correspondence." He slumped in his rocker. "I know that for a fact because, for a long time, she stored the box in my attic."

"Is there anything of value in it?" Mark asked.

"Probably not." Mooney started rocking again. "I went through every file myself and gave some stuff to that university back east, Yale, I think it was. At any rate, it can't hurt to ask her. When I became Hotel manager, I cleared out my attic and gave her the box and everything in it."

"Julius, you've been a big help," Abby said. She managed to lean over and give him a quick peck on the cheek.

"By the way, Julius," Mark said, as he reached for Abby's hand, "are you sure you don't know the father of the Pine Lake Madam?"

"It was just a rumor, Mark, just a rumor." Julius shook his head. "Sorry I said it. Best forget it." He suddenly came out of his chair. "Yes, just forget it." He put his drink on the porch railing, and started for the stairs. He had only taken a couple of steps when he turned around, and smiled at Abby. "If you have any more questions, you know where to find me."

"Yes, and *we* will almost certainly have more questions," Mark said. He wanted to be sure Julius knew Abby would not visit him alone.

"Thanks for being beside me," Abby whispered to Mark as they left the veranda and retreated to Abby's room. "It's too late for a visit tonight, but Miss Cooke will be our first priority tomorrow."

"If the Madam holds a key to this puzzle, we'll have to include her when the treasure is divided, don't you agree?" Mark opened the door and threw the key on the bed.

"Yes, of course, but what about Julius?" Abby asked. "He's helped, too."

"Well, yes, I guess so."

"You don't sound convinced," Abby said.

"That folksy way of his . . . I have a feeling that what you see is not always what you get. That's all I'm saying." He threw his jacket on the bed and started to undress.

Abby snapped her fingers. "How could I forget? I'm out of shampoo. I'm going to the lobby and pick up a bottle at the sundry desk. Be right back." She held the door open a crack as she started out and smiled as she peeked around it. "Don't go anywhere."

"Don't worry; it'll take more than the lack of shampoo to get rid of me."

The front desk had the shampoo Abby needed, but as she turned around, she spied Blue Hair in the Solarium, talking quietly with a gentleman she didn't know. *But he looks familiar. I hate to be a snoop, but their conversation looks quite serious from here.*

Abby remembered a secret entrance to the Solarium from behind the candy counter, a small opening the kids used for unseen escapes from boring adult conversations. *Good. Xeno is nowhere to be found. Left for the day, I'm sure.* Abby slipped through the opening into the Solarium and was soon behind the potted palms, only a few feet from the conversation taking place.

"Sir, you underestimate me." Blue Hair was suddenly sitting straight up in her chair, eyebrows arched as high as Abby had ever seen. "Eyes and ears have I, in the Hotel," she sniffed, "and all are as keen as yours, even more so, I dare say."

"Really?" The stranger's eyes began to twitch and blink, and he shrugged his shoulders several times. "My eyes on the *Shoodle* will be sufficient for my purposes before this caper is closed."

"Detective?" Blue Hair pulled up her gloves and gave them an extra tug. "Do you mind a personal question?"

Wait, did she just call him "detective?" Abby didn't move. *What's this about?*

"Not from you, my dear Mrs. Vandivare."

"Very well. Each time we meet to discuss our mutual interest, you have several episodes—if I may call them episodes—when you blink; your eyelids blink rapidly up and down." She gave another tug to her gloves. "Is it the result of . . . a wartime injury perhaps?"

Abby pushed a couple of palm leaves apart for a better look at the stranger's face. *Only a partial profile. Pencil mustache under a round nose.*

"I hoped you wouldn't notice," the detective said, "but I suppose everyone notices. I flew the Mosquito bomber for the RAF back in '43. One day, the Germans got lucky, and I had the misfortune of having my tail shot off by one of their anti-aircraft batteries."

"Heavens, I'm so sorry."

"I survived, as you can see, but on that day, I began experiencing an involuntary twitch of sorts, and that's the burden I carry to this day. I rather wish it would go the way of the Fuhrer. I'm sorry if it offends you." He brushed his moustache nervously with two fingers, which Abby thought, *only serves to draw attention to his facial tic.*

"Oh my no, it most certainly does not offend." Blue Hair tucked her purse under her arm and stood. "I know you will be happy to return to your home when you finish your business here."

"Yes, this is a lovely place, but I do harbor a yearning for my garden in the Cotswolds." He extended his arm and escorted Blue Hair through the far doors of the Solarium.

Abby quickly retraced her steps back to the lobby and her room.

"That was odd, really odd," she said to Mark as she recounted her experience. "There they were, talking about their 'eyes' in the Hotel and elsewhere. She even called him 'detective' at one point." She turned her back to Mark. "Unbutton me."

"Did they mention us?" Mark asked, as he slowly began to unbutton Abby's blouse.

"No. Not by name. At least, not while I was listening." Abby suddenly turned to Mark. "I hope the Madam can help us. She must."

"Turn around, my dear," Mark said, giving her a twist, "I'm not finished."

Abby heard a low chuckle from Mark.

"What's so funny?"

"I only met the Madam once. Well, I guess I didn't meet her really; I was standing behind her at the Post Office, waiting to buy stamps. A long-haired young man rode up on his Harley, walked right in, and straight to the window next to her. He was wearing a pair of black motorcycle boots and *nothing* else. I swear. Nothing. People around him were shocked and not sure what to say or do. The Madam took one look, stared him straight in the eye, and said, 'Young fellow, you simply must have a talk with your tailor.' With that, she turned and walked out the door. I never laughed so hard in all my life. What a character!"

"She is that," Abby said, as she walked into the closet to hang up her blouse. "We lived next door for a long time. She had a habit of getting up early to spray down her porch, ostensibly, to wash away the morning spiders. Mother and I often watched her daily ritual. Of course, the men liked to come by to see what she chose to wear while spraying spiders. And it was always white lingerie, usually several layers. I was shocked one morning when she appeared on her porch dressed in a long gossamer web of a gown. She caught me staring at her, and said, 'Honey, I'm wearing the Royal Treatment Corset today; do you like it?' I was speechless and tried to nod. I didn't even know what it was."

Mark laughed. "I'm glad you're not wearing one right now. That blouse was hard enough."

Abby unzipped her skirt and let it fall to the floor. "Let's make that one easy for you."

Mark looked her up and down. "Aren't you worried tongues will be wagging tomorrow?"

"About what?" Abby pulled his shirttail out of his waistband.

"About me entering this room with you on my arm. Two single people, one of whom is well known to the Club, the other well known to locals, and did I mention, both single?" He threw his trousers over the nearest chair.

"Only employees of the Hotel will notice our comings and goings, and they're not likely to be telling anyone." She pulled Mark toward her, and together, they fell into the middle of the bed.

"But tongues will be . . ."

"Wagging?" Abby thought Mark's objection was totally faux. "Let 'em wag," Abby said. Feather pillows bounced wildly up and down as well-worn bedsprings had their way. "Old walls and floors are nothing if not a perfect soundboard for everything that moves in these rooms," Abby said, laughing.

**

Hot showers refreshed them both. Wrapped only in the Hotel's large, terry cloth robes, Abby and Mark popped the cork on a bottle of Chateau Saint Pierre which the management had sent to Abby's room as a "welcome back" gift.

"To gold!" Mark said.

"And to us!" Abby cheered.

"Even better," Mark said, as they lifted the Hotel's Longchamps stemware and tipped their crystal rims together.

After a long sip, Abby plopped on the bed, careful not to spill a drop from her glass. With tilted head and softened eyes, she asked a question that had been on her mind since they first met. "Mark, were you ever in love?"

"I wondered if you would ask." Mark joined her on the bed and rolled as close as he could.

"Girls always want to know." She snuggled closer and smiled. "That's essential information."

"Well, the answer is yes, once, in London during the war. She was the most . . ." A lump in his throat kept him from finishing the sentence. "Her name was Sarah, and . . ." He gulped the remainder of his champagne down and set his glass on the floor.

"Yes?"

Mark started over. "During the war, she was a frequent volunteer at the American hospitals outside London, tending to wounded Americans. I met her while doing a story on some of her GIs." He smiled. "She was committed to saving every one of them."

"What happened?" Abby set her glass beside his and gave Mark rapt attention. She wanted to know every detail.

"Every day she drove into London from her family's country home." His voice dropped. "One morning—the war was nearly over—an Army truck made a sudden left turn in front of her car. In the crash, she suffered a spinal injury, and a few days later . . . she died." He paused a long time, and Abby gave him an understanding, soft touch on his arm. "Just like that, she was gone," he blurted out. "I thought my life had ended." He rolled over on his back. "And that's when I asked AP for a transfer back to the states. Europe was not the place for me anymore."

"I'm sorry. I'm very sorry." *So many destinies altered by that damn war.*

"Talk about guilt, I was overcome with guilt," Mark said. "I thought I should have been driving the car. For years, I blamed myself. But the truth is, there was nothing I could've done to prevent it, nothing at all. Our life together . . . simply was not meant to be." Mark jumped off the bed and poured another glass of champagne.

"But you seem to have come to terms with it."

"I work on coming to terms with it every day." He gave the champagne another long sip. "What about you? Do you feel guilty about your Robert?"

"Yes, of course." She rolled across the bed in the opposite direction and stared at the wall.

"I thought so. I saw your face that first morning as we were cruising *Holly-Hoo* out to Gull Island. I saw it change. One moment you were happy, even ecstatic, the next, the picture of profound grief. And I understood."

Abby turned back to him. "You saw that?"

"Yes. You probably felt guilty even being there with me, didn't you?"

She nodded, but felt her face redden. "Was it that obvious?"

"Guilt is a powerful emotion, and difficult to hide, that is, for those capable of feeling guilt at all. I expended an enormous amount of energy on all the things I should've done differently, but one morning—thankfully—I woke up, and heard a voice loud and clear: 'Get on with your life; write those new chapters.'"

Abby responded with a soft kiss to Mark's lips. "I thought happiness had abandoned me, too."

"I only know I have walked this path before you." He touched her cheek and, with a thumb, wiped away a single tear.

"Oh, Mark, if you only knew the full extent of the pain within me." When she thought of Robert, her chest tightened, and her breathing became labored. *The pain is so intense and very real.*

"Only knew?" He gave her a sideways glance. "I think we know each other well enough for you to tell me anything." He reached over, pulled a Kleenex from a box on the dresser, and gave it to her.

"I can't speak of it. The pain hurts too much." She crushed the Kleenex with both hands, and then pulled the tissue apart. "It runs too deep."

"Abby, nothing is so painful that you shouldn't talk about it, ever. Try me." He cleared his throat. "'Only yourself can heal you; only yourself can lead you.'"

"What—or who—was that?"

"A line from a Sara Teasdale poem. Remember her? She wrote what I've been trying to say, and much better, I have to admit."

Abby was astonished to find anyone who'd even heard the Teasdale name. "Sara knew my family. She was a Saint Louis poet who wrote many of her poems while vacationing right here in Charlevoix."

Mark lifted Abby's chin and gave her a gentle kiss. "And she was a wise woman because she believed you have the power within to *heal yourself* and *lead yourself* out of this pain."

After a moment of quiet contemplation, Abby let it out in one difficult emotional burst. "Robert and I had a child . . . a boy." She began to sob. "Born in the spring, just weeks before the D-Day invasion. I never had a chance to tell Robert."

Mark said nothing, but wrapped his arms around her.

"A boy," Abby said. Between sobs, she repeated over and over, "a beautiful baby boy."

"Did your parents know?" Mark reached over her shoulder and pulled another Kleenex from the box on the dresser.

"My mother knew. I told her about the pregnancy, but I could never tell my father. He just wouldn't understand."

Mark placed the Kleenex in her hand. "Well, I understand." He pulled away and looked into her eyes. "Where . . .?"

"I was attending Agnes Scott College, just outside Atlanta. When my time came, I checked in at Sisters of Joan Home for the Unwed, and that's where baby Robert was born. It's where all the unfortunate girls at Scott went to have their babies."

"Did you think of yourself as, um, 'unfortunate'?" He brushed away a single tear that had traced its way to Abby's chin.

"No, not at all. But Robert was not there, and I knew I could not raise the baby alone." Abby dabbed her eyes several times. "A single woman? No, absolutely not."

"Did you give him up for adoption?"

"No. I couldn't do that either; that would mean breaking my tie to the baby altogether, a tie that kept me close to Robert. When I explained all this to mother, she arranged for my Aunt Margaret in Atlanta to raise him. It was supposed to be a temporary arrangement, until Robert came home. But when he didn't come . . . and the months went by . . . Aunt Margaret persuaded me to let her keep him. She said the Finlay family didn't need. . . " She paused, looked at Mark, and spit out the words, " . . . didn't need to have its reputation sullied in Saint Louis society by the news that Abigail Finlay had birthed, and was now raising, a child out of wedlock."

"I'm sorry that you listened to her." Mark gave Abby gentle kisses on both cheeks.

"Really? You don't think me a terrible person?" She searched his face to be sure of his support.

"Abby, I'm the one who loves you, remember? I'm the one who will stand by you, always." Mark held her even tighter than before and kissed her forehead. "You need to stop blaming yourself for every perceived wrong turn you've made. You did everything you thought was right at the time." He gently wiped tears from her face, including one that was ready to drop from her chin. "You know what I think?" He lifted her chin again.

"No." She sniffled and looked into his eyes.

"I think I'd like to meet this young man. When our search is done, I think you ought to invite . . . young Robert . . . to come to Charlevoix."

Abby was speechless, and stammered. "I—oh, Mark!" She threw her arms around him.

"Besides, I like that name, Robert."

Abby beamed. "Aunt Margaret calls him Bobby."

"Well, maybe Bobby will become a journalist and help me at the paper." Mark winked. "But, of course, he may have other ideas, and that would be fine."

"Mark, I can't believe I found you, right here in Charlevoix." She ran her hands under his robe and squeezed his bare skin tightly.

"Don't sound so surprised. I think Robert asked you to meet him here, not Saint Louis, because he knew Charlevoix would be the best place for you to regain your happiness should the war prevent him from returning. You're where Robert wanted you to be." He gently pushed her hair back over her ears. "And honestly, Robert is here, too, isn't he?" Mark paused as his eyes examined every unblemished inch of her face. "In all those northwest breezes that caress this girl." With one finger, he slowly outlined her face. "In all those multi-colored, ever changing sunsets that feed your soul." He kissed one cheek and then the other.

She felt a tingle down her spine and began to smile again

"And especially, in all the perfectly blue skies that lift your spirits . . . every minute . . . of every day." Mark took her hands in his, and she smiled a broad smile. "I love to see that smile," Mark said. "I never tire of it." He gave her a gentle kiss on the tips of her fingers. "Abby, I would never say, 'forget the past.' The past travels with us every step we take and makes us who we are. Robert will always be a part of you, and that's as it should be, but . . ."

"Yes?"

Marked stepped behind her, his voice, nearly a whisper. "Robert would be disappointed if you didn't . . . " He wrapped his arms around her, pulled her close, and kissed the back of her neck several times, whispering between kisses, " . . . if you didn't choose to live . . . to celebrate again . . . the love you once knew . . . again."

Abby turned toward Mark, kissed him, and gave him the tightest squeeze she could muster.

The full haloed moon outside lit up the entire room, revealing the sharp outline on the far wall of two people making love. The two lovers were so tightly entwined that when Abby finally glanced at the shadow carved there, she saw only a single silhouetted image, and felt a supreme happiness she had not known since one afternoon, long ago, on Park Island.

Chapter Twenty-Five
The Seventh Messenger

As Mark and Abby slept, a lone figure in a flowing white robe made his way silently down a narrow, back hall beneath the Hotel. With one hand, he swept away cobwebs; with the other, he pulled a key from within his robe and unlocked a narrow door, the only exit from a carefully disguised dead end. The door opened onto a narrow landing with stairs that dropped into a black void below. As the robed figure began his descent, he lit a small candle. It flickered a moment, then brightened. In the dim light, the steps were barely visible. Their worn out planking sagged with his every step, and squeaked loudly as he counted each one. " . . . Ten . . . eleven . . . twelve." There was no handrail to steady him, but he needed none. The robed figure had come to his cellar sanctuary many times and knew twelve steps would bring him to the dirt floor. From the last step, a path of river pebbles led to a wooden table pushed against a rock wall. The table was partially covered in a tattered altar cloth. Near its tasseled edge, someone had embroidered, in gold thread, *"Till I Come."* In the center of the table sat a stone slab, a basalt stele. It was quite small—about twelve inches square and two inches thick. On its surface was an inscription in some alien language. Six winged figurines, about seven inches in height, stood guard around the table's edge in a protective, half-moon arc.

In the flickering light, the robed figure stood before the table and began to pray, first in whispered tones, and often so softly that only his lips moved.

Then—silence.

For a long time, he stood motionless, his face reflecting a tangle of ghastly fears supplied by his imagination. His breathing came short and fast. His right hand gripped a candle that burned halfway down its wick before he could find the courage to speak.

"Father Jezreel, Most Holy Sixth Messenger." His voice quivered and hands shook. "I am surrounded by infidels and non-believers in search of the treasure of Brother Strang's kingdom. Even now, they approach the residence of the Madam. Fearful am I that—"

A low frequency rumble bubbled from the basalt stele on the altar, then a guttural sound. "Is that you, Father Jezreel?" The robed figure leaned forward, as if leaning would improve his ability to discern a message from the sound, a sound that soon became a pulsating hum, so powerful that waves of air set in motion by its force involuntarily rocked the robed figure back and forth in sympathetic rhythm to its pulses.

The robed figure was suddenly aware that the ambient temperature in the room had fallen dramatically. He shivered and pulled his robe tightly about him. "I have read the Flying Roll, which you prepared, but I can find no answer for this most serious matter among all the sermons of the previous messengers."

The air in the room began to move once again, slowly increasing its physical intensity. Dust particles on the wooden table rose from where they lay, danced across the table, and onto the floor. The candle he held glowed even brighter, and somewhere in the distance a church bell tolled. An eagle in Pine Lake Meadow screeched its displeasure when the silence of the night was broken by the untimely tolling.

The robed figure stood transfixed in the center of the room, his palms outstretched, his eyes closed. Slowly, he lifted his arms to the ceiling. A brilliant, white light pulsed near the apogee of the domed ceiling, and hovered briefly before descending the arced wall to its midpoint. Slowly, the light began to spin around the full circumference of the room. As its velocity increased, the light became a blinding belt that lit up the crude cathedral with the brilliance of ten thousand lumens. Pulsating waves of air finally subsided, and a voice emerged from the light, a murmur at first, before finally cohering into language.

Each word was spoken softly, but with an edge that resonated around the room with the cutting brilliance of fine crystal.

> *"If thee will obey my voice and keep my covenant, thou shalt be a treasure unto me above all people; for all the earth is mine. I shall go with thee, and soon, I will give thee rest and a just reward. Now, go and keep my covenant."*

The robed figure fell prostrate before the table. "Yes, Father Jezreel, I will keep your covenant. I will use the gold to gather the House of David faithful from the four corners of the earth and lead them to Palestine. There we shall remain and await the Second Coming."

The robed figure clasped both hands over his ears in anticipation of the next event. In an instant, the brilliant light disappeared, and the low rumble began anew. The rumble pounded his eardrums with a painful intensity, the pressure stretching them like the head of a concert tympani.

With great difficulty, he struggled to his feet, his legs unstable, his balance unsure, and made his way back to the stairs. He placed a foot on the bottom-most tread, and the candle he held immediately gave up its light without so much as a single wisp of smoke. The low rumble that had shaken the room was gone and so was the oxygen. The robed figure gasped for air, his coughing echoing against the cavern's walls.

Suddenly, the cool room felt very warm. He flung open his robe as he weaved his way back to the stairs. One step at a time, he pulled himself up to the narrow landing at the top. There, holding the doorknob firmly for support, he turned it and fell into the hallway. The whole experience had left him shaken and weak. He wiped the sweat from his face with the sleeve of his open robe. Back in his room, he leaned against the door to catch his breath. Exhausted, he collapsed on the bed, his body suddenly cold and quivering.

The grandfather clock in the Hotel lobby struck three a.m.

Chapter Twenty-Six
Buckingham Palace on the Pine Lake Club

Just thinking of the Pine Lake Madam brought a smile to Abby's face. *What will she be wearing when we arrive this morning? Something outrageous, I'm sure.*

Condensation fogged her mirror. For a moment, she had forgotten about the man in her bathroom, running hot water, shaving his morning whiskers. *A man shaving in my bathroom!* It had been ten years since she'd had a man in her bathroom.

As fast as she wiped away the condensation, the fog reappeared. Quickly, Abby finished applying her mascara and touched a dab of perfume behind each ear. When Mark entered the room, towel wrapped loosely around his waist, she gave him a flirtatious smile and an equally flirty, "Good morning."

He leaned over and touched his lips to hers, then to her forehead, her neck, and—

"We have to go; Miss Park awaits!" Abby wiggled from his arms but never lost touch with his body.

"Are you sure?" Mark drifted a bit closer.

"Yes!" Abby laughed and gave him a teasing push away. Without losing eye contact, she picked up her wide brim straw hat, the one with the blaze of fall colors for a hatband, and placed it on her head. Her right hand gave it a finishing tap. "I'll go down and get a table in the dining room and wait for you." Abby laughed again as she opened the door. "You will be fashionably late for breakfast and offer apologies when you arrive." And with an exaggerated bow of her head, she said, "I will accept, of course."

Both laughed as she gently closed the door.

Soon, they were enjoying English muffins and a fruit plate for two in the dining room. Filled with anticipation for the day ahead, they finished breakfast in record time.

"I know we're in a hurry, so I'll sacrifice coffee . . . for now," Mark said, as he pulled Abby's chair out from the table. "Maybe the Madam will offer coffee when we arrive."

"For you, waiting will be a real sacrifice; I know how much you like coffee first thing in the morning." As Abby grabbed Mark's arm, she gave it a tug and asked, "Did you hear church bells in the middle of the night?"

"No, you must have been dreaming. Church bells?"

"Yes, I heard them clearly, and loudly."

"Look around," Mark said, with a sweeping motion of his arm. "If there was such a noise in the middle of the night, this entire room would be abuzz with conversation about it."

"I guess you're right. Just a dream." Abby decided not to give it another thought. *But, it seemed so real. I can't believe no one else heard the sound.*

As they walked briskly across the Hotel lobby, Abby stopped just long enough to pick up an ashtray from a table near the door. "I'll need this later." She slipped the ashtray into her purse.

Mark raised an eyebrow, perplexed by her pilfering. "You don't smoke," he said, "or do you?"

"No, silly. At least, never in public." She pretended to pull a cigarette from her lips and blow smoke into the air. "But, I know someone who does." She winked. "You'll see."

Mark pulled his jacket tight and zipped it up to shield himself from the brisk morning breeze. "Tell me more about Miss Phoebe Cooke, aka, the Pine Lake Madam."

As they walked along Ferry Avenue in front of the Hotel, Abby explained that Miss Cooke, a spinster, proudly proclaimed her virginity at every opportunity. "She also made clear, in no uncertain terms, that she enjoyed quite the bohemian life in another time."

"How could she be a virgin and enjoy 'the bohemian life?'" Mark asked. "I'm confused."

"You'll be more than a little confused after you meet her. I was never able to find anyone in the Club who could speak with authority about her past." Abby was quiet a moment. "Or, if they knew about her past, they were unwilling to speak of it."

"Sounds like she was intentionally misleading," Mark said. "And that makes this reporter ready to ask even more questions."

"Now, you must promise not to get too personal with your questions. She might choose to give you a silent, frosty stare. It's legendary." She gave Mark her version of a frosty stare.

"Hmmm . . . maybe there's a feature story here," Mark said, as they turned the corner on the lower terrace. "Whoa, is that her cottage?"

"Now you know why Club members call it 'Buckingham Palace on Pine Lake.' You'll see; it *is* different." Abby whipped off her hat and let it flap along the picket fence surrounding the cottage. "The pickets have been painted alternating colors of crimson and gold for as long as I can remember."

"The colors definitely give the place a royal touch." Mark raised an eyebrow. "This lowly newspaper editor is speechless."

"And the architecture? It's in a class all its own, yes?" Abby teased. "A combination of English Baroque and Queen Anne finished off with, shall we say, an overabundance of gingerbread trim."

Mark recovered enough to say, "It's certainly in a class by itself."

"Mark, no need to be polite." Abby shook her head. "Say it."

"All right then, it's a Halloween nightmare. I . . . what the hell?" Symphonic music filled the air, blaring from speakers hidden in trees and bushes surrounding the cottage, and so loud it made conversation impossible. Finally, someone turned the volume down, and Mark caught his breath. "Well, ahem, isn't that the Overture from Handel's Royal Fireworks?" He tried to whistle a bit of the music.

"Very good." Abby was impressed.

"This is definitely feature material." Mark cocked an ear to one side. "This lady has an obsession."

"Oh, it's not so bad," Abby said. "Besides, it only plays five minutes daily, according to an agreement she reached with Club management." As if on cue, the music suddenly stopped. "What'd I tell you?"

"I guess not everyone is a royal fan." Mark chuckled.

"Some in the Club are convinced she has Royal family connections," Abby said, "but you and I know otherwise, unless you count King Strang as royalty."

"I don't," Mark said, with a grin.

"Well, don't be surprised to see a table in the front parlor set for formal tea. She says it's there 'just in case the Queen stops by.'"

"Are you kidding? She's *obsessed* with the Royal family." Mark stepped through the gate and held it for Abby.

"Be forewarned; she also can be coarse and raw," Abby said."

"I assure you, Abby, I'm not easily shocked."

And there she was, standing at the front window, assessing her guests as they stepped hand in hand up the cobblestone walk.

"Even from this distance, I can see she's wearing the boldest colors you've ever seen." *But something's missing from her distinctive aura*, Abby thought. "Do you see a cigarette?" she asked Mark. "She's always been a chain smoker of the first order, never seen in public without her precious Benson & Hedges. She never seemed to have an ashtray handy when it was needed most."

"What do you mean, 'needed most?'"

"Visitors learned to bring an ashtray along or be willing to stick out a bare palm to catch the ash." She held out her left hand and tapped the ash from an invisible cigarette into it.

Mark gave her a disbelieving look. "All I see is a woman who uses too much make-up around her very large eyes."

"That's to enhance her smoky, sultry look." Abby tossed her head back and batted her eyes slowly.

At that moment, the door opened, and the Madam twirled over the threshold just like Abby had seen Loretta Young do countless times when opening her television show. She wore a summer party dress with puffy sleeves and a tight waist, *no doubt*, Abby thought, *to show off her hour-glass figure.*

Abby extended the Hotel ashtray immediately, only to be met with an icy, "What's *that* for?" The Madam didn't wait for an answer. "I haven't had one now in nearly five years. Not that I don't want one; I simply have not had one. And your mother is to blame." She rolled her eyes. "Your mother came over one day, found me sick in the bed, not breathing very well, and waiting for the doctor. Well, believe it or not, your mother—a woman who did *not* smoke at all—pulled up a chair by the bed, and lit up two cigarettes. 'Now, Phoebe,' she said, 'we're going to smoke this last one together.' Your mother coughed every time she inhaled, and I listened to her cough as long as I could stand it. Finally, I asked, 'Frances, why are you doing this?' She told me, 'Sunrise at Pine Lake is as good as it gets, Phoebe, and I want you to see a few more.' At that moment, I knew my smoking days were over."

The Madam extended her arm and, with a flick of her wrist, she snuffed out her last imaginary cigarette in Abby's purloined ashtray. An exaggerated cough followed before she said, "Well, don't just stand there; come in!" She gave Abby an affectionate kiss on the forehead. "Abby, you darling girl, so good to see you!"

Abby stifled a gasp as the door shut behind them. The air was heavy with the fragrance of perfume, so heavy and sweet she found it hard to breathe.

"It's English Lavender," the Madam said, "my favorite. Well, perhaps not always. It became my favorite when I discovered it drives out those disgusting spiders if you spray enough around. Have a seat in the parlor. You'll see crumpets waiting for you there. I'll be right back with a freshly brewed kettle."

"They look like small pancakes," Mark whispered to Abby. "And what's that on top?" He wrinkled his nose. "Do you think she would be offended if I asked for a doughnut?"

"Shhhhh. She'll hear you."

"Jam and butter on top!" Mark said, as he bit into the nearest cake. "Crunchy on the outside, spongy on the inside." He grinned broadly. "Mmmmmm . . . has a real snap to it."

"You think it has snap now; wait'll you try it with my tea," the Madam said, as she walked into the parlor with a fresh pot of tea. "You'll have the best sex of your life."

Mark choked on the small cake, coughed hard, and his eyes watered. Finally, he managed to get the whole thing down.

With her back to Mark, the Madam mouthed to Abby, "And you will, too." She gave Abby a broad smile and winked. "How long has it been, Abby? I don't think I've seen you since you were a little girl. You used to come over looking for free candy, and you always had that dog with you. Oh, of course, not a real dog, just Tige. Buster Brown's dog, wasn't it? And you drove me crazy singing that stupid jingle over and over, 'Hi, this is my dog Tige. He lives in a shoe. I'm Buster Brown. I'm a heel, too.'"

"No, no, 'look for me in there, too,'" Abby said.

"See, I told you it drove me crazy." With an abrupt about face, she placed her hands on her hips. "All right, who is this good looking man?"

"Oh, I'm sorry. Miss Cooke, this is Mark Day, editor of the *Clarion* and a very good friend."

"A *very* good friend?" She repeated each word slowly. "A . . . very . . . good . . . friend." And she gave Abby another wink. "I see . . ."

Abby, embarrassed, jumped in to explain the reason for their visit and to make sure the Madam knew Julius had suggested they talk with her. His suggestion didn't seem to make any impression. Finally, they asked the Madam directly, if she would be interested in helping them find the rumored gold of King Strang's Royal Treasury."

"Royal Treasury?" Abby had never seen bedroom eyes glow so brightly. "Of course, I'll help," she said, without a moment's hesitation.

"Wonderful," Abby said.

"Now, if you're wondering why I'm not sitting, it's because this waist is so tight I'm afraid I'll pop the snaps open if I sit." She inhaled deeply. "I can't hold it forever." With a red face, she exhaled just as fully as she had inhaled. Her voice slowed as she strained for the words at the end of her breath, "What else . . . did Julius . . . tell you?"

"If you are asking if he told us of your personal family history, yes, he did, but don't worry, the details are safe with us. No one will ever know."

"Abby, I'm grateful for that, but I suspect Julius did not tell you the details of his own life, did he?

Neither of them said a word.

"I didn't think so. Well, you need to know Julius has more than a passing interest in your search. You didn't give him any hint of where the gold might be, did you?"

"Well, no. We haven't found it." Abby exchanged an anxious glance with Mark.

"Good. You must not trust Julius with any critical information. I'll tell you why. Julius Mooney and his family migrated to this area about thirty years ago. He must have been about twenty years of age. They were part of a group of Southerners—from Alabama, I think—persuaded to move north and join the House of David, a religious colony out there on High Island."

"Damn!" Mark put down the second small cake he was about to eat. "Was Julius a member of that group?"

"Well, yes, he had to be if he was to live there. It's a terrible tale. The group's leader, one Pernell Richards, insisted that Holy Scriptures made him responsible for shagging all the virgins in the colony before they could be married. In other words, he had a biblical justification for raping the island's young girls. But, of course, he was not the first man in history to get creative in his lust for young maidens."

How many times have religious leaders justified their depraved actions by invoking Holy Scriptures or some sort of Divine intervention? Abby thought. *Truly disgusting.*

"Richards came a long way for an uneducated broom maker, don't you think?" The Madam gave them a wry smile. "The only real talent he had was for twisting straw into brooms and twisting Scripture to keep his flock in line." She shook her head. "Someone should've used a broom on him." She wrinkled up her nose and pretended to be sweeping something disgusting from near her feet.

"How did our future Hotel manager, the young Julius Mooney, get along with Richards?" Mark asked.

"Not well. Not well at all." She put the imaginary broom next to a floral, wingback chair, and took a seat. "One night, I was told, Julius overheard a 'cleansing of the blood' ritual, as Richards called it. I never knew the details. The way I was told, Julius left the group not long after and came here. But, he was on High Island long enough to hear all the rumors about Strang's buried gold. Many, including Julius, believed the old king buried his gold on High Island." The Madam straightened her skirt and picked imaginary lint from it. "Julius looked everywhere. He was determined to find it and restore Strang's kingdom."

"Strang's kingdom?" Abby asked. She wasn't sure she had heard correctly. "Not Richards'?"

"No, no. He hated Richards for what he had done," the Madam said. "But, I'll tell you this: if Pernell Richards couldn't find the gold, it wasn't likely Julius Mooney could either." With a smile and a wink, she added, "Richards, after all, was the all-powerful Seventh Messenger."

Mark jumped to his feet. "Excuse me, did you say 'Seventh Messenger?' Pernell Richards?"

"Oh yes, but you couldn't have known him. You were just a baby, Abby, too."

"But, we know *of* him." Mark shook his head. "This is not good." He slumped in his chair. "Not good at all."

"No need to be concerned," the Madam said. "Pernell is long gone. Unfortunately, he died before they could convict him of anything. The colony disappeared altogether in the mid-twenties, but I've heard some members of the H-O-D can still be found downstate." She reached for the nearby pot. "More tea?" and filled her cup.

Abby sighed deeply. "Well, someone is claiming the title today."

"Really?"

"Yes, I've received several warnings—"

"Threats, really," Mark interrupted. "Explicit threats."

"Okay, threats from someone pretending to be the Seventh Messenger," Abby said. "From someone trying hard to persuade us to abandon our search for Strang's gold."

"Oh, shit. Pardon my French," the Madam said, jumping up. "I don't know who's behind the threats you've received, but I can tell you this: Julius has become increasingly obsessed with his search for Strang's gold since his wife, Henrietta, died a few years ago. He brings it up every time he sees me. Finding the gold and re-establishing Strang's kingdom on Beaver would give his life a meaning, which he feels has eluded him." She plopped in the middle of a crimson velvet settee. "I hope he is not involved in these warnings."

"I've never seen you so serious," Abby said.

"I've never been so serious, Abby. I'm very concerned about Mooney's emotional state. I passed him in the Hotel garden last week and he was staring at the lake, uttering words I've never heard—foreign, you know, definitely not English—and when I spoke to him, it was as if he didn't hear me." She shook her head. "Sad."

Abby looked at Mark. "Maybe the rumors about him wandering around East Park at night in a trance were true?"

"I hope you didn't lead him to believe you've found the gold, or indeed, that you're even close to finding it. That would *not* be good. As soon as you were out of his sight, he'd be searching high and low."

The Madam looked into their faces. "Oh, no, you *did* tell him too much." She tip-toed away from them as if trying to avoid stepping into something unpleasant.

"Mrs. Vandivare suggested we talk with Julius," Abby said, "to see if there was anything in the records of the first caretaker, John Johnson, any information at all that could help. When we told him our search had hit a brick wall, and that's all we said, he sent us here to ask if you have any of Johnson's records from the early days."

"You've probably told him too much." The Madam tip-toed back to them, holding her nose all the way. "I hope you weren't taken in by that fake Alabama drawl of his. Don't be fooled by that 'aw shucks' persona. He just puts that on when he is trying to make a fool of you. I suspect he's looking where you've looked right now." The Madam checked the bottom of her shoes as if looking for something that ought not to be there. "But you came with a specific question, didn't you?"

"Yes." Abby struggled to focus on the current conversation while tugging at the back of her mind, trying to think of anything she might have revealed to Julius in her naiveté. She told the story of Strang's diary, how he placed three clues for Elvira's children inside, with instructions to present one to each of his children on their twelfth birthdays. The Madam's eyes flashed when Abby spoke of how Mary Perce had planned to move the gold, and how, after Strang's death, she had put a single clue to the location of Strang's gold in his diary, a clue that would lead her daughter to the gold. "But, the diary and Mary's clue have been lost."

"Mary Perce, you never cease to amaze me," the Madam said, looking up to the ceiling. "What a woman! You *are* extraordinary, just like me," she said, laughing.

"Do you have any of James Strang's correspondence?" Abby asked. "If so, there may be an overlooked diary there, too."

"The king's correspondence!" The Madam slapped the arm of the settee. "That box in the attic!" With a burst of energy, the Madam bolted down the hall to a photo of the Queen Mother's 1923 wedding. She removed the photo from the wall, held it close to her breast for a moment, then placed it on a nearby table. The wall, however, was not a wall; rather, a door, and behind the door, a narrow stairway climbed steeply to her attic.

The Madam led the way, with Abby and Mark close behind. At the top of the stairs, she fumbled for a wall switch that illuminated the entire attic in a flood of light. She wasted no time in moving boxes around, reading aloud the label on each. "Mosaic Egg . . . The Octagon Library." She picked up a third and blew a light covering of dust from it. On its side, the initials, "ER."

"Elizabetha Regina," Abby said.

"Elizabeth the Queen," the Madam said, with a royal air, as if announcing the arrival of the Queen herself.

Trinkets of all kinds were spread all over the attic. A clutch of Wedgwood jasperware was displayed on an ebonized game table; a vitrine filled with mouse figures sat in a corner; and a box, titled, "wreath made of human hair," was on the floor in front of Abby. The Madam tried to give it to Abby, but Abby shook her head vigorously when she read the label. The Madam smiled, enjoying Abby's shocked expression, and slid the box out of sight as she continued to push her way through the cluttered space.

"Where are those boxes?" the Madam asked aloud. And then, she froze. "Ah, here, *here* they are!" She glowed with excitement as she picked up the first box and held it high as if it were the Holy Grail. "All of my notes from the 1952 coronation are in *this* box." She spread a white linen cloth across the floor, smoothing out each wrinkle she found. Next, she placed her coronation box in the middle of the cloth with all the care and precision of one of the Queen's Beefeater guards. As a final gesture of royal fealty, the Madam covered the box with a second white linen cloth, and only then did she stop a moment to take a breath. She turned around abruptly without looking, bumped another box, and nearly knocked it over.

Abby grabbed the box before it fell and noticed someone had dashed off a label on its top that read, "Strang's Stuff." She held it at arm's length and blew away several layers of dust which induced a coughing fit in all three of them.

"I never cared a shit about his stuff," the Madam said. "I was told Grandmother Elvira brought it from Beaver when she came to Cross Village after the murder, and she gave it to my mother. I do remember my mother saying 'there is absolutely *nothing* of interest in this box.' So, I never opened it." She shrugged her shoulders and turned her attention back to her linen covered royal collection.

"Well, maybe it's time to take a look." Abby couldn't hide her excitement. "I volunteer to be the first to open it." Her fingers trembling, Abby began rifling through its numerous folders. "Somewhere in here, I feel it, is an answer to this mystery." Near the middle of the box, Abby discovered a folder labeled "US Patent Office." When she pulled it out, a yellowed scrap of paper, which had stuck to the back of the folder, came loose, and fell toward the attic floor. Abby grabbed it in mid-air. "A handwritten message, clearly not from the Patent Office. Listen: 'To Charles, Clement, and my dearest Eva, a clue I give to each of thee. Open the clue on thy twelfth birthday only. To Mary, I pray thee will forgive my—'"

"Yes?" Mark's voice was rising in anticipation. "What else? What else?"

"That's all," Abby said. "Whatever followed is missing, torn away, I suspect, by someone intent on keeping the contents secret."

The Madam murmured something as she pulled out another box from the back of the file.

"Did you say something?" Abby asked. *She knows more about this Strang business than she lets on.*

The Madam ignored Abby's question. She held out a plain wooden box with no markings, just a single leather strap and a small key

lock to secure its top. "Maybe something in here will help. Mmmmmm .
. . locked tight."

Chapter Twenty-Seven
"Catch a Gleam of Glory Bright"

W e don't have time to be delicate." Mark looked around, picked up a broken table leg, and gave the lock a sharp whack. The simple lock, its leather fasteners softened by time, gave way easily. Mark reached inside, and grabbed a thick packet of correspondence. "Looks like a dead end. Here's one labeled, 'Meteorological Journal, Records of December 1850 to July 1851.'"

Abby picked up the rest of the correspondence. "Mmmm . . . an interesting title, 'Fishes of Beaver Island Harbour,' and look at this, 'Vibrations of Mercury in the Thermometer.'"

"I know something about that," the Madam said. "My grandmother told me, Mary recorded her scientific observations for the Smithsonian. They asked her to travel to all the islands in the archipelago and record anything and everything related to climate. I guess she did." The Madam pulled out an official looking piece of paper with an engraved masthead. "Take a look at this," she said, and handed Mark a letter from the US Patent Office.

"Looks authentic," Mark said, "dated October 1, 1852." And he began to read.

> *'Honorable Mr. James J. Strang: We are pleased to record your invention among the records of creative innovations in the US Patent Office.'"*

Mark stopped reading and glanced down the page. "Mostly bureaucratic boiler plate, nothing important."

The Madam gave Abby several more pages. "These must go with the Patent Office letter."

"Indeed," Abby said. "It appears we have the original patent application." She continued flipping the pages. "And the next several pages describe some kind of lock."

"You don't think I just broke Strang's lock, do you?" Mark asked.

"No, but Rube Goldberg would have been proud of *this* one," Abby said, as she pointed to a single page of intricate mechanical drawings.

Mark took the drawings and quickly scanned them. "These drawings make no sense whatsoever."

Slowly, Abby returned each page to the correspondence box. "Worse, there's no diary here, no sign of a clue that might lead us to our objective." She fingered each file, and was straightening several to make sure they would fit inside, when her eyes fell on a small notebook laying on its side near the back, almost completely hidden by the correspondence files. "Oh, my God!" Her hands were suddenly shaking. "Mark, I think this is it!" With both hands holding tight, she pulled out a leather bound notebook, its spine peeling away. Edges of some pages, she noted, had already begun to crumble and flake away. "This just *has* to be Strang's diary," she said, beaming. The cover crackled with age as she opened the book. "I hope, I hope . . ." she whispered, as she quickly flipped to the inside, back pages. "But, there's nothing in the back, nothing where Mary found the original clues meant for Elvira's children." The excitement on her face was suddenly replaced by abject disappointment. "There's nothing here." She collapsed cross-legged on the floor, diary in her lap. "Nothing here." Her voice dropped like a lead balloon.

Abby offered the diary, open to the first page, to Mark who began turning each page quickly. "Looks like undecipherable scribbling to me," Mark said, and began reading aloud.

"'*NIIF.OwUb.I.PEIN.I.IETb.FIYI:*'" He repeated the line several times. Finally, he looked up at Abby, and his eyes brightened. "But it's not undecipherable, it's simply one man's coded language."

"What do you mean?" Mary asked. "Do you really see something?"

"Maybe," Mark said, as he put his finger on each word of the first line. "If that's a complete sentence, Strang may have put a period at the end of each word and a colon at the end of the sentence. The capital letter "I" could be a vowel of some sort, but who knows?"

"Who knows, indeed?" Abby couldn't hide her skepticism. "How can you be so sure; how can you be so confident?"

"All the boys in my neighborhood pretended to be spies for the Army when we were growing up and dreamed up all sorts of ways to send coded messages to each other." He smiled and gave Abby a wink. "Our parents never figured out what we were saying about them."

"So, what does James Strang say, Mr. Morse?"

"So far, nothing is legible to me, except the author's name on the title page."

"You can translate his writing later," Abby said. "Right now, we need to find evidence of something in his book that can be attributed to Mary Perce, not James Strang."

Mark shook the book as if expecting a note from Mary Perce to fall from its leaves. A few speckles of dust from the deteriorating binding drifted to the floor.

"No, no," Abby said. "That's no way to handle a book of one hundred plus years. Let me see it." She reached over, checked its spine, and closed the book slowly with both hands. Starting on page one, she began turning pages, one at a time. "Nothing but a few stains from, umm . . . unknown sources." When she came to page twelve, she suddenly stopped, and turned to the Madam. "Do you have a magnifying glass?" she asked.

"Yes, of course." And from under one of the linen sheets, the Madam handed Abby a large reading glass. "This one has the Queen's Royal Seal carved on its ivory handle."

Abby didn't look up. Her eyes were already focused on the alphabetic letters magnified under the glass.

"Oh, my," Abby said. Abby's nose nearly touched page twelve as she examined it closely. "Oh, my." She looked up at Mark, and with a broad smile, spelled out, "N-e-t-t-i-e."

"What was that?" Mark looked over her shoulder and squinted at page twelve. "I don't see anything."

"Mary Perce could have been a member of your boy's club spy ring," Abby said, "and she wouldn't need a decoder ring, not even the one from Captain Midnight."

"Abby, stop teasing," Mark said. "What are you talking about?"

"I'm talking about a very clever woman. Take a look." She handed the magnifying glass to Mark. "You'll see that every letter James Strang wrote was written on the ruled lines of each page. Look closely, and you'll notice that someone has underlined selected letters on this page and the next.

"FIYI.NJeb.I.tPtIIq.I.yiYIe"

"But, *all* of the letters are written on ruled lines." Mark said. "Wait, I see it, a heavier line under some letters, darker than the rest."

"That's it!"

"I don't want to disappoint you," Mark said, "but couldn't Strang have done it himself?"

"No, I don't think so." Abby's voice exuded the confidence of a person certain of her deductive powers. "Why would Strang go to the trouble of a complex cypher language if all he was going to do in the end was create a message with underlined letters?" Mark and the Madam listened in silence. "Answer: He wouldn't. But I think Mary used James Strang's own letters to create a message, a clue meant for one person— her daughter, Nettie."

"Why are you smiling, so?" Mark asked.

"I think she chose this method of creating a message to mock her husband's attempts at secrecy and deception."

"Perhaps…" Mark looked closely at the text while the Madam picked up the magnifying glass and began reading.

"N-e-t-t-i-e," she read in a bouncing soprano voice. "Nettie. That's what it says, sure as the hose in your pants, uh, I'm sorry, I mean, the nose on your face."

Abby turned Cardinal red. She couldn't believe the Madam would make such an indiscreet remark. She looked at Mark through the fingers of one hand and attempted to hide her glowing face.

Mark ignored the Madam's comment. "Let me see that glass." His eyes suddenly widened, and he whispered loudly, "I can't believe it! N-e-t-t-i-e . . . there it is."

"Pay dirt," the Madam said.

Mark lifted Abby off her feet, held her as high as he could and gushed, "My little genius."

"Of course, I am." She gave him a wink, and handed him her pencil and paper. "Write down the letters as I call them out, and when I get to the end of a line, I'll give you a signal. If Mary tried to imitate her husband's rhyme, we'll know when it's time to begin a new line."

For the next few minutes, Mark wrote, as Abby, with assistance from the magnifying glass, transcribed the message Mary had underlined in Strang's personal diary. When Abby could find no more underlined letters, she stopped. "That's it. The message, or clue, ends on the bottom of page sixteen."

Mark began to read aloud.

"God, help thee scale the utmost heights
And catch a gleam of glory bright.
Ever higher, do not falter
Heav'n waits 'neath High's great altar."

"So, the Indians were right after all," Abby said. "High Island, it is."

"I'm shocked," Mark said, "because that island has been combed from one end to the other."

"Has anyone looked under 'High's great altar?'" Abby asked. "This clue makes clear we have to climb 'the utmost heights.'"

"Well, the high dunes are on the west," Mark said. "And that's where most people have searched in the past. I've heard there's an even higher point on the east side, but it's in the Darkening Mist. You saw it yourself when we went out to Gull the first time. No one goes there."

Nodding, Abby said, "Well, maybe it's time for someone, like us, to go there and solve that mystery, too." Her voice was determined. "Besides, I'm tired of people warning me not to go into the Darkening Mist."

"That's my girl," the Madam said, closing the diary with a snap that sent a cloud of dust into the attic air.

"Careful, careful," Abby said. "It's a hundred years old!"

Chapter Twenty-Eight
Best Laid Plans

T his place feels eerie to me," Mark said, as he squeezed *Holly-Hoo* through the narrow entrance to the small harbor on High Island's east side. "The water in the bay, calm as a swamp, and the sky . . . impossible to see through this blue mist. And why does the air feel so clammy? Too early in the day for humidity of any kind."

Abby and Mark had spent the night in Mackinac in order to get an early start on their long awaited day of discovery. But Abby knew the day held as much opportunity for disaster as discovery. "After all," she told Mark at breakfast, "the Seventh Messenger seems to be walking in our footprints wherever we go."

"Let's hope we don't meet him today," Mark said.

Abby pointed to a rock just beneath the surface. "Hard to port!"

"I see it." Mark steered *Holly-Hoo* around the submerged rock and slowly maneuvered her closer to shore.

"Look, someone's dinghy." Abby pointed to a tiny wooden boat not far from the beach. "I think it's tied to that bottle, some sort of makeshift buoy."

"Yes, but that dinghy means they'll be coming back. They'll tie up a much larger boat to their buoy, take their dinghy to the beach—and come looking for us." Mark slowly circled the little buoy with *Holly-Hoo*.

"But, we don't plan to be here long. Let's 'borrow' their buoy and take a chance on getting back before the person who owns it returns." Abby was surprised at her own boldness. "Are you willing to take a chance?" Suddenly, she was no longer risk adverse.

"Sure, m' lady. I'm with you." Grabbing his gaff, Mark snagged the partially submerged bottle and tied *Holly-Hoo* to it. "I don't think much of this buoy; it's half full of water."

With the 'borrowed' dinghy, they quickly made the beach. Before they left the dinghy, Mark picked up two lines someone had stowed under a seat. "I don't think we'll need these, but we might as well 'borrow' them, too."

Abby slung a back pack over her shoulder, and double checked the only supplies she'd packed for their excursion: two sandwiches, one apple, and a flashlight.

"Don't you have a change of shoes with you?" Mark asked. "Or are you going to wear those deck shoes all the way to the top? They'll be full of sand."

"I'll be fine," Abby said. "Besides, they're all I have. "Let's go!" And they stepped off with Abby in the lead. "Over here," she waved a moment later, and aimed for a winding little trace ahead of them. "It's the only thing that looks even remotely like a path." The way felt soft to her feet, covered as it was in layers and layers of slowly decaying pine needles. On either side, the brush was thick, and densely matted with countless cycles of autumn death and spring rebirth. Suddenly, they stepped into a clearing with three large mounds in the middle, surrounded by a carpet of lengthy sedge grass beaten down by rain.

"This is not the path we should take to the top," Abby said. She didn't move.

"What's the matter? Why not?" Mark stepped beside her and put his backpack down.

"Take a look. Over there." She pointed to several malformed and oddly shaped trees. "Did you notice they're all about the same size?"

"What does that have to do with—" Mark started off in the direction of the trees, but Abby stopped him.

"They're Council trees, planted by Indians when they were saplings to guard the burial site as they matured." Abby took a couple of steps backward.

"Cemetery, eh?" Mark picked up his backpack again. "Let's take a closer look."

"No!" Abby grabbed his shirttail and held tight. "Don't you see? All around us, a circle of trees."

"Yes, crooked ones at that," Mark said.

"Not by accident." Abby said. "Those trees were intentionally bent that way, tied by the Indians, so they would grow crooked and discourage lumbermen from taking them."

"It appears to have worked," Mark said. "What do we do now?"

"It was said the Indians often chose one—perhaps two—of their tribe to live nearby and guard their 'Spirit House." Abby slowly scanned the forest surrounding the circle of trees.

"Surely there are none here today," Mark said, as he glanced over each shoulder.

"We're not staying to find out," Abby said. "Let's go that way." She pointed to a path leading toward a much steeper incline.

Ten minutes later, Mark raised his arm and stopped. "What do you make of that?" He pointed to a spot straight ahead that appeared to be the remains of a small campsite. "Not another burial ground, I hope."

"Hardly, but it is somebody's campsite." As they approached, Abby felt a sharp stick underfoot and looked down to see the shredded remains of tent canvas and support poles.

Mark shook several layers of sand from a large scrap of tenting. "I don't think anyone has slept here in quite some time." He bent over and pulled up a couple of tent stakes. "These wooden stakes look like something you might buy in an Army surplus store."

"Look at this, a cot, maybe, and what's this . . . a journal?" From under the cot, Abby retrieved a small notebook, curled at all edges from exposure. At first, it appeared blank, but several pages into it, she stopped to read a page, titled, "*Ruminations of Sgt. C. J. Strang.*"

Mark dropped the tent stakes and came over to take a closer look. "Maybe it's the journal he wanted me to publish."

"Regardless, he was *here!*" Abby began thumbing through the pages as fast as she could. "Somehow, he figured out the gold was on High Island."

"So, what does he say?" Mark looked over Abby's shoulder.

"The first page is titled, '*Search for Great-Grandfather's Gold.*'" She leafed through several pages. "He comments about the humidity he endures in the mist. He doesn't like it, and what's this?" Abby scanned the next page as fast as she could. "I think you'll find this of interest. He writes, '*Charles and Eva concluded Old Pine clue was of no use. They formed partnership to search Gull. Clement pulled out.*'"

"Don't stop." Mark sat down on what was left of the old cot, and it immediately collapsed. He jumped to his feet, wiping sand from his sweaty legs as he stood. "Don't worry about me; read on."

Abby, in a somber tone, continued. "Mostly a few phrases strung together, some of it incoherent. '*Disappointed but will persevere.*' At the bottom of the page, there's this: '*Charles and Eva never found gold. They searched entire length of Gull. Conclusion: gold does not exist— never did. Charles and Eva, confounded by father's true intent in leaving clues. If great-grandfather thought his progeny interested in his line of work, he was mistaken. Not one of us . . .*'"

"Yes? Go on. 'Not one of us'. . . what?"

"I don't know. He just stopped writing." Abby turned several more blank pages.

"You mean, that's all there is?"

"Wait, near the back pages, he starts again," Abby said. "'*Back from the war, finally. Praise God. Indian in Cross Village says ancestor offered a golden sacrifice to the gods on the highest point of High.*'" She flipped the page. "'*Sacrifice made in no man's land. Indians say no one has searched no man's land and returned. Indians believe gold was offered in good faith, and accepted. Not a good idea to take the offering back.'"* Abby put her finger on the next sentence and looked up at Mark, astonishment written all over her face.

"Why did you stop reading?" he asked.

"He says, quote, *'I tried to convince Mrs. Vandivare the gold was buried on High but she did not believe me,'* end quote." Abby punctuated each word in the sentence with her finger as she read it, and exhaled deeply. "She knew the truth but didn't believe it. John Johnson, the early caretaker told her the truth." Abby was quiet as she reflected on the story Blue Hair told of Johnson's final visit at the death bed of Mary Perce.

Mark gently took the journal from Abby's hands. He read the sergeant's words to himself for a moment. "It's a very sad ending," Mark said finally. "And here, on the last page, he underlined every word several times."

"What does he say?" Abby asked, softly.

"'But I am here,'" Mark read. *"'Audie Murphy is not the only one to go to hell and back. I did it, too, and he got all the glory. Well, he can have the glory, I just want the gold.'* Every word is underlined."

"Such sad desperation," Abby said. *"*Another tormented soul from that horrible war."

"That last entry is dated August 1, 1951." Mark scratched his chin. "What could have happened to him?"

"An Army veteran is not likely to leave his gear behind, is he?" Abby asked, as she picked up a tin cup, hatchet, and a roll of butcher twine.

"No. My guess is something—or someone—interrupted the sergeant's search." Mark scanned the full circumference of the clearing as if he expected to catch someone spying on them. "We best keep an eye out for other seekers of the king's gold."

"I think you've read too many Jules Verne tales." She put the diary in her backpack. "Still, let's get to the top of the hill, now!" She jumped to her feet. "Summit, ho!"

At the top, Abby surveyed an unimpressive landscape. "Just large rocks and boulders scattered about and—wow, look at this—the ground is wet everywhere. Do you see anything that looks like an altar?"

"Here's a flat piece of rock," Mark said. "Could have been part of an altar, perhaps the altar's top, but it looks like it was just tossed aside. Now, it's half buried in damp clay."

"Maybe Mother Nature did the tossing," Abby said. "Earthquakes are rare but do occur in these parts. These stones are too heavy for any human to have moved them."

"But, an altar could have been right here!" Mark said, as he kicked a few loose stones out of his way. They bounced over the edge of a small crevice. "Abby, come over here! Bring your flashlight. Several rocks fell in, but I didn't hear them hit bottom."

"It's almost as if the earth opened over this spot during an earthquake," Abby said. "I'll tie a line around the flashlight, and you can lower it in." She had no intention of getting closer to the edge of the crevice until she knew it was safe. Besides, Mark was already there. With the full extension of her right arm, she handed Mark a light and stepped back quickly.

Mark tied the light snugly to the end of the line and lowered it. "I can't see much, but wait, there's the bottom, about fifteen or twenty feet down," Mark said, "and . . . what's this . . . that black thing, a rock?"

Suddenly emboldened, Abby crawled to the edge of the crevice. "That's no rock!" Abby said. "That's a chest—a chest fit for a king!"

"I think you're right! Now all we have to do is figure out how to get it up here with us."

"The crack is not even wide enough for *me* to slip through it," Abby said. "And even if we could, twenty feet down is a long way to drop to an uneven surface. You could break a leg."

Mark stuck his head over the crevice. "I'm not sure the chest would fit through this narrow crevice. It's about an arm's length wide, and we don't even know how much of it is buried in the sand."

"What if we made the hole wider?" Abby stood up and walked to where the "altar top," as Mark called it, was half buried, to look for something to use as a shovel.

"Wider? I suppose we could." Mark began loosening some of the rocks along the edge of the crevice and tossing them aside. "But, we have to be careful."

"You didn't pack a shovel, did you?" Abby asked. "Because that would be—"

"Arggggggggghh!" Mark let out a cry, as a gaping hole opened in the crevice. Rocks and stones, which had been held together by their own weight, fell into the hole, followed by Mark, his flashlight, and the line that held it.

"Mark!" Abby screamed, as she abandoned her fears and raced to the crevice edge. All she could see below was total darkness. "Mark!" she cried. "Are you okay? Is anything broken?" There was no response. "I have to get down there." Frantically, Abby looked around for the second line, all the while calling his name. "Mark! If the flashlight works, turn it on!"

Finally, after what seemed an eternity, she heard his voice. "I can't pull my leg out from under this rock."

"Wait! I'm coming down." She picked up the second line where Mark had left it next to his backpack.

"How? There's no ladder up there."

"Yes, but I have line." She began tying a series of knots in the line to use in the climb down into the crevice.

"No, don't come down. One of us has to stay up there. Besides, I just got my foot unstuck. My leg is bruised but . . . yowww! It's a bit sensitive but still working."

"Can you stand?"

There was a moment of silence, followed by a loud grunt. "I'm standing now," Mark said, sounding a bit out of breath. "I *need* that flashlight! I can't see any . . . wait, I found my light. It was caught in the rocks."

"Does it still work?" Abby was afraid it might be broken beyond repair.

Mark shook the light several times vigorously, smacking it in the palm of his hand. "Damn, the switch doesn't work."

"Shake it, then try the switch again." A moment later and a beam of light erupted from the crevice. "Ah, you did it!" Abby finished the knots she had been tying in the second line.

"Whew! Something smells bad down here," Mark said, "and the ground is hot and sticky."

"I don't smell anything," Abby said, peering over the ledge. "Right now, we have to figure out how to get you and the chest out of there." There was no response. "Mark?" Still no answer. "Mark? Are you okay? Say something."

"Oh, my God!" Mark said. "I don't believe it."

"What's going on? What happened?" Abby couldn't see anything in the darkness below.

"Over there." Mark pointed his light toward the clay wall. For a moment, Abby couldn't make out anything, and then she saw it. A skeleton in Army fatigues lay on the ground curled up in a fetal position. She gasped. "We didn't expect anything like this, Mark. Do you think it might be the sergeant?"

"Charles J. Strang? Yes, at least, that's what it says on these dog tags." Mark reached across the skeleton and turned the dog tags up. "There's the serial number under his name and another marking, 'T43.' Hmmmm . . . we know he got a tetanus shot in 1943."

"This pretty much answers the question about why he suddenly disappeared from Charlevoix. But how'd he get in this hole?" Abby tied the line around a large boulder and nervously played it out as she inched toward the edge of the crevice again. *I'm willing to go down there, but I don't want to. I must continue to tell myself I am willing. I am willing.*

"I think he found the gold. Perhaps it had fallen through the crack already, or maybe it fell in when he fell with it. Somehow, he got into this hole and couldn't escape."

Abby was now at the edge of the crevice. "Then, he would have starved to death." Abby shook her head. "No one should come to such an end." Abby felt unsettled about having Mark in a hole with the skeleton of one who died of starvation because he had no way out. "Mark, we can talk later; I just want you out of there."

"I want out myself. Do you have the other line close?"

"Yes." She grabbed the line. "I've already tied it off. Catch it when I throw it over the ledge and shimmy up."

"What? You want me to shimmy up? It's twenty feet . . . and I've got at least one hundred eighty pounds of muscle and bone to, uh . . . 'shimmy up' there."

"Oh, quit complaining." Abby smiled. She enjoyed showing off her skills to Mark. "You won't need to do much shimmying. This sailor knows her way around knots, you know. I've already put an Alpine Butterfly knot every four feet. Tie the end around the chest, and when you get up here, we'll pull the chest up after you."

"Don't think I'm opposed to this shimmy business," Mark said, "but let me check to see if there is any chance of finding another way out." Slowly, he began to make his way around the cavern's walls.

Abby could only watch and follow his light.

"Nothing, absolutely nothing," Mark said, as he touched the warm, dripping surface of the clay walls. "Probably hot springs trying to find a way to the surface." At that moment, he stepped on something brittle that cracked loudly at first, then gave way under his weight.

"What was that noise?" Abby asked. "Did something break?"
"Yes, unfortunately, someone's rib cage grabbed me and won't let go."

"What'd you say?" Abby called down.

"The sergeant wasn't the first to explore this hole," Mark said. Then, with a loud "Oomph!" he extricated his foot from the skeleton's rib cage. "Here's an Indian who must have fallen back in the last century."

"How do you know it's an Indian?"

"This poor fellow was wearing moccasins and a leather vest when he fell," Mark said. "That much I can see. Hard to identify anything else. The skeleton appears half buried in the clay, and he's got a well-used flint tomahawk in one hand, dull blade." Mark ran his fingers across the blade and stuck the tomahawk in his belt. "And something shiny in the other. Let's see it." He reached down and pried the skeleton's grip away. "Abby, catch this!"

"Don't throw anything !" But, Abby was too late. At that moment, a gleaming gold disk appeared in the air above the hole, just out of her reach. "Oh my God. Is that what I think it is?"

Mark caught the coin as it fell back into the hole. "Yep!" He flipped it over, then called out, "1832 gold sovereign! I think this is Mary's friend, Ogawee."

"Ogawee!" Abby whispered. "He did return." *But look what happened to him.* She stood up, coiled the line over one arm, and prepared to throw it. "Mark, I don't care to find any more lost souls. Look up and get ready." She tossed the line over the ledge. "I've got the other end around the biggest boulder I could find up here."

Mark grabbed the line and quickly tied the open end around the chest and through its two handles. With the knots Abby had tied to hold his weight, he wasted no time working his way up the line and over the ledge.

A few minutes later, they were pulling the chest upward. "Steady, very steady," Abby said, as much to keep herself calm as to keep the two of them from jerking the line and perhaps causing the chest to break loose and fall back into the cavern below.

Slowly, the chest rose until it was close enough for Mark to touch. "It's going to take both of us to pull it over the ledge," he said. "Here, hold it steady while I tie off the line on that boulder. I'll be back to help you pull." And then he was gone, with the rope over his shoulder.

Abby grabbed one corner of the chest and held it as best she could, but it moved every time Mark gave the rope a tug. "Hurry!" She was leaning over the ledge a bit and was afraid it would start swinging again. "I mean it; hurry!"

When Mark thought the line secure, he let it go, but the knot slipped. "Damn!" It slipped once more and then held. The jerk on the line was just enough to cause Abby to lose her grip and send the chest swinging back and forth, inches from their grasp.

"Abby, hold my legs, and do not let go for anything." Mark extended the full length of his upper torso into the crevice and grabbed the handle of the chest. Abby sat on his legs. With one great lift upward, Mark got the chest to the lip of the crevice. "Not . . . far . . . enough," he gasped, his knuckles turning white.

Please don't let the extra weight open an even larger hole.

Abby could see that Mark was about to lose his grip. She jumped up, leaned over the ledge, and grabbed the only visible part of the handle she could find. A knowing nod was exchanged between them, and with Abby's shout of "*Now*," they pulled it up and over the ledge.

The chest they had long sought was in front of them. "I can't . . . believe . . . we did that," Mark said, gasping for air. He rolled over, still out of breath, and grinned. "You are one strong lady."

"I've trimmed many a sail. Of course, a little adrenaline never hurt any great enterprise." Abby smiled back and attempted to roll toward Mark, but exhaustion left her flat on her back, out of breath. "I'm also covered in wet clay." For a long moment, they lay next to each other, and then, Abby let out a loud, exhilarating cry. "King Strang's *l'armoire de fer!* The king's personal iron chest."

"Doesn't look like the repository of a king's royal treasury," Mark said. "Just a plain and ugly iron chest, if you ask me."

Abby, up on her elbows, felt the edges of the chest. All seams were welded tight. "Forged, no doubt, by the king himself." Next, she examined its sides. "Lots of iron strapping." Her fingers found a round handle. "Feels like a wheel of some kind, maybe." She gave it a twist. "Hmmm . . . seems to move in both directions, clockwise and counterclockwise, with little difficulty. If it's a lock, it must be broken." She gave it another twist to demonstrate to Mark how useless it seemed.

Mark hunched over the chest and took a close look. "This little handle must be the lock," he said. "But, how does it open? I suspect there's a piano hinge inside, and the entire top opens . . . but *how* does it open?" With some effort, Mark turned the chest over. "There's even iron strapping on the bottom. But there's no hole for a key anywhere. It reminds me of a child's bank. Remember those? You put the coins in easily, but you had to smash the bank in order to get the coins out."

"Yes, and I never liked them," Abby said. She stared at the chest a long time; then suddenly, she grabbed Mark's arm. "Didn't the patent abstract we saw at the Madam's house describe a keyless lock Strang had designed?"

"Yes, but unless you know precisely how to open it, you might end up with an iron chest rusted shut forever." Mark tapped the chest on all sides as if, Abby thought, it might open magically with the right series of thumps.

"Or, we could take a sledge hammer to it," Abby said, with a gleam in her eye.

"If it's really well made," Mark said, "we'd probably end up with a broken lock and a chest with a large dent in the side."

"Okay, fine," Abby said, "let's get back and take another look at the instructions in the Madam's attic."

"I'm cool with that," Mark said. "Besides, we may have visitors soon." He pointed skyward. "Hear that?"

A small airplane engine whined overhead. "I don't see anything." Abby squinted into the mist above, which parted a moment later, and for an instant, revealed a small patch of blue sky. "There!" Abby shouted. "We're outta' here." She lifted one end of the chest. "To the boat, *now*."

Mark picked up the other end. With a considerable amount of grunting and groaning, and several stops to rest, they carried the chest down the hill as fast as the terrain and their strength would allow. Near the bottom, Mark asked, "Need another rest?"

"No, keep moving." She waved him forward. "We need to get off this island."

"Whatever you say," Mark said, picking up the pace. "I'm with you!"

They were about to step onto the beach when Abby dropped her end of the chest. "Whoa!"

"I thought you didn't need a rest," Mark said, as he set his end of the chest down.

"I think our hosts came back early." Abby pointed to another power boat at anchor, about a hundred yards from *Holly-Hoo.* "I guess their buoy was in use, and they decided to anchor elsewhere."

"No one onboard," Mark said, as he picked up his end of the chest. "They must have come ashore already."

"All the more reason to waste no time." She grabbed the handle again, and together, they practically ran for the dinghy. They almost reached the dinghy when they heard a scream from the direction of the forest. Turning, both froze as they realized it was a brown skinned man, his body covered in war paint, arms flailing wildly, and sprinting toward them.

"*Another* Indian, a *live* one this time," Mark said coolly, as if he were not as shocked as Abby.

All Abby could see was the knife he was waving and another one between his teeth. "That's not a welcoming party," she said.

Calling on all his reserve strength, Mark lifted the chest into the dinghy with one adrenaline assisted grunt. "Get in!" he shouted to Abby. "Quick!"

"It's no use, Mark! He's going with us unless—" Abby reached for an oar in the bottom of the boat. She was going to make one last desperate attempt to fend off the attacker.

Just as the Indian was about to make a flying leap for the dinghy, Abby saw a flash of light from the trees and heard a rifle shot echo off the rocks at the harbor entrance. The Indian stopped, turned, and stared toward the forest before falling forward on his face. That's when Abby noticed blood flowing from a wound between his shoulder blades. "Oh, no!" Abby started toward the fallen figure. "Mark, help me . . ."

As she stepped out of the dinghy, Mark caught her arm. "No! Abby, get back in."

"We can't leave him." She pulled off her scarf and was preparing to treat the wounded man.

"Abby, whoever fired that shot probably has the same in store for us." He grabbed her and attempted to push her into her seat.

"But Mark, he needs medical attention." Abby slipped Mark's grasp and put one leg over the gunwale.

"We have to get out of here!" Mark pulled Abby back into the dinghy, slapped oars into their oarlocks, and began pulling in long, rhythmic sweeps straight for *Holly-Hoo*.

Abby's eyes watered as she watched to see if there was any movement at all from the Indian lying on the beach. There was none. She continued to watch in silence, as their little dinghy moved farther and farther from the shore.

Once at *Holly-Hoo*, Mark strapped the chest to the water level rear transom. "Too heavy to pick up and put on deck," he said. "I don't have enough strength." He wrapped a couple of leather straps around the chest. "That'll hold it just fine for the ride back to Charlevoix."

Abby remained quiet. *People are dying over their lust for this gold. This was not supposed to happen.*

Mark touched her arm and pointed in the direction of the island. "Look." A man dressed in a bush jacket, shorts, and pith helmet emerged from the brush, rifle under his arm, and watched them a moment before disappearing into the brush. "See what I mean. He's not from around here, that's for sure." Mark quickly started *Holly-Hoo's* engine and headed for the open lake.

"But, he looks vaguely familiar," Abby said. *Where have I seen him . . . mmmm?*

For the rest of the trip, the two huddled in the cockpit in their sweatshirts and slickers, checking the chest periodically to be sure it was still attached to the transom. Abby was quiet for most of the return trip, but finally, she asked Mark, "Aren't you bothered a little bit that people are being hurt, even dying around us, around our search for that maniac's gold?"

"Any who've been hurt, or worse, would not be the first to have their judgment clouded by greed."

"But—"

"Abby, you can judge the actions of others if you want to, but it's a waste of time. You don't have the power to grant them a moral code of conduct. In the end, each of us must assume responsibility for our own decisions, and that goes for the people who have tried to interfere with our search."

"I know you're right," Abby said, "but something good, something positive *must* come from all this."

"You feel pretty strong about this, don't you?"

"Yes! This experience has taught me . . ." She gave Mark the thoughtful look of someone about to share something of themselves not usually shared. "I'm determined, I'm persistent, and I'm certainly not risk adverse, but any death in pursuit of a bucket of gold coins is an affront to any ethical man or woman. I don't want the deaths to hang over us the rest of our days like the albatross that haunted the ancient mariner. I fear the penance we would have to pay."

Mark turned toward Abby, her hair flying wildly about, occasionally covering her entire face, and pushed it under the hood of her slicker. "You astonish me, my dear; you astonish me."

"Oh, don't be astonished. I'm quite the ordinary person." Abby pulled her jacket tight and shivered. "But, I don't enjoy being near such evil as we have seen. That's all."

"Just remember, *we* didn't bring harm to anyone. The mariner, of course, that's another thing." Mark smiled and pointed to a small dot in the sky. "That's not an albatross, but it is of concern. When we get back, we're going to need a place to keep the chest safe from that guy, while we figure out how to open it."

"Don't worry," Abby said. "I know just the place—a place where only the bats will know our secret. You'll see."

Chapter Twenty-Nine
Boathouse Secrets

Rats, the *Shoodle!*" Mark said, as they cleared the channel and spotted a lone vessel in Round Lake. "Should've been hauled for the season by now."

"I'd recognize her anywhere," Abby said. "It's about the only Mackinac fishing boat left on the lake."

"Not sure why it's out, but I don't think they see us," Mark said. "Look, the captain has turned her into the wind to lower her sails."

"Too busy handling that large jib to notice us," Abby said. "Good."

Mark turned the helm toward O'Malley's Marina but stopped when Abby nudged his arm. "I have a better idea." She pointed in the direction of her family's old boathouse, a two-story hideaway tucked away at the end of Pine Lake bayou. "O'Malley's is a little too public for our cargo. No need to invite even more attention."

Mark nodded his approval and guided *Holly-Hoo* slowly into the bayou.

"Up there, on the right." In the twilight, the structure was barely visible.

"That place?" Mark squinted at the weathered building just ahead. "Looks about ready to fall in." Cedar planking on its exterior walls curled at the corners, and in some places the planking had pulled away entirely.

"Never mind. Can't you go a little faster?"

"Not unless you wanna' draw a crowd. If we create too much of a wake, we are certain to have a welcoming party."

The closer they got, the more dilapidated the boathouse appeared to Abby. "It's seen better days," she whispered. One of the cupolas on the roof was slightly askew, its four windows shattered or panes missing altogether. Two large wooden doors, each five feet wide, stood guard at the entrance to both slips. Rotten wood barely held the hinges in place. So extensive was the rot that Abby feared the doors might fall into the water when she tried to open them.

"How do you propose we get inside, my dear, other than brute force, of course?" Mark asked. "Surely, you've thought of this possible obstacle."

"Surely." She smiled and pointed to a spot on the corner of the structure. "Stop when you're alongside."

Mark reduced their speed to dead slow.

"That's it. Steady, hold steady." She leaned over the side of the boat to gain a closer examination of the cedar planking. "These planks are secured with wooden pegs instead of nails, but none of them is pounded in their full length, the better to hide a key feature of the boathouse. Watch this."

With one hand she grabbed the third plank to steady herself, and with the other hand, she reached for a brass peg, barely visible near the bottom of the plank. She smacked it with a paddle to loosen and free it from the grip of moisture and age. "I hope this works." To her surprise, she found the six-inch peg easily extracted. She held the brass peg to her lips, asking for silence, and listened. They heard no sound. No sound at all. Abby slammed her fist against the side of the boathouse. Again, nothing. Then, from inside, she heard the unmistakable screech of a rusty wheel turning. Abby smiled as she realized two large counterweights, their gravitational weight released, were pulling the twin doors inward.

"Very clever," Mark said. "Any other secrets here?"

"No. My father designed it so family members could enter the boathouse at any time of day or night. He didn't like the idea of an open slip any time—thieves, you know. I love to think of all the personal inventions he brought into our lives."

Dry hinges and pulleys made a great creaking noise. The whole structure acted like a giant sounding board, converting the noise of the opening doors into energy that reverberated across the water in all directions.

"If that doesn't wake the dead around here, nothing will." Mark looked around to determine if any of the neighbors had become curious. Seeing no one, he lined up *Holly-Hoo* with the open bay, then gave the engine a short burst of reverse thrust, before shutting it off and letting the boat glide silently into the slip, which it did with just a few inches to spare on each side. "Now, how do we close the doors?" Mark asked. "It's dark in here."

"Got a flashlight?" Abby extended her palm.

"Sure." From under the console, Mark pulled out a flashlight and handed it to Abby as she jumped to the catwalk.

"Now, to find that lamp. Father never installed electricity; I'd pay anything for it . . . wait." From under the workbench, she pulled out an old kerosene lamp. Blowing as hard as she could, she removed only the top layer of dust caked on the lamp by years of neglect. "Where are those matches? Ah . . . taped to the lamp, of course. Swedish fireplace matches, the kind that light no matter where you scratch them." She snapped the first one across the nearest planking, and its head burst into flame. The lantern's light was rather weak at first, but grew brighter as she raised the wick. Soon, the entire boathouse could be examined from corner to corner.

"Yuck! This place is filthy," Mark said, "smells like moldy straw and mildewed canvas."

"Never mind the smell," Abby said. She wheeled around, searching for the door mechanism. "We've got to get the doors closed." With help from the kerosene lamp, Abby quickly located the mechanism for closing the doors. The principal gear was a brass wheel that could be turned by its wooden handle, but Abby found its gears clogged with dirt and not a small amount of corrosion. It wouldn't budge. "Gotta' get those doors closed." She found an oil can her father always kept near the brass wheel and squirted oil on every movable part she could identify. "Now move, damn it!" A whack with a monkey wrench was next. Then, another whack. Abby stepped back and waited. And then, she pushed the handle forward with all her strength. Slowly, very slowly, the wheel began to move. She could move it, just barely, but she knew she couldn't stop. To stop was to risk the wheel freezing up again.

"May I help you?" Mark asked. Abby's red face was obvious even in the lantern light.

"Okay, but don't . . . let . . . the wheel . . . stop." Abby kept turning as she spoke. "Keep it moving."

Mark grabbed the handle and began turning as Abby let go. Another full turn was enough to bring the doors to their fully closed position. Abby had made her way down the catwalk to the doors, and when they closed, she quickly reset the counterweights.

"You did well," Mark said, with a congratulatory kiss to each cheek. "Fortunately for us, the catwalk is almost even with the gunwale, but getting the chest off the boat is still going to be a challenge. Any ideas?"

"Just one." She held a finger up and slowly pointed to the ceiling. "That block and tackle was all Father needed to haul the boat out every fall. Let's get it down." She started to reach for the hoist, but stopped with a kind of exasperated squiggle on her face, as she examined the line. "It doesn't look like it's in very good shape." She wiped her forehead and pushed her hair back. "Doesn't anything remain the same? I hope it still works."

Mark loosened the straps, stiff and dusty from years of nonuse. "Something's been chewing on the leather." Abby examined the straps but stopped when she hear a loud fluttering from high above. "Just bats," Mark said, "and they just left through a broken window."

"We won't need the straps," Abby said. She wouldn't let herself think about the bats, just then. "We'll use a line with a hook to lift the chest. It shouldn't take but a minute to raise the chest clear to the ceiling and tie it off."

As she glanced to the ceiling, Abby spotted a loft that was not there the last time she was in the boathouse. "What possible use would my brother have for such storage?" A wooden ladder led her up to a second story loft. Peering over the topmost rung, her mouth dropped open. "I always wondered what my brother did with all the stuff he cleared out of the cottage," Abby said to Mark, standing at the foot of the ladder. "He was supposed to sell it, but he didn't. He saved it! Boat records, scrapbooks, an assortment of tubing . . ."

"Tubing? What was he going to do with that?" Mark asked. "Oh, never mind . . . you better come down."

"He had many uses in mind. Someday he'll tell you. Oh, good grief, what's this? 'Used Motor Oil.' An oil drum full of it, and a fire hazard, if you ask me."

"Forget that stuff," Mark shouted up the ladder. "We've got work to do." Abby turned in time to see Mark lowering the block and tackle to the deck of the boat. In the next minute, he slipped a hook through one of the two chest handles. "Hold the chest steady as long as you can," he said to Abby. "That should keep it from swinging back and forth while I snug it up to its hiding place." The chest soon reached the full height of the boathouse rafters.

"That's about thirty feet in the air." Abby squinted into the blackness above.

"Yep, only the bats will find it up there." Mark tied off the chest to the nearest cleat. "Now, to the Madam's cottage, and, uh, I hope she doesn't have visitors." He reached for Abby's hand.

"Oh, stop that." Abby slapped his hand and gave Mark a reprimanding stare for suggesting some untoward activity might be taking place at Miss Cooke's cottage. "Just the same, maybe we ought to stay on board tonight. We've come a long way in search of King Strang's royal treasury. I'd hate to lose it simply because we left it unguarded a few hours."

"I agree." Mark reached for the lamp and lowered the wick. "Besides we don't know who was piloting the plane that left Gull with motor trouble." In the flickering shadows of the boathouse, Mark spoke softly. "Or the man on the beach in Bermuda shorts who shot the Indian."

Abby shuddered. "Anyone that interested in our exploits could be anywhere around here by now."

Mark searched the shadows around them. "Especially if they looked for us at O'Malley's Marina and didn't find the *Holly-Hoo*." In the next instant, he blew out the lamp. "I'll sleep on the deck tonight. We don't want any more night visitors like the ones who siphoned our gas tank the first time we visited Gull."

"And I'll take the aft berth," Abby sighed. "Nothing can keep me from a 'deep repose for these limbs with travel tired.'"

Mark laughed. "You can think of Shakespeare at a time like this?"

"I'm too tired to think of anything except my limbs are utterly exhausted." And she gave Mark a gentle kiss.

But Abby slept fitfully. "For some reason," she told Mark the next morning, "I dreamed about the infamous Holy Island gallows, and not an empty gallows. At first I saw Billy Merrill swinging from the gallows, and the gallows squeaked loudly. In the next scene it was James Strang himself on the end of the rope. And in a final scene, it was a man without a face, a man in a white robe. And beneath the gallows, a chest of gold. Throughout the dream, someone was laughing, someone in the woods, sitting by a fire, laughing."

"Hold on, Abby. Don't get carried away," Mark said, as he handed her a doughnut. "You need some breakfast. "What you heard was the iron chest swinging from side to side during the night, blown by the wind rattling the broken windows in that cupola." He pointed upward. "The block and tackle squeaked every time the rope stretched."

"But who was he?" she asked Mark.

"He?"

"The robed figure in my dream."

"I don't know; perhaps, it's someone you've met along the way?"

"No. I don't think so." She was quiet a moment. "Why would such an image appear in a dream of mine?"

"Abby, I'm a newspaper editor. I try to stick to facts, not fantasies." Mark took a large bite from his biscuit. "I'm glad we saved them; they're the last." He grabbed Abby around the waist and lifted her to the catwalk. "Don't you think it's time for our visit? It's almost mid-morning and the Madam is surely awake by now."

Abby nodded, but was quiet, reflecting on the images in her dream. As they stepped into the morning sun, she was brought back to reality when the boathouse door closed behind them with a solid clunk, and the latch fell hard into place.

"Did you know the door would lock automatically?" Mark asked.

"Of course."

"So, you have a plan for opening it when we return?"

"You'll find out." She winked and gave him a pat on the butt as she pushed him toward Miss Cooke's cottage.

A rap at the door brought no answer. She gave the door a second rap and then, another. Abby was about to try a fourth time when the door flung open.

"Abby! You darling, come in!"

Abby stood speechless for a moment. The Madam, dressed in a floor length, white robe with faux fur around the collar, waved them in with a flourish. Underneath that robe, Abby could clearly see a full-length corselette, and thigh-high stockings with a garter at the top of each.

"Jeez!" Marked gasped.

"Settle down, young man," the Madam said. "You're welcome, too."

Abby covered her smile as Mark turned red. "I'm sorry to disturb you again, Miss Cooke but—"

"Oh, you haven't disturbed anything," the Madam responded. "Come in." A screen door slammed at the back of her cottage. "Mark, you need a shave. Abby, you need a comb. But you know that. Please have a seat."

"No time," Mark said. "We need to take a look at that patent abstract in your attic. We think we found Strang's prototype lock installed on the chest that holds his gold."

"Really? I mean, *really*!" Her eyes popped wide open. "The gold? You found it?"

"Well, we found Strang's chest," Abby said. "We're about to confirm once and for all that King Strang did have a treasure worth hiding . . . or, uh, not."

"Right this way," the Madam said. She made a perfect pirouette, her robe swirling about her. "I can't wait!" In a few moments, they were rifling through Strang's correspondence again.

"Patent Office. Patent Office." Abby flipped through one file after another. "Ah, here's the letter. Let's see, lots of numbers referring to classes of locks, I guess, background on the invention and . . . yes! Here's the abstract." She handed it to Mark, but he returned it.

"Hey, you fixed the radio on *Holly-Hoo*; you dared to take us through Merrill's Mirage; you tied a perfect Alpine Butterfly knot; and so, you deserve first shot at interpreting this thing."

Abby's eyes sparkled, and she blew Mark a kiss.

The Madam rolled her eyes as she observed their flirting. "Back to business, you two."

Abby smiled, then quickly scanned several pages, stopping from time to time for a closer look at the mechanical drawings.

"As I said the last time I saw these, it's a true Rube Goldberg contraption." She flipped through several more pages. "'*A lock of Strang's own invention,*'" Abby read from one dog-eared page. "This has to be our lock." Abby's fingers traced every line of the abstract, as she struggled to interpret the drawings.   "In this drawing, it has locking ears that are inserted through the opening in the chest wall and turned until they lock into place. That holds the lock, but . . . how does it open?"

She scanned the lines as fast as she could. "Listen to this.

'Most thieves will try to remove the lock by pulling or turning, but almost never by striking, for fear of damaging the mechanism permanently.'"

"Strike it?" Mark said. He shook his head in total disbelief. "Are you sure?"

"Yes, and there's more.

'The lock must be pushed into the box until a loud engaging snap is heard. The snap is the release of two pistons, held in place by tension placed upon them by two heavy duty springs. Once the tension has been released, the lock can be turned by the concave locknut on the exterior, which also serves as its handle. A full half turn to the right with the concave locknut allows the pistons to be released. Once they have released their hold, the top will open on its hinges.'"

"That's it? I can't believe the lock is that simple," Mark said. "Anyone could give it a whack at any time, and it seems to me it would open easily."

"Well, maybe not. Listen to this.

'Warning: The concave locknut must be aligned properly before striking, or it cannot be opened no matter how hard one strikes the central shaft. Therefore, BEFORE the central shaft is struck, look for the triangle carved inside the concave locknut. Each

point on the triangle has a letter designation F, A, E,
corresponding to the Father, Adam and Eve. The operator must
turn the locknut until the "F" point on the triangle points to
Heaven. A sharp strike with a wooden block or the palm of one's
hand will push the lock far enough into the chest wall to release
the pistons.'"

"Now you understand why no one, including the U.S. Government, was interested in buying one," Mark said. "Because if you don't know the meaning of the letters, F, A, and E, you have little hope of opening the lock."

"As I said, old Rube would be proud of old Strang."

"But when the instructions are followed exactly, the lock is easily opened, right?" the Madam asked.

"Easily, your Majesty?" Mark said. "We'll let you know how 'easily,' the next time you see us." Mark pulled the instructions from the file and stuffed them under his belt. "Right now, we have a treasure chest to open." He grabbed Abby by the hand, dashed down the stairs, and out the front door.

Outside, Abby picked up the unmistakable smell of burning timbers. "Fire in the bayou!" Abby shouted. In the distance, smoke bellowed into the sky as the two raced toward the source. "Oh my God, it's our boathouse!"

Chapter Thirty
FIRE!

Abby could feel the air growing warmer even though they were several hundred yards from the boathouse. With each breath, the bitter taste of carbon ash was renewed on her tongue. By the time they reached the lower terrace, fire crackled from every window of the ancient structure.

"Faster, Abby! Faster."

Mark's stride was a few inches longer than Abby's, but she kept pace. "I'm right behind you." Flames were already licking the roofline.

They were a full one hundred yards from the boathouse, when a lone figure, running hard, emerged from the smoke. Abby, at first, could not make out the face.

"Who's that?" Mark shouted.

"Oh, my gosh! It's Xeno! Xeno Miller," Abby said, "you know, from the Hotel."

"Xeno? But, isn't he blind?"

"Yes! He is!" Abby couldn't believe her own eyes.

"Blind men don't run like that," Mark said, his breath coming in short bursts.

"Well, I *thought* he was blind." Abby, winded by their dash, called out to Xeno, but he never looked in their direction. The next moment, he disappeared into a thicket of sugar maples behind the bayou. Somewhere inside the boathouse, window glass shattered. Smoke and fire belched from every opening, touching nearby tree limbs.

"Come on. We've got to get *Holly Hoo* out of there," Mark said.

The intensity of the heat-smoke combination seared Abby's eyes. "That hurts!" She covered her eyes and turned away. "What about the gold?" she gasped, as she peeked through her closed fingers in Mark's direction.

"The gold is about the only thing that's safe," Mark said. "It might melt in that chest, but it won't burn. Let's make a run for the boat. I'll crank her up and cast off. If there's time, you can release the line holding the chest from its cleat. But we have to save *Holly-Hoo*."

"The roof appears ready to cave in," Abby said. "Where's that key?" She started to run her hand along the top of the doorframe.

"Forget the key," Mark shouted, as he hurled the full force of his two hundred pound frame into the door and blew it open. A wall of smoke, pushed outward by a wave of heat, stung their faces as they tried to enter. Mark ripped off his shirt and tore it in two. "Here, hold this over your mouth and nose." He grabbed Abby's hand and pulled her along the catwalk surrounding the boat. "On three, jump!"

"*Three!*" he shouted, skipping "one" and "two" altogether. Holding hands tightly, they jumped to *Holly Hoo's* deck. "Black as sin, but still there," Mark said, staring into the darkness high above them. "Whoever started the fire must be disappointed they didn't find the gold."

"Or mad as hell," Abby said. "What! The slip's double doors are open!

"Someone else knows your father's method of secret entry," Mark said.

"I don't care; I can't get this line free." Abby jerked the line holding the chest in the air, frantically working to loosen the knot. "I can't get it off the cleat," she called to Mark. "Must have gotten wet and shrunk. I need a knife!"

"No time!" Mark shouted. *Holly-Hoo's* engine roared to life. "Let's go!"

"Too tight," Abby said. She struggled desperately to loosen the line's grip. "I *will* get it down!"

"Forget it!" Mark shouted again.

All around her, Abby heard timbers crashing to the floor. Some splashed into the water and disappeared with a steamy sizzle. Suddenly, she heard a thunderous crash, and the whole structure trembled. The drum containing her brother's used motor oil had fallen to the catwalk, turned over, and was spilling its contents into the water. A second later, the surface of the water erupted in flame and black smoke.

"We can't stay here. We have to go, *now!*" Mark shouted, and grabbed the helm.

"My God, who is *that?*" Abby yelled.

At that moment, a figure appeared at the top of the companionway, dressed head to toe in a flowing white robe, his face hidden by an oversized cowl, and around his waist, a sash of gold satin. Locks of silver-grey hair outlined the robe's cowl, and a snow white beard, nearly obscured by the smoke, hung half way down his chest. In the chaos of the moment, with a fire raging all around her, Abby thought she might be hallucinating. A rafter, high in the ceiling, fell to the catwalk, spewing splinters and a fountain of sparks in every direction.

"Welcome to the House of David, ye servants of the Seventh Messenger." A monotone voice penetrated the air, cutting through the noise of the firestorm around them.

"What'd you say?" Abby glared at the figure. "*Why* are you here?" Her vocal chords burned with the irritation of tiny cinders floating in the air. Choking, her voice croaking, Abby demanded, "Say something!"

"Where . . . is . . . the . . . Father's gold?" the voice asked. The figure stood motionless. The folds of his robe made him look like an angel, Abby thought, *without any wings.*

"You!" Mark was outraged. "*You* set fire to the boathouse!" He shouted above the noise. "Why?"

What . . . is that thunder? Abby wondered. *Even the boat is shaking. An earthquake? Abby Finlay, remain calm.* Abby heard the engine cough once and die. "Oh no! No! Not the time to quit, *Holly-Hoo*."

Suddenly, the robed figure charged at Mark, pushed him against the console, and pressed a dagger against his throat.

"Satan smote the timbers. If you wish to avoid a slit throat, deliver the treasure to the Seventh Messenger, *now*!" He flicked the tip of the dagger under Mark's earlobe, just enough to draw blood. Then, he drew the blade across Mark's arm, and much more blood spurted toward the gunwale.

"You bastard!" Abby shouted as she jumped on the robed figure, and pulled backward on his robe with all her strength, choking him. The robed figure staggered backward a moment, shook her loose, and flung her to one side. He threw the dagger at Mark as he charged again. Mark ducked but not enough to escape the dagger entirely. The blade sliced through the biceps of his left arm, and he fell to the deck, clutching the wound tightly. Mark tried to grab the dagger, but the robed figure was faster. With the dagger now tight in his fist, he turned toward Mark to finish him off.

Thirty feet above, Abby saw flames brighten as they skated up the line that held the chest. The line, weakened by fire, snapped, and the weight of the chest–gold and all–brought it down, striking a crushing blow to the head of the robed figure, throwing him backward and overboard into the burning water. The chest hit the mahogany skin of the boat with a splintering thud, and slid across the deck. Abby caught the chest with an anchor chain just before it was lost over the side.

"Shit!" Mark said. Blood spurted over the deck in pulsating streams. "I think he hit an artery."

"Put some pressure on it with your right hand, and hold it till we get out of here," Abby said. She clamored toward the console. "That should be enough to stop the bleeding."

"Can you handle the boat?" He plopped down beside her.

"I'm already at the wheel." Abby said. "And hold that wound tight; I can't turn the wheel loose to help stop the bleeding."

A small explosion of heat and flame erupted as the fire reached the resin heart of a pine rafter directly above them. "Go *Holly-Hoo*. Go!" Abby yelled, as she turned the ignition.   The engine roared to full throttle, coughed, and then, quit. Roof trusses nearest the fire fell first. Abby knew they would soon fall like dominos and surrender the strength that held the structure together.   "What do I do now?" She turned to Mark with panic in her voice.

"Back off the choke. Don't flood it." Mark said.

Abby slammed the choke shut.

"Now, turn the ignition again, and hold it until the motor turns over."

Abby held the ignition key in the start position and resisted the urge to give it gas, even though she wanted to. When the engine roared to life a second time, Abby didn't wait for anything else to develop. She jerked the gearshift backward into full reverse. "Grab the gunwale," she shouted to Mark. "But don't take the pressure off that arm."   Mark raised an eyebrow at her instructions.

One roof truss after another began falling into the water where *Holly-Hoo* had been, and walls of the boathouse fell inward, consumed in flame. Black smoke erupted from the water every time a resin soaked timber hit it.

"I can't see anything except what's behind me," Abby said, "but I'm fine with that."   As soon as they were safely away from the boathouse, Abby slammed the gearshift forward and raced toward the channel. When they reached Lake Charlevoix, Abby turned to catch the city's lone fire truck arriving and firefighters pouring water on the boathouse. "They'll never get close enough to do much good," Abby said. "It's too hot."

"Forget 'em." Mark said. "We've gotta' disappear quick, or we'll have no choice but to turn this chest over to the authorities." He took a step toward the chest. "Look what it did to my deck!" Mark leaned over to pick up some large splinters, and for a moment he forgot he needed to keep applying pressure to the wound. "Ooooow!" he screamed, as blood began to flow again.

"Keep the pressure on!" Abby shouted. "As for *Holly-Hoo,* I suspect she's seen worse in her life."

Mark leaned against the gunwale. "Okay, okay . . . pull into the old beet factory." He pointed to a dark spot on the shoreline with no lights visible.

"How will you know where to tie up?" Abby asked.

"I worked here most summers when my family ran the place." He grabbed Abby's arm. "There . . . the loading docks! The whole place is abandoned. It'll be safe enough until we figure out whether or not I need to find a doctor."

"You won't need a doctor when I'm finished with you," Abby said.

"What do you have in mind?"

"You'll see." She gave him a flirtatious wink.

"I can't wait." Mark said, and winked back. "I can't wait." He slinked back into the captain's chair.

A few minutes later, Abby successfully maneuvered *Holly-Hoo* into one of the slips at the beet factory. When the boat was secure, Abby grabbed her bag from under the seat and began a frantic search through it, tossing contents all over the deck. "No tourniquet. Damn! I thought I had one with me." She turned to Mark. "Let's use this." With that, she pulled her scarf from around her neck, and as fast as her fingers could fly, tied it around Mark's upper arm. "This will slow down the bleeding while I sew you up."

"You'll what?" He started to get up.

"Sew you up. You need stitches." Abby held a needle high in one hand and a length of catgut suture in the other.

Mark nearly jumped out of the captain's chair. "But—"

"You forget. My father was a doctor." Abby motioned for him to come closer. "Please, sit down."

Slowly, Mark eased back into the chair. A bit uncertain about this development, he began to fidget nervously.

"You'll have to be still, too," Abby said, as she finished threading the needle. "It's lucky for you that I'm here with my trusty needle. The dagger didn't hit an artery, but it may have nicked a vein."

"Nicked? Sounds serious." He paused. "Did you say . . . a vein?"

"Well, it *is* a large vein, and a long cut." Her eyes were very wide, her expression somber. "But in all honesty," she smiled, "it's hardly more than a surface laceration. I'll have you stitched up in no time."

Mark turned in his seat to position his arm directly in front of Abby. "Are you sure you know how to do this?"

"Well, you can do it yourself if you prefer." Abby offered the needle to Mark.

"No, no. I don't doubt you." Mark recoiled with a thin smile.

"Lie down on the deck and, uh, don't watch. This will take a couple of minutes, I hope. Unfortunately, I don't have anything to deaden the area around the cut, but you'll be glad to hear, I'm using a thin needle and the thinnest sutures in my bag."

"It's okay, I was a war correspondent, remember?"

"Yes, of course. I forgot. In that case, you can watch." Abby smiled as she wiped the wound clean. When finished, she announced, "Only six needed, that's not bad."

"You're done? I hardly felt a thing."

"I told you I was a doctor's daughter. But I assure you I'm no Florence Nightingale. You'll have to take care of yourself from here on." She laughed as she covered the wound with a large bandage and taped it tight. "You'll be fine in the morning, but your arm will be a little sore for a couple of days."

"Thank you, doctor," Mark said, smiling. "How much do I owe you?"

"Oh, you can't afford my rates," Abby teased. She snuggled up to his chest, gave him a teasing kiss. "However, I'm sure I'll think of some appropriate remuneration before morning."

With his one good arm wrapped around her, Mark gave Abby a long, lingering kiss. Several times, Abby allowed her lips to move slowly and sensually along his. When they finally broke their embrace, Abby whispered, "Well, that was a good down payment, but you owe me a lot more than that."

"Fine with me, my dear, but right now, we better get serious about hiding the boat *and* the chest." Mark gave her a gentle kiss on the nose, and slowly turned to untangle the lines that operated the several hoists on the dock in front of them.

Abby came up behind him and poked him gently in his rib cage. "Just don't forget where we were."

"No danger of that." He brushed her hair back over her ears before returning to the tangled lines. "What's wrong with these lines?" He pulled hard, but the first couple of lines wouldn't operate the hoist at all. "Frozen," he said. "Frozen in place, I suspect, as it was the day the factory was shut years ago."

"We could use some of that oil my brother was saving in the boathouse," Abby said.

"Look under the first mate's seat, Abby. There should be an oil can in my toolbox."

Abby got down on her knees and rummaged around in his toolbox. Finally, she found a rusty can of Liquid Wrench. "Will this do?"

"Perfect!" In a few minutes, Mark had one of the rusty hoists completely oiled up inside and out. "We'll wait a few minutes for the magic to be done, and then we'll try the hoist again. Liquid Wrench is one of the three essential tools in a man's, or woman's, tool chest," Mark said, with a smile. "Can you guess the other two?"

"Surely they are a good hammer and screwdriver." Abby said.

"Not quite. You need an adjustable wrench, heavy enough to do double duty as a hammer, and most important, a roll of duct tape.

Everyone knows duct tape will repair anything in an emergency." Mark started to laugh but stopped when he noticed Abby's eyes were suddenly downcast. "Uh-oh. Now, what's the problem?"

"It's Mooney, Julius Mooney," Abby said. "I wish you had been in position to catch him and keep him from going overboard back there." She sat down hard on the black chest. "He wasn't the man I used to know."

"Who? The guy in the white robe? That was Mooney?"

Abby nodded.

"But how could you tell?"

"His boots. I recognized his snakeskin boots before he fell over the side."

"Are you sure?"

"Of course. He wears them everywhere," Abby said. "Julius Mooney *is* the Seventh Messenger!"

"Correction, he *was* the Seventh Messenger," Mark said. "I don't think he came up after the chest knocked him overboard." Mark touched her shoulder. "Rescuers were there when we left, Abby, but I doubt if they will be successful in saving him. He took a really hard hit."

"I know, but still . . . " She was quiet a moment, a tear trickled down her face, and Mark handed her a tissue. "I just have a terribly sad feeling when I think of the man and his wife, Henrietta. Even though I was often uncomfortable in his presence, he was liked by nearly everyone in the Club . . . at one time."

"Abby, he lived through a terrible loss, and then, given an opportunity to make a choice for his life after Henrietta's death, he chose poorly. Why? Who knows?" With his one uninjured arm, Mark lifted Abby from her seat on the chest. "Why don't we open the chest right here on the deck while we wait for the Liquid Wrench to do its job? That'll give you something to smile about." Mark held onto her hand as he searched about the deck for a tool. "I just need the flat side of that paddle over there and, yes, my adjustable wrench."

"I saw the wrench under the console," Abby said, "and I have Strang's instructions right here." In a few minutes, the chest was in position for "the whacking," as Abby called it. "I'll read the instructions for you.

> '*A full half turn to the right with the locknut is the first step in releasing the pistons that hold the chest shut.*'"

Mark rotated the locknut to the right. "Wasn't there something before that, something about pointing the nut toward Heaven?"

"I almost forgot," Abby said. "It's gotta' be aligned properly. We're supposed to turn the locknut until the "F" carved inside points to Heaven. Then, whack it with a wooden block or the palm of your hand." She watched as Mark turned the locknut, his hands shaking.

"So, first turn the locknut until the "F" inside points skyward. Done! Stand back! I'll use the strength of my left arm to hit it."

Abby leaned over and gave Mark a kiss. "One more thing," she said, as she put her hand under his shirt and tickled the hair on his chest, "even if the chest is empty, I'll still love you, and we'll chalk it up to another life adventure we enjoyed together."

"I like that word, 'together,'" Mark said. "Tell you what, why don't you hold the paddle, I'll hold the wrench, and we'll strike the locknut, together." He kissed her as she held the paddle in place. With his uninjured arm, Mark gave the lock a whack with the wrench, a whack so hard he sent the cylinder into the chest a full two inches. Abby heard a loud "snap" as the shaft pushed inward. Mark gave the locknut a full half turn to the right. Abby heard a distinct "thwang" this time, followed by a firm "pop." Spring loaded pistons released a hold they had held for a century.

"But it still doesn't open," Abby said, as she tried to give the locknut a twist. "Maybe it was in the water too long. Rust, you know."

"Hand me a screw driver and hammer," Mark said, scratching his head. "I've another idea."

Abby again searched for tools under the console and pulled out the first tool she found. "Will a cold chisel do?"

"Even better." He held his palm out. As soon as she placed the chisel in his hand, Mark began probing for a crack where the top of the chest was welded to the chest walls.

"Ah, I see," Abby smiled. "The old tried and true 'when all else fails,' pry it open approach."

Mark was already perspiring as he attempted to muscle the top open with brute force. Finally, he found a crack big enough to accept the chisel's edge and pried the top open a couple of inches. That was enough for Abby's hand. As her fingers touched the velvety smooth surface of the first coins, her face beamed, and she whispered, "Gold." Then, much louder, "Gold coins, and lots of them! Some are stuck to each other, probably the effect of the heat from the boathouse fire." She stirred them vigorously until they snapped apart. When most were free, Mark turned the chest on its side and the coins cascaded onto the deck.

Abby couldn't believe the sheer number of coins. "No wonder it was so hard for you to lift." But, as Abby began stacking the coins in columns of ten, another wave of sadness swept over her. *We should be euphoric, but I don't really feel like celebrating.*

"What is it now?" Mark asked. "Are you still thinking about Mooney?"

"I look at these coins, and I think about all the people who have died in the grip of its luster: Sergeant Strang, Ogawee, Billy Merrill, and yes, Julius Mooney." She held her palm up to Mark. "That's four!"

"Don't forget the Indian guarding the resting place of his ancestors on High Island," Mark said. "He died on the beach."

"That's right," Abby said. "That's five, and only God knows how many more."

Silently, the two of them continued to work, extracting the coins and stacking them in neat piles of ten each. Soon, there were twenty rows of ten coins each, and many more lay on the deck. As Mark finished the stacking, Abby reached inside a final time to determine if she had missed any. She didn't find a coin. The only thing left was a note, and she handed it to Mark.

"Another clue?" Mark asked, as he began to read:

'*Honor your Father when you stand before the bar,*
He will lead you onward to a better world by far.
You shall wear a cloak of gold, His Kingdom to restore,
Trust but one – your Father – and live forevermore.'"

"Those words, no doubt, were meant for Elvira's three children," Abby said. She began returning the coins to the chest for safe keeping, but a moment later, touched Mark's hand and said, "For the sake of the people who have died in this adventure, let's do something with the gold 'for a better world by far' in the here and now."

"Agreed." Mark lifted her hand and gave it a gentle kiss.

When all the coins were safely returned to the chest, they secured the hoist around it. "C'mon, let's do this together," Mark said. "Grab on, and pull on my signal." He motioned for Abby to join him. "Now!" Mark whispered loudly. With one great pull, the hoist lifted the chest above the deck. They swung it over the dock, and lowered it to the bottom of the storage bin under the factory floor. "Here, take a few of these planks and spread them over the beet bin."

"A cool place for a hot package," Abby said. "I think we should spread some around in haphazard fashion, so it doesn't look like it was done to hide something."

"I love your brain," Mark said. "Of course, I love you, too."

Abby smiled and started to wipe soot off her face. "Even now?"

"Especially now. Let's go." With *Holly-Hoo* secured in the slip, they began their long walk, hand in hand, back to the Hotel. "One more question," Mark asked. "How do you expect us to enter the Hotel unnoticed?"

"There's a rear entrance," Abby said. "If you don't know where it is, you'll miss it. The servants use it to move unnoticed throughout the

Hotel. When I was a little girl, we kids had more fun playing in the back halls than any of the organized activities of the Club."

Twenty minutes later, the two entered the Hotel through a tiny, recessed door at the rear. Once inside, Abby led Mark through a labyrinth of narrow halls and worn down stairs. A series of bare bulbs dangled from the ceiling and provided the only light for their steps, as they squeezed single file down the hallways.

"Watch your step," Abby said. "The stairs here are even narrower than the hallways." At the top of the stairs, she found the small door she was searching for. "Seems smaller than I remember, more like a cabinet door." Through it they stepped into a pantry, which led them to another door, marked with a small Roman numeral "II."

"This is our floor," Abby whispered. "I can't wait to get into bed. What a day!" She began shedding articles of clothing at the entrance and created a trail of discarded clothing all the way to the bed. "I'm exhausted," Abby said, as she collapsed onto the bed.

"And you were right; my arm *is* very sore," Mark said, as he collapsed beside her.

"You won't even have a scar when it heals, so stop complaining." She smiled and gave him a playful tickle as he rolled toward her.

"Should we ask the front desk to send up more champagne?"

"Tomorrow, my dear, tomorrow," Abby said. She put her hands behind his head and pulled him toward her. She was tired of talking, or doing anything that wasn't focused on her new love.

Chapter Thirty One
The Consecration

Room service delivered a sumptuous breakfast: eggs over easy, a rasher of bacon, strawberries and a single hot biscuit on each plate. "I'm starving," Mark said, as he spread a sheet of butter over half a biscuit. "The only thing missing is a bit of Michigan honey."

"Really? Wait here," Abby said. "I know just the place. I'll be back in five minutes." She had in mind a jar of crystalized, Michigan honey, and there was only one sure source on Club grounds: the candy counter in the Hotel lobby.

As she headed for the door, Mark sat up on his elbows. "Do you think Xeno Miller will be there? You said he was always there."

"I would be shocked to see him. If he's smart, he's long gone." She pulled up her jeans, tucked in her blouse, and headed for the door. "I'll be right back."

The lobby appeared deserted when she slipped in. *Good, I'm not really dressed to be seen. I'll just get the honey and dash back to my room.*

At the candy counter, she found, as always, a good half dozen jars of crystalized honey. She pulled the first one off the shelf but nearly dropped it when Xeno Miller got up from his chair behind the register.

"Xeno, you're here!"

"Yes, I'm—"

"Always here, I know." Abby looked over her shoulder to check for eavesdroppers. "But why? I saw you running from the Finlay boathouse just as the fire began yesterday, and wh—oh, good grief—

what happened to your hands? That's more than a scrape from a cash register drawer. And your arms . . . the hair is singed!" Abby put the honey jar on the counter and gave Xeno a penetrating stare. "*And*, by the way, you're *not* blind."

"Shhhhhhh!" Xeno looked around the lobby. Certain they were alone, he leaned across the counter. "Abby, I'm sorry. I'm sorry for everything. Mr. Mooney made me do it."

"Do what, Xeno? What?"

Xeno shook his head. "Mr. Mooney's been crazy lately. I can't talk to him about anything." Xeno looked around the lobby again. "Are you sure you're alone?"

"Yes, but, how could Julius *make* you do anything?"

"You don't understand." Xeno reached for her arm. "The man has become the devil's right hand. Pure evil, and I don't like to speak of evil."

"Why don't you start from the beginning, and lower your voice. "Did Julius know you can see?"

"No." Xeno paused, and heaved a great sigh. "He thought I was blind, and why not; he was there the night I lost my sight."

"What—what do you mean? *Where* did you lose your sight?"

"Come around the counter." As Abby stepped around the end of the counter, Xeno led her behind a large potted plant. "We were both on High Island during the time of Pernell Richards, the man who claimed to be the Seventh Messenger. Mr. Richards regularly raped the young girls before he gave them to the husband he had personally chosen for them."

"What?" Abby's voice was far above a whisper. *I must remember to whisper.* She pulled Xeno a little closer. "Do you have any proof?"

"Proof? I was there for one such rape."

"What?" Abby's voice grew louder again.

"Shhhhh! The girl he raped that night was not just any girl; she was . . . my Joanna." His voice trailed off on the name. Xeno hung his head. "I pleaded with him, but he paid no attention. No attention at all."

"Where did this crime occur?" Abby placed a hand on Xeno's arm, hoping to offer some comfort.

"He called it Shiloh, his Font of Holy Blessing. It was anything but a blessing. It was a hole in the ground beneath his cabin, a horrible place where he took all the young girls for their consecration."

"Consecration? That's what he called it?"

Xeno drew in a deep breath. "Yes. He said it was to make sure they were counted among the faithful followers of the Seventh Messenger when Jesus Christ comes back to rule Palestine for a thousand years."

"And you believed that?" Abby caught sight of someone crossing the lobby at the far end and held up her hand for silence. "Never mind; we must hurry. What happened the night he took Joanna down to his so-called Shiloh?"

"His eyes were like two burning coals that night. Even when you turned away you could feel their heat on your neck. He was an awful man."

"Xeno, take your time, and keep your voice down. Tell me what happened that night?"

"I cannot tell you every detail. I cannot." Xeno closed his eyes. As he began, Abby noticed his shaking hands, and they never stopped as he relived the terror of that night. "But I will tell you all that I remember."

"'God remove me from this room. I beg of you.' That's all I could think to say, as Mister Richards tied Joanna to the four corners of a table. She tried to scream but couldn't. Mr. Richards had stuffed a rag in her mouth. But her eyes . . . her eyes . . . they screamed for help. When he was finished tying her down with leather strappings he kept for this specific use, he picked up a filet knife from one corner of the table.

'Sit down,' he commanded, and shoved me into a chair. 'You will watch the blessing of young Joanna.' In the next instant, he used the knife to pop the fasteners from Joanna's skirt, and with a growling snort, he ripped the skirt away. She was totally exposed. I turned away. But I heard Joanna sobbing, and sobbing, and then, a thud as something heavy hit the floor. As I turned around, the Messenger was on his knees, hands clasped together, praying. 'Let Joanna be consecrated to Thee.' While he was kneeling in prayer, I picked up her skirt and covered her as best I could. But . . . but when Mister Richards saw me near Joanna, he flew into a rage. He slammed his fists on the table and threw the knife at me. The knife missed and ricocheted off the fireplace.

'Thy eyes are cursed.' Those were his exact words as he grabbed my wrists and held them. Those burning slits looked into mine. 'Did the devil send thee here?' He pushed me into a chair and grabbed me from behind. 'Ye deserve nothing but the punishment of Satan's Gloves.' He tied me to the chair with more leather straps. I was paralyzed with fear. From somewhere under the table, Mister Richards pulled out a pair of leather gloves and slipped one on each hand. 'How dare thee watch!' he said. He stepped behind me, jerked my head backward, and closed his gloved fingers over my eyes. The index finger of each glove held a small nail. I lost consciousness after that. I know that I screamed, but I don't remember anything until I woke outside . . . lying in the snow . . . and not far from Mister Richards' cabin. I don't know how much time passed before Julius Mooney found me and took me to his cabin to tend to my wounds. I must have been nearly frozen."

"Holy Jesus!" Abby whispered loudly, as again she checked the lobby for early risers. When confident no one saw them, Abby put her arms around Xeno. *Words cannot heal such pain,* she thought, and so she said nothing for several minutes. Xeno finally opened his eyes. Abby could see that reliving that horrific moment had ripped open a deep scar. Tears poured down his face, now pale as kaolin. And for a long time, Xeno stood behind the potted plant with Abby, his eyes closed, body trembling. Abby thought Xeno had finished his story, but then he took another deep breath and exhaled slowly.

"The rapes didn't stop, Abby. They did *not* stop." He spit out the words in disgust. "One night Julius Mooney overheard the rape of another young girl. I heard it was his sister, and I guess that was the last straw for him. A few nights after that, he put me in his boat, and with the help of one of the girls Mister Richards had abused, the three of us set sail for the mainland, finally landing right here in Charlevoix."

"This is a side of Mooney I've never seen," Abby said.

"Then you should know Julius Mooney returned to High Island several times—always in the middle of night—to provide other young women the means to escape Mister Richards. All were pregnant, and he knew nobody wanted anything to do with them."

"Pregnant? All of them?" Abby's mouth dropped open.

"I know you don't believe it, but it's true. He put them up until they could find a home, or at least, until they could find someone willing to take care of them until, you know, their time. Several were adopted by families of Pine Lake."

"Really? Pine Lake?"

"That's what I was told." Xeno turned to take a step back to the cash register. "No one cared about what happened to me that night except Julius Mooney. He found me, picked me up, and took me in. I was always grateful for that. I told him so, and pledged him my loyalty from that day forward."

"But you really could see in one eye?"

The sound of footsteps stopped their conversation. Two elderly members of the Club passed on their way to the Dining room. As soon as Xeno was sure no one could overhear, he continued. "I couldn't see anything at first. A year passed before my eyes began to heal. My left eye was blinded permanently, but my right eye finally healed to the point that I could see some images, mostly shadows, and only if they were moving directly in front of me. Even now, images are pretty dark."

Two more guests passed by, and at the far end of the lobby, Abby glimpsed someone sitting down to read. *This place is entirely too public.* "Didn't you ever think of leaving?" she whispered to Xeno.

"I wanted to be loyal to the man who saved me from the Messenger. But when Mizz Mooney died, well, that's when Julius

Mooney started behaving strangely. If I did something wrong, he'd whack my knuckles with a maple branch until they bled. If someone started asking about Strang's gold, he made me write notes in the name of the Seventh Messenger to scare them off. Sometimes Louis, the bellman, had to write the notes. It always worked until you came along. I was glad you don't scare easily."

"No, I do not," Abby said, with her most determined tone. "But I'm curious, Xeno, what else did he do that seemed different or, strange?

"Well, not too long ago, I heard him talking to Miss Cooke, you know, the one they call 'the Madam.' He had Miss Cooke believing he wanted to rid the islands of the influence of the House of David and restore Strang's kingdom if he found the gold." Xeno turned to face Abby. "Miss Cooke never figured out that he was committed to the *opposite*. He had come to see himself as the true Seventh Messenger and was convinced Pernell Richards was a fraud."

"So, what happened at the boathouse?"

"Mister Mooney asked me to meet him there. I didn't want to, but, you know, I agreed. I knew there'd be trouble when he arrived, dressed in the Messenger's robes, including that fake beard. He lit a kerosene lamp and told me to sit down. That's never a good sign. Then, he said I must confront you and Mister Day and demand that the gold be turned over. I didn't even know you had the gold. Anyway, I decided this was not going to end well, and I better get out of there."

"I guess that's when Julius learned for the first time that you had some vision?"

"Yes! You should have seen the look on his face. When I took off through the boathouse door, he gave chase, cursing with every step. I think he would've caught me if he hadn't tripped over a loose floorboard. That board flipped the kerosene lamp into the air, and when it crashed, it splattered burning fuel all over the place."

"And that's about the time I saw you running from the boathouse."

Xeno nodded. "I suppose so."

Abby shared with Xeno all that happened when she and Mark entered the boathouse, how the gold fell from its rooftop hiding spot, hit Julius Mooney on his skull, and knocked him into the burning water. "We barely escaped with our lives!"

"Somehow, it doesn't surprise me that Mr. Mooney came to such an end," Xeno said. "Visions of an earthly kingdom blinded him just as surely as the Messenger's gloves blinded me."

The stranger who had been reading at the far end of the lobby approached the register and picked up a morning paper. Xeno stepped behind the cash register to accept the stranger's dime. "Highway robbery." The stranger uttered only two words before turning briskly for the dining room.

Abby finally got a good look him. *That's the man I saw talking with Blue Hair in the Solarium, the one she called "detective."* Abby watched as he put the paper under his arm and headed in the direction of the dining room. Suddenly, she remembered another time when she had seen him. *He was also on the train the night I traveled to Charlevoix! I caught just a glimpse of him, but that was enough.*

"They all say the same thing," Xeno said, with his first smile of the day, "and most of them can buy the newspapers that are trying to make a living on that one thin dime."

Abby smiled as she stepped in front of the counter. "I have to go, Xeno, before someone else sees us, but I want you to know that you did nothing wrong." She took a step away but returned to lean over the counter. "But there are likely to be a lot of questions about what happened last night," she said in a low voice. "You don't want to become involved in that. You may want to leave Pine Lake, at least for a while. Perhaps one of the resorts around Harbor Springs could use a good man who can tell the difference between a five dollar bill and a one dollar bill 'just by feel.'"

"You're probably right. Lord knows I don't want any more trouble. I'd ask Louis, you know, the bellman, to go with me, but I haven't seen him in several days—"

"Xeno—" Abby cut him off. She'd heard enough. "How much for this jar of your finest crystallized honey?"

Xeno laughed. "Hardly anyone buys it anymore. Take it, with my thanks. And take this newspaper. The Traverse City Times was just delivered." He grabbed her hand and shook it vigorously. "You are a good soul, Abby Finlay."

When Abby returned to her room, she shared her encounter with Mark, who kept repeating, "I knew it. I knew it."

Slowly, Abby split a biscuit and spread crystalized honey across both halves. "We'll split the gold with the others as we promised, but I don't think we ought to share the news about Xeno. That's best kept as one of the untold secrets of the Pine Lake Club."

"I agree," Mark said, smiling. He picked up a biscuit and took a bite. "It won't be the first or the last secret protected from Pine Lake ears."

"And there's one more thing," Abby said, as she stared into the blueness of Mark's eyes. "There's no point in mentioning the pregnant High Island women who were brought here, or the children they may have given up for adoption to Pine Lake families. If it's the first the members have heard of it, the news can only cause trouble."

"I'm fine with that," Mark said, as he picked up the newspaper. "But what should we do about the detective?"

"I don't know. I don't know how he fits into all this, but I have a distinct feeling his presence does not bode well for our little enterprise."

"Oh my God, look at this," Mark said, pointing to a headline on the front page of the Times.

Chapter Thirty-Two
Secrets in an Angel's Face

Hotel Manager Hero of Boathouse Fire." Abby grabbed the paper from Mark and quickly scanned the story.

"The *Times* is fast. It only happened yesterday. Read on." Mark plopped down on the bed.

"It's a short story with few details," Abby said. "It says the only fatality of the fire was Julius Mooney, but listen:

> '*Charlevoix fire chief, Thomas Mahoney, said Mooney died while fighting to save one of the oldest boathouses on the Club. The county coroner reported Mooney's death was most likely caused by a falling timber. Cause of the fire is unknown. Details, when available, will appear in a later edition.*'"

"Is there any mention of a boat leaving the scene at high speed?" Mark sat up against the headboard with a pillow behind his back.

"Mmmmmm . . . no."

"What about the white robe Julius was wearing? Any mention of that?"

"None, whatsoever. See for yourself." And she handed the paper to Mark. "The rescuers probably didn't know what to make of it, so they didn't mention his costume."

"And when my newspaper carries the story in next week's *Clarion*, there'll be no mention of it either." Mark flipped quickly through several pages of the paper. "Whoa, what's this? Bottom of page six: '*Bellman Killed in Boating Accident near North Fox.*'"

"Xeno told me he had not seen Louis in several days." Abby frowned and bit her lower lip.

"Here's the rest of it," Mark said.

'The body of Louis Spellman, longtime employee of the Pine Lake Hotel was discovered yesterday on the beaches of North Fox Island. Preliminary reports indicate that Spellman, a bellman for more than thirty years, drowned when his boat broke apart after hitting rocks in an area known as Devil's Reef. It appears he was alone at the time. It remains a mystery why Mr. Spellman, seldom seen on the waters around Charlevoix, would be cruising in an area of the lake that holds such high risk for the uninitiated.'"

"And still another life is added to the list of those whose lives the gold has destroyed." Abby put her hand on Mark's arm to stop his reading. "What about Sergeant Strang, a decorated war hero? Is there no mention of him anywhere?"

"They don't know about him, yet. I'll probably be the first to write about him." Mark folded the paper and put it on a side table.

"Well, you will make him the hero he truly was, won't you?" She was always saddened by loss of life but especially when the life lost was that of a soldier. *Each death reminds me of the pain I felt the day I learned Robert had been killed at Normandy.*

"Don't worry. I know what I have to say; I can read it in your eyes."

"Good." She turned away and pulled up the covers again. "I suppose we'll never know whether or not he crossed paths with Robert." There was unmistakable sadness in her voice. "But, I guess . . . I guess it doesn't matter . . . anymore."

**

Abby and Mark spent the day calling the other members of their Pine Lake detective cabal, and arranging for their celebratory dinner in a private alcove of the Hotel's dining room. All were invited to meet at seven o'clock at the Club's Casino for cocktails, followed by dinner at the Hotel.

At the appointed hour for dinner, all were in attendance except Mrs. Vandivare. "Odd," Abby noted. "She's never late for any engagement." When the waiter showed them to a circular table near the window, overlooking the lake, Abby pointed to the seat nearest the window. "Howard, I think your cigar will prefer *that* seat next to the window." She gave him the stern look of a teacher who expected her suggestion to be obeyed. Howard moved to the window seat, and the others filled in around the table: Mark and Abby on his left, Phoebe Cooke on his right. They saved one chair for Blue Hair. Abby smiled as she realized they must look like a New Year's Eve party anxiously awaiting midnight. *Chatting excitedly, saying nothing, waiting for the clock to signal the zenith event of the evening.*

When the waiter filled their champagne glasses, Abby lifted hers into the air and offered a toast, "To our success!"

"Here, here!" the others responded, as glasses clinked together.

What an odd collection we must seem to the wait staff, Abby thought. *There's the Madam in that low-cut gown—all white, of course— and high heels, too. And me in my emerald gown, emerald necklace and matching flats. She probably thinks I'm Dorothy from the Wizard of Oz. And Howard, he must have selected the loudest jacket in his closet. I wish he'd get rid of that cigar! Mark is the only one who looks halfway respectable, white dinner jacket and pink carnation.* She batted her eyelashes at Mark. *Respectable and quite handsome, too.*

Abby leaned closer to Mark and whispered, "I hope nothing has gone wrong. Mrs. Vandivare is never . . . wait, there she is!" Abby pointed to the entrance and gasped. She cupped her hand around Mark's ear to keep the others from hearing. "That's the stranger. That's the detective I told you about, the one talking with her in the Solarium, and later, the one reading in the lobby!"

"I don't like the looks of this," Mark said, "but I guess we have to play out the cards we're holding."

"Mrs. Vandivare—at last," Abby said, rising to give Blue Hair a polite embrace. "You are right on time."

Blue Hair glared at the detective. "I am *late*, young lady, and *he* is the reason why."

"Please, won't you introduce your guest," Abby said. "He is certainly welcome to join us, too." She motioned for the waiter to find another chair.

"I'll let him introduce himself." Blue Hair gave a half-hearted bow in the direction of the detective and took her seat.

"My dear chaps, I am Detective Theodore Campbell, representing the Queen's Royal Treasury and Scotland Yard." The detective made sure all could read his official credentials.

"Uh-oh," Howard said, and put his glass down. "A detective on duty, that's never a good sign, no sir."

"I have been working donkey's years on the oldest case in our files," the detective continued, "and you dear chaps have helped me crack it. I must, therefore, begin by expressing the deepest gratitude of the Royal Family for your considerable assistance."

"Whoa! What are you talking about? What old case?" Howard asked. Howard was the only one who seemed able to find his tongue. All but Abby were dumbfounded, and she had decided to hold her questions.

"Britain's Royal Family has been searching more than a century for the gold you found, not so much for its monetary value, as to demonstrate that the Crown does not suffer theft—any theft—gladly. As far as the Crown is concerned, there is no statute of limitations on theft from the Royal Treasury. You have found gold that rightfully belongs to the Queen, and I am here to reclaim it for Her Majesty. And make no mistake, James Jesse Strang stole *his* gold from Queen

Victoria." He collapsed his lanky frame in the empty chair the waiter had just that moment placed behind him.

The waiters, always discreet, disappeared into the kitchen.

"But the gold was in New York, not England," Abby said. "And even if the gold we found belonged to the Queen, how would you prove it?" *We've come too far to concede defeat now.*

The detective cleared his throat, and turned his attention to the entire group. "If you must know, one of Strang's children came here seeking employment, but she made one revealing mistake. According to Club records, Eva Strang, the king's daughter and first dance instructor for the Club, possessed a gold pendant and . . . and well, Mrs. Vandivare, if you please. You are more familiar with the details. Besides, the details are, indeed, delicious." He smiled and rubbed his hands together.

Before Blue Hair had a chance to speak, the detective added, "You should know that several years past—several decades, really—the Yard contacted Mrs. Vandivare in hopes of enlisting her services as, shall we say, a listening post. Mrs. Vandivare has been far more than that—far more. She has been the Yard's contact point in the Club since the early 1920s. And, I must say, she has not disappointed. She can separate fact from Chinese whispers faster than anyone I know. Please do proceed, Mrs. Vandivare."

"You are too kind, sir," Blue Hair said, pulling her wrap more tightly about her. "It took me a while to piece the details together, but here's the gist of it. When Strang's daughter, Eva, came to the mainland after his death, she worked as a domestic for several families around Charlevoix. Eventually, she worked for the Bishop family at the Pine Lake Club and lived with them in their cottage, *Sunrise*, next door to the Hotel."

Abby sat straight up. *Sunrise played a role in the discovery of Strang's gold?*

"One day, something quite astonishing happened," the detective said.

"Sir, something astonishing is always happening at the Pine Lake Club," Howard said, and he bit off the end of his cigar. "Always."

"Shhhh!" Abby hoped Howard would stop interrupting.

"When the Bishop family commissioned the carving of a medallion for their dining room ceiling," Blue Hair said, "they asked the artisan to carve the face of an angel in its center. When Eva saw it, she was immediately taken with the image and became quite excited. She offered her gold pendant to be melted down and used as gold leaf to gild the angel's face. She said it reminded her of her own mother."

"I know about that old thing," Howard said, leaning across the table. "The Bishops didn't like it, thought it garish, and put it in storage. Somebody found it and gave it to the Hotel." Turning to the detective, Howard said, "Say, do you know that your eyes blink a lot when you're talking?"

Blue Hair shot Howard a dagger-like stare. "Howard! Mind your manners." Turning to Abby, she said, "And the Hotel put it in the center of the Solarium when that room was added. Abby, I thought you might remember the medallion when I pointed it out the day you and I met in the Solarium."

"I'd forgotten all about it," Abby said. "Mother never liked it. A waiter in the Hotel told her a tear falls from the angel's face at least once every summer. I never believed it and Mother never liked it, so, we ignored it."

"July 9, to be exact," Blue Hair said.

"July 9?"

"Yes, that's the anniversary of King Strang's death. I've been here every July 9 for the past twenty years, and I can assure you, a single tear falls from the angel's face at sunrise on each anniversary of James Strang's death, including this very summer."

Abby looked about the table and glanced into the speechless faces of her colleagues. She picked up a menu and placed it slowly but firmly in the center of her dinner plate. "Well, I predict there will be no more tears, Mrs. Vandivare." Abby adjusted the emerald pendant around her neck and cleared her throat. "No more tears from the angel in the medallion . . . or anyone here." She picked up her menu and pretended to be looking it over. "There will be no more sadness, *period*."

Mrs. Vandivare looked down the table at Howard who smiled and blew three perfect circles of cigar smoke into the air. And then, he leaned over and whispered into the Madam's ear, "Our Abby is home."

Abby paid no attention to Howard; she was only interested in determining the role of the medallion in solving the mystery of Strang's gold. "And how did you uncover this fanciful tale about the medallion?" she asked Blue Hair.

"Years ago, as I was searching through Club records for information that might be useful to Scotland Yard . . . " Blue Hair gave the detective a satisfied smile. "Suddenly, there it was, a note stuck in Club annual reports, a note written by Henry Bishop himself around 1925, explaining how the medallion came to be . . . gold leaf and all." She nodded to the detective. "Now, your turn, sir."

"Thank you, but I have nothing to add," Campbell said, "except to say, it is far from fanciful, Abby, 'tis true. Now, do any of you chaps have further questions?"

Howard turned his cigar between thumb and forefinger as if examining it for the first time. "If the king gave Eva a gold piece," he said, looking straight at the detective, "don't you think it likely he gave a coin to *each* of Elvira's children?"

"Of course," Campbell said, "He could have given a gold coin to each child, but we have no evidence of such gifts. The other coins, if they were given to his children, have never been found. We are only certain of Eva's gold coin."

Abby gave Mark a knowing glance. Mark's grandfather had a gold coin, she knew, passed down from Clement Strang, which he gave to the Mormon Church in Utah. "If only he knew the source of the gold that covers the statue of the Angel Moroni on the Salt Lake Temple," Abby whispered in Mark's ear.

"I have a bad feeling about this," Howard murmured.

Abby decided she would ignore Howard's comments for the rest of the evening. "Detective, I don't believe you answered my earlier question. How did the Queen's gold come to be deposited in a bank in New York?"

There were several insistent nods around the table. "Yes, let's get back to that," the Madam said, as she adjusted the straps to her gown.

"My, my." The detective looked the Madam up and down. "My dear, my dear."

The lecherous once over from a British detective is something you don't see every day. The Madam doesn't seem to mind. Hah! She's giving him the once over, too.

"Very well, dear chaps, I'll try to make this brief." His eyebrows danced up and down several times. "Not long after Queen Victoria was crowned in 1837, President Martin Van Buren had the brass neck to ask Her Majesty to invest in America. Your country was in the worst economic depression of its young history, primarily due to bank speculation in land and easy credit to people who could not afford to pay it back."

"In case you don't know, we've been there several times since," Abby said.

"More champagne, please." Howard lifted his empty glass to catch the waiter's attention.

"Shhhh!" The Madam took a turn at shushing Howard. "Let him explain, please."

"Thank you, Miss Cooke. As I was saying, you Yanks were at the end of your tether. Your President Van Buren needed an infusion of gold immediately. The Queen agreed in 1841 to place a substantial amount of gold in selected banks around the country. The first bank to receive the gold was in your state of New York. It was also the last because someone—James Jesse Strang, by name—stole the sovereigns not long after they were deposited. Then, he did a Lord Lucan to the American frontier."

"What's a 'Lord Lucan?'" Howard whispered to the Madam.

"Shhhhh! He disappeared, you idiot." the Madam said.

Abby shook her head in disgust at both of them.

"We've known for some time that Strang hid the gold before he died," the detective said. "We had a Fifth Columnist, if you will, on the island, a chap by the name of Alexander Wentworth."

"I would like to be a Fifth Communist some day," Howard said. Everyone laughed. Howard had stopped whispering. "But, I would need to know my job."

"Well, you'd be a spy for someone; that would be your job. And if you were caught, you'd be shot at dawn," Mark said.

Howard put his cigar down. "In that case, I withdraw my application for the job."

No one laughed. And the only sound was a low puttering from a motor boat returning to the harbor for the night. Detective Campbell gazed out the window and watched the little boat until its stern light disappeared down the channel. "On the night Strang was assassinated," the detective continued, staring into the approaching darkness, "Wentworth accompanied Thomas Bedford to the waterfront where the deed was done. Wentworth had been instructed to restrain Bedford, but he did not expect the cowardly Bedford to shoot Strang in the back. As a result of the botched mission, the opportunity to discover the location of the Queen's gold was lost. We learned later that Strang, on his deathbed, gave clues to the whereabouts of the gold to his wife, Mary Perce, with instructions to deliver them to Charles, Clement, and Eva, his children by Elvira. But, we've only seen the one clue. You have seen them all— three, yes?" He looked directly at Abby.

"Four," Abby said, "Actually, there were four, if you count the one written by Mary Perce."

The detective's eyes began to twitch and blink out of control. "And?" he said.

Abby related the story told by John Johnson of how Strang's first and only legal wife, Mary Perce, moved the gold to High Island after his death and wrote a fourth clue she planned to give to her oldest surviving daughter, Nettie. "Her plan was to make certain that only Nettie could find the gold."

"You don't say!" the detective said. Even his hands began to twitch. The detective leaned closer. "And was the fourth clue also found in the coded diary of James Strang?"

Mark had been sitting quietly, listening as others talked about how the mystery was solved, but his suddenly beaming face had everyone turning to him. "Detective, you are quite correct. The clue was in Strang's diary all right, but it took our Abby to unravel its meaning." Mark gave Abby a little squeeze. "The clue was written in code by Mary Perce *within* the coded words of James Strang."

The detective's mouth fell open. "It was in the diary *all the time?*" He glanced at Blue Hair, whose expression revealed nothing.

"Yes!" Mark said, wide-eyed and grinning from ear to ear. "It was Abby's deciphering that led us to the gold Mary Perce had hidden on High Island." Mark began to draw a map of the islands out of table salt, and soon described the entire archipelago for the dinner party. "It's really not far from Gull to High Island. This pepper mill represents the Beaver. They're all very close."

"I congratulate you, Miss Finlay, on your excellent deductive powers," Campbell said, clearing his throat and stroking his chin. "At this point, I suppose it doesn't matter how many clues existed." He turned and looked directly at Howard Hancock. "One more thing confounds me. From the moment Miss Finlay bought her ticket in Saint Louis, I have tracked her every step, including her gathering of clues from Howard Hancock and Mark Day. Mister Day, as all of you know by now, is a descendant of James Strang, and his clue was obviously handed down through his family." Detective Campbell paused, his eyebrows flying up and down. "The enduring mystery is this: how did Mr. Hancock acquire the clue in his possession?"

Howard shifted back and forth in his chair. "I was very young." The pain on his face reminded Abby of a little boy forced to confess that he had shoplifted the fat wad of gum he was chewing.

The room was silent.

"Okay, Eva had a daughter, Mary Beth." Howard heaved a great sigh, as if he had just revealed the world's biggest secret.

"Yes, we know that; Julius told us," Abby said. She thought Howard looked a bit deflated when he realized his secret was out.

"But he couldn't tell you the most important part because he didn't know it," Howard said. He leaned to one side in his chair and then to the other. All of a sudden, he wasn't so sure he wanted to tell the rest.

No one moved. No one spoke, and then slowly, Howard began a revelation he had held for half a century. "Mary Beth's mother raised her right here in the Hotel, and as soon as she was grown, she followed her mother as a dance instructor for the Club. She even gave me some lessons in the early 1900s." He stopped, looked down at his shoes, and muttered something under his breath before looking up and blurting out, machine gun fashion, "We had a good time; she was very grateful; she gave me a clue. Okay?"

With that, he took a new cigar from the humidor on the table, lit it, and began taking long and slow puffs, as if, Abby thought, he wished to be transported by the smoke to a better place and time.

"Mary Beth *gave* you a clue?" Mark asked. "Really?"

Howard nodded and blew a large, single ring of smoke toward the middle of the table.

"Why? What, pray tell, did you give her?" Abby asked. She was sure of the answer but wanted Howard to confess it for all to hear.

"I gave her a daughter, if you must know. She sits at this table." Slowly he turned to face the Madam. "Phoebe . . . Phoebe, I'm sorry everyone has to find out this way."

Julius was right, Abby thought. *But Howard Hancock?*

"I did not know until years later that Phoebe was my daughter," Howard said. "Mary Beth was pregnant by the end of the summer that year—1914, I believe—and gave birth in the spring while I was away on a cruise. By the time I returned to Pine Lake, she had already given the baby girl to the Cooke family. Only recently did I learn from Phoebe that I was her father." Howard stopped and stared at his feet. "I'm so sorry, Phoebe."

The Madam gave a tug to the straps of her gown, moved closer to Howard, and patted his arm. "Don't say you're sorry. Don't ever say that. I'm certainly not sorry." She gave his hand a gentle kiss. "You're a fine looking man, and I'm proud to be your daughter."

Someone let a spoon drop. It hit the linen tablecloth with a soft "thud." Another person played with the ice in his water glass. And still another started to call a waiter but thought better of it. Finally, Abby said, "Julius Mooney once told me, 'As the lake changes to the seasons of the year, so does the Club change to the chapters of one's life.' All of us have experienced chapter changes this year. Dramatic chapter changes. Every one of us."

All were quiet for what seemed a full minute.

Abby tried to mentally review her recollection of events. "Detective Campbell, how did you know I received a clue in Saint Louis?" She had concluded there was more intrigue here than had been revealed. Her eyes were fixed on the detective. "Detective?"

"The US Government has been aware of the Queen's interest in finding the lost gold for quite some time. Indeed, your Treasury Department had followed the activities of James Strang's descendants to no avail." His eyes began to twitch and blink once again.

"When the lost letter from Lt. O'Donnell was found by the U.S. Post Office, the letter first went to the Defense Department, where alert eyes learned that it held a clue to the Queen's stolen sovereigns." He held his hands high and pretended to move the letter from one hand to the other as he demonstrated how the letter traveled from one US agency to another. "The letter next went to Treasury, and your Treasury Department contacted us. From there it was a simple matter of forwarding the letter to Abigail Finlay in Saint Louis and letting matters unfold. Agents of the U.S. Government could have brought the clue to Charlevoix, of course, and conducted a search themselves, but were not likely to receive assistance from locals, now were they?"

The Madam shook her head.

"Of course not. And Mrs. Vandivare was not going to work with them; she was already in the service of the Queen."

Blue Hair raised an eyebrow and nodded slowly.

Detective Campbell, who had not taken his coat off until that very moment, threw it across the back of an empty chair.

"So, the gold belongs to the Queen," Howard said. "We found it, but she gets it back. And that's that, right?"

Abby thought he seemed resigned to emerging from this experience with nothing to show for it, and she wasn't about to let that happen. "Detective, surely the Queen would agree that simply taking it from us, after all we've been through, would not be fair. I realize—"

The detective held up his hand for silence before the others could chime in. "If you will permit me, I have something more to say that you may find of interest. The gold was valued at fifty thousand pounds British sterling at the time of the theft. A reward of two thousand pounds was offered for its return. As the years passed, the gold's value increased, as well as the reward. Thanks to collectors and speculators, the gold coins, more than one hundred years later, are worth nearly two hundred thousand pounds. Collectors have indicated the coins might bring as much as three hundred thousand pounds at auction. The Queen, of course, does not want the gold to go to auction and is prepared to offer three hundred thousand pounds for the safe return of all stolen coins."

Abby heard an audible sound of relief, as nearly everyone exhaled deeply.

"Therefore, if those gathered 'round the table agree, I shall arrange to have that exact amount—not a half-pence less—transferred to any bank account you designate in America. You may then divide it up among yourselves, while I am winging my way back to the homeland with the Queen's gold sovereigns. It should keep you in beer and skittles for quite a long time."

Detective Campbell searched the eyes of each person at the table. "What say you?"

326 || Roland McElroy

Abby looked into the faces of her colleagues in the quest, and hearing no objection, exclaimed, *"Done!"*

"Done!" they echoed, raising their champagne flutes high into the air.

"Tell me, detective," the Madam said, "When you get back to England, do you think you might encourage the Queen to pay us a visit? She would be welcome to stay with me."

The room erupted in laughter. "No more champagne for Phoebe." Howard made a slashing sign across his neck.

At that moment, the waiters returned from the kitchen carrying the entrées ordered earlier. Blue Hair took one look at Abby's choice for dinner, and said, "Abby, what *would* your mother say? Chicken tetrazzini? Not white fish with parsley and lemon?"

"She would say, 'a girl can change her mind, can't she?'" Abby winked at Blue Hair, then looked in the direction of the detective. "Detective Campbell, you will join us for dinner, won't you?"

"I am delighted to accept," Campbell said. He pushed his chair up to the end of the table. "Mrs. Vandivare, will you be my dinner partner?"

"Oh my, no, it's far too early for dinner," Blue Hair said. "I'd like to take a walk to the Solarium for another look at the angel's face in that exquisite medallion." She paused, looked Abby straight in the eye. "Abby, won't you join me in the Solarium?" Abby sensed this was more than a polite invitation. Abby nodded, and followed in Blue Hair's footsteps. She wondered what more was of such import that it required a private meeting.

In the Solarium, the two stood beneath the medallion, gazing into the angel's eyes.

"Does the angel really shed a tear once a year?" Abby asked.

"Yes, always at sunrise on July 9, the day James Strang departed this vale of tears." Blue Hair was suddenly very quiet.

Abby thought she seemed to be avoiding eye contact. *She just keeps looking up into the angel's face.*

"There is another secret, one that has been held far too long," Blue Hair began, as she fixed her stare on the angel's face. "Abby, you've heard, haven't you, about the pregnant girls from High Island who came to Pine Lake in the 1920s, after Richards was arrested?"

"Yes?"

Blue Hair turned to Abby, and spoke softly. "One of those girls came to my house. Her name was Constance O'Reilly. Constance, just seventeen years of age, was already eight months along and not physically well when she arrived at the Club. Your mother came to my house on the night Constance was due and assisted in the birth of a healthy baby girl. The sickly young woman was most troubled about the prospect of caring for her new child. The shame of an unwed mother was a heavy burden to bear."

"Not much has changed, has it?"

"No, I'm afraid not. As Constance watched your mother care for her newborn, she asked Frances what she should do. Frances, bless her soul, said, 'Constance, never you worry. If you are willing, Elisha and I will raise her to be a devout Christian and see that she gets the education she deserves.' Constance agreed, and three days later, she took the night train to Chicago, confident she had made the right decision, and indeed, relieved to know her little girl would be in such good and capable hands."

"Was the hair of the baby's mother blonde?" Abby asked.

Blue Hair was suddenly very quiet.

"And the baby's hair, was it blonde, also?"

Blue Hair's face was one of shock, and then, relief. "You knew?"

Abby nodded, and bit her lip.

Blue Hair sighed. "Yes, you were that little baby girl, Abby. You were that little miracle."

Abby sat down on the wicker loveseat under the medallion, and Blue Hair sat beside her. "I knew I was adopted. Mother told me long ago, but I knew nothing of my birth mother," Abby said, in a near whisper. "Nothing, until today."

"And all these years since your mother's death," Blue Hair said, "I have worried about how I was going to tell you. That Frances Finlay, she made sure to spare me the task."

"Mother explained it by telling me her first pregnancy had been very hard, and she was not confident she could have another baby. When the opportunity to adopt me came along, well, she never hesitated."

Blue Hair sighed again. "Frances and Elisha Finlay were the best two friends I ever had."

"It was only yesterday that I learned of the pregnant girls from High Island, who came here in the early '20s," Abby said. "I was born in '24 and adopted in Charlevoix. When you and I met in this very room a few days ago, you said I resembled my mother. 'Your hair is blonde, like your mother's,' you said. I wondered if you might have been thinking of my biological mother because Frances Finlay's hair was auburn."

"You are most clever and perceptive, my dear child," Blue Hair said, smiling. "Nothing escapes your sharp eye . . . or keen ears."

"It doesn't take a genius to figure out the likely trail of my lineage. Tell me, Mrs. Vandivare, why did mother keep the details from me? Was she embarrassed?"

"Abby, in the 1920s, when babies were adopted, it was assumed the circumstances were suspect. Many birth mothers were shunned, especially if they tried to raise the child themselves. She probably thought it best not to mention the details, but if you had asked, I'm sure she would have given you the honest truth."

Abby shook her head. "I never asked."

Blue Hair put her arm around Abby's shoulders. "You suppressed your curiosity? Why?"

"I'm not completely sure, but I've given it a lot of thought since coming back to Pine Lake, and especially since Mark came into my life."

"Yes?"

"All my life, I've had a fear of separation and isolation. Maybe it's because I didn't have a chance to bond with my natural mother, I don't know. Maybe it was the fear of another separation that made me refuse to accept Robert's fate. By denying his death, I could preserve my commitment to him, my bond to him, until I saw him again. Does that make sense?"

"Yes, but what a burden to carry every day."

"To me, my commitment to Robert was not a burden; it was the only thing that kept me going. Besides, I knew in my heart, the details of my birth would not change anything. As far as I'm concerned, my 'real' mother will always be Frances Finlay. Everything I am, I owe to her. Whatever I have become, for better or worse, I attribute to her nurturing, her teaching, her compassion."

Blue Hair embraced her warmly and kissed her cheek. "Abby, a young man waits for you at that table," she said, nodding toward the dining room. "Frances Finlay would be happy that you found such a man to share your life." Both smiled. "I think Frances knew you would eventually come to Charlevoix and find Mark."

"I believe that, too," Abby said, her voice cracking. "Mother would wonder what took me so long."

Blue Hair smiled as she grabbed Abby's arm and started for the dining room. "Mark is a bit of a liberal, you know, but you can work on that."

Chapter Thirty-Three
A Castle Fit for a King

The Capitol Limited, B&O's night train from Saint Louis, pulled into Washington's Union Station at precisely 8:14 a.m. In the dining car, Abby sipped English tea as Mark enjoyed a bold cup of dark Sumatra coffee. "Why have all the major milestones in my life occurred in train stations?" she asked Mark. He shrugged and gave her a quizzical look. "The most traumatic," she recalled, "was the day I kissed Robert goodbye and watched as he ran for the train at Pine Lake Depot. I was sure he would be gone only a short time, but he . . . he never came back."

The car slowed gradually and swung gently from side to side before coming to a full stop. Mark reached across the table and took her hand in his.

"Last August," she said, "I boarded a train at Saint Louis' Union Station, and traveled alone to the Pine Lake Club, a place I vowed never to visit again until Robert returned." Abby touched Mark's hand as gently as he had touched hers, and put her tea on the table. "And last night, I boarded yet another train, headed for another Union Station, the one in Washington . . . and this time I was not alone." She smiled broadly and looked deep into his "Charlevoix blue" eyes.

Mark leaned forward and met her lips with a teasing peck. "*And* last night, I discovered the answer to one of the great mysteries of my youth," he said.

"And that is, or was?" She smiled. *This will be a good one, I'm sure.*

"When my father taught me the correct way to shift gears in his Chevrolet, he always instructed, 'let the clutch out slowly so the car won't jerk your passengers; pull away smoothly just like a Pullman.' I finally know what he meant. A Pullman really is the smoothest way to ride the rails."

"You're more like Howard Hancock every day," she teased him. "You'll soon have an anecdote for every occasion," and she leaned across the table to steal another kiss. This one ended with a playful smack of her lips.

For a long while, they enjoyed touching hands, squeezing them from time to time, never uttering a word. Abby thought about the dinner they had shared last night and the surprise Mark had for her.

**

A violinist strolled the dining car playing "Unchained Melody." While the music played, a porter appeared with a bottle of Mouton Rothschild Pauillac and placed it quietly in a sterling silver bucket of ice, while Mark simultaneously slipped a small package across the table. Abby's face turned ashen, and at first Mark thought he had done something terribly wrong. With a great flourish, he had written her name on the card attached to the package, and after her name, he used his pen to place three small dots on the card. Abby felt a lump in her throat.

"Mark? Three . . . three dots?"

"Oh yes," Mark said, "when my father traveled he always left a note on mother's pillow for her to read before she retired for the evening. He signed his name the same way each time, with three small dots to signify—as she told me much later—'those three little words we can never hear enough.' Why do you ask?"

"Robert always put three dots after his signature in all his letters, his special way of saying 'I love you.'"

Mark took her hand and clasped it between his two.

"Abby, before the war, you knew you would marry Robert. You even knew where the two of you would live, how many children you would have, and most assuredly, you knew where you would vacation together. But now . . . now, Robert is gone." Mark caressed her hand and held it silently for a long time. "You keep a journal, recording in it everything you do each day. But remember, you won't be the one who writes the last entry on the last page, the last day of your life. Someone else will write that entry, won't they?" Mark looked up from her hand and gently brushed away a tear forming in the corner of her eye. "Come with me, my love, and let's give them something to write about."

Abby smiled. "And will there be a locomotive bell clanging away in that last chapter?"

"I hope so," Mark said. "I laugh every time I think about your introduction to that bell. After you left my office, I was certain you thought me a crazy eccentric for holding on to such a misplaced relic."

"Hardly." Abby laughed. "But it *was* loud."

**

Mark snapped his fingers and waved a hand in front of her eyes. "I don't know where you are, but it's time for us to get off this train."

Abby suddenly became aware of a porter standing beside them. "I brought your coat, miss," he said, as he held Abby's for her. "Everyone else is off already."

"Oh, I'm ready," Abby said, jumping up. "This is going to be a big day for us."

Outside Washington's Union Station, Abby threw her arms open to show Mark the blemish free panoply above them. "It's a Charlevoix sky, Mark, very rare for the Nation's Capital."

"A precursor of spring, that's for sure." Mark raised his arm to hail a taxi for the short trip to the Smithsonian Castle.

"Let's walk," Abby said. "It's not far, and besides, it's a perfect day for a walk down the National Mall to the Castle."

As they entered the Castle's Great Hall, they were greeted by two small posters, one directing them to an exhibit of James Strang memorabilia in the East Wing, and the second to an exhibit in the West Wing commemorating the fifteenth anniversary of the D-Day Invasion.

"I'm sure the curators are not aware that the two exhibits have at least one common thread," Abby said, as she stood between the posters, "a simple handwritten verse on a scrap of paper, exchanged between two soldiers on the night prior to the assault."

"That's true," Mark said, "and who could have imagined that little verse would help solve the mystery of the Queen's missing gold sovereigns?"

Members of Congress and invited guests poured by them, some turning to the left, others to the right, as they assembled for the separate but consecutive opening ceremonies. "Mark, look—a framed copy of the speech General Eisenhower delivered to his troops before the invasion began on June 6 of '44." Abby continued to walk along the hall, reading the captions on documents and photographs. She stopped at one photo, an aerial shot taken the second day of the invasion. From the air, a string of small objects appeared on the beach making a dark line along the entire length of the previous night's high tide. "They look like small logs," she said to Mark.

"Abby, I think we need to find our seats at the Strang exhibit," Mark said, as he attempted to pull her away from the photo display.

"Oh no," she gasped. Abby turned away quickly when she realized the photo showed not logs, but hundreds of bodies, washed up on the beach after the initial assault. "Oh, my God, no." She stopped to catch her breath. "I'm sorry. I'm sorry."

"This way, Abby." Mark pulled her toward a sign that read, "East Wing Exhibit, Beaver Island King," and pointed her to a list of

Strang memorabilia. "Take a look at these photos of Strang's five wives."

Abby, pleased to find something on which to refocus her attention, examined them closely but stopped when she saw the image of Mary Perce, Strang's first and only legal wife. "She looks strong to me and yet vulnerable; is that possible?"

"Yes, but in the end, she showed more strength than weakness," Mark said. "Say, look over there." He pointed to a number of objects in a corner of the room. "I wasn't sure they wanted that old wooden weathervane from my newspaper office, but I'm glad it's here."

"I was surprised—no, shocked—when the museum staff told us it was an early representation of Moroni, patron saint of the Mormons," Abby said. "It takes some imagination to see a patron saint there."

"Oh, it's there." Mark pointed to a couple of weathered spots where a face might have been carved at one time. "The weather has been hard on this old 'vane, but it's Moroni, all right." He glanced up to the ceiling. "Thank you, great-grandmother for saving it."

Two seats had been reserved for them, directly in front of a glass case that housed Strang's personal diary. Abby donated the diary, but not before making a copy for Mark's research.

Most of the Smithsonian officials had made their way to the dais, and conversations faded away. "I think I've finally broken James Strang's code," Mark whispered to Abby as they sat down. "Someday the diary will be published in its entirety."

"And tourists will want to visit Strang's home on Beaver Island," Abby whispered back. "After all, he almost became the leader of the Mormon Church. Maybe we should invest in a ferry service to Beaver?"

"Who wouldn't want to visit James Strang's *sanctum sanctorum*?" Mark said, smiling.

Abby shushed him quickly. The Vice President was about to speak.

"And of course, the *Clarion* needs a new press," Mark whispered, as Nixon approached the podium.

Abby smiled and nodded her approval. While Nixon spoke, she thought about the other recipients of the reward money, none of whom were present on this occasion. Abby understood. *Most Club members are not looking for more publicity, for themselves or the Club.* She had visited all of them before she left Charlevoix. The Madam was off to London to have tea with the Queen, and Howard was driving a newly restored Deusenberg to California, a young blonde by his side. And of course, there was Mrs. Vandivare. She invited Abby to join her for tea in the Solarium before she left. Her sole purpose was to make a gift of her share of the reward money, with the condition that Abby and Mark use the funds to buy *Sunrise,* the Finlay summer cottage. *I was overwhelmed by her generosity and promised our first daughter would be named Josephine. She liked that.*

**

A new summer and a new life lay ahead for Abby and Mark. As they walked hand in hand from Pine Lake Depot to *Sunrise*, the family cottage, Mark noticed Abby's expression had become a bit sad. "What happened to that smile of just a minute ago?"

"I'm not unhappy," she said, as she turned to Mark. "It's just that life does change, and I've discovered I have little control over those changes. I sometimes wonder if we control anything, really. For instance, I suspect that'll be the last time we take the Resort Special to Charlevoix. Everyone seems to be coming by automobile these days."

The Resort Special gave two short toots of its whistle and slowly began chugging toward the railroad bridge for the short trip across the channel to Charlevoix depot. "Even those little toots sound a bit sad," Abby said. "Stage coach and steamboat travel were the first to become obsolete, and I have a feeling the train will soon follow."

They stopped for a moment at the steps leading up the terrace to *Sunrise,* and turned to admire the magnificent view of Lake Charlevoix.

"If that's true," Mark said, "what's the future for all these summer cottages along the lake?"

"Pine Lake Club will always be here," Abby said, as she began walking toward the front porch of *Sunrise*. She stopped when the aroma from the Hotel kitchen next door filled her nostrils. "All those wonderful smells mixed together—cherry pies baking, lake trout frying, chicken being fried." She closed her eyes. "All these things *must* be here, always."

From the porch, Abby turned to take another look at the little train depot. "I love the morning train. 'Youth comes on the morning train,' Mother always said, 'and age departs on the night train.' In my view, youth on the morning train represents all the new chapters in one's life waiting to be written, all the unknowns yet to be known."

"You wait here and enjoy the 'unknowns,'" Mark said. "I'm going inside to call my office. I want them to know that your son, our son, Bobby is joining our staff this summer and will arrive later today. It'll do him good to get a little ink under his fingernails." Mark examined his nails and frowned at the black ink he pretended was there.

Abby smiled, kissed him on the cheek, and said, "I'll be waiting right here."

The sun was no longer peeking over the horizon. It was high enough to bathe every inch of the two-story Hotel, its wrap-around veranda, and the lawn in front. Abby thought it must seem like a Hollywood movie set to strangers. She turned from the sun's glare and strained to read the name of the boat that just entered Lake Charlevoix from the direction of Round Lake. *Can't make it out, too much peeling paint.* She spied a couple of sailboats out early. *They've almost made Two-Mile Point already.*

The sun's reflection off the water made it difficult to see any activity at Pine Lake station, but Abby could make out a couple of porters putting away step stools, and another loading luggage on a small livery wagon. The stationmaster was manually changing the sign announcing arrivals and departures. Seagulls, their wingtips occasionally touching the tops of small waves along the lakeshore, seemed to glide forever before soaring to the top of the station's cupola. Their squawking soon drowned out the sound of the departing train.

A lone passenger approached a luggage cart and picked up the only remaining suitcase. *No one came to greet him, I guess.* The passenger stepped off the platform and began making his way toward Abby.

"Oh!" Abby gasped. "I, no, no . . . " She was startled by *whom* she saw walking toward her. Still a long way off, but the face was familiar, a little older, but she knew it well. The figure walked slowly, a slight limp in his stride. At first she was silent. Then, another breathless gasp escaped her lips, and she clasped both hands to her chest.

"R-R-Robert?"

The End

Author's note

The Seventh Messenger consists of two stories told in parallel. The story of James Jesse Strang is based on the life and times of an excommunicated member of Joseph Smith's fledgling Mormon Church who took his followers to Beaver Island, Michigan, in 1848, and anointed himself "king of God's kingdom on earth." James Strang "reigned" until his assassination in 1856. Strang's story is true although the existence of a royal treasury was never more than a rumor the island folk enjoyed telling and retelling.

The second story is entirely fictional, its characters, fictional composites of individuals who might have lived in and around the town of Charlevoix, Michigan and the Beaver Island archipelago in mid-twentieth century. Most of the action of the fictional story takes place in 1954. Any resemblance, however, to individuals, living or dead, is purely coincidental.

**

Five Wives and Fourteen Children of James Jesse Strang

Wife #1: Mary Abigail Content Perce, m. 11/20/1836, at age eighteen
Four children:
Mary Elizabeth (Little Mary), b. 7/5/1838, *died at five years of age*
Myraette (Nettie) Mabel, b. 5/23/1840
William J., b. 1844
Harriet Anne (Hattie), b. 1847

Wife #2: Elvira Eliza Field, m. 7/13/1849, at age nineteen
Four children:
Charles James., b. 4/6/1851
Evaline (Eva), b. 4/18/1853
Clement J., b. 12/20/1854
James Jesse, Jr., b. 1/22/1857[*] (14th and last child born)

Wife #3: Elizabeth (Betsy) McNutt, m. 1/19/1852, at age thirty-one
Four children:
Evangeline, 1853
David James, 1854, *died in infancy*
Gabriel, 1855
Abigail Utopia, b. 1/1/1857[*] (13th child of Strang)

Wife #4: Sarah Adelia Wright, m. 7/15/1855, at age nineteen
One child:
James Phineas, b. 11/11/1856[*] (12th child of Strang)

Wife #5: Phoebe Wright (cousin of Sarah), m. 10/27/1855, at age eighteen
One child: **Eugenia Jesse, b. 10/28/1856[*] (11th child of Strang)**

[*]**Four children were born *after* Strang's assassination**